Bhagavan's Guitar

-As Light Is-

Sandeep Patel

Gabi
thank you!

*Dedicated to the young and old
of today and tomorrow*

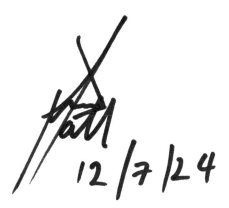

12/7/24

Gabi
Thank You!

Contents

Prologue

Bhagavan is a noun that is used highly in Hindu, Jain, Gujarati, Buddhist and other communities to say God. However specifically *Bhagavan/Bhagwan* and *Bhagavati* (feminine of *Bhagavan*) is one's personal connection to the Supreme Soul. Thus *Bhagavan* is the Spirit of God (*Shiva, Shankar, Shakti,* the Evolutionist). Whereas God in teaching from *Bhagavad-gita* is *Paramatma* (Supreme Soul, *Supreme Brahman* also known as *Lord Vishnu,* the Preserver and His avatars, especially *Sri Krsna,* the Father). Concluding the trinity form of One Light is *Brahma Dev* (not to be confused with *Brahman*) who is the Creator of what God/Life has to offer. He is the reason why humans over time have dissected science and made war in order to understand God stronger and much better. *Brahma* trait in that of *Paramatma* is as simple flesh. All three forms of God make the *Tridev; Brahma, Paramatma* and *Bhagavan.* When one is enlightened to *Paramatma* they follow a life of *bhakti-yoga* (connection to the Supreme Soul) and are to be considered as *Bhagavan.* Hence one who has the Spirit of God is *Bhagavan.* I am *Bhagavan.* You can be *Bhagavan.* We are therefore *Bhagavan.*

"Oh, my soul... You are not alone...
There's a place where fear has to
face the God you know."
Casting Crowns (2016)

The Monopoly board game was designed by a lady called Elizabeth Magie (United States, 1903). At the time of design the game was called, 'The Landlord's Game.' In 1935, the Parker Brothers first published the game with the toy company Hasbro. Now Monopoly is widely known around the world with many designs and a well known one being that of popular streets and rail stations of London City (England, United Kingdom).

Monopoly means to be in total possession or control of a particular market; let that be of a supply, trade, commodity or service. For one specific body or company to be the most superior in a market and totally own the necessity is to have monopolised that need.

Unrequited love is love that is not openly returned. This is more prominent in males i.e. a man cannot easily say, 'I love you,' even though they deeply feel so. Bhagavan's Guitar is to overcome the unrequited feeling and substantially monopolise love; so with *Bhagavan* I have conquered unrequited love and I'm pleased to say, "I love you."

O Lord of the Universe

Chapter 1

...mmmm. Start by rolling double numbers. Start by doing this to understand that not everything falls to the will of the individual. There is a chance that most things that acts towards or against life is by chance regardless of how tight one holds onto the straight and narrow. Taking this on board know that chance can make major changes in one's life. What is also known is that chance is also governed by something as chance is within the realm of the four corners of the universe. What controls chance is beyond any man's view of life but chance does exist and chance is an expansion of something somewhere. So respect the chances when the wind blows. Therefore take a chance on rolling double numbers to get started.

The year was 2021, the land was London, United Kingdom, and the home was a one bedroom apartment that centered a face of all four points of a compass. Shankar Gopal lived there. He had been there for ten years observing nature, enjoying humanity and in control of his consciousness in a city that was as diverse as the whole world in one place together. What led Shankar to be there was his misfortune, necessity to survive, the chances left on him by the will of life and his wait for the summoning of the Almighty One.

On a bright beautiful clear blue sky day which to Shankar was everyday regardless of the British weather of rain, snow, sleet, fog and shine he could travel in all directions of the compass as free as a bird. As the date was 2021, Shankar had access to the world both by body and by spirit. The summoning of the Almighty One was soon to come as the people of the time were losing their minds with communion.

London, the world's first multicultural land. There was no surprise that stability would be key. Everyone fought for their own, everyone fought against each other, everyone had different views from each other, and no man spoke up against the woman and no woman spoke of love towards the man, and where no child had foundation or admiration from where they arrived from, they all voted equity without effort for equality.

Shankar was waiting for the sky to rumble and crackle, roar and pour, and the stars to be set aside to make way of the birth of the One. The One who would bring balance to the desires of people that had been left astray fighting for justice and to those who were holding the righteous word of God in their hearts. The One to come was to be known as Krishna. Shankar was to teach Him everything he knew to liberate the world and make them know Krishna will be the most exalted in providence, He to be the 'Supreme Personality of Godhead,' He to be the One Light.

Civilisations had changed dramatically in the last twenty years than it had for hundred years before. Unimaginable differences through to the time of World War I and II, to the birth and growth of Sikhism, to the order of Islam, and to the time before the birth of Lord Jesus Christ, ancient kingdoms of Maya, demigods and goddesses formations in Bharat, Empires of the Orient, mythological Greek Gods, Pharaohs of Egypt, and other spaces in time to the present day.

The reasons for the greatest extraordinary change on civilisations were threefold; one) aviation had outstandingly changed the world on making life easier for people to converge into one another, two) the birth of the world-wide-web brought every individual of the era to be just a push of a button or a tap of a screen away from one another and, three) the desire of the majority to end segregation and bring passion of individual cultures to coincide in union with other cultures. In short the change was communication in an internationally multicultural growing world.

With a world that had changed massively in such a short space of time there was growth of grandeur in liberal movements. That to say not many bravely spoke against another in debate, not many listened well with another, not many humbled themselves, not many took blame, not many changed circumstances, nor did many agree with each other at the best or worst of times, therefore many were left to walk a path that was mixed as all flavours of ice-cream in one tub.

There was a system people followed set by law, politics, money, sex, outlaws, corruption, terrorism, media, envy and other propaganda that a single life was as a mouse in a maze with no way out and very little cheese to share in trust. Biblically the devil had his claws all into the earth. An individual spoke easily about a devil but as people together spoke nothing of the sort. All excuses and no solutions that Mother Earth was to cry out to the far ends of the universe to save the goodness in people she had spawned so no further generations could be taken by the grasp of extreme liberal ignorant miscreants.

The birth of the One was to be the birth of the Light again in form of a child to enter the Earth's domain from His abode. He was to come again to resolve His own right of rule on Earth. Meaning to say His own life for complete liberation yet had not occurred. Krishna to be born again onto the earth of the world and fulfilling His purpose would grant Him and His realm of heaven liberation.

Over hundreds of thousands of years that mankind inhabited Earth the time was to come again for the Light to make all the wrong experiments He bestowed on the land right. But first the duty of Shankar was to find Krishna and ignite the light within the Supreme Light to straighten the time to His opulence. Shankar himself was the bank of resources of divine nature that had accumulated from practices of all faiths and cultures since the beginning of time. He had *Bhagavan* within him; as a matter of fact Shankar was *Bhagavan*. The Light's practices from all life from the far reaches of the universe were saved in Shankar. Shankar was waiting for the One to return so to awaken Him on the ongoing ordeals He had left as options for mankind. For the age of the digital era Shankar was to be uploaded into Krishna, *Bhagavan* was to be uploaded into The Light, and The Light was to be refreshed and downloaded into mankind.

<u>O Lord of the Universe (Hymn)</u> /
<u>*Om Jai Jagadish (Mantra)*</u>

O Lord of the Universe, praise,
Om Jai Jagadiś, hare,
Mighty Lord of the Universe, praise,
Swāmi* Jai Jagadiś, hare
The agonies of devotees,
Bhakta janoṃ ke sankata,
The sorrows of devotees,
Dāsa janoṃ ke saṅkaṭa,
In an instant, you make these go away,
Kśana meṃ dūra kare,
O Lord of the Universe, praise.
Om Jai Jagadiś, hare.

He who's immersed in devotion,
Jo dhyāve phala pāve,
With a mind without sadness,
Dukha bina se mana kā,
Lord, with a mind without sadness,
Swami, dukha bina se mana kā,
Joy, prosperity enter the home,
Sukha sampati ghara āve,
Joy, prosperity enter the home,
Sukha sampati ghara āve,

A body free of problems,
Kaṣṭa miṭe tana kā,
O Lord of the Universe, praise.
Om Jai Jagadiśh, hare.

You are my Mother and Father,
Mātā pitā tuma mere,
Whom should I take refuge with,
Śarana karu maiṃ kiski,
Lord, whom should I take refuge with,
Swāmi śaraṇa karu maiṃ kiski,
Without you, there is no other,
Tuma bina aura na dūjā,
Without you, there is no other,
Tuma bina aura na dūjā,
For whom I would wish,
Āśā karuṇa maiṃ jiski,
O Lord of the Universe, praise.
Om Jai Jagadiśh, hare.

You are the ancient great soul,
Tuma pūraṇa Paramātmā,
You are the in-dweller,
Tuma Antarayāmi,
Lord, You are the in-dweller,
Swāmi, Tuma Antarayāmi,
Perfect, Absolute, Supreme God,
Pāra Brahma Parameśwara,
Perfect, Absolute, Supreme God,
Pāra Brahma Parameśwara,
You are the Lord of everything and everyone,
Tuma saba ke swāmi,
O Lord of the Universe, praise
Om Jai Jagadiśh, hare.

You are an ocean of mercy,
Tuma karuṇa ke sāgara,
You are the protector,
Tuma pālana kartā,
Lord, You are the protector,
Swāmi, Tuma pālana kartā,
I am a simpleton with wrong wishes,
Mai mūrakh khalakhāmi,
I am a servant and You are the Lord,
Mai sevaka Tuma Swāmi,
O Lord, grant me Your divine grace,
Kripā karo Bhartā,
O Lord of the Universe, praise.
Om Jai Jagadiśh, hare.

You are the One unseen,
Tuma ho Eka agochara,
Of all living beings,
Saba ke prāṇapati,
The Lord of all living beings,
Swāmi saba ke prāṇapati,
Grant me a glimpse, Grant me a glimpse,

Kisa vidhi milūṃ dayāmaya,
Kisa vidhi milūṃ dayāmaya,
Guide me along the path to thee,
Tuma ko maiṃ kumati,
O Lord of the Universe, praise
Om Jai Jagadiśh, hare.

Friend of the helpless and feeble,
Dīna bandhu dukha harata,
Benevolent saviour of all,
Thākura tuma mere,

Lord, benevolent saviour of all,
Swāmi, ṭhākura tuma mere,
Lift up Your hand,
Offer me Thy refuge, At Thy feet,
Apane hāth uṭhāo,
Apani śaraṇa lagāo, Dwāra paṛā hūn Tere,
O Lord of the Universe, praise.
Om Jai Jagadiśh, hare.

Removing earthly desires, defeating sin, Lord,
Vishaya vikāra miṭāo, Pāpa haro, Devā,
Lord, defeating sin, Lord,
Swāmi, pāpa haro Devā,
With all my faith and devotion,
With all my faith and devotion,
Śradhā bhakti baṛhāo, Śradhā bhakti baṛhāo,
Eternal care unto Thee,
Santana ki sevā
O Lord of the Universe, praise.
Om Jai Jagadiśh, hare.

Body, mind, wealth is all Yours,
Tan, man, dhan sab kuch hai Tera,
Lord, everything is Yours,
Swami, sab kuch hai tera,
What's Yours we return, Lord, What's Yours we return,
Tera tujh ko arpan, Prahbu, Ji ka prabhu ko arpan,
What is it to me?
Kya laage mera?
O Lord of the Universe, Praise,
Om Jai Jagadish, Hare,

O Lord of the Universe, Praise,
Om Jai Jagadish, Hare.
Mighty Lord of the Universe, Praise.
Swami Jai Jagadish, Hare.
The agonies of devotees, The sorrows of devotees,
Bhakta janon ke sankat, Dāsa janon ke sankata,
Thou instantly make go afar,
Kshan me door kare,
O Lord of the Universe, Praise.
Om Jai Jagadish, Hare.

Birth of Krishna

Chapter 2

Beneath the night sky there was an intense argument that was leading into chaos and cursing between a brother and sister. In New York, Manhattan no one hears cries or joy high above the ground at night let alone the day. In one of the skyscraper's deluxe apartments named Mathura, Devika had gone to share the good news of her pregnancy to her brother Kaans Kapoor, but he was not taking the news as good.

Kaans was an extremely rich arrogant man that had most luxuries a New Yorker could have. He was a wolf of the trading market and money was his primary passion. Kaans not alone had overflowing banking investments in many businesses in New York, but also he had links to other people at all ends of the world. Kaans' reputation overshadowed many high end rollers. He was known as the King of Spades and ruled over many demonic people in the financial industry.

King Kaans was fond of his sister Devika, but not her marriage to a man at a higher state of caste than himself. Vasudev Yadu was of the Yadu Dynasty and Kaans' psychology to relate with Devika's husband was not admired nor appreciated.

The Yadu Dynasty was much different from Kaans' by them being superior with an angel touch of frosting. Vasudev's father had started his empire in the stock market and allowed good relations for his buyers and staff that the Yadu business was very well respected. Therefore Kaans demanded even more so for Devika to stay away from Vasudev.

Reason for Kaans to hate his sister's in-laws was that they provided everything for her and Vasudev. There was plenty of money, jewelry, garments, relations and an outstanding home for them. Truth was Kaans was not to provide his sister with anything but the fact that she had found someone who did was a reason for betrayal towards him. And further above the highest mountains or below the deepest oceans Kaans wanted to outsell and conquer Vasudev's family even if that meant to dispatch his demons to destroy all relations of the Yadu Dynasty.

"How dare you bring a spawn of that immigrant into my household?!" shouted Kaans.

"Don't you dare say that! The child is ours! You will be an uncle!" shouted back Devika.

"Your child will be nothing of mine!"

"... You have been with many women and yet you haven't settled to bring your own child into this world, and yet you insult my child that will carry on our father's name."

He turned his back to Devika and added, "I have had no father and nor will the child if you affiliate it with me!"

Kaans said this whilst Vasudev stood and watched in silence not to aggravate Kaans or give him any reason to escalate his anger further.

"You're an asshole! Vasudev has not stepped on your toes, as a matter of fact he has bowed to them," continued Devika.

"Ha! Ha! Ha! Ha! He doesn't even have shoes to step near me or to touch my toes," Kaans mocked.

"You will not change! I had come here for your blessings and you destroyed me," Devika forwarded to save herself from Kaans' insults. "Why do you consider yourself away from me? I helped raise you when we had nothing and all for you to turn your back on me?"

Kaans walked over to pour himself a drink. The good news of him being an uncle was killing him. Narcissist behaviour had fuelled him since he learnt he can bully to get his way. As this was a situation that he had no control over or that he felt he had no reward in he was burning up with anger. He thought why should anyone be happier than him? And why should a Yadu like Vasudev take his only family away?

"Let it be! You don't care! You won't care! We will raise the child and soon the child will know what the world is and you shall be sorry! That's if your own ego doesn't destroy you first!" Devika declared.

"Go and do as you wish! You are not welcome here! I'll send you a cheque via post once in a while for insurance purposes," Kaans said with a smirk.

Whilst stepping towards the apartment's door with Vasudev, Devika finished with, "Well I guess... love you sister and thank you will not come from those lips. I thought you would have changed. We will raise the child without your help as we are very much happily in love!" and she stormed out with tears running from her eyes and slammed the door closed.

"Go! Leave! Bitch! Lover of infidels!"

None of what Kaans said had made sense. Kaans walked over to his intercom and called the porter at the front desk, "Call the police. The lady leaving the building in a purple dress has been seen as selling herself. She had also threatened me with a knife for money as I didn't accept her offer. She is accompanied by a frail looking man. They both are very dangerous."

By the time the lift had reached the ground floor there was screeching of tires and sounds of sirens outside Mathura Building. Devika and Vasudev were not questioned, nor was the porter, and nor was the caller by the time the handcuffs were on them and they were put into the back of a police car.

Not at all baffled about who had made the call to the police but shocked on the extent of Kaans' hate Devika should have known that he was looking for any way to remove Vasudev. Her brother had no love for anyone so for him to spill a drop of blood for someone else would make him as weak as a kitten. Deeper weakness had already been exhibited in Kaans for doing this to his sister, her child and his brother-in-law.

The second hand of the clock moved slower than the minute hand, the minute hand moved slower than the hour hand, Vasudev's heart beat moved even slower than the time ticked. The time had fallen into the early hours of the next day. It was about one in the morning and Vasudev sat on a concrete bench in a cell next to Devika's. He sat there drifting in and out of sleep with his head against the wall behind or in his hands in front. There was a water dispenser within his sight but that happened to be behind the sergeant's desk. So close but yet so far. Life was just mocking Vasudev. Yet Vasudev wasn't thirsty he wasn't anything but. And if he was feeling anything then that anything would be numbness.

Outside the moon was on the east horizon covered by thick clouds that gathered over Manhattan. The crackling of thunder was heard. Louder the roars of thunder came. At half one in the morning when all was quiet in the materialistic world life was completely opposite in the spiritual one. The atmosphere between the ground and the sky had split. The atmosphere between the sky and space had too split. The stars and their constellations had become divided. Areas of light had moved away from itself and blackness occupied the northern hemisphere. Then came the rain in heavy fall, and then there came the lightning without mercy over all life sleeping on the mighty island of New York. The wind howled through the concrete jungle as the rain poured and the lightning struck the atmosphere making thousands of horizons on the Manhattan line.

An aura of inauspicious and auspicious character had accumulated over the outer Earth's atmosphere. The stars had drifted away from their stationary points of the universe. The space between the planets of the universe had expanded. The energy assembled over the Earth's atmosphere filtered itself onto northern hemisphere and finer still over that of New York, and finer still over Manhattan.

Outside the police station the rain had eased and fell gently. There was feeling of sweet pleasure that occupied the air. There was good fortune in the air with peace and prosperity. And as far as India the lakes filled with beautiful lotus flowers that began to bloom. Animals, fish and birds as peacocks began to dance full heartedly without the fear of people. Cows began to become pregnant and produce more milk. Cosmic vibrations covered the Earth fully in transcendental form without the materialistic existences becoming affected.

Vasudev awoke by an alarm bell that began to ring within the police station. He got up on his feet and looked around to see that no one was attending to the sound. The only sergeant manning the station was fast asleep at his desk. Surprised Vasudev felt but all of a sudden his consciousness was hit by the screams of Devika. Vasudev turned to the screams and began rattling the gate to his cell. To his surprise the gate swung open. The screams sounded in rhythm of loud breathing. Devika had gone into labour. He made haste to her jail cell. The hinges to her cell were broken and the gate was open. He touched the edge of the jail bar and maneuvered his body in reaching for Devika. She was sitting half on the concrete bench with her feet off the cold floor in a labour position trying to give birth to their child. Vasudev grabbed a pillow and helped Devika. After a while of cries of pain and exhaustion came cries of a baby.

"He's a boy, Devika! We have a boy!" said Vasudev with a smile.

"How did you get in here? Where is everybody?" asked Devika as she caught her breath.

As Vasudev got some water from a basin to clean the child a gold-light from the baby's eyes began to shine. Time stopped still and then the whole body of the baby began to glow gold. In the hands of Devika and Vasudev the child became heavy as iron and gave rise to His own weight. From the gold-light that radiated from the baby the jail cell illuminated brighter as The Light consumed Himself into a distinguishable shape. The shape resembled that of a grown man with four arms holding something in each hand. Then a voice came into the ears of the couple.

"I am The Light. I am the Supreme Soul of the universe. I am the Source of all you know. I am the will of the good, the rights of the passionate and the reason for ignorance. I am within this child. I am this child. I am the hearer of prays and I am the granter of love. I am the reason for evolution. I am a preserver of My own wishes. I have been known by many names. I am now *Kalki*, but hide Me from this world and name Me, Krishna.

"I am the Lord of the Universe, but as far as you know Vasudev I am of Yadu Dynasty. I am the Ocean of Milk that underlines the universe. Whoever is not with Me is still within Me and I choose to do what I feel best for those within Me. I can see what you do and I can see everything, but within Me I do not see anything but the bright whiteness of light that I am. I am the highest blissfulness of life. I am the heart in every living creature and the life of every plant on land and sea. I am spiritual strength. I am the law of gravitation and cosmic bonds. I am the light that shines from every star. I am the face of the moon.

"Listen to My instructions from the start. Take this body of Mine from here, follow the path where the rain falls slowly and stops to deliver Me to a foster family I have prepared in waiting. When the rain stops give me to a place with the name, 'Vrndavan.'

"My child, My mother, My sister Devika, you will have to remain here for the time being not to bring suspicion to your brother Kaans. O child, O father, O brother Vasudev, give Devika a holy kiss and take Me now through the open gates of this building and open paths of this city to where I will grow to soon come back to declare justice on Kaans. I could free you from the chains I had put upon you. I could liberate you now but I am to love the material world before this to happen. So return soon not to raise suspicion to Kaans. Again I am with you as you are with Me."

Lord Vishnu that shines light into the universe making stars, nebulas, planets, moons, cosmic dust and black holes stands with four arms holding an item in each hand. A conch-shell, a spinning disc, a golden club and a lotus flower began to take form. The conch-shell represented the communication that He has with His devotees; which is also symbolised as the sound of creation (Om). The discus represented how He protects His followers from evil and symbolised the power of the mind. The club/mace represented His mental and physical strength. And the lotus flower represented the existences of worldly liberation.

Vasudev saw Him to have jeweled ornaments of immense value, a *Srivatsa* mark on His chest (the mark of *Goddess Laxmi-Ma*), and a full lock of hair.

With a hum the gold light faded out leaving the space to return back to normal. A small *shyam* (dark skinned) baby was left on the jail floor playing with His feet which were coloured as a lotus flower.

Devika and Vasudev sat for a while just gazing at the baby whilst He moved with His eyes closed. As Vasudev gazed at the baby he felt the transcendental, material and cosmic nature of God co-existing within Him. Devika reached for baby Kirishna to cuddle. She knew to obey The Light on His commandments without any other concerns. She was speechless, so was Vasudev. They both were instantly liberated and free from Kaans seeing the Lord in His eternal form. Vasudev kissed his wife and began to prowl across the jail cell. Every now and then he kept looking at the child in his wife's arms. He then stopped and looked at his wife.

"It's okay. Here take Him. Take Him and go," Devika instructed Vasudev.

Without any disagreement or choice in the matter Vasudev approached Devika and his boy. Devika wrapped the child tightly in the sheets of the bed and kissed Him several times before handing Him to Vasudev. She looked at Vasudev and blessed him.

"I love you. Don't worry I'll be fine. Just go and quickly return," Devika said and looked away.

Vasudev hugged her tight and gave her a holy kiss on the forehead whilst holding baby Krishna, "I will soon return," he said.

Adoption in Vrndavan

Chapter 3

The police station was still adrift from the auspicious nature of the atmosphere. Vasudev walked out of the station collecting his belongings which were on the sergeant's desk. Vasudev flagged down a cab which was passing by and asked the driver to take him home. Upon arriving he immediately got into his car and drove out of Manhattan.

The roads of Manhattan were deserted and several traffic lights showed green. Vasudev took these signals as a sign and surely enough the rain that poured down was less noticeable on his windscreen. He found himself hooded by a shadow that hovered above his line of sight. This shadow drifted left and right and so Vasudev turned left and right in correlation to this unknown manifestation. Soon Vasudev found himself crossing the Delaware Bay and by the time the rain had completely stopped he was in Dover, Delaware. He pulled over to see his child churning in His sleep.

"So You are the One hey son? You are the One I have prayed to my entire life," Vasudev said to his boy as he placed his finger in his son's hand.

Sure enough his son held onto His father's finger. They both smiled; Vasudev with his eyes open and the baby with them closed.

When Vasudev gained his breath and his anxiety lowered he looked around to see what he could see. The time was about five in the morning now and soon to be a sunrise. Vasudev saw a gas station clerk setting the prices to the new day and towards the foreground a restaurant that read, 'Taste of Vrndavan'. Surely that was the place to knock.

Vasudev parked in front of the doors. He got out the car and approached the building. He looked up and over the horizon and saw a plaque made in concrete near the centre below the roof. The plaque read 'Vrndavan 1820'. He then looked to see if any lights were on when suddenly the door to the right of him opened and out came a man as fit as a fiddle dressed in jogging attire coloured white, red and black. The first thing this man saw before he had shut the door was Vasudev standing there. They stared at each other for several seconds without either one with concern to look away.

"Good morning! Are you okay there? Anything I can help you with man?" said the man.

Vasudev was taken away by this man's deep fearless voice and stuttered, "My name is Vasudev. I... I... I have come to see the one that has been said to raise my... child."

"Excuse me? Pardon? Did you just say, 'to raise your child?'" enquired the man.

Vasudev forwarded, "I was told to come to Vrndavan from Manhattan."

"Yes, this is Vrndavan and I'm Nanda-Raja Gokul, the owner of Taste of Vrndavan," replied the man, "but bringing a child to my doorstep I see as going a little far for a gratitude service tip," Nanda-Raja said with humour.

Vasudev didn't know what more to say to Nanda-Raja as Nanda-Raja observed him and the car that he had come in. Nanda-Raja heard a small baby mummer from within the car. Vasudev looked at Nanda-Raja looking into the open window and thought to do nothing but drive away.

"Sorry, I must have been mistaken. Sorry to bother you. I will be on my way," said Vasudev to Nanda-Raja, and began to walk to the driver's side of the car.

Nanda-Raja took a deep breath and murmured, "Oh my God, I don't believe it," and then in a firm voice said, "Stop! Come into my home Vasudev."

As soon as they entered baby Krishna began to cry and made Himself known to His surroundings. This in turn was heard by the lady of the house, Yashoda Gokul. She awoke mid-sleep by the crying of a baby. Nanda-Raja walked into his lounge and asked Vasudev to take a seat. Before Vasudev could take comfort heavy striding footsteps were heard from the ceiling above him and then coming down the staircase and straight into the lounge stormed in Yashoda.

"Was that a baby I just heard crying?" asked Yashoda.

She answered her own question as she saw and heard baby Krishna in Vasudev arms. She stood in silence mesmerized at the appearance of Vasudev and baby Krishna. She then gestured with her eyes to Nanda-Raja only something that he could understand.

Yashoda walked to Vasudev and looked at the baby. Tears of joy started flowing from her eyes. She chocked on her own tearful joy and took the baby in her arms from Vasudev. Resting on Yashoda's bosom baby Krishna stopped crying. Yashoda rocked the baby in her arms in joyful bliss and walked to the kitchen which was beside the lounge with baby Krishna.

"His name is Krishna," said Vasudev.

"Vasudev you're still standing, do sit," asked Nanda-Raja by signally Vasudev with his hand to the couch. "Believe me I am bewildered as you are."

"I beg to differ," replied Vasudev.

"So tell me first what brought you here?" enquired Nanda-Raja as Yashoda walked back in with water for Vasudev and formula milk for baby Krishna.

Vasudev inhaled deeply then om'ed for a few seconds and began to tell the story. He began with himself and Devika, her brother Kaans, their relationships, the fowl arrest, and the birth of the One with the apparition of God to what The Light had instructed. The couple listened with many moments that divided into seeing Vasudev, baby Krishna and staring into dead space. Once Vasudev was done he leaned forward and motioned for his baby. Yashoda eased the baby back into his arms and sat beside Vasudev.

"*Jai Sri Krsna!*" praised Nanda-Raja, "Hail The Lord! Hail The Lord! That's unbelievable! …Yet I do not feel uncomfortable towards this."

Vasudev had felt that Nanda-Raja and Yashoda were expecting something as such but had no clue on how and why? The time had come for them to speak so Vasudev lifted his jaw and raised his eyebrows without looking away from Nanda-Raja as a sign for him to speak. Vasudev dilated his eyes in acceptance to whatever Nanda-Raja had to share.

Nanda-Raja cleared his throat, "This is not the first unexpected child that has come into our home. Four years ago Yashoda had fallen terribly ill due to depression after we could not conceive a child of our own. She prayed to *Lord Vishnu* as she always does and I began to pray too for her wellbeing. One day whilst she suffered from night sweats and nightmares I took it upon myself to sacrifice my liberal ways in order for her to become better."

Yashoda gently interrupted, "He gave up his modern lifestyle of drinking with friends, partying and eating whatever was thrown at him to begin giving more love to me. He dived into a more spiritual sense of living," added Yashoda. "Nanda broke ties with his own family and resisted their generic influences on him all in order to make me better."

"She did get better. She got better very quickly. The spirit within me knew I was to make amends for my ways and felt sincerity to my sacrifice. So when I saw Yashoda start smiling I knew that was something I had to hold onto by letting go of the other side of me."

"I was smiling so much as I was with child," chuckled Yashoda.

Vasudev smiled with Nanda-Raja to Yashoda's comment of own delight.

"But the child that Yashoda was to give birth to was not mine too. She was conceived by the Spirit of God as we had not made love for the child to be mine. The night that she told me she was to be a mother I had been approached by a man in the restaurant. He was with his spouse; both were dressed in gold and white and were talking whilst laughing to themselves about Vrndavan. They were talking about a lady about to give birth to their child as a surrogate mother and all because of a man's sacrifice," Nanda-Raja leaned back on his couch, looked at the ceiling and nodded his head. "Of course I thought nothing but with the pitch of his voice and her sweet sound I could hear everything. I believe they wanted me to hear.

"They had finished their meal and He looked directly at me to ask for the bill. I walked over and the lady got up and brushed by me whilst the man took the bill by touching my hand. There was a sense of auspicious belonging. I couldn't move and was like they had pinned me to that very point in time. He signed his receipt and returned it back to me. I remember the lady had already had walked to the door and he was getting on his coat. So I rushed to the till to process their payment and by the time I turned to look at them again they were gone..." Nanda-Raja paused.

Yashoda felt her husband Nanda-Raja becoming overwhelmed in the story and continued on his behalf, "They had left a huge gratitude for a tip. The tip was actually three tips, one was for the food which was very much more than reasonable. One was a cheque signed for a sum of a million and one dollars. And one was a note that read: 'Thank you for the delicious meal at Taste of Vrndavan. Accept our gratitude as two newly born sons; one to come to you now and the other to come soon to your doorstep – *Laxmi* and *Vishnu*.'"

"Holy Mighty God!" said Vasudev.

"We thought the cheque would bounce but was passed into our account. All I could think was that they must have had a lot of cows," laughed Nanda-Raja remembering the time of the happening.

"So the other son is from the Lord you say? Is he here with you? What is his name?" asked Vasudev.

Not answering the questions Yashoda continued, "That all happened four years ago and I gave birth to a bright bubbly boy whom has been a bundle of joy. However in the last couple of days he has been acting really strange. He has happened to have built a huge appetite for butter."

When she said this baby Krishna in Vasudev's arms gave out a little cute laugh.

"Yashoda had a dream just the other night about our son at the side of her bed saying to her that his brother is soon to come. His younger brother will be coming," added Nanda-Raja. "And yes he is with us. His name is Balaram. As older brother of the Divine he is the external potency of strength for the Almighty Lord in human form as he continuously lets us know."

The door to the lounge opened softly and a boy no more than three years old came tiptoeing in. He looked at his dad and then his mum but more so at the baby in Vasudev's hands. He stretched his body upwards like a person trying to see over a wall and looked at baby Krishna.

Balaram brought himself really close to the baby and touched his forehead with Krishna's and said, "I told you didn't I? I told you that my brother will be coming." He then gave baby Krishna his finger and Krishna's skin glowed slightly.

A clock on top of the fireplace gave a ring on the hour and Vasudev knew that the time had come to leave. Vasudev couldn't stay as even as the ripples of water were the same for him and Nanda-Raja they too were still separate from each other. No two baptisms were the same even though they were to come from the same cup. Vasudev gave Balaram a hug and a holy kiss and he did the same to Krishna. He embraced Yashoda and Nanda-Raja Gokul. Vasudev got back into his car to head back to Manhattan leaving the lights of Taste of Vrndavna for another day not so far away.

The dawn of the new day had come very quick. Before they had known that the sun had rose on the day there was knocking at the back door to the Taste of Vrndavan. Nanda-Raja went to open the door as Yashoda cared to her holy sons.

Hare Krishna, Hare Krishna, Hare Hare
Praise Young Brother, Praise Young Brother, Praise Praise
Hare Rama, Hare Rama, Hare Hare
Praise Older Brother, Praise Older Brother, Praise Praise
(Priase Light, Praise Light, Praise Praise)

Nanda-Raja opened the back door leading to his kitchen to find his master chef who was a *brahamanas* standing all dressed to impress. His name was Ganesh. *Brahamanas* were known to be devotees of *Lord Vishnu* and were considered to have extreme wealth passed down from generation to generation. Whereas Nanda-Raja was from a caste of *vaisyas*, a workman for protectors of cows and agriculture.

Ganesh had not much money but on this day one would not be able to know that. He was in his late twenties and was dressed in branded threads.

"Get that water, milk, yogurt, butter, cheese, paneer and the rest into the kitchen fast fast!" he shouted to a truck driver and the rest of the kitchen crew delivering the days ingredients. "We don't have the whole day to give charity like cow-herders…"

"Good morning, brother!" said Nanda-Raja.

"Praise The Light, boss!" Ganesh replied.

"Hey boss, did I hear right? You have fostered a boy? Man you are the man!" said Ganesh whilst moving into the kitchen.

"Huh? Where did you hear that from?" asked Nanda-Raja with a puzzled look.

"Oh, my home girls all been texting each other for the past half an hour and they wanted me to ask you if it was true. So what you and Yashoda-Ma got a brother for Bala huh?" he carried onto saying without any remorse whilst he prepared the kitchen as his own.

"Yasho? When? How? What? Well of course she did," he began to laugh trying to hide his embarrassment for not knowing what his wife may have told to her best friend, Rohini. There forth Rohini must have forwarded the message to her entire contact list. "Umm... a hum. Yes, yes, Ganesh, yes. So you do a grand job today and I'll give you a two-hundred-thousand percent bonus, okay?"

Brahamana Chef Ganesh walked over to Nanda-Raja and gave him a huge heavy hug, "Say no more, I've got you and I'll do it for free Nanda-Raja."

By peak time of the day's service at Taste of Vrndavan the place was filled and vibrant. The waiters and waitresses were moving with a secret code amongst themselves to make the service flow easier. The phones were ringing off the hook for reservations and collections that Nanda-Raja was shocked on the demand for the menu for that day.

Yashoda had made a baby shower event out of the day and even gave the day a name. She called the day *Janmastami*, (Birthday of The Lord). Rohini called all their girlfriends who called their girlfriends and all women came dressed glamorously, smelling of seducing scented cosmetics. They piled into Taste of Vrndavan with slender hips to firm breasts to give love to baby Krishna and receive blessings of protection from Him.

Everything inside and outside of the restaurant was decorated with painted minerals of red oxide, yellow clay and peacock feathers. The celebrations continued at the Taste of Vrndavan for throughout the day and well into the hours of the night. All relations of Yashoda and Nanda-Raja celebrated the adoption of Krishna to Vrndavan.

Kaans Accepts His Fate

Chapter 4

Moments after Vasudev had exited the police station Devika started to feel pains again coming from her womb. The pains were similar to that of child birth. Exhausted from giving birth to baby Krishna she had not thought that Kaans would enquire about the missing child. Her womb began to expand and before she had time to comprehend her own thoughts she was giving birth again to another child. A baby girl was born.

Throughout the night Devika held the baby girl in her arms wondering what she would say to Vasudev as soon as he arrived back. She began to pray to *Lord Vishnu* baffled about would to do next. She began to fear for her life as she knew the anger of her brother and she was in fear for her husband.

"O Father of mine in Heaven, give Your servant enlightenment, give Your servant peace!" she said out aloud. "Give Your servant reason for Your will."

A response unexpectedly echoed off all walls of the building and entered her ears into her mind. Her heart beat began to pulse harder to accommodate for the voice.

"O My wonderful beautiful daughter and mother, the laws of life cannot be violated. Kaans' sister Devika, Kaans cannot kill you as this would ruin his reputation and would be cursed further than beyond. Your name still sounds in his heart and his fellow colleagues are in envy of him as of this and therefore he cannot harm you enough to kill you so stay strong."

"O *Lord Vishnu* I pray You guide me through what I should do with this child," returned Devika. "He is uncivilized. Kaans will try to take this child from me as soon as he hears of this birth. Kaans will come with anger and weapons of legislations to imprison me forever and worst still bury all that he wishes. You are the eternal forms of self sufficiency and You also recite in Kaans as for Your will he acts as such. This is Your form of cosmic manifestations. Why do You need to have for Yourself material gain through Kaans?"

"O daughter Devika, thank you for coming into My home. I am to kill all the wrongdoings of *Brahma* that I set him out to do in My name for the world to come to this point in time. In contrast to *Brahma* desiring to increase populations for personal passions, you and Vasudev had gone through severe austerities. For over twelve-thousand years Devika you have been pure in heart, mind and spirit, that even if you had not you were excused.

"I am to kill all bad royal princes, their followers and soldiers, and too all demonic rulers as of My *Brahma* in your brother Kaans. Nothing shall happen to this child as she is a creation from Me to lure Kaans away from Krishna. She is of My material energy. She is Krishna's internal potency. Her name is Yogamya, and she keeps hold of My five elements of nature; earth, wind, water, fire and ether.

"O My Devika, daughter of love, you are not to live in darkness, disease nor death. You are blessed and I am proud of you as you are a rescuer from the fearful world, free from anxiety and so you were married to Vasudev of Yadu Dynasty, a devotee from the time before you've known.

"With My appearance alone through you will vanquish misaligned ignorance I ensure you this. Krishna's transcendental form along with His material love will elevate people to higher heights in goodness, bliss and knowledge!"

"My lovely Father, please hide Your form I have seen from sight. Lord enjoy serving Your devotees as I am sure You have prepared a way to see to Kaans as You have to everything else," and as she said this she had satisfied *Lord Vishnu* which ended her pray for guidance. "We wait to return to You."

Meanwhile on the drive back to the police station Vasudev was in trance on his love for Krishna. As he thought of the space of transcendental nature between his mind and that of Krishna's he began to become enlightened to His being. Vasudev saw that Krishna was simultaneously everywhere as well as in His own universe. Both areas co-existed. Both the body in Earth form of nitrogen, carbon, chlorine, salt and protein was with the water, wind, air, fire and ether of Earth. Krishna's single entity was surviving as a flow of milk as huge as an ocean and had millions of life forms within Him. The material body didn't actually exist in the material world. The effluence actually expanded over the entire universe just as the material energy of the sun cannot be merely covered by the clouds. Krishna recited everywhere to nowhere. Krishna was the Super-soul of everything and had given each individual a soul of His very own but with the freedom of choice.

Vasudev laughed to himself as he concluded that the Lord was practically enjoying Himself in a universe that was His home. All souls and life were like a child's imaginary friends where the child happened to be God. Vasudev also thought was he laughing or was the Lord actually laughing through transcendence?

Vasudev could also feel the modes of material conscious behaviour within himself; that of passion from greatness even in acts of violence (*Brahma Dev*), that of blackness, peace, annihilation, evolution and ignorance (*Baba Shiva*), and above all that as the 'Supreme Personality of Godhead,' (*Sri Krsna*), as ultimate goodness and mercy. Even as The Light was all forms He too was not affected by them when in form as the Ocean of Milk. Though He recited utmost as the nature of goodness, perseverance and expansion.

When Vasudev arrived back to the police station in Manhattan the aura was still in the same auspicious flex as when he had left. The station was sound asleep and the ambience of the building was in a fixture between time and space. Vasudev immediately went to Devika and saw the other child in her arms. Devika explained to him about Yogamya and

Vasudev reassured her about the Gokul family for baby Krishna.

The alarm bell throughout the night had stopped ringing just at the time of sunrise the next day. Devika and Vasudev felt the nature of the night being lifted. Vasudev gave Yogamya a kiss and returned back to his cell. The new born baby began to cry which woke the gatekeepers and immediately they called the paramedics and Kaans about the delivery.

Once Kaans heard about the baby his soul sent shivers down his spine. He immediately bailed his sister from jail but only on the grounds that she stay in close proximity to him.

Kaans arrived at the hospital where Devika was sent. She was resting in bed and Vasudev sitting on a nearby chair. He closed the door to the room and walked his broad rugged figure with wired mind over to the child.

"So here is the birth of my cruel death…" Kaans said whilst looking at the baby.

Devika heard the sound of disapproval and resentfulness in his voice, "My dear brother, she is a female child, she will grow and work for you. She is no threat to you brother Kaans. Let her live in peace and safety. Don't listen to the demonic voice."

Devika said this in a way to test if Kaans would be humble in the face of negative acquisition. But surely enough Kaans did not listen or become humble to Devika. For self-gratification he picked up the baby to drop her to the floor in sight of Devika.

"Nooo!" Devika screamed as she reached for the baby.

Yogamya didn't touch the cold white tiled floor. She hovered an inch above the floor and the hospital room's temperature became very cold very quick. A force of energy pushed Kaans away and Yogamya floated in the space between them and the ceiling. The body of the baby began to glow gold and white and grew to a shape of an adult woman. Eight arms with eight hands extended from the body and every hand held an item; a bow, a lance, arrows, a sword, a conch-shell, a disc, a club and a shield. Clothes appeared on the glowing body that of opulent garments and jewelry. The room began to rain flower petals that appeared out of nowhere and vanished to nowhere.

A voice from Yogamya echoed around the room and addressed Kaans, "I am *Amba-Ma*. I am Goddess of God. I am God within this child. You rascal Kaans, how can you kill Me?! A child has been set to kill you Kaans. He is your Maker as you wished for one. He is elsewhere in the world where you will have to spend much of your fortune to get Him before He gets you. He could kill you with a clap of His hands but there is many more works to be done after you have gone. Don't be cruel to your only sister, however I guess that caution is well pass due. Now away with you! *Om Tat Sat!*"

And just like that the energy that was summoned into Yogamya was gone and she lay there giggling in her baby basket. Kaans couldn't believe his eyes and ears and stood in shook as a statue. Kaans wasn't a religious man or even a man of any God. Kaans was all about numbers and power rather than compassion and spirit. Kaans stood striped of his pride and ego. He then accepted that everyone including himself was under the control of a superior power.

Kaans privately repented in the coming years and became enlightened into transmigration from one thought to another. His sister Devika comforted him over the years as the inevitable was surely to approach him and that he should not fear but be pleased to be liberated from his stupendous bondage.

Every living entity is born ignorant and in misunderstanding of the material/fleshly influences of the living world. In ignorance people create enmity with friendship, which can lead to envious behaviours, greed, illusion, and lamentation. With this the living would forcefully forget one's relation to the Super-soul, which is to acquire ultimate goodness.

Immediately the day after next from witnessing *Goddess Amba-Ma*, Kaans was obliged to undertake the situation in the respect to his pride and temptation. He ordered his council of perpetrators to send out a message to the Lord, whomever and wherever He may be. The message was for the Lord to come and get him as he was committed to killing Him.

Because Kaans had also questioned Devika and Vasudev, he had learnt that the lack of love in the world was indeed the bringer of the Lord. Thus the Lord would recite in the hearts of His saints and devotees. Kaans ordered his demon companies to harass the saintly people and even to reduce their duration of life. Destroying and mocking the saintly lotus feet of Supreme Godhead would lead to sinful activities of the people as there would be a loss of hope. This would lead to godless civilizations that would disturb humanity and so lure the Lord out of hiding to free Kaans from his curse on Earth.

Shankar Meets Krishna

Chapter 5

The news hadn't had travelled far from Delaware of the arrival of Krishna before the atmosphere of the Earth's nature had changed in its own force. The news hadn't had also been in existence for more than a year before the elements of wicked nature had become alerted to the form of change. The air and wind was in high saturation of oxygen, the waters had lowered in sewage and animal waste, the plants were flourishing across the globe and the trees were producing larger than normal leaves, birds sang sharper and caws merged from blind spots, and the rain fell more purified than previously.

The heat of the sun became more manageable especially in tropical countries and the radiation of the sun's heat waves was not signaling any need for concern by astronomers. The shift in climate and weather forecasts in the year of 2021AD didn't follow the probability of what was occurring a decade before then. Because there was no need to be alarmed of the change in the climate the news was announced as a natural phenomenon rather than any act of man's efforts.

One man however analysed the change of natural phenomenon to a person regardless of what the news or weather channel broadcasted. Shankar in London, England, had felt the arrival of the One whilst he meditated which left him with a question; where would the Almighty One be?

From the last few thousands of years since the first coming of *Sri Krsna* (~3000 BC), who had come to make wrongs right had brought rise to an era known as *Kali-Yuga*. The Light had come to live life in the era of the Golden Age (*Satya-Yuga*), however after He had died and left Earth, the next era commenced, the Iron Age (*Kali-Yuga*).

Sri Krsna had died accidently by a hunter known as Jara who was forgiven for firing an arrow into *Krsna's* ankle whilst He slept amongst deers. This fatality returned *Sri Krsna* to His abode without Him achieving His own liberation.

Kali-Yuga then unraveled a time where man would purge one another due to envy from sex and money. They used religions over cultures as an excuse to take either a path in personal passion or ignorance towards growth of humanity. The Age of Kali also was known to be a representation of demigod *Kali-Ma* (Goddess of Death). Her image wore a skull necklace and a tongue dripping with blood standing on *Baba Shiva*, that symbolized cycles of life and death as the Lord of Evolution slept delegating His duties to her.

The end of *Kali-Yuga* had approached. 2021AD was the mark of time for a make or break outcome for mankind. As for the coming of the Lord the hope was to awaken *Baba Shiva* in Shree Krishna to strike the people of Earth and bring them out of madness into an Eternal Golden Age. Henceforth the circles of ages would come to a close and into an eternal beginning.

Shree Krishna of 2021AD would be the next avatar of *Lord Vishnu*, also known as *Kalki* (Day of Tomorrow). He would be for the generations to follow all in order for the mission for humans to reach together the final frontier of unknown time and space.

One fine day the door bell to Taste of Vrndavan rang. Yashoda came to answer the door. She looked through the peephole and saw a sharp well dressed man. Feeling no sense of fear she opened the door.

"Hello ma'am, good day to you," said Shankar.

"Yes? Morning, how can I help you?" asked Yashoda.

The man looked at Yashoda, smiled and replied, "My name is Shankar. I have come to bless you and your family on the good news for your newly born child."

"I'm not sure what you mean," said Yashoda surprised on how this man knew of them and of baby Krishna. "I'm sure you have the wrong address," she added without enquiring on how this man knew.

Yashoda fell silent to defend herself and provide protection for Krishna. She thought not to say anymore or allow Shankar to raise suspicion about her white lie.

Shankar felt he made her uneasy, "No problem. Give me call when you're ready, here is my card."

He firmly handed Yashoda his card without concern of what she must have thought of the auspicious encounter with him. He then turned around and walked to his car as Yashoda closed the door. She looked at the card she was handed. It was a black card with gold font that read:

O Shankar Gopal
Diplomat of Foreign Relations (UK)
Om Shree Krishna
UK: +44.207.437.3662
USA: +1.214.827.6330 / IND: +91.90584.83337
shankar.gopal@houseofcommons.gov.uk

Immediately after baby Krishna began to cry. Yashoda ran to nurse Krishna. She cradled Him in her arms and rocked Him to and fro but still this did not stop the crying. She called for Nanda-Raja to bring some milk but this too did not stop the crying. Nanda-Raja carried baby Krishna in his arms and played with His lotus feet, but this still did not stop the crying. Balaram also heard the crying and came to see his little brother and yet this did not stop the crying. The crying continued above that of normal and began to shake the foundations of the building. The crying also was accompanied with multiple moments of piercing screeches that ripped through their eardrums and became unbearable for Yashoda, Nanda-Raja and Balaram to withstand. To natural reaction they placed baby Krishna down and moved away and out of the main door to get away from the immense crying and screaming.

Shankar happened to still be standing there. He was standing crossed legged leaning on his car lighting a smoke whilst he saw the foster couple hurdle out of the house hand over foot. He chuckled to himself and let away the flame to his lighter. Shankar approached the couple clearly being able to hear the crying from inside.

"I'm sure I can help with that Mother Yashoda," he said with a tone of reassurance.

Nanda-Raja turned to him and stood amazed at the stature of Shankar, "Who are you?"

"This was the person that just knocked on our door," said Yashoda. "How do you know my name? Have we met?"

Shankar chuckled, "I guess we have met 'sometime' Mother Yashoda. Sometime indeed we must have crossed paths. But spiritually speaking we meet every time you pray."

The couple didn't know what to say. Yashoda handed Nanda-Raja Shankar's card. Nanda-Raja looked at the card and Shankar looked over them through their doorway and into their home. He then out aloud bellowed a loud but gentle, Om.

"OmmmmMmmmm."

The vibrations of Om filled the building and reached Krishna's calling. As Krishna heard Shankar's Om He immediately stopped crying.

"Let me in O beautiful family of our Father and let Him see me. Let Him see His *Bhagavan*," Shankar insisted with an oxymoron statement.

The statement stated that *Lord Vishnu's* Father was *Baba Shiva*, and *Baba Shiva's* Father was *Lord Vishnu*.

"Come and let me sit with you O love of our divine bliss and grace. I shall tutor you for the years to come to understand and nurture the child to fulfill the prophecy that He had set to mankind long ago."

The sound from the building had fallen silent as a mouse. As the couple led Shankar to baby Krishna there was a change in the aura of the living place. The air had softened and there was a sweet smell of sandalwood that assembled itself. The light from the sun through the windows came in brighter as the clouds moved away allowing the whole room to lighten and welcome Shankar. Shankar looked at baby Krishna and baby Krishna looked at Shankar. They both smiled a gorgeous gracious smile to each other. Shankar leaned down and kissed baby Krishna on His forehead, and with His baby hands He held onto both of Shankar's cheeks as they touched foreheads. Shankar then marked Krishna with a black spot made of kohl behind His ear. This was to spiritually protect Him from wicked sights or talks that would surround Krishna's life as an infant.

"Can I be rude enough to ask for a glass of water?" asked Shankar to Yashoda.

"Sure, sorry I'll bring some right away."

Shankar drank some of the water and poured some into his hand. He then wiped water onto Krishna's brow and eyes for calmness, relaxation and purification.

"Peace be upon You Shree Krishna," blessed Shankar.

"O Yashoda and Nanda-Raja, mother and father to the Lord," began Shankar. "I have come to you with knowledge and philosophy which you will find most beneficial on understanding the Lord in His human form. I have been waiting and meditating for His arrival as I am he who has protected His coming to mankind for over thousands of years. Within me recites the Spirit of God and that to say the Bank of God. I am the one that the Lord turns to make deposits and withdrawals so to speak and so He remains seated," he said whilst giving away a small smile. "Allow my spirit of *Baba Shiva* to bestow wisdom of *Lord Vishnu* and *Brahma Dev* to enlighten you with what will be needed to understand Krishna Consciousness."

The Gokul foster parents of the Lord sat more at ease after Shankar introduced himself in this way. Balaram came into the room and sat on the sofa crossed legged in a lotus position. As Shankar looked round to young Balaram, Balaram's reserved energy strengthened ten-fold.

"*Om Tat Sat* – Supreme is Eternal!" began Shankar. "First I need you to understand something from long ago. This is developed knowledge that had led to wisdom and encounters of three worlds in which Krishna, the Lord Light Almighty recites. Without Krishna in these worlds the worlds are numb however they still co-exist and one is not far greater than another. That being said one world does overcome the others and that is the world that *Lord Vishnu* is in as the Preserver; the rule of thumb as spoken is to preserve. So what was to preserve is a law called, 'The Absolute Truth.'

"*Paramatma* is *Lord Vishnu,* The Light, and here beside us in this baby form is He. The Light is the Lord and that is also death. Light is life and death. To be with The Light is better than to be in The Light. As if one is in The Light then they are nothing and have become nothing for The Light to see. In other words that's hell, as even The Light would have nothing to see not even black. As of a person's wicked actions God was not able to make new energy from that soul. Therefore judgement fell to harvest the soul back into The Light until time occurs whenever for The Light to make something, anything from the energy within the Ocean of Milk once again.

"*Brahma* and *Bhagavan* are the other two worlds. *Brahma* is counted as the Creator and His first love. The son of the Lord, born from the navel of *Lord Vishnu* at the time of creation, The Big Bang. A spark plug ignited from what was once all white to something now that is the ever expanding universe. *Brahma* is *Paramatma's* first love.

"Whereas *Bhagavan* is where we all rest. We are all *Bhagavan,* and I am the most highest in respect to such peace. *Bhagavan* holds the entire universe. He was created as due to a fight between *Brahma* and *Paramatma* to see who was greatest. They fought in Heaven and *Bhagavan* asked them both a question. As *Vishnu* answered truthfully and *Brahma* lied, *Lord Vishnu* i.e. *Paramatma* received the right to have prays directed to. His love took his right hand and His spirit took His left."

The form of *Tridev* occurred again by the teachings of Lord Jesus Christ, who informed about the Trinity; Father, Son and Holy Spirit. In cosmic energy and heavenly realms the Father would be *Vishnu*, the Son would be *Brahma*, and the Spirit would be *Bhagavan.*

Shankar felt them becoming uneasy, "Rest assure the words that I have spoken taste sweet as honey in the mouth but in the stomach they are hard to digest at first. Have the night to mediate on this and you'll feel better in a few days making what I have shared more sound and golden.

"Furthermore 'The Absolute Truth,' as stated long ago are the three worlds where *Sri Krsna* rests His consciousness. These conscious worlds of life, love and peace parallel that of goodness, passion and ignorant natures of human material and spiritual interactions. These I'll explain some time else but the aim is to have more good nature and equal amounts of passion and ignorance."

"With these three worlds of conscious nature, one would see an element coloured black to find peace, an element coloured red to feel and replenish love, and an element coloured white or as light to resemble the normal act of unknown life.

"Peace can be found anywhere and especially that of the horizon line where the land meets the sky. Peace is not darkness. Yes, black is a dark colour, but the feeling of darkness is not that of the feeling of peace. With excessive light one must have black.

"Love is considered as red as all life especially that of human has blood that is the colour red. Human visual sight has a huge affinity for red. The Lord uses red to admire us and weigh our dues. So that to say red, if not love, is what we should grow, as without red there is no life and surely life would not have love. *Sri Krsna's* eyes see with peace and love.

"So finally on that note leaves the light or white, as The Light. If one has too many bad memories or that one person's life has affected another's but not in a pleasant way then not to return hurt to the blood of that person but to give away to The Light. This would mean to look at a candle flame, a light source or the sky above. Looking at light off water also helps me. To live and let go with Light is what I say.

"The Absolute Truth has evolved. I have shared this with baby Krishna as I spoke. Evolution of the truth has been given a new name, 'The Eternal Truth'."

Nanda-Raja was taken back by Shankar's directions. He was overjoyed to hear that there was a system of life outside that made by politics. He was overjoyed that his child Krishna was to share and place the test to life. He smiled, looked at a switched off bulb and gave out a huge yawn.

"Mother Yashoda, can you bring water in four glasses so we can finish with a purification *abhishek* on the final part of The Eternal Truth?" requested Shankar.

"There are two more factors to consider with the three worlds of conscious behaviour and they are how to control the physical movements of our limbs especially that of hands, and also how to control the senses of our audio interactions with our own thoughts and that of others. With our hands we are to place together if nothing else. Finger and thumb on each hand helps. This is so the pulse of our blood flow becomes stable and rhythmic, thus saves oneself on waving their hands in the air like some frantic person. Simple and highly affective. Leaning on things and lifting weights and work appliances are all a sense of exertion and letting go is the sense of inertia.

"That leads me to the final factor of The Eternal Truth, and that is the ambiguous sound of Om. Om vibrates the universe from the time of its creation. From the time the spark plug ignited to the end of time and space Om is. The 'O' part has happened at the time of the creation, now and forevermore sounds the 'mmm' part. Out aloud or within the mind. So thus constant time of just ...mmm... Furthermore Om can be played with a beat as music or as a mute dial. Do you understand what I mmMean?"

The Gokul's returned in love, "mmmm."

"Mmmm," came from baby Krishna.

Shankar looked over at Krishna playing with His lotus feet and he tickled them. He moved his fingers in a walking motion over Krishna's body to His belly to tickle Him more. Then he walked his fingers to His eyes, ears, mouth and nose, head, shoulders, knees and toes, knees and toes. Krishna giggled and spluttered saliva from His mouth and nose.

"Ugh, so gross Your excellency!" Shankar said whilst laughing.

"Now everyone have a drink of water to purify the mind and bring end to the baptism into new reborn life I declared. Mother Yashoda, Father Nanda-Raja and Brother Balaram, what I have shared to you is just the basic fundamental basis of life for consciousness of Krishna's pastimes. He will have more pastimes some even I will not be able to put together. But let these be known as faith. The Eternal Truth existed once as the *Sanatana Dharma* (Eternal Faith). To bond with this is to be with the Source of Life and thus is the highest form of yoga, *bhakti-yoga*: To be in a continuous bond with the Supreme by loving devotional service," concluded Shankar.

The sunlight was shining through the blinds and reflecting off Shankar's body. He looked directly at the sun and squinting his eyes to allow a little sunlight at a time to come into each eye. The sunlight enhanced his strength and appraised him on sharing the good news. He then executed back into present time. Nanda-Raja and Yashoda felt Shankar exult himself and they too looked at the light coming from the sun.

Karma-yoga Knowledge

Chapter 6

Proceeding from the last day the following day
arrived. Shankar was warmly invited to stay with the Gokul
family and had spent one night under the roof of Taste of
Vrndavan. He had enjoyed food prepared by Ganesh and
Nanda-Raja alongside the company of baby Krishna and
Balaram. Yashoda harnessed new found peace from Shankar as
well as the wisdom he had shared.

Time was approaching the winter season of the year
and in Delaware people could be seen starting to wrap up warm
and become cosier. Shankar being used to the cold weather of
London did not mind at all of the weather. Regardless of the
weather being hot, rain, snow, sleet, hail, fog, cold, mild,
medium or heavy wind to Shankar everything was okay. Just
get on with the day and let the weather do whatever she wishes.
If there was immense heat carry a water bottle and shades. If
there was immense rain cover under an umbrella. If there was
immense wind hold on tight and walk through or stay indoors.
Overcome whatever weather comes but don't complain or even
compliment even though more days than few for Shankar were
bright blue.

The British would only talk about the weather as a
conversation starter and absolutely nothing of that of any
drama. The reaction to have no bond to the weather was an
example of *karma-yoga*. Before Shankar was to leave the
humble home of Yashoda and Nanda-Raja, he sat with them
once more to explain to them about The Light's further
consciousness for a wholesome life; the art of *karma-yoga* and
transcendental knowledge.

Shankar began, "There will come a time when Krishna will be known as Govinda Gopal, and pass all that I have taught you to a young man of His age at the time of great need. He will write all that I have said for the time to come from the time that has passed. And after such words have been practiced into formula Krishna will rise as Shree Krishna, and become liberated Himself to pass the Earth's sun and situate back to His Throne in Heaven."

The fireplace to their lounge was roaring and the family of Taste of Vrndavan sat in comfort to take note of Shankar's words of wisdom.

"There are many 'fruitative desires,' and they are vast and branched in their own categories. Fruitative desires is what you can think of that the people of mankind like and want rather than what one deserves and needs. Fruitative desires are not a contraindicated form of living after all the fruits of life is what makes life more enjoyable and a reason to live and love. Above all Shree Krishna Himself will be a fruitful desire as something for people wanting rather than needing. What must be embedded is that with this desire of what one wants over needs needs an element of peace, hence this is a part of Krishna Consciousness known as *karma-yoga*, also known as *bramini*. In lemans terms; to have fruitative desires but not to sink frequently into the nectar. Devotion into the holy name of Krishna makes *karma-yoga* easy and sublime."

"Does that mean not to add or eat too many chillies all the time?" comically asked Nanda-Raja as he knew Yashoda had a desire for chilly way above the norm.

"Absolutely right! Chilly, garlic, olives, salt, beers, alcohol, money, infatuations, jewelry, sex, cars, books, newspapers, whatever you can think of that someone just lives by is what they have to control and overcome to return back to the Source," Shankar said as a wave. "*Karma-yoga* allows one to keep their desires and also refrain on becoming indulged into them. So that said, your children who you love very much must leave their nest and that's a parent's duty to set them free in a direction of safety and security, understanding and agreeing to such is known as *sannyasa*."

"I have heard of *sannyasa*, that's when the soul of the body has to remain active for the body to function. That's like saying a human soul has a life and must be engaged with the Super-soul otherwise an illusory energy of material modes are experienced. Thus as you say, one may over drink, over eat, over temper and anger, or even have a habit of excessive lying and manipulation," added Ganesh.

"You are wise and well informed Ganesh. *Sannyasa* is a purification process and one should do the best to set *sastras* (disciplines) to engage with Krishna Consciousness. One can have best of both worlds from within their soul to the touch of their flesh if the direction of necessity is seen to be given back to Life. He who chooses to refrain is a pretender and a cheater of knowledge and peace, whereas the opposite enters the Kingdom of Life. The fruits of others desires overtime build the fruits of today, hence sitting and praying all day in a transcendental mode is not beneficial for the majority. Krishna Consciousness knows this and suggests respecting the work of others that have evolved the fruits of the spirit, for e.g. the telephone to the mobile phone to the smart phone. To understand and agree is to have sacrificed to Lord of Life, *Vishnu*, so the material bondage has been broken, a *yagna* (sacrifice and/or charity), has been formed and thus the individual gains liberation (*moksha*)," Shankar added.

"Sense-gratification overcome by Krishna Consciousness and satisfaction for such by *karma-yoga*," whispered Yashoda to herself.

Shankar leaned back on the couch and placed his left finger and thumb together, "The effect of *karma-yoga* with Krishna Consciousness is so great that even though I have sense-gratification from smoking, I still deliver work in the name of the Lord at such a higher state from most others. It is a form of *yoga* that I too have to achieve perfection, however the beauty of the *yoga* is that one does not need to but to be in consciousness of the desire that's fruity.

"So I'll need a *yagna*. What would my *yagna* be? What would anyone's *yagna* be? What after praying to demigods and goddesses across all faiths and religions, what would one boil their *yagna* down to? After getting what one desired from any person, god, goddess, workload, child, inheritance, fortunes and even misfortunes (which in turn is someone else's fruitative desire being churned into another's soul) what would that *yagna* be?" Shankar asked.

"Shree Krishna," said Nanda-Raja.

"Yes, hundred percent! To provide blissful love and devotion to 'Supreme Personality of Godhead,' and hence the wellness of fellow men. To give tax or to sanctify food as sacrifice so to speak. To give to *Praja-pati* i.e. *Lord Vishnu*, He who is of all worlds in space and in the heart of all creations. He is the life source and all beauties of all worlds. The Protector and Preserver of everything! In short, Hail Light, for Life!"

Baby Krishna giggled from in His cot that was heard sweeter than sparrow's singing in a single tree altogether. Balaram carried on that laugh and so the others chuckled in too.

"Going back to where we were before we got rudely interrupted by the baby," said Shankar in a tone directed to elude Krishna's soul. "*Yagna* is very important. Take for example, Hindu people who eat meat would worship demigod *Kali-Ma*. Other people that wish for love worship Jesus Christ, and other people that wish to have fortune they worship *Goddess Laxmi*, and furthermore people that wish to have strength they would worship demigod *Hanuman*, and further still people that wish for a belonging worship from Prophet Muhammad.

"A *yagna* will have to be paid back to the Source, to worship The Light, *Lord Vishnu*, i.e. to bring one's soul back to the Source of all things. Men that worship demigods and receive their gifts will ultimately have to sacrifice that in the name of God. They are to return the gift to reach Shree Krishna to receive the highest form of liberation. The desire of air, light and water for the body and soul is to steal the light but to then shine light in God's name. This is deeply desired in formation of Krishna Consciousness."

Shankar carried on, "Wholesome food and meat products are only produced by goodness. Metals as mercury, magnesium and other elements as sulphur too go back to The Light. Including moonlight, sunlight, rainfall and even the breeze are all enjoyed making an ultimate reach for life free from entangled material form. Henceforth you should refer to self as being *Santas* – devotees of the Supreme Lord, and always in loving service with Krishna Consciousness. You shall perform sacrifices as you already have on fostering Krishna to represent *Santas* and live peacefully in sinful times."

"*Santas*, I like the sound of that. I am a *Santas*," amusingly agreed Nanda-Raja.

"Even the Lord who is omnipotent had given *yagna* to Himself which made the universe. Animals help growth of plants, trees, vegetation and vice versa animals grow by consuming them is a form of *yagna* in the animal world and plant kingdom. If one just satisfies their own god then that's unauthorised sinful work.

"The *Brahmans* are an example of throwing flowers over statues that their hands have made, but give nothing to the people or people of other countries. This is the fight that Krishna is about to face; to break the passion of ignorance and get goodness to thrive for the alien as well as the familiar. He is to fight what *Vedic* literature calls, '*vikarma*'."

"*Vedas* are old school right? There are four I have heard..." enquired Ganesh.

"There are four; *Rig Veda, Yajur Veda, Sama Veda, Atharva Veda. Veda* in Spanish translates to the word, 'Life'. In Vrndavandesh Temple in Vrndavan, India rest letters of the

Vedas. Vedic literature scribes the Lord to be so powerful He can impregnate by just the glance of His eyes. 'He who can glance over material nature and Father all living entities.' Then to return home and allow the conditioned souls to find liberation and *yagna* in the name of Shree Krishna."

Shankar then got up and walked to the kitchen. He turned on the water tap and flowed water in his hand and wiped his brow. Refreshing his brow and his eyes he returned back to the others with a lightened mind and pureness in his sight.

"One that is fully satisfied in Lord Krishna as the Lord Almighty, there is no duty for that one. A self realised man in Krishna Consciousness as *bramini* does not see duties as work. There is no attachment to themselves and human work. They are working on behalf of the Lord and have gained personal non-attachment. Whereas those with personal attachment are good and non-violent but that is their attachment to life. It's like saying 'I'm good, I do no bad,' that is the label they live by but provide little to humanity and Krishna love," said Shankar.

Nanda-Raja then looked up at the ceiling as he had drifted to another thought, "I have heard of *Lord Rama's* wife Sita's father, King Janaka being in great affinity to the transcendental sense of God that he taught his people to work for a good cause, as a matter of fact to even fight for good. King Janaka intervened to help people follow the right path and to avoid war at all costs by such teachings of transcendental knowledge."

"The people at that time were much more ignorant than they were innocent. The realized soul of spiritual life stunted them to know how to work only. Common men follow great men and great men's standards the world pursues, Nanda-Raja. An *Acarya* is a teacher who teaches the *sastra* (scriptures) to his people as did King Janaka. First though he had to behave as such before he could teach. He was a great king, and the people of the time of over seven thousand years ago were a whole lot more innocent as they are in today's time. Which obviously states that today people are that much more ignorant," Shankar said and forwarded, "Well-being is the responsibility of generals, politicians and leaders of all sort to move the people morally and spiritually.

"Let it also be known that the Lord is working even O Family of God, He is not apart of the three worlds. The Lord senses everything as opulent so there is need for rules and regulations to exist for social tranquility amongst civilised men in and out of their household. Krishna is here to ordain the Lord's rules and regulations so unwanted populations don't grow as then the Lord would encounter a shit-storm to destroy those ways of living," Shankar announced.

"Whoever knows The Absolute Truth as I mentioned yesterday as being The Eternal Truth, knows that self-gratification and desires of material nature are meaningless. They would feel no attachment to that but would be in bountiful supply of wonders with the truth. Without Krishna Consciousness music would be heard but not felt and self-gratification would make one forgetful. *Karma-yoga* allows us not to waste time on ignorant people but let them hear the name Krishna, making them free from material bondage and free from oppression.

"So I have heard; not every man should do another man's work even though they could do it better. God and demigods should not be imitated but followed. Meaning one cannot lift a hill or do *rasa-lila*, but can follow Shree Krishna, this is known as to perform *isvaras* in *bramini* as *karma-yoga*."

Shankar closed his eyelids half way and concentrated on his *atma* spot (between his eyebrows) and exhaled. He did this to clear his mind on the thoughts that could have begun to accumulate. Shankar was a master *yogi* and knew the arts of *yoga* for daily living with Krishna Consciousness. He could control and make people dwell in his perceptions of thoughts to benefit his self-gratification defying everything he had just taught. However he refrained from this mystical art and kept his mind with the Supreme-soul.

"O mighty hearted Nanda-Raja, the Lord would not have chosen you and Mother Yashoda by chance but with great admiration. *Karma-yoga* in action with Krishna Consciousness ends upon renounce. Renounce is to be free from emotion of good and hatred. All knowledge gathered in life to be devoted to the Lord than to work life without. This will free you from material bondage when things in life be lost or not gained. There has to be a form of detachment for material desires. This detachment should be an attachment to Krishna Consciousness. For one to see, live and benefit for the Lord, the living entity of the body should be one with the Supreme Spirit Body, thus one would have the best of both worlds," stated Shankar. "You, the Lord's dear loved ones are in the hardest but most rewarding forms of living entities as you will have to raise Krishna as well as let Him go totally from body, mind and spirit. How can this be possible from all that I have said?"

Shankar continued, "Just like the lotus leaf stays dry on one side with no reactions to the world below so you should liberate your consciousness. To work knowledge that I have shared and to renounce it altogether is what I am asking. And the only way this is possible is to serve what the Almighty Life desires. The Super-soul is within every heart of every living being but the connection has been lost through entanglement of material world desires and conflicts.

"As the human body is a 'City of Nine Gates,' two eyes, two nostrils, two ears, one mouth, an anus and genitals, there is an exchange from inner to outer conceptions of the universe without effort. This is the way the Super-soul in the heart rests. Agree that purification is not something to be worked upon as much as that is something not to be ignored and that space between is transcendental Shree Krishna."

There was a wooden cuckoo clock on the wall and the time was five in the afternoon. The wooden cuckoo bird came out of its little wooden door and cuckooed five times and went back through the little wooden door into the wooden clock.

"Time to feed Krishna-wishna and Bala-wala," said Yashoda looking at the boys. "I'll prepare something for you too Shankar. You can take a taste of Yashoda with you on your flight," she cheekily added.

As Yashoda, Nanda-Raja and Ganesh had become liberated they were familiar to pious and impious nature of reality. Working, living and breathing in the name of Krishna would have final verdict for their judgment. And as their day of judgment had been sealed they were given purpose free from worry and cleansed. They had self-realisation and self-realisation of others towards others. Living in a multicultural nation as the United States was a valuable attribute to have. They had steadiness of the mind, steadfast of intelligence, humble in nature, confident in voice, powerful in strength, fearless for peace, and sacrificial love in the name of Krishna.

All the qualities of realisation is that of *Supreme Brahman*. Every new born on Earth is *Brahma* with the Super-soul of The Light in their hearts. Once the person is reborn knowing that then *Bhagavan* grows from there. That is what Shankar was teaching. Krishna would have to grow from being *Brahma* to *Bhagavan* and infiltrate human hearts in order to sacrifice them all to become of His nature and hence achieve *Brahma-nirvana* (the absence of material miseries).

An intelligent person that concerns themselves with material entanglement and miseries but enjoys living The Eternal Truth can happily be in *Brahma* all the way to their death bed. However whoever practices Krishna Consciousness and works *karma-yoga* would keep their fruits from their life of material and spiritual advancements. Their works would be preserved that even renouncing them by *yagna* would grant one reaching a superior state of mind.

Baby Krishna to Juniors

Chapter 7

The year now was 2022 and baby Krishna had become one year old. *Janmastami* was for a traditional ceremony of *abhishek* (bathing). Baby Krishna was bathed in water to remove all sinful *karmas* and to cleanse His body for the year ahead.

Outside the ceremony there was a high wind gathering. The wind was becoming more and more powerful making trees and road signs shake. The light of the day was disappearing as the speed of the wind moved clouds above Delaware denser together. Inside the ceremony the light was as bright as they had thought the day was outside.

Baby Krishna was in His cart crying for His mother's attention and kicking His lotus feet on the wooden panels. Yashoda had not heard His cries and before she did baby Krishna had broken the cart into pieces. Yashoda then noticed even though the other children tried to warn her. She came running to feed baby Krishna. He however didn't drink the milk but carried on crying. Yashoda began to play with His lotus feet and immediately the crying stopped and baby Krishna began to drink. Mother Yashoda twitched her own toes as she made herself more comfortable with her son.

Nanda-Raja looked over at the beautiful sight of his wife feeding The Light and became overwhelmed in grace that he gave a toast, "Ladies and Gentlemen, thank you for coming to my son's first birthday! On behalf of my wife Yashoda, we would like to offer you a donation to a charity of your choice. Please write your chosen charity with your name and add it into my business card jar and we will donate to them! Here! Here!"

After Yashoda was done feeding baby Krishna she laid Him down and went to attend to her guests. Baby Krishna could feel the wind increasing in strength outside which rattled the walls of the building. He crawled to the nearest window and suddenly a gust of wind within the atmosphere picked Him up and whisked Krishna high above the building. The wind had turned into a whirlwind that then into a tornado across the land. The guests and the household were becoming concerned about the nature of the weather and went out to see. To their surprise they saw a light within the whirlwind which grew brighter.

Krishna had made light within the force of nature and made Himself heavy as an anvil that tore through the forming tornado ripping the wind apart. He broke the dimensions of the demonic wind and slammed the wicked energy into the ground destroying the currents of hot and cold air. The environment immediately calmed from the force of the natural disaster.

The men of the party then began to speak cowardly of sinful thoughts regretting that no worse happened. Mother Yashoda ran to baby Krishna as He lay there listening to the men. As she picked Him up and walked pass the men His light was still shining which turned the men's thoughts to ploy to Krishna's nature. He conditioned the souls of the men as a fictional movie does to please its own audience. As a pastime activity Krishna did this for His own enjoyment. Krishna's goal for human life was to please His devotees and make friendships. Thus this escapade of events did exactly that.

Shree Krishna had many pastimes, some that He enjoyed on His own and some with Balaram and His friends. As Krishna grew from baby to infancy to juniors He loved to tease and flirt with Yashoda's girlfriends and their daughters. They were all very much fond of Him. Not knowing that He was the Lord Almighty they still had an intense affinity for Him and Krishna encouraged that. His eyes showed passion for love, His lotus feet showed courage of strength and His thick locked black hair showed peace and tranquility for all to love Krishna.

A few years later when baby Krishna was in his infants Yashoda heard some cluttering coming from the kitchen and then a huge smashing sound. She ran as fast as she could to the kitchen to find that the butter pots had been broken and the special butter called, '*makan*', that was churned within them had been tampered with. Much *makan* was also smeared across the table tops and small hand prints of *makan* had decorated the kitchen. There were two sizes to the hand prints. Immediately she knew that Krishna and Balaram had their hands in this. She went to find some rope first to tie up the brothers as a way of punishment before she went to find them. She found Krishna and Balaram on the roof of their home.

"Krishna, come here! Did you break the pots of butter downstairs?" she asked sincerely.

"It was the monkeys. They had come into the building and Balaram and I tried to fight them off but they were too fast and the pots broke," replied Krishna.

"Monkeys huh? And where are the monkeys now?" played along Yashoda.

The brothers looked at each other in amazement that their mother had changed her tone and after a short pause Krishna replied, "They've gone back to the zoo."

"The Delaware Zoo might that be?"

"Yes. How did you know? That's where they also came from," said Krishna.

"You two are the little monkeys, little monkeys," she said trying not to laugh. "So answer me this, why is there human hand prints of butter all over my kitchen?"

Krishna and Balaram stood speechless.

"Open your mouth you little butter thief, *makan chor*," insisted Yashoda.

She grabbed Krishna's cheeks and made Him open His mouth to look in. She was expecting to see and smell the texture of the oily sweet butter in His mouth but she saw something else altogether. She was mesmerized. Her eyes widened and pupils dilated. Her breathing became so faint that her heartbeat almost stopped. Yashoda on the roof top of Taste of Vrndavan, holding her son's face in her hand saw in His mouth the vast four corners of the universe. She saw planets, stars, moons, comets, nebulas, shooting stars, all of the galaxies, and a golden rim surrounding it all of which she saw lay rest in harmony with everything else. For a few seconds what represented time as light years she was perplexed.

Krishna then licked his lips and said giggling, "Okay mother you've caught this butter thief gold handed."

As He said the words the whole vision of Heaven and the universe vanished back into a normal mouth cavity.

"Um, I don't know what to do with You," Yashoda first said trying to overcome what she saw and remain as the adult.

"Why don't you tie Krishna up so He doesn't cause anymore mischief to gain your attention just for reassurance sake?" smartly added Balaram. "Is that not why you have brought that rope, momma?"

Outsmarted by Balaram, Yashoda replied, "Oh yes you're right, Bala. And this way I can keep you both separate from one another. You can come and help me clean up the kitchen, cheeky pants."

Playing His mum Krishna quickly added, "Yep my big brother Bala is strong, much stronger than me, he can help you momma."

Yashoda stood and moved Krishna to a small square vent they had on the roof and began to tie Krishna up.

"Now don't try to escape and I'll come free You later," she said whilst circling the rope around Him.

She managed to get Him secure to the vent but upon tying the two ends they came a couple of inches short. She undid what she had and tried again knowing she had plenty of rope but again the rope came short a few inches.

"What's wrong with this? I'm sure the rope was long enough," she said starting to become frustrated.

"Try one more time mom I'm sure you will be able to get Him tied," suggested Balaram.

From his tone of voice Yashoda caught on and caught on further about what she had witnessed from Krishna. Embarrassed, flushed, and overwhelmed at the same time their mother set the rope down and sent both the brothers out to pass time to leave her in peace from the moment of grandeur.

A few years later Krishna was in His juniors. He and Balaram had joined the local farm to help with the animals and harvesting of the land. His pastimes allowed the cows to produce more milk, the hens to lay more eggs, and the sheep to produce more wool as the seasons changed. Furthermore when the seasons changed into autumn there were more offspring of the animals too.

The farm was owned by a man named Rama Patel, and he lived on the farm with his second wife and eight children. Five were boys and three were girls. Krishna and Balaram spent their time at the farm when there was no school.

From youth the cowherd boys would dress up like Krishna and play alongside Him and their many animals. They would all dress nice and carry a wooden stick to help them walk across the land but also to battle with one another. A flute was carried by Krishna and so therefore did the other boys. The cowherd boys had a whistle that sounded like a bullhorn that they used to call one another and startle the cows. To call the sheep from the fields they had three dogs named George, Jake and Sean. They were very good shepherd dogs who loved assisting Krishna on calling the sheep.

The daughters of Rama Patel were continuously being teased and strengthened with affection by all their brothers, Krishna and Balaram. They had called themselves '*gopies*' for Krishna. This was a personal name that was made whilst together, however Krishna also liked calling them cowgirls.

"Echo!" said one of the boys in the barn.

At times an echo of 'echo' would bounce back for all to be amused of the sound of one's own voice.

"Om!" said Krishna loudly which at times resonated within the confinements of their space.

"George Harrison!" said Balaram and everyone shared laughter whilst the name echoed.

The Super-soul i.e. Shree Krishna, was in all the children's hearts led the cowherd boys and cowgirls to follow Him and play games as hide and seek, tag, counting lights, describing clouds, naming and imitating the animals, and playing with *amalaka* fruits (which were like golf balls), all to present themselves as devotees to Krishna. Thus He being the enjoyer, nature and preserver as One in their pastimes together.

Whilst the friends played a phone call from Mother Yashoda rang at the farmhouse.

"You're mother is on the phone and she wants you boys back now!" shouted Rohini, (Rama's wife).

Immediately as Krishna heard this both Rohini's and Yashoda's breasts became filled with warmth that they began talking to one another ignoring their own instructions they had given to Krishna and Balaram.

The daughters of Rohini also felt a shift in hormonal balance and distracted the brothers not to leave. Rama had too become distracted in what he was doing from all the higher energies of the females speaking. He came to have a look at all the excitement and saw Krishna and Balaram standing stern in posture whilst what looked like his girls cornering them.

"Okay boys, time for you to go, see you tomorrow now," he said whilst pushing them out.

The brothers laughed along with Rama and waved their friends goodbye. As Rama did this he was aiding the Lord to be relieved and saturate a male role model leader of love. Hence he, who gives to the Lord is a million fold winner; 'bestowed of all benedictions.'

A few days later the brothers had come back to Rama's farm to accompany the newly born calves with their cowherd friends and friends of friends. The farm was sectioned to the rest of the land by woodlands. The children loved to play in the woods and the calves would naturally follow them whilst the cows grazed in the fields. One evening as the friends were about to leave the woods they saw a small campfire that was unattended.

"Stay here my friends. I will go and see to the campfire," said Balaram.

Balaram went closer to the campfire. As he walked closer he tried his hardest to not make any noise but the sound of leaves and twigs crackling under his feet was unavoidable. As Balaram got even closer to the campfire he sensed that there was something or someone else in the woods with them. The daylight was fading making visibility into the surroundings difficult.

All of a sudden the fire roared several feet high and began to set fire to the trees. Birds flew as fast as they could off the branches and nests into the sky which gave the friends a massive fright. As Balaram looked back to see Krishna and his cowherd friends he was approached by a large dark shadow.

A demon named Palambasyria, who had been watching the children for many days had become overcomed by their opulent appearance. He thought to kidnap one child for ransom. Little did Palambasyria know of the external potency of Krishna that rested in Balaram that he was no match for Balaram. Krishna saw the shadow appear over his brother and so did their friends. As the demon grabbed Balaram who was half his size the woods bellowed in crackling. The shine of Balaram faded out and all the friends became worried. The fire was engulfing the trees and the smoke was making the air very difficult to breathe let alone see through. Krishna stood shielding His friends.

"Help, Krishna! Help, Ram!" cried the friends.

Krishna saw Balaram through His third sight and then saw His brother by eye contact between the raging fire and thickening smoke. As Krishna saw his brother about to take action on the demon He opened His mouth and a huge gust of wind came in between the trees. As Krishna was shielding the friends they were not moved but the fire all around was extinguished.

Then ... crack, crack, crack, crack, thud came a sound that shook the leaves off the trees around them. The light of Balaram returned brighter than before. Demon Palambasyria was undertaken by Balaram's strength and was thrown across the woods far from sight where he landed dead as wood.

Balaram returned back to his friends. Krishna smiled at His brother and placed His arm over Balaram's shoulders. The cowherd friends became extremely joyous and praised Krishna and Balaram for saving them. The farmer's children and their friends of friends with the calves walked back to the barn beside the farmhouse in delight. There was nothing that was impossible or to be concerned with when they were with Krishna and Balaram.

The news of this happening had spread as fast as a forest fire throughout the school the brothers attended. The farmer's children had told their friends, and their friends of friends had told their friends. Soon before the week was over the whole town of Dover knew of the incident and the victory over the fire and the demon.

Supreme Brahman i.e. Krishna as Shree, and the Super-soul as *Lord Vishnu* filtered into all the hearts of the people that had heard the story. Before long no person became afraid of the sound of thunder or a strobe of lightning. All individuals were protected by a higher sense of affection from the brothers.

The State of Delaware became a greater state in treasury as the people were happy so they worked happier which brought costs down and the land flourished. Rain and evaporation of water from Delaware River brought further condensation and precipitation to the land which granted trees water. There became a natural flow of taxation to the state. The people were rewarded by making their land a safer place to live as well as influencing trading in the financial markets.

Description of autumn in Dover, Delaware, United States began to brighten the hearts and illuminate the souls of many people. The land itself was seen with rainbows overhead when the rain settled in the skies. The acts of material existence associated itself with states of nature energy of *Goddess Durga*, (the internal potency of Shree Krishna). *Durga-puja* was the biggest ceremony in autumn, where too the festival of *Navaratri* happened. In autumn the life of nature grew lotus flowers and lilies. Animals too would become pregnant (cows, deers, birds).

Autumn bonded strongest with governmental contracts. Best citizens would overthrow thieves. The male sexual drive of 'Supreme Godhead,' encouraged a mating season. As for the females the breeze of the season was more unfortunate for them especially the *gopies* not embraced in Lord Krishna. And those without cause to mate kept in devotional service with great enthusiasm, patience, conviction, and clean from excessive material bondage. For many people that meant an increase in sitting back and watching sports and being a sport. Autumn brought by Krishna and Balaram accustomed a work lifestyle that coincided time of transcendence and material existence. As in nature people, preachers, politicians, and public folk could not do business in the rain thus they built profit on tax and knowledge in the ecosystem as the trees do from the rain.

Clear rain water, fresher air, recycled pollutants and anxiety of life from the summer prior with new grass carpeted, fruits and dates ripened with blackberries. The earth was turned and deeper mud got water which grew fresh vegetables similarly new consciousnesses grew in mankind. Farmers began to find new ways to reserve water as the oceans calmed in autumn. The night the sky was a wonder of innocence. As the moon makes the night brighter with the stars the Yadu Dynasty around Krishna made His peace dwell deeper.

Four works of human societies according to *Vedic* literature are *brahamanas, ksatriyas, vaisyas,* and *sudras*. Here good people lived in harmony away from anguish, regret, depression and disbelief. Believers to the miracle sang, 'Hari Krishna,' (He who takes away).

Krishna and Brahma

Chapter 8

A convoy of yellow school buses made their arrival to the high school in which Krishna and Balaram attended. Students from twelve to eighteen years of age departed from the school buses and made their way into the grounds of Dover High School. Some students made their way to the lockers to exchange their books and others to exchange conversations of their lives. Some students made their way to the cafeteria to wait for other friends to arrive and some students pastime in the outer grounds of the school. The school's bell rang for the first period of class and all students made their way to the classrooms. The yellow buses departed their position outside the school and made way to the garage and parking bays.

High school was a pleasant time for Krishna. He was smart, intelligent, handsome, famous and wealthy in savings. He dressed everyday to impress His fellow friends and be an inspiration to others. He motivated all students of every subject from math to languages to art to humanitarian studies to sports to home economics to history to science and through to drama.

He was fifteen as of date attending high school classes and Balaram was in his senior year. Everyone knew of the brothers but Krishna was the one who had all the females' attention as well as most males.

"How was your night last night?" asked Radha-Rani to Krishna.

Radha-Rani was the fairest female in all of Krishna's life. Out of all the females He knew from His community that all had affection for Krishna, Radha-Rani had the most love for Him. She was implacably infatuated with Krishna. No other girl could get close to Krishna without Radha-Rani knowing about that. And all other females in the whole district of Dover knew that Radha-Rani was head over heels about Krishna and that Krishna had a similar interest towards her too. Radha was her name but the people called her Radha-Rani as for the relationship she had with Krishna.

Radha-Rani was kind, respected, and in a league of her own which all the other girls admired. They all respected Radha-Rani as she held her own status. Krishna was the only one that could affect her wellbeing and as Krishna never let Radha-Rani down there was no concern of their love ever vanishing.

They fought, they laughed, they comforted, they appraised, they dwelled, they studied and they ate together whenever possible. If a male had something to say to a female he would consort Radha-Rani first and get her approval as she would consort Krishna. So if nominations were to be made or anyone needed advice then Radha-Rani they would first sought.

"Fine. Forever new but nothing out of the blue," replied Krishna.

"We're going to be in college next year. Are You excited?" Radha-Rani asked.

"Excited or not-excited is neither here nor there, but the moment of now that I spend is what is most important in My world of life, love and peace."

"I'm excited," said Radha-Rani as she stretched a fake posture to point out her chest. "Does the moment of now mean the moment with me is important?"

"When is there a moment with you never important?" said Krishna with a smile.

"Mmmmm. You know not to woo me too hard before class, I can't concentrate."

"Oh look there goes the Peacocks!" Krishna said looking at the school's football team.

Krishna called the football team, 'peacocks', as the uniform was blue as well as the team were all proud splendid males (whereas they were the 'Senators'). But as peacocks they liked to show off to the females their might, brawn, beauty and dance. Furthermore Krishna calling the male members of the team peacocks was His own way of showing admiration and affection to them. Henceforth this was a reason why everyone loved Krishna, as not only did He have a way with women and men but also with the school as a whole.

One day that was no different from any other came something different beyond measure. There walked into Dover High School a new student. The new student was not from Delaware, let along America. He was from Leicestershire, Great Britain. He spoke in a strong British accent and was of same ethnicity of that of Krishna and Balaram. He knew the Indian culture very well and with great respect and intellect. He was charming in a gentle type of way, but yet stern to the sight from unwanted attention. The students were drawn to him. Not out of love as they were to Krishna, but out of interest as he was an alien to them. The student's name was Brahma, and within one year he had adopted the nickname, British-Brahma.

Brahma had his own style of grandeur. He drove to school in a scarlet red Mustang and all days of the week he wore something that was red. Sometimes that would be red shirts (many shirts), red shoes (many shoes), red strapped watches, couple of red badges, red caps (many caps) or whatever else he had like books, files, pens and pencils. Brahma loved the colour red which attracted others around him to him.

Of course Krishna and Brahma bumped paths and knew of each other's reputation. However no matter how hard Brahma tried to seek attention from the females and males of Dover High School, the name of Krishna and Radha-Rani always came out.

Brahma in all respect was an inspiration to the students but he did have a tendency to have his head move in five directions to view females. The students, staff and all other members of the school knew how to distract Brahma was to just have an attractive female walk by him. As his material nature was limited and Krishna's transcendental nature was limitless, time happened to always be fresh and rewarding to hear about Krishna even though Brahma stood out.

As the academic year was coming to an end Krishna had decided to organise a day out to, Bombay Hook National Wildlife Refuge. He invited all His male friends and invited Brahma too. He picked a location at the bank of Delaware River for the friends to meet. Most of His friends including the cowherd boys came to the gathering but Brahma had not come. They sat on the soft grass under the hot summer's sun talking and mocking each other as Krishna watched Blue Grosbeaks and ducks walk, swim and fly from the bank of the river.

Krishna was wearing a blue Dover High School football jersey with black denim jeans and so were His friends. Under the jersey Krishna tied a cloth around and above His waist line to hold in and tighten His abdomen. He also used the cloth to hold a flute. Krishna loved to play the flute and was very good. When He played the cows would begin to produce limitless amounts of milk and the cowherd girls along with Radha-Rani would melt in love for the music.

Krishna pulled out the flute to play for His friends whilst they had lunch. He closed His eyes and played sweet music with depths and peaks in rhythm as His friend's hummed in symphony. The animals as birds, foxes and turtles all began to enjoy the music coming from Krishna's lips.

From a short distance away Brahma had pulled up in his Mustang with several females from his neighbourhood. As he turned off the engine they all heard the sweet music that occupied the air. The females immediately had sunk into the rhythm of the music and looked to see where the music was coming from. Brahma saw Krishna and His friends by the bay.

"Come let's see if we can call them over here girls," said Brahma.

From the top of the hill side Brahma flashed his lights and the females got out of the car to attract Krishna's friends. Some of Krishna's friends saw the lights and the females waving in their direction. They stopped what they were doing and went towards them as Krishna played with His eyes closed.

After a short while Krishna opened His eyes and pushed His flute back into His cloth. Without assuming that His friends would have gone too far He opened His lunch pack and prepared for lunch. Krishna had a butter sandwich, cherry yogurt, rice, and pieces of fruit and salad. Krishna faced the river and had not noticed that His friends were missing. He placed a lump of yogurt and rice in His left hand and was about to consume when He realized His friends weren't there.

Krishna looked around and saw that not only that His friends were gone but also the animals had dispersed too. Immediately He got up to search for them. He searched far and wide for them and began to become worried on their whereabouts. First Krishna thought the friends were playing a joke on Him, but after an hour of searching caves, bushes, and the woodlands He knew that something was wrong. Krishna knew He couldn't return home without them so He went to the car park. Krishna saw Brahma's car and felt that he must have stolen His friends from Him.

Krishna sat and looked between the trees and between the horizons. He focused on the transcendental nature of peace. He expanded Himself to reach His mind over the land of the park. He expanded Himself over the town of Dover, over all homes and all spaces within spaces. He summoned His inner peace. The warm breeze of the day slowed and the sound of the environment faded out. And in a loud deep voice that echoed to and under the sky He holla'd, "OoooMmmmMmmMmm!"

"MmmmMmmmm! OmMMMMmm!" He holla'd more which resonated across the land.

Slowly His friends came over the hill and back to Krishna, "Krishna, our friend, we don't know what happened. We were subdued by the females. We had never seen them before and we forgot all about You. Sorry. Forgive us," said one of His friends as he approached Krishna.

"We didn't mean to leave You. We just thought we would be back as soon as we could but Brahma's friends had us entangled in his web and we couldn't set ourselves free from his light," carried on another.

"That is why I said, 'Om'. My peace strengthened you away from the new unknown flesh that had you all aroused," Krishna sympathised.

Krishna had not only enriched His friends with the power of His light, but also brought happiness to the females as their hearts began beating from Krishna's voice as the males left them. The animals too heard Krishna's voice and were released from their self-gratification by Brahma's passion.

"Brahma had stolen your hearts and thus you went missing. I expanded My light and called out a word from My lips that overcomes the love from the life he was offering," explained Krishna. "You are My cowherd boys and you are faithful to Me as I am faithful to you. Thus I protect you from such entities that can resemble a temporary part of Me too," continued Krishna still holding the lump of yogurt and rice in his left hand.

Brahma was a part of 'Supreme Personality of Godhead,' as in the form of *Brahma Dev*. He had all qualities as that of *Brahma Dev*, and could save the Earth but would also destroy much too. Creation was the name of *Brahma Dev's* game, not preservation. He would create new people out of Krishna's friends that would follow sense-gratification lives rather than self-awareness in brotherly love. *Brahma Dev's* existence of dying love over a twelve hour cycle would be a multiple of four million, three hundred and twenty thousand times more within a timeline. Meaning that one moment of

Brahma Dev's time was equivalent to a solar calendar year. Hence Krishna's friends with Brahma felt they were with him for a lot longer than what were merely a few minutes.

As Krishna and his friends got into their cars to head back home Brahma came into the light to see why his mischievous ways hadn't had worked. He knew not to be over mischievous with Krishna. He saw all the friends of Krishna in another light, the light of *Lord Vishnu*. They all presented traits of himself, *Vishnu* and *Shiva* in form of Krishna. There was a mystic power over the living entities that he saw before him that associated as a reservoir of all truth, knowledge and bliss of *Sri Krsna*. Brahma fell to his knees and as soon as he had he too became liberated. As sunlight would hit water, Brahma's soul became that of Super-soul's and filled in royalty of *tulasi* leaves and jewels.

"I am humbled at Your being Krishna. Your Eternal Truth that You share exceeds all material wealth and desire," sincerely spoke Brahma.

Krishna summoned His inner soul and opened the curtain of His internal potency. His internal potent energy that rested in his sister Yogamya severed the top head of Brahma's five directions on conditioned souls. Brahma as *Brahma Dev* was left with four heads that resembled the compass of the universe. The fifth head that rested on top of the four was severed for feeling affection from people that he had touched. Yogamya's mystic nature gave peace to Brahma.

Krishna Consciousness from Heaven fell as a golden stick on Brahma and his other four crowns fell to the lotus feet of Krishna. Freed Brahma saw Krishna's divine nature and he saw himself as a friend of God. He began to pray loud and carefree showering Krishna with compliments. Prays that Brahma did for Krishna were that of *samadhi*, meaning to concentrate the mind on the lotus feet of the Lord.

"My Dear Lord, You are the *Supreme Brahman* and Super-soul to Absolute Truth," boasted Brahma.

Krishna received the praises and gave Brahma permission to return to His abode, *Brahmaloka*. That moment of pastime seemed as a year with Brahma passed all pleasing and all attractive in brotherly love. Thereafter Krishna consumed the lump of yogurt and rice that was still in His left hand.

Kaliya-Naag Online

Chapter 9

The internet had made its presence marked in the twenty-first century and the majority of humans on the planet had access to the world-wide-web. Even if a person didn't have a home they most likely had a mobile phone and that mobile phone was a smart phone. Smart phones had access to everything the internet had to offer. People could buy, sell, trade, exchange information, see the news and socialise all in the tap of a screen. Humans were very much at home when they had their mobile phone with internet connection even more so than just being at home. Truth was fair to say that the mobile phone was just as important as a person's wallet. As a matter of fact the mobile phone with contactless function pretty much had become a person's wallet.

There were great good things that the internet had brought. People could search for whatever they thought of interest and people could advertise whatever they thought of interest even if that interest really was of no interest. The best thing about the internet was social media platforms that built a bridge throughout the globe for people to connect. With all great good things there would be an element of an opposite.

The internet also provided wicked hearts and cruel intentions to be spread as viruses. Even though social media providers narrowed the aspects of cyber-crime and abuse from the wicked to the vulnerable there were still many who lived joy in creating misery to others. The internet did have its fair share of polluted individuals and due to data laws in subscripts for freedom of expression extreme toxicity existed.

All were aware of broadband speeds and unlimited usage packages available. Also all needed to have wi-fi connections when in public and private locations. There was nothing wrong with that technology and so worked wonders for humanity. As the world of computers rose immensely from the early parts of the twenty-first century so did the demand for skills in the careers of computers and e-commerce.

Krishna was born in a time where He knew not of a world without computers and the internet. The whole generation of young adults knew that the internet was here to stay and to occupy time to pastime. The future was of a digital age and to embrace was far more important than to dismiss or reticule.

Dover High School had a computer lab where the students would pastime browsing the internet or completing assignments. The school also had many computers connected to the web in the library. Furthermore the students brought their own devices such as tablets, phones and laptops to school.

During a time in school there came across talks in the corridors and classrooms that the students were not able to access the internet. The students had tried many times to enter their details but something was blocking them on entry. The staff had the same problem. Instead of the usual login there were web pages of indecent pop-ups to buy drugs, weapons and women. The school technicians had to close down the service for the students as the adverts were becoming far too dangerous and way out of control. There was a breach in the network that needed to be sought before valuable data of the members were lost to whoever was causing these poisonous websites to appear.

Over a week had gone by and there was no luck on gaining access to the internet safely. This caused a massive problem for the students and staff as work had to be stopped and deadlines to be cancelled as no one had access to the shared files. As the school drank from the resource of the internet during school hours they became poisoned on every attempt to check if the internet was back on for them. Some students had to seek counseling and some students had also received threats so they stayed away from school altogether.

Krishna was not affected by such cruel intentions from anyone. He had an art of mystic *yogis* known as *yogesvara*, that He used so nothing out of the blue would alarm him. He volunteered to get to the bottom of this and find the source of the evil.

He branched out His own laptop which He had flourished with components that He had built out of scratch. He typed in His password 'kadamba tree' (a tree with yellow flowers). He tightened His belt cloth and flexed His hands and dived right into the ocean of the internet to surf the waves of files using the school's wireless connection.

Krishna's own computer was at risk of becoming hacked by this mysterious virus but to please His fellow peers He loved the most. Krishna tapped His lotus feet to the ground and began to surf the water of digital data. Immediately with Krishna's presence to the world-wide-web the reservoir of information on His laptop raised the banks of data by a thousand gigabytes.

As soon as He had entered the illegal, crude, poisonous waters the unnecessary websites began to appear on screen. Instead of closing down the windows that opened He maximised them without a second thought of all the people that were watching. He openly showed everyone surrounding Him what was trying to be shown with no concern or importance. He maximised a dozen pop-ups and then a dozen more. More kept on coming on screen and whilst this happened the life of the laptop was at risk of breech and also that of the school's data system. His peers around Him began to become worried whilst *yogesvara* Krishna opened all the pop-ups that were invading their space.

He then pushed a few buttons on the keyboard in a rhythmic sequence that sent out a tumult sound through the wireless connection to the modem which pulsed through the phone lines and electrically short-circuited the source of the trouble. All the pop-ups from the internet were then replaced by a repeating video of a venomous serpent with a hundred heads slithering upright on a river's surface.

"I am Kaliya-Naag. Who is this that has awoken me from my sleep?" screeched a voice through Krishna's speakers. "Show yourself!"

Krishna opened His webcam channel.

"No don't do it!" said one of His peers.

However Krishna had already clicked on the light to the webcam. Kaliya-Naag saw Krishna glowing in glory with ornaments of gold around His neck and a gold band keeping His hair locks tied. With the beautiful image of Krishna smiling that Kaliya-Naag saw he became angry in envy. Kaliya-Naag bombarded Krishna's laptop with coils of computer codes which made His laptop and the other computers flicker in strobe fashion. Everyone became worried but Balaram seeing Krishna take the hits with a smile was not afraid.

The three worlds of Krishna Consciousness vacated His space and all staff and students developed ecstatic love for Krishna for bringing the demon out to surface. As there were other computers they all went on to the terminals to see how they could help Krishna. Balaram looked over at them to safeguard the school from infiltration of this being. Krishna felt that He had placed the emotion of His failure and death upon them. Feeling their unhappiness He sat upright and replaced the coils of strain on Kaliya-Naag's codes.

Krishna began to dance codes of syntax over nine Ghz per second on the hundred hoods of the serpent. His fingers and lotus feet danced on each of the jeweled heads of Kaliya-Naag. As Krishna carried on this digital martial arts of anti-hacking Kaliya-Naag became fatigued. Eventually Kaliya-Naag came to consciousness and instead of venomous fumes of a serpent on screen a video interface appeared of an old feeble man dressed in riches sweating and vomiting. Krishna had beaten each head of Kaliya-Naag's inscription codes and gained access to his location. As Kaliya-Naag surrendered he became liberated.

"Grant me mercy O Light of the age," wished Kaliya-Naag. "I praise you!"

"Grant our beloved mercy, O young One," came voices of *Naagapatnis* (Kaliya-Naag's wives). "Keep our location away from the law as we cannot lose the one we serve, and so we give our offspring to You as insurance that we will do no such acts of crime. We pray to You, do grant us this."

From behind the scenes the *Naagapatnis* were watching the moves of Krishna and knew from then that He was the shelter of souls. He found the ones without devotional service to The Light and still they were reached by Krishna. The lotus feet of Krishna came across the world-wide-web and channeled the demon to give prays and obeisance a million fold over.

Krishna granted their wish and gave immunity to Kaliya-Naag, but he had to leave the internet's ocean with his *Naagapatnis*, children and belongings for their own well-being and for the love of Krishna's mission. They agreed humbled at Krishna's mercy and the computer screens turned back on to normal. Life returned to the development of digital communication for the school and prominently the world.

Forwarding a few sunrises the sun again lowered behind the west horizon bringing a surreal red sky. Nanda-Raja had made plans with his lead chef Ganesh to have a meal at a newly opened restaurant. Yashoda, Krishna and Balaram had also agreed to join them as a family to inspect and give an audit to this new restaurant. The restaurant was beautifully situated next to the River Delaware which was not so far from Dover. The restaurant was called Govardh Hill, and was owned by a man named Narad Shah. Ganesh was hoping to take partnership with Narad and needed Nanda-Raja's approval upon settling into two business contracts. If the meal and meeting went well then there was no reason for objection from all parties.

Upon arrival there were many trees surrounding the backdrop of Govardh Hill Restaurant. The place was peaceful and tranquil all at the same time with the sound of the river nearby. However a disturbing fragrance of intoxicating nature accompanied and hovered in the air. As the family stepped out of their vehicle the first thing they smelt was this toxic air and looked immediately around to where the smell could be coming from. They noticed a group of teenagers beside a few cars with the music on smoking marijuana. The family ignored them and thought nothing more, but before they could walk away Narad had come out of the restaurant to get the teenagers off his property.

"Excuse me fellas can you vacate my grounds?" Narad asked the teenagers.

"Yo man just chill we will be gone soon," said one of the male teenagers.

"You've been here for some time now and the smell and noise is disturbing my business."

"Dude I said we will go, now go and look after yourself," said another male teenager.

"Calm down Nalak," intervened a slightly drunk female who happened to provoke the male instead.

"Don't you know who we are? We're sons of Kuravia, the governor of where your restaurant is and I guess we could ask you to leave. So go back where you came from darkie!" added Manigreav, the brother of Nalak.

Narad's pride was hurt but also his patience with these rude individuals. The females ignorantly laughed along with the males as they mocked and ignored Narad. Kuravia was a rich man by wealth and respect but his sons were quite the opposite. They were consumed on desires for alcohol, drugs, gambling and women. The spiritual attachment of Kuravia's household was forgotten but Narad tried again to instruct them with another gentle approach.

"Lads, you are respectful sons of Kuravia and you hold your father's reputation. Be free without shame of these ordeals you have. Become a tree of life rather than smoke the tree," Narad said to them.

Nalak and Manigreav were as ignorant as trees and as a tree cannot help being ignorant the teenagers smoked in damaging ignorance. But worst they verbally abused Narad which gave the third strike to them trespassing on his property. He grabbed one of the boys and pushed him against a tree and with the other hand pushed his brother too. The females became frightened on the unexpected strength of Narad.

"I'm doing this for your own good boys," Narad said whilst pinning Manigreav to the bark of the tree. "Stay here crucified into this Arjuna Tree whilst I call the cops on you!"

Krishna after a hundred seconds of a hundred years of the life of the Arjuna Tree moved forward to stop Narad from doing something that he may later regret. On Krishna's approach with Balaram on His side, the Kuravia sons saw the immense beauty of Krishna and felt the broken branches within Him. The females were too arosed by Krishna's presence. Their breasts began to swell and they became flustered. They began to cover themselves. There was blazing fire surrounding their vision as the Lord approached them. Nalak and Manigreav felt ecstasy of Heaven approaching them and became numb.

Narad felt the boys' bodies become loose. He let go of them and stepped back. Krishna walked to the boys that were still frozen into the trees. He stepped up close to share the space between the brothers. He pulled Nalak and Manigreav away from the trees which allowed their souls to be released after the hundred tree years that consumed them. Kuravia's sons began to praise Krishna and became liberated from their demons.

From the encounter between Krishna and Narad, Krishna as a young man felt that He had a relation to Narad from past lives.

Later Ganesh's proposal to join Narad after a delicious meal and an exchange of baskets filled with money, gold, jewels, fruits and grain in the presence of the family of Taste of Vrndavan at Govardh Hill Restaurant for years to come was agreed and sealed.

Krishna Meets Shankar

Chapter 10

"Flight four – o – nine, it's landed! We're going to be late!" said Krishna as He searched His app for arrivals from Heathrow, London to Delaware New Castle Airport.

"Calm down Kanaiya, he still has to get through baggage and customs," replied Nanda-Raja.

"I know, but I want to be the first person he sees when he comes from the gate."

"Hahaha, I'm sure he'll see You first."

"What's was that laugh about?"

"Krishna, You have never really seen Shankar and the last time Shankar had seen You was when You were a baby. There's no way he will recognise You first and most likely he will recognise me or Your mother," teased Nanda-Raja.

"I'm wearing the Dale Earnhardt Junior cap. Also I've sent him photos online. I've sent him videos and we have been talking I'll have you know."

Nanda-Raja looked over at Yashoda and rolled his eyes.

"Good for You," he said.

Yashoda, blew Krishna a kiss.

"I bet you he will see Me, as he knows Me better than anyone else," Krishna said in defence.

"You know Krishna, he will see you guys last as You know he'll see me first," added in Yashoda.

"Hahahaha. You're probably right as he does tend to save the best for last," Nanda-Raja replied.

"'By the best you mean Krishna and I right?" added in Balaram.

Yashoda's ecstasy burst a little and she replied, "Honestly you're right he does happen to look at men with more of a passionate feel than women, but then again he won't be seeing You first at all Krishna."

The family made their way to arrivals and waited in anticipation for Shankar to come through the gate. They had flowers in their hand and a smile on their faces. Time had ticked over fifteen years since they last saw him in person and were very excited to meet him again. From Yashoda receiving his diplomat card to being Krishna's Godfather, the foreign exchange was something out of this world. The gate to arrivals opened and after a few passengers exited there walked out Shankar. The smiles on the family grew larger as they waved to acquire his attention. He with smile just as large smiled back to them. And as Yashoda predicted he did notice her first but by his peripheral vision the family were all in the picture.

"Namashkar," said Shankar as he approached them with his right palm raised.

"Namaste," the men said.

"Namashkar," said Yashoda.

He looked over at the whole family and hugged Nanda-Raja and Yashoda. He gave Balaram a handshake and a hug too and then moved deeper into sight of Krishna. Krishna's eyes were glowing in love looking at Shankar. Shankar with his eyelids half closed admired Krishna. He opened his arms to reveal his brawn and hugged Krishna as tight as he could. The warmth of energy between the two transcendented throughout space and a flow of love fuelled through the universe. When Krishna naturally hugged Shankar cosmic energy fused between the two souls. In such a moment both entities became one and Shankar preserved bodily energy as Krishna's spirit energy evolved. There developed the universal form of Supreme Godhead as *Bhagavan*.

"Wow, just as I imagined!" said Shankar as they approached Govardh Hill Restaurant.

After freshening up Shankar sat with the family at the restaurant during the hours of lunch. The restaurant was serving patrons of the town. From breakfast to dinner Govardh Hill was open for business.

"Parvathi," called Nanda-Raja to a waitress. "Can you bring water please?"

Shankar looked over at the direction Nanda-Raja spoke and saw a lady that took his breath away. However he maintained his composure and tried not to show anyone that he had become attracted to her.

After a few moments Parvathi returned with a tray of glasses and water. She served the Gokuls and came across Shankar. Whilst pouring the water she spilled some accidently onto the table and on him.

"Oh I'm so sorry," she said whilst looking deep into his eyes trying to dry the water with a napkin. "I don't usually make a slip-up like this."

Nanda-Raja and Yashoda found her behaviour unusual. Yashoda realised instantly that Parvathi had become flustered around Shankar. She could see that Parvathi was attracted to him as even after she left the table her sight and mind was on Shankar. They thought to say nothing of this, as really after all this was only a little water that poured out her hands and onto their guest.

"I see you are all living in good fortune," said Shankar as he looked around the place. "You've lifted this hill of Govardh well and the people seem protected in your presence."

"All thanks to your blessings," replied Yashoda.

"I have learnt from my contacts that Vasudev (Krishna's father) has a priest, Garga-Mun, a member of the Yadu family You belong to Krishna, and has approved the wellbeing of both Krishna and Balaram. He has said and I quote, 'Krishna will grow to great wonders and to protect Him and His loved ones. That no evil or demon would ever come close to you Nanda-Raja, and that you will be a great devotee to

Lord Narayan, (He who has sat in the position of the Lord as the Lord is with us). And so *Lord Narayan* will give you great fortune and defence as He protects the devotees of Krishna," informed Shankar.

He drank some water as Parvathi crossed his line of sight. Nanda-Raja sat back and exhaled a sign of relief on what Shankar shared first. Nanda-Raja was a devotee of *Lord Narayan* and remembered his parents talk of amazing stories about the Lord as *Narayan* and His wife as *Goddess Laxmi*. The stories were in full opulent nature with people that lived in bliss and beauty in gardens of life and colour; particularly the stories were of people living in Heaven. Nanda-Raja felt blessed to have his foster sons equal to *Lord Narayan*.

"So tell me how have the boys been behaving? I only hear one sided stories by this feather boy, so tell me Mother Yashoda has 'He' been a good boy?" asked Shankar.

In an aloof tone Yashoda replied, "Well you know how life is, boys will be boys. Krishna and Balaram, have grown very much fond of each other and with their male ego that they both torment the girls and even my girlfriends at every chance."

"We so do not!" the brothers said.

"She clearly thinks too high of herself," said Krishna pouting as He was teased in front of Shankar.

"Oh really? Like You 'especially' haven't stolen butter from our kitchen numerous times and then gone to ask for milk and yogurt from the farmer's girls? If that's not teasing then it's flirting, little Kanaiya," forwarded Yashoda.

"Well I get bored you see and as a pastime I just go and occupy the time with the neighbours. You know to keep them on their toes. That's all I am doing," Krishna replied.

"You go and release their calves from the barn and then the cows have to go looking for them. Before anyone has realised where they've gone, You, Balaram and the farmer's children are in the woods with all the animals. I get a phone call from Rohini, blaming me that I'm not being a good mother."

"Ummmm.... forget I asked," said Shankar looking over at Nanda-Raja with an auspicious smile.

Nanda-Raja added "Well life is a man's world."

Yashoda looked at Nanda-Raja with an unpleased face, "Well life doesn't mean anything without a woman or a girl. So I took away His ornaments didn't I? Thus He couldn't find the butter. That's what grew them both out of messing up the kitchen and wasting my time," said Yashoda to the air as to pat herself on the back on a victory.

"Remember the first time you found Krishna with His hands in the butter mom? You tried to tie Him on the roof but then you saw that there wasn't butter in Krishna's mouth, there was..." Balaram added to say.

Yashoda quickly interrupted, "That wasn't how that really was and you two know that. See what I mean Shankar, they can be very mischievous but their smiles are so sweet that I end of giving in and not chastising."

Shankar looked at her in a way that overwhelmed her with an aura of motherhood and she embraced that sight filling passion of love for Krishna and Balaram.

"Well see Shankar, they get all the love and I get nothing besides the bills," sarcastically chuckled Nanda-Raja.

Nanda-Raja then lifted his glass of water and claimed a toast. He intentionally did this to see if Parvathi's gaze would fall on the water and Shankar's admiration to her. And as surely as he did this he was right, "Cheers to a safe travel and new beginnings!"

"Have you seen a change in your environment of where you live in the last decade?" asked Shankar. "There should have been an opulence of the Absolute, meaning people should have attributes of Krishna."

Krishna looked puzzled, "What do you mean? They should have attributes like me?" He asked Shankar.

"Just as You love Your friends they love You and want to share love to their friends from the love of You, my Lord

Krishna," replied Shankar. "You have six opulent traits; strength, fame, wealth, knowledge, beauty and renunciation. These six flow with You and slowly flows to others. Your friends and Your people will acquire, grow and show these six wonders of You. Soon You will have to come with me and show this nature to a man I have for seen that will be in great need of Your consciousness my Lord. Krishna, Your consciousness in time will be a dear friend to him and mankind will benefit of Your discourses."

"Who is he? What is his name?" asked Krishna.

Ignoring the obvious question Shankar moved on to say, "No demigod or great sages know of Krishna's full opulence and foolish to think otherwise. As I am Your *atma*, Your spirit, who You had chosen before time began and created from Your eye, I know best to teach You in Your second coming. If You had known when You arrived then the human body would not have been able to harbour that form of knowledge, wisdom and energy."

Shankar smiled as he felt that Krishna was feeling concerned. Krishna knew in return that Shankar was always there for Him and so smiled back. Shankar raised his glass and Parvathi came to refill with water.

"You are reborn Krishna from a form that was once before and reborn into this form You are too unborn. Meaning as You must have felt that You are neither here on Earth nor somewhere You ought to be. You are between places of everywhere.

"Your actual form of Absolute had created my actual form of *Baba Shiva* and other demigods as *Brahma Dev,* along with planets, stars and moons, with all that inhabits them from life to stone to water. You are in human form and we are in Your divine presence," carried on Shankar. "People that act under You knowing that You are the reborn and unborn Supreme Lord are *Sannyasi*, or as I, *Yogi*. We don't need to dress up as pseudo's to serve as we believe and know You as the Supreme Lord as a part of us. We shall go to Heaven and we shall come to Your humble abode even if in Your present form Krishna You don't agree."

Krishna returned in modesty, "I'm not as good as you think I am. I have bad moments too you know."

Shankar laughed, "I know. You don't have to tell me, and if You do I'll only can say, I told You so," he laughed furthermore.

Whilst Shankar was laughing he couldn't help but cough at the same time. The moment was like a contest between laughter and coughing but simultaneous was very arousing. He didn't want to stop laughing so he carried on coughing alongside laughing. He noticed Parvathi look towards him so he drank a little water.

Turning his conversation towards Nanda-Raja and Yashoda, Shankar said, "As He develops further to Shree Krishna He will present and influence many more. *Yasas,* is when a great devotee brings man fame. And the friend of mine in dire need of Krishna will also bring Krishna great fame being a great devotee of His. Thus Krishna, You are to have *Sannyasis*, meaning as a Jehovah's Witness to work for cause and not money. This will allow for penance. The people will fast for penance and deliverance for a better life from troublesome suffering just as one of the prisoners crucified beside Christ Jesus.

"You shall do this by *tusti*, not over gathering goods or equity, hence remain gracious and humble, therefore in *samata*; equilibrium to attachments. People will become in *ahimsa,* full utilization of the human body and live for non-violence; they will have fearlessness, *abhayam*. Only if one is in Krishna Consciousness they will have this and too have pleasure and happiness in abundance of spiritual knowledge, *sukham*. This mother and father role will allow control of senses, emotions, money and relationships."

"*Samata,*" Nanda-Raja said to himself.

"And so forth refraining the mind on thinking unnecessary thoughts I use Om. Om works well when we run away with our thoughts. Om gets one to think that why do we think thoughts that we wouldn't expect so?" said Shankar and looked at Krishna to answer.

"I guess 'I am' testing what action one would take," replied Krishna.

"Is that a question or an answer?" asked Shankar. "Never mind I thought the same. As the Supreme Lord that controls everything so what is out of my control is in His, and so He is the One making me think the things which thus as You say, 'I am' being tested to ignore. I guess He is using us to filter out thoughts that He does not want. Therefore that leads to *satyam*, truthfulness that benefits others in relation to *ksama,* having tolerance and forgiveness especially on excusing minor offences. This allows *asommoha,* freedom of doubt and illusion. This leads finally to many gaining intelligence and confidence with others and especially with You, Supreme Lord."

"Hmmm, I am the Creator of all life on all Heavenly planets and exist in spiritual and material worlds yet I don't feel that special," mumbled Krishna. "So would be nice to hear a thank you once in awhile."

They all laughed several chuckles.

"When the time of each individual person is right and they imitate You with devotional service within their love then they will know that You are no ordinary man. For their soul to realise this they may need a few than many life cycles, but once they do they will understand their reason for existence outside the material world and that is to worship Your greater form," mentioned Shankar.

"How would they know?" asked Nanda-Raja.

"Attachment to material energy; physical body, sense pleasures, material possessions, envy that pollutes the mind and transcendental consciousness enables one to reflect a pure image of supreme bliss i.e Krishna."

"Whow. Sounds immense," Balaram added.

"Indeed that is Bala, but when a soul in a person finds this *moksha* they are not to sit in glory and pray in awe and give offerings, but to work in the name of the Lord for bettering mankind. That's where the difficulties can come in play," advised Shankar. "Furthermore they should dwell in Krishna to gain transcendental joy. Children as boys and girls find things amazing as they are new to such things, whereas they get older things become more common and they too should enjoy that movement of things in peace. That is when one knows they are in transcendence."

Krishna earned great enlightenment of transcendental happiness when conversing about Himself as Shree Krishna. He realised the joy He got to hear about Himself was an honour and that same feeling would be for many of His devotees.

"When you two brothers come across appraisals then you have your own duty to accept humbly and in mind say, '*Hare Krishna, Hare Rama,*' to pass that moment of a second to higher planes of intelligence and consciousness," advised Shankar. "People in liberation with You, will acquire that their love (*Brahma-jyoti*) is passed to Your humble abode of the Supreme Planet of the Lord, *Goloka Vrndavana.* This planet is of mind waves as a plant that is watered. The water would travel to the roots to pulse more material for the plant to grow. They are the plant, the love is the water, and the blessing is Yours for them to grow."

"*Hare Krishna, Hare Rama,*" said the brothers.

"*Hare Krishna, Hare Rama,*" said their parents.

"*Om Tat Sat,*" Shankar added. "So now I guess I will fill you in on the highest stage of life, *buddhi-yoga, buddhi* means intelligence. One person that has reached the highest of heights in their development of life and in Krishna Consciousness would not be able to go further, however if Shree Krishna pushes them they acquire, *buddhi-yoga.* I spoke about *karma-yoga* to you last time and with *jnana-yoga,* that are practices of people with fruitative desires with worship of Krishna resulting the mental consciousness to become *buddhi-yoga,* also known as *bhakti-yoga*; in relation at all times with the Supreme Lord free from entanglement of the material world. All three *yogas* (mystic elevation) lead back to the Supreme Lord in one's life time or the next."

The family of Krishna sat with their mouths open. The *yoga* system of ancient times began to make sense with each other and life as they lived. Intelligence developed into the hearers on the surrounding tables as well as the immediate recipients. Mercy was shown by Shankar and the light of knowledge shined in the hearts of his company that destroyed the darkness of ignorance. As sunlight is always shining, the hearts of people would reside as the sun and beat in admiration for love as all would have the greatest gift of all; intelligence of Shree Krishna's truth which also coincides with His grace.

"O Krishna, You will be all that no demons or demigods can understand and yet they will bow to You. Your own internal potency You know best as You are the universe! I am *Bhagavan* as You are *Bhagavan*!" uncontrollably boasted Shankar in full ecstasy.

"*Om Namah Shivaya,*" said Krishna.

"MmmMmm," added in Balaram.

"*Hare Krishna, Hare Rama,*" replied Shankar.

Parvathi walked across the restaurant floor to the table with her chest pounding in excitement, "Would you like me to bring the dessert menu?" she asked.

Yashoda smiled and nodded. Parvathi understood not to bring menus but to straight desserts of warm chocolate brownies with vanilla ice-cream.

"Mmmm. Okay, something cold and with sugar. Doesn't that now sound just about right?" said Parvathi hinting signs of flirtation to Shankar.

Shankar cleared his throat and chuckled, "Sorry got a little excited. Nevertheless the jet-lag has worn off."

All hearing ears went back to their meals but couldn't get Shankar's deep British accent out of their minds especially to what he was saying.

"As You have many forms especially of the history of bygone ages, *puranas*, there would be difficulty in staying with Your true form in remembrance. Take this as the image one remembers in memory of another. At what age, in what appearance, in what clothes, in what surroundings, and in what light typically if they had met the other person many times? Would You remember me in Your days to come as how I am now or how I was when You first met me?" carried Shankar to another absolute truth.

"The memory can be illusive and real. Memories can be occupied by demons and sins, but Krishna You have *yoga-maha* that protects one from such memories. Time takes over and eventually they are renounced but in the meantime one sees You in materialistic form i.e *bhava,* and sees God in all things. The eyes will see material but the mind will think spiritual and both are intertwined. So all the memories one has of You is what they chose or is in *yoga-maha.*"

"I have a sister named Yogamya. She waits for me in Manhattan," said Krishna looking over the horizon outside.

"I know of Yogamya. She is Your internal potency of energy, hence she holds the memories You have and passes them to others to remember You by. With *yoga-maha*, the reading remains fresh despite repetitive. You have given her responsibility for Your memories as You have given Balaram responsibility for Your strength."

"This question may sound dumb, but could I see His memories if I ask Yogamya?" asked Nanda-Raja.

"Why ask her when you can ask Krishna here?"

"What Me? I have no memories to share. I'm just learning who I am. Besides how would she know if she is younger than I?" said Krishna all puzzled.

"Let's say she has Your smartphone and password. This was given to her by me and my father before me and his father before him," replied Shankar. "But that's not of concern as You have many transcendental pastimes that are all of spiritual activity. You are saturated with memories of many life forms over time from all heavenly planets that how You did Your business only You know," claimed Shankar.

"Sounds a little too far-fetched to Me, but I can understand how *yoga-maha* can help Me forget memories as well as remember what I want. I do have thoughts of such things that at times makes no sense so I just Om and return to here and now," Krishna replied.

Shankar saw Parvathi walking full body towards the table holding a tray of desserts. She walked slow with a sway to her hips and didn't take her sight off Shankar as she approached. She came to the table and placed the chocolate brownies with vanilla ice-cream on plates for each person and placed spoons alongside. She looked at Krishna. She picked up His spoon and placed into His ice-cream. Then she looked at Shankar and placed his spoon into his ice-cream.

"Is there anything else you would like?" said Parvathi in seductive way to Krishna.

"No thanks Parva-didi, that will be all for now, you can go," He replied sincerely.

"As You wish," she said and gave a little curtsy, swung her hair and walked back to serve others.

"What was all that about?" said Nanda-Raja.

"I think she fancy Shankar and using Krishna as bait to get his attention," said Balaram. "It's obvious as many girls at school do that to me to get to Krishna."

"Aren't you still with Radha?" asked Yashoda.

"Radha-Rani and I are not an item. We're just friends."

"Oh... Radha-Rani hey? Hahaha. This is all falling to my master plan," mocked Shankar alongside to divert them from topic of him and Parvathi.

"Hey, this is not about Me, this is about Shankar and how he likes sister Parvathi."

"Oye, I didn't say I liked her! Where did you all of a sudden get that from?"

"I'm God and God knows," declared Krishna.

"Very well as You say so confidently. But I will get back to Nanda-Raja's question," returned Shankar. "You asked to see the memories of the Supreme Lord. So yes I will show you the splendorous manifestations, but only prominent ones as Krishna's opulence are limitless. The energy of Krishna's manifestation in the material world expands over common man and the spiritual world energy is also a manifestation that is different to the world's perceptions.

"Impersonal or pantheist cannot understand the opulence of the Lord, let alone see Him. And Krishna You are soon to find that people are more impersonal in this world than any governing bodies. Don't worry the people in this restaurant will not see what is about to be revealed to you," Shankar said to Nanda-Raja. "Krishna can You please just come over here and stand just here beside the table?"

Without question Krishna moved out of the bay and beside the table as Shankar requested. Shankar picked up the spoon that was in Krishna's ice-cream and looked at the spoon with his third eye. He rolled the spoon around his fingers faster and faster. He then released the spoon that flew in the direction of Krishna and hit Him square and hard in His throat. Krishna started chocking and as soon as He did, Shankar pushed his hand into the frame of where Krishna's diaphragm would be and winded Him out. Krishna started to turn blue and in a flash of golden light Krishna revealed His universal form that occupied the whole restaurant.

Material forms of life on planets were seen illuminating out of the body of Krishna, and also stories of memories played over the infinite things they saw. There were children playing with animals to father's crying over the death of their children.

There were high buildings made to melting ice-burgs. There were sounds of ambiance and sounds of destruction. The material and spiritual worlds of many planets all moved in harmony with the Supreme Light.

The room then was occupied by the voice of the Supreme which came as seven thunders as One in harmony.

"I am the Super-soul, the entire universe is My opulence and twelve *adityas* of One is I. I am *Vishnu* and lights. Of the demigods, I am *Indra* – the King of Heaven. Of the senses I am the mind. And of all living beings I am the living conscious force Supreme and Eternal. From *Rudras,* I am *Sankara – Baba Shiva*. From *Yaksas* and *Raksasas,* I am Lord of Wealth, *Kuvera*. From *Vasudevs,* I am fire, *Agni*. From mountain of natural resource, I am *Meru*. Of great sages, I am *Bhrgu*. Of vibrations, I am *Om Kara*. Of holy names of chant, I am *Japa*. And as immovable things, I am the Himalayas. Of all the trees, I am a Banyan Tree. Out of perfected beings, I am *Kapila*. Out of weapons, I am a thunderbolt. In *Krsnaloka*, I am *Surabhi* (cows that give milk indefinitely). I am a sex desire for good sons, *Kandarpa* for sense gratification. Out of many hooded serpents, I am *Naag*, I am *Ananta*. Out of departed ancestors, I am *Aryama*. Out of Lord of Death, I am *Yama*. Out of animals, I am a lion. Out of birds, I am *Garuda* (*Vishnu*'s carrier). Out of wielders of weapons, I am *Rama*. Out of Rivers, I am *Ganges*. Out of creators, I am *Brahma Dev*. I am the beginning, middle and end of spiritual science. Supporting an argument, I am *Jalpa*. Defeating opposition, I am *Vitanda*. And coming to a conclusion, I am *Vada*. All truth is *Krishna*. Out of the alphabet, I am the letter A, as *Veda* begins with an A, without A there is nothing, *Akara*. Out of the compounds, I am the duel compound, *Hare Krishna, Hare Rama*. Out of all annihilating fire, I am time. Of birth and death, I am all future endeavours. Out of consciousness of goodness, passion and ignorance, I am Goodness. Out of hymns of the *Veda*, I am *Sama Veda*. Out of *mantras*, I am *Gayatri-mantra*."

Krishna in human form looked up and across to see His own existence. He could see exceptional infinite opulence. He saw the millions, billions of lives that rested in Him and He felt the millions and billions of hearts that beat for Him. Krishna felt His power over all demigods and suns. Further still Krishna felt the millions and billions of minds that He could influence, and at that thought He became scared and returned back to the body as a mare young man.

"*Hare Krishna, Hare Krishna,*" preached Balaram. "*Hare Krishna, Hare Krishna.*"

Across the restaurant floor no person appeared to have seen what the others had and heard. However as Shankar looked around the place he saw a pair of bewildered eyes looking straight at Krishna. They were of Parvathi's. She was standing in shock not moving as all other people moved around her. Shankar realised why she had witnessed the Supreme Lord when no one else had. As he was fond of her and she was of him the minute that they met, the Lord allowed her to see as she was to be family and not impersonal to Shree Krishna.

"Call her over Shankar, she now sits with us," requested Krishna.

No one can suppress Krishna in victory, in enterprise or in strength. He is the gambler of cheaters, and out of splendour He is splendid. When a soul is with the Super-soul much love can be formed. Furthermore when the Super-soul is with a soul then lives can be changed. Those that don't agree to that energy are in *maya*, hence that of which is not. Whereas the extraordinary beauty and opulence of a person originate from Krishna's spark and that is the reason He called over Parvathi for Shankar.

Shankar returned back to the table with Parvathi and she first placed her hands together in namaste to Krishna. Namaste is to do with greetings and goodbyes but also to say that the light within self welcomes the light within someone else. Krishna raised his right palm and blessed her.

Parvathi had a little of all the seven feminine qualities needed to be seen as glorious in the eyes of the Supreme Lord; fame, as with her righteous man being glorious, fortune, as she was to be with Shankar, fine speech, she could speak three languages, memory, as she was a graduate of remembering subject matter, intelligence, she could read many books and interpret and apply, steadfastness, as overcoming unsteadiness, and patience, humble and gentle in ecstasy and sorrow. She was a perfect match for Krishna's spirit, Shankar.

"Why don't you give Shankar your number?" suggested Krishna, "You know he is just sitting there in silence or that close to silence just mediating to ask."

Shankar pulled out his card and handed to Parvathi. She gripped her lower lip with her teeth and by touching his hand discretely she took the card.

Govardh Hill Raised

Chapter 11

At a table in Govardh Hill, Ganesh sat with his laptop open and online with Nanda-Raja at Vrndavan. They were discussing business strategies that would benefit both restaurants with most minimum costs. They both were supplied by the same markets and farmers for their ingredients but transport of the food from them was becoming too costly. Life would have that Govardh Hill and Vrndavan to be supplied by different sources for their ingredients but then the same taste of food that built Vrndavan would not be the same for Govardh Hill. One way or another a sacrifice was to be made to keep the customers satisfied and bonded to both restaurants as one.

Krishna was called by Nanda-Raja to shine light if any on the path to take for their dilemma. Around the regions of Govardh Hill Restaurant, what sacrifices would there need to be made so that Ganesh could profit from the business of Taste of Vrndavan? Krishna knowing Ganesh since childhood and the area of Govardha Hill Restaurant He knew there were benefits for both the customer and business if something could be done about the transportation, storage and quality of food to both businesses from one source.

To start the strategy plan Nanda-Raja asked Krishna what sacrifices would have to occur for making perfect sense for the source to provide more food at a reasonable price. The food source would make more money as they would dispatch more and less food would go to waste, so why would they charge more? He suggested that the *yajna* (sacrifice) should be paid in taxes from those managing the food and as the buyer of a larger amount of food should not have to pay more than twice the amount. Nanda-Raja mentioned that at that value, he and

Ganesh were paying the food source's taxes and the government was in no incline to help. To Ganesh the government twisted the people to get food readily available when there was no shortage of food in the world.

Liberal arts and stress or discomfort from economic, traditional and ceremonial passages should ultimately have liberation. The wealthy can have fine dinner parties and experience extremely delicate cuisines with no concern about the lower castes that had no bite of bread and wine so to sip.

Ganesh was not taking this as hard or personally as Nanda-Raja but he still had a problem. And therefore the only other assumption that Ganesh could make was that did the government not want to feed easily who they could not afford to educate? As Vrndavan was in a high scale part of town whereas Govardh Hill was just developing was that the reason?

"I see what you're asking me for father," said Krishna. "On one hand the governments are right with an increasing uncontrollable population of many people with many views and paths of life there would be anarchy if there wasn't some form of system or control. Why feed them if one cannot educate them is a valid point."

"I can understand that son, but we can educate people by providing a good quality service through our businesses which in turn affects the community," replied Nanda-Raja. "If we were to open a restaurant without food hygiene control and not make that attractive to the community then we would get business, but the community wouldn't glow in growth. I do not attend to do that. I want to light up my lands. I..."

"We," interrupted Ganesh.

"We attend to make a common relationship with the people through our food and therefore through the businesses. When a man says, 'I loved that meal at Vrndavan,' he would think of Govardh Hill and when a woman says, 'I like that place Govardh Hill,' she would think of Vrndavan. That thought of taste can radiate to good living," replied said Nanda-Raja.

Nanda-Raja was optimistic but not delusional optimistic. Krishna felt all warm from inside and smiled at Ganesh through the webcam. He nodded a sign of approval for their request for His knowledge.

"I'm not going to say this will be easy. After all someone is to pay a sacrifice for what you require, however I am willing to help on this matter. I would suggest testing the waters of the supply of food to Vrndavan, and make the supplier angry that his business of selling and delivering the ingredients has taken a surprising turn," analysing the proposal Krishna forwarded, "Father we can stop showering them with money for their service and also stop our locals from wanting the normal menu. So to stop worshipping for the food from King Indra Food Industries, and so stop the *Indra-puja.*"

Nanda-Raja pondered about what Krishna said for a few seconds and replied, "That idea is not half bad. That could potentially work. *Yajna* Vrndavan first and so the first class physician will be succumb to death, hehehehe," he laughed eerily on the ingenuity. "But then again, why would they care?"

"We shouldn't need to think about that but be free from praying to King Indra's supply of water and food as rain. Again I remind you that there are four classes of workers; the *brahmanas:* who would be the religious leaders that study literature (especially that of *Vedas),* and who associate godly interfaces with human civilisations, the *ksatriyas:* who engage themselves with protecting the citizens, the *vaisyas:* who would be a community of agriculturists, traders and protectors of holy cows and food, and the *sudras:* who should provide service to the highest classes i.e. the above three.

"In our case here we are *vaisyas* in this moment of time and so is our duty to farm, trade, agriculture, produce, protect cows and bank this work for future financing. King Indra and his food industry is a demigod to us and in this moment of time should present himself as a *sudras.* Due to the three modes of material nature, King Indra has no authority to our lives and so we must do what we should do," taught Krishna with wisdom to Nanda-Raja and Ganesh.

"Sounds like a fresh idea Krishna, but if we sacrifice Vrndavan what type of *yajna* would you provide to keep the business open?" asked Ganesh. "There's no reason for a complete closure."

"We can go through a season of traditional basics for *yajna*. Let all men and women know of a ceremony to save both our territories of Govardh Hill and Vrndavan together. We should use grain and *ghee* to prepare rice, *daal*, *halava*, *pakora*, *puri* and milk preparations of sweet rice, *rabri*, *rasagulla*, sweetballs, *laddu* and *sandesa*. Invite all *brahamanas* of all faiths to give obligations to the fire of human *seva* (care). They to give the food as *prasadam* to all, but first starting with the dogs and the lower class people – the untouchables (*candalas*). So instead of an *Indra-puja* there will be a *Govardhana-puja*. This would satisfy Me immensely."

"So inevitably Govardh Hill would be worshipped and no more of the '*Indra-puja*'?" asked Ganesh for confirmation.

"The women will come dressed to impress on the royal auspicious occasion to both Vrndavan and Govardh Hill. They'll come riding six by six horses around the mountain and they'll come with the men driving their horse-power engines all decorated as handsome as cows once were. The local farmers and their wives and their workers will attend to the sound of the music of My flute. They will come to be cleansed and to receive blessings for the wellbeing of their children and their children's children. They will not only worship but idolise a new *puja* and then they will go home."

The sacrifice at once began by sending an email from Nanda-Raja and Ganesh to King Indra's Food Industry to suspend the delivery of food until further notice for Taste of Vrndavan and Govardh Hill Restaurant. The laptop screens were then closed.

When the news arrived to King Indra he became angry as predicted by Krishna. He thought for many years he had not had a problem from Vrndavan so why all of sudden this huge loss in his business. He enquired of the family household for both the restaurants and came to know of Krishna being an associate for both. King Indra controlling the food supply as rain water was outraged on how a youth had out smartened him.

He ordered the networks of his food chain to pour out food at the most ridiculously cheapest value to all people in the region of Govardh Hill. Ganesh would have debts to settle and thus bankruptcy of the restaurant. Therefore to the destruction of Krishna's plan on providing better for the people.

King Indra produced a storm of supplies around Govardh Hill that Ganesh was not able to keep his business a float for any longer than a week. Krishna and Nanda-Raja with their support of Taste of Vrndavan workmen went to Govardh Hill as they were suffering from a major financial flood.

All the people that had made Krishna their shelter were all in mercy of Krishna as He tested King Indra's passion. There were just a short of a fraction of two hundred people that were being frightened of King Indra's wrath of pride and egocentrism against them. Krishna saw the people terrified to even accept what King Indra was offering over the land. The cheaper food showered upon them was unwanted charity from King Indra to make a means to an end. The people felt the food was poisoned of pity and acted not to trust Indra, however they also did not know where else to go to satisfy their hunger.

As soon as Krishna saw that worships and *puja's* would fall into the hands of King Indra and that the people would turn into his reign of power He led as many people as possible under the roof of Govardh Hill. With minimal effort as that of the pinky finger He lifted the people's spirits and the restaurant for a week. The *Govardhana-puja* was carried out throughout the day and night where all people ate and lived in happiness with food that was already prepared by Nanda-Raja and Ganesh.

By the mystic power of Krishna, King Indra was astonished when hearing from his workers that no person received the orders from them but all were under the roof of Govardh Hill, laughing, singing, dancing, talking and eating merrily. King Indra immediately departed the clouds of his storm and the wind of his power stopped. However the festivities at Govardh Hill carried on for a few more days before all people returned home. Not one *gopi* went home with her stomach empty.

Nanda-Raja and Vrndavan relations praised Krishna in the most wonderful ways. News had travelled back to Dover faster than they had returned. The news was as Krishna left to help Ganesh and Govardh Hill relations He was dressed in red, white and gold ambiance. When He arrived to raise Govardh Hill as an elephant would a lotus flower i.e. without any effort, He had a face with skin that was *shyam* (shiny dark red/black), so Krishna was also known as *Shyam*.

The bountiful of mercy, beauty, love and peace in abundance shown by Krishna to the relations of Vrndavan and Govardh Hill, King Indra was thrown back and liberated. The king of heaven of food supplies gave obeisances to Krishna as he was out smartened. King Indra adjusted a long term contract to provide for both restaurants fairly. King Indra and his business was elevated to *brahamanas.* A brand new logo with a *surabhi* cow was added to King Indra Foods.

Moral was progression for the just raised jealousy to the horizon. Jealousy is a natural feeling as one cannot control what one likes and would like for themselves. But when jealousy becomes envy i.e. one hating another for having something of need or want then that should be rectified and controlled in form of sacrifices for the good of others. As nature produces a fruit full of sweet nectar and flowers produce sweet smells over the other, curiosity comes into consciousness and that curiosity should be given conscience to elevate demigods to work a holier state of mind.

O Flute and Females

Chapter 12

Electricity: a wonderful science that man created to be a necessity around the world. From founder Benjamin Franklin harnessing the current of electrons in a lightning bolt from a kite to a string to a key there was more to be seen. Between an English man and a French man, alternate current and direct current electric lines on pylons stretching over vast amounts of land and terrains brought light bulbs to light. That light bulb created by the science of Thomas Edison, who the world takes his spirit for granted should be in gratitude. But then again with the intense power of the scientists' spirits to bring electricity out of thin air one could only guarantee themselves rather than give gratitude for a sight of light in the modern age.

Another thing that electricity provides besides the ion exchange that keeps the heart beating for all life that has hearts is an amplifier of a microphone to a surround sound speaker system. Why this is as important as anything else that runs off electricity is in the eyes or let's say the ears of the hearer. As common as electricity is to a light is as common as Krishna's lips to His flute.

Krishna had many flutes of differing lengths and materials. One flute made of bamboo He kept close to Him everywhere He would go and every time He would play for Taste of Vrndavan. His lips would touch the bamboo wood of the flute that the females were jealous of as they wished for His lips to touch theirs. The sound made would resonate to the microphone which would be amplified to the speakers surrounding the four corners of space in the restaurant.

When Krishna played His favourite flute that was kept tucked under a cloth around His waist all life coming and going from Taste of Vrndavan would bloom in beauty. Plant and wildlife such as birds and farm animals as cows would come into trance (*samadhi*) from hearing the sound as He would pass passing time. When performing the sweet sound that would leave vibrations in the air for the entire universe to hear there would be absorption of all activities on the senses of a particular living being. That thought would be delivered back to the 'Supreme Personality of Godhead' as the highest union of *yoga*. Krishna would dress in yellow-gold and Balaram would dress in blue on times when Krishna pastime in Delaware from Vrndavan to Govardh Hill.

Transcendental nature of the sound from Krishna's lotus lips would satisfy all His male friends and their company. The females and cowgirls (*gopies*) in Krishna Consciousness would receive the flute's vibrations as blessings of the highest offering. The *gopies* and their company would always be in loving ambiance to the flute. Surprisingly the *gopies* were jealous towards some animals around the fields and they were the female deers who gave obeisance to their deer husbands, something that Krishna's women could not do for their husbands when the flute played. Some *gopies* most close to Radha-Rani knew that the bamboo flute to Krishna was highly respected over a human. That being said Krishna needed no female for any work they were entitled to do due to the sound of His flute.

Water allows trees to grow and water allows bamboo to grow. The trees are pleased with bamboo as the bamboo is pleased with the touch of water. When the lotus lips played the flute with the farmer's family the cows would hear the sound as smooth as water streams that they would lengthen their ears to hear more. The calves of the cows being fed by their mother would stop sucking and become engaged to the fluid of the milk and the flute. They would bond heart to heart with the Lord.

When aborigine girls heard Krishna playing the flute in passing or at the restaurants they would become full breasted and have thoughts of lust. As they couldn't encounter more than the sweet sound from Krishna to the flute to their hearts they would come smear *kunkuma* (red-oxide powder) on their faces and breasts as foundation for expelling their love/lust desires.

The *gopies* on the other hand would compliment everything from Vrndavan to Govardh Hill. So when the sound of the flute was heard from the River of Delaware to the islands there was a sense of full ecstasy. The mayor of the state, Mayor Caitanya, had come to understand that the best worshippers of Krishna were the *gopies*. Even though they were not as educated as families of *brahamanas* and *ksatriya,* the *vaisyas* were in thoughts of Krishna twenty-four seven, three-six-five, and a quarter.

Women and girls that had heard of Krishna playing the flute from their friends and friends of friends closest to Krishna were all in beckoning to experience the sound from His lips. News had filtered to Krishna that there were wives of many other faiths and cultures all wanting to hear and see the Lord in His playing. He knew that once the wives of the women other than that of *gopies* had experienced His blissful nature they would become better wives to their husbands and women to their households. Nevertheless Krishna full in opulence is not as easy to bear for quick and easy and needed to structure a way to accompany the women in succession. The first rule of thumb was to invite the wives of *brahamanas* who performed sacrifices as to respect them above all others (besides His *gopies*) to His humble abode.

There came a time when Krishna was with Balaram and His cowherd men in Rama's field where the boys had become hungry. He instructed the cowherd men to go to mandirs, churches, mosques, synagogues, gurdwaras, temples and other places of worship to speak to the women whose tongues practiced old religious literature and let them know of the names, Krishna and Balaram. He said to them that their names would confuse and baffle them so to say instead, 'we accept your sacrifices' and hence to give the cowherd men food.

The sacrifices that the wives of *brahamanas* performed were of ten-fold; they would either be that of paraphernalia (*mantras*), hymns (*tantra*), place (*desa*), time (*kala*), fire (*agni*), teachers (*rtwik*), demigods (*devata*), performers (*yajamana*), sacrifice self (*kratu*), and procedures of faith (*dharma*).

So the cowherd men went to find the wives of *brahamanas* who weren't either that of *ksatriyas* as Balaram or that of *vsaiyas* as Krishna. When the men met the wives of *brahamanas* around their district coming and going from their places of worship they did not say what Krishna had complimented them on sacrifices, but instead became overjoyed in Krishna and told them how wonderful He was. So evidently they returned back to Krishna and Balaram empty handed.

"They neither said yes or no to our request for food," they told Krishna.

Krishna replied, "One man's fortune and luck is not the same in every location. Hence only God can satisfy everyone everywhere as One. As the sand can be everywhere so there can be love and life moreover. Go back to the wives of *brahamanas* that perform sacrifices and say Krishna and Balarama have asked you dear mothers..."

The men of Krishna went again. And as they said what they had been told the women agreed to come see Krishna and Balaram. As a request of this kind from Krishna should never go a miss the wives disobeyed their husbands, fathers, sons and brothers to go see Krishna on a specific date and location which they did share with their families.

When the sun was highest in the sky on one spring day within the woodlands of Rama's farm the wives came to see Krishna and Balaram. When the wives arrived they saw Krishna, Balaram and their cowherd men being affectionate and tending to the cows. The wives of *brahamanas* saw Krishna with a *shyam* face complexion wearing gold robes and His cap with a peacock feather. He was dressed to impress with red and white roses on hand. He spent time addressing them as, 'O dear wives of *brahamanas*' and shared with them mystic *yogis* and cosmic space wisdom with narrations, novels and literature.

After they had become one with Krishna they gave food to Balaram and the other men. They all ate peacefully together and then the wives returned home to serve their men stronger for God. The men of their households began to repent as for not giving a straight answer and not offering their food to their wives for Krishna. However even though they had repented, learnt, and knew more about Krishna they were much afraid of losing their material gain and spoke nothing of the sort to their fellow peers.

The wives of *brahamanas* prior to becoming married would perform fasts and sacrifices to their Lord in order for Him to find His most suitable partner for them. As a matter of tradition many women from different faiths and cultures would do the same in hope of marrying the right guy. So as when Krishna had come to being the Lord of His land and His people from Vrndavan to Govardh Hill and beyond, the unmarried *gopies* would pray for a husband as Him.

Chance had that there was a time when *Sri Krsna* had become jealous if not upset that His *gopies* were praying to demigods as *Goddess Durga* or *Baba Shiva* for a good husband and not Him. To Shree Krishna commonsense was if one wishes to have a partner as Him then they should pray to Him and even more so that He was the Light Almighty.

Traditionally girls from ten to fourteen years of age would start praying to *Goddess Durga* for a month in term to actually have a husband as *Sri Krsna*. Since then time had changed and the location of such acts were not seen as common practice of living. Then again the acts of girls particular to a baseball batter, or football quarterback or mathematical genius, or literature poet, or basically the lead singer in a band can have them all thirsting for their attention. With this scenario they would thirst for Krishna's attention.

Once upon a time several of His fanciers (*gopies*) had gone for a swim in Delaware Bay which was forbidden to go bathing. The local ranger had called the police, who had called Mayor Caitanya, who had called Krishna knowing that the attitude of the *gopies* to Krishna was like that of no other. Their lust for Krishna was highly different from any other type of love/lust relation with any other man. Mayor Caitanya believed the service of natural *karma* which doesn't yield fruitative results accompanies the women of Krishna. Hence to fulfill them as behaved girls and let themselves know that He has seen them naked would make them wives with Krishna as their husband.

Krishna was obliged to carry out the request of Mayor Caitanya to 'teach the *gopies* a lesson,' but moreover to accept the *gopies* as His wives in spirit. Arriving at the bay where the *gopies* were taking a swim He quietly stole their clothes and climbed into a nearby tree.

Then He said surprising them, "You have all forgotten your ways of this land and that you worship other gods for your needs. I have taken your clothes and if you wish them back then you must come individually to Me and comply with Me."

First the *gopies* found this amusing and laughed at the expense of Krishna. But when the sun started to set and the water became cold they started to shiver. They pleaded with Krishna to have their clothes back or they would tell His dad and the media of sexual harassment. But Krishna replied that His father is old and that He is strong in conviction. The *gopies* respected Him and slowly came out the river covering their tight waists and beauty with their hands.

As their desire was to marry Krishna and only a husband is allowed to see the woman as naked, Krishna fulfilled their request in this way. Spiritually He too knew that the *gopies* were in favour of The Light, with them being covered or not, they would be naked in the eyes of the Lord. As the girls were simple souls they were obedient to Krishna in great love and servitors. Krishna returned the clothes individually and out of divine love they mentioned nothing to others.

After that the thought of a woman in Krishna's mind would come as that the woman is married to Him and she is one of many wives to The Light. The children she would bare to a husband she loves would be that of God's abode; with cowherd men and Balaram in a landscape full of trees and beauty to rest, eat, and drink, whilst listening to sweet vibrations of music coming from the flute touched by the lotus lips of the Supreme.

Hide and Seek Gopies

Chapter 13

Ready or not here we come.
Don't hide from us forever,
We are always for You here,
You are the light in our eyes,
And the beat in our chests,
That beckons for your magnificence.

Your lotus face, Your lotus feet,
Your cunning smile, Your flute's sound,
Your kisses, return Your kisses.

Where have You gone?
Where can You be?
We will go ask every tree.
As madwomen we'll copy You as cats,
Just come back to us *gopies,*
Just come back to Radha-Rani.

Your lotus face, Your lotus feet,
Your cunning smile, Your flute's sound,
Your kisses, return Your kisses.

Let go right off the shoulder our strap,
Dust off Your lotus feet.
We worship no *Brahma* or *Shiva,*
Or even ask wealth from *Laxmi-Ma.*
You're Vrndavan are blessed and fortuned,
But we're unhappy as we can't see You.

Your lotus face, Your lotus feet,
Your cunning smile, Your flute's sound,
Your kisses, return Your kisses.

You're the lotus of all beauty,
You're the avenger of death,
We are Your slaves,
We are Your wives,
So come and kill at Your will,
You're the Supreme Lord of living entities.

Your lotus face, Your lotus feet,
Your cunning smile, Your flute's sound,
Your kisses, return Your kisses.

We're Your maidservants and slaves.
Dear Krishna look at us with lotus ways,
Let our breasts touch Your brawn,
Speak to us with Your nectar scent,
Your Eternal Truth we hold with us,
But without You we're nothingness.

O Lord, O Krishna, O Heart Throbber.
We're absorbed by Your Life,
Regardless God if You not love us,
O *Atmarama.*

We're many thousand *gopies,*
Of sixteen thousand ladies,
Hundred and eight prominent calling Your name.
Embed us Your internal potency so we not forget,
We wear fine linen and *kunkuma* on our breast.
Seat comfortable made for two
You're just so beautiful too!

O *Isvara*, O Krishna, O Supersoul
Which three world's do You prefer?
O Life, O Love, O Peace
Your lotus face, Your lotus feet,
Your cunning smile, Your flute's sound,
Your kisses, return Your kisses!

I am grateful for your love and promises,
Even though I need no love or romances.
Here I am your lotus love,
Not to be hidden from you,
Your butter, milk and forever water.

Siva-ratri Road Trip

Chapter 14

The season was that of autumn and the time had fallen upon *Siva-ratri* (*Vidyadhara*), which was the celebration and worshipping of the demigod *Baba Shiva*. Upon admiration for their friend and Godfather Shankar; Nanda-Raja, Krishna, Balaram and several of Nanda-Raja's friends and associates went for a road trip to give prays to *Baba Shiva*. They did not practice the cults performed during the ceremonies but wished to take adventure in respect for Shankar.

Nanda-Raja, Krishna and Balaram knew of the *Bhagavan* character of Shankar and even though *Baba Shiva* was said not to take incarnations they knew too well that He had in the form of Shankar. The universe as a whole black eternal expanding space was that of *Baba Shiva's* entrusted upon by *Lord Vishnu.* So life just wouldn't be right if Krishna did not go to take an audit on ceremonies in the twenty-first century.

Even though the relations of Vrndavan respected demigods as *Baba Shiva* and *Brahma Dev*, the Evolutionist and the Creationist, they believed and worshipped in their young friend, Shree Krishna as the Supreme Godhead, and that as the Preserver. After the change on land and sky of Dover, Delaware they believed no more than that of Krishna to be their Saviour. They had hired a minivan that seated twelve people and travelled over Chesapeake Bay on Route 50 to Washington D.C. to reach Sri Siva Vishnu Temple.

"Amazing isn't it?" said Balaram.

"As it is, that it is," replied Krishna.

"So much tranquility and peace. Imagine how life would be in Gujarat, India," continued Balaram.

"Busy and with huge crowds," added Nanda-Raja. "But the weather would no doubt be good."

Balaram forwarded, "When we get there I'm going to ask about how it would be in the homeland."

"You can just call Shankar and ask him," said Krishna.

"Yep, he would know for sure," said Balaram.

Pilgrimages in Gujarat, India that celebrated this auspicious worship of *Baba Shiva* resided by the rivers that flowed from the Himalayas. Great rivers as Ganges, Yamuna, Narmada, Godavari, Kaveri, Ambikavana and Sararmati which long ago was called Sarasvati, all had villages and towns that gave refuge to those coming for *Siva-ratri.* Temples for *Baba Shiva* were built by the river banks to follow a bathing of purification (*abhishek*) for worshippers who came there.

Alongside temples of *Baba Shiva* there would also be a temple for His wife, *Goddess Durga* also known in some Vedic literature as *Goddess Parvathi.* She who was most exalted of women and doesn't live outside association of *Baba Shiva.* Within the temples of *Baba Shiva* would be a s*hivalinga*, decorated with flowers and paint of special authentic markings. Next to the s*hivalinga* would be a statue of a cow sitting. The cow's name was *Nandan*, and was the transport for *Baba Shiva.* There was more to the *shivalinga* but utmost symbolized man and woman genitalia (projection and base) as seed and earth, as maker and maintainer, as peace and strength (*Shiva-Shakti*). *Shivalinga* would have milk and water poured onto the stone as *abhishek* for *Bhagavan.*

The men arrived at Sri Siva Vishnu Temple just after high noon. They removed their shoes and walked into the temple. People immediately noticed Krishna as His image and ambiance was striking at first glance. Krishna being all of the three worlds could walk anywhere and draw the crowd to Him. He however practiced over time to be distant from the three worlds of material nature and consciousness but they were always with Him.

Both men and women kept stealing glimpses of Krishna's handsomeness. Some people stared, some people gazed, and some people glanced as they carried on their duties and worship. Nanda-Raja and his friends as for tradition and accustom gave charity in the form of money and sweets to the *brahamanas* that maintained the temple. They all placed their hands together and gave obeisance to the statues and *shivalinga* that were there. They placed garlands of flowers to Nandan giving *Baba Shiva's* transport respect too. On finishing their pray they said, '*Om Namah Shiva*ya' (All Bow to Peace).

On the drive back on Blue Star Memorial Highway (Route 50) to Dover they crossed over the Severn River, through Sandy Point State Park, across Chesapeake Bay Bridge, through Stevensville to Kent Narrows on Kent Island, where they decided to take a break and stay the night. When they arrived to the hotel the stars were shining in the night sky and there was nothing to do besides have dinner and get some shut eye. The party had reserved rooms at Hilton Garden Inn, which had spectacular views of Chesapeake Bay.

Nanda-Raja and his friends after dinner decided to go for a stroll around the vicinity of the hotel. They laughed and walked alongside the bay that had various boats and yachts docked. They spoke about what they enjoyed the most and that was cricket especially that of the India Premier League.

The six friends walked along the dock in their own world when there approached a disturbed individual. He had a tattoo of a serpent around his neck and an appearance of someone that was set out to make trouble. He walked passed Nanda-Raja and his friends with an awry perception of them and then turned back around and towards Nanda-Raja. This individual came up behind him and swung his arm around Nanda-Raja's throat cutting off his breathing and made him weak in the legs. Nanda-Raja's friends started to beat the individual but even six men were no match for this person's hatred for life. He attacked the friends with his other arm, and kicked and head butted them too. The serpent tattooed man was not out to rob money he was out to rob life.

A friend of Nanda-Raja stepped back and called Krishna on his phone, "Krishna! Krishna! Come out quick Nanda-Raja is being attacked! We're on the docks!"

Krishna and Balaram ran quickly to them and saw the man choking Nanda-Raja. Krishna ran towards the man looking at him with furious anger. The man saw Krishna coming and prepared himself but as soon as he saw Krishna's eyes of fury he had already knew he had lost. Krishna with one hand grabbed the wrist choking Nanda-Raja and squeezed so hard that He broke the bones of the man immediately freeing His father. With the other hand He thrust into the man's serpent tattoo knocking him off balance with his head having nowhere to go but to the stone-cold ground. Using the force of gravity the man's face hit the ground in a state to bring concussion as Krishna held his one arm and stood His lotus foot on back of the man's skull.

"Mercy! Mercy! Mercy!" screamed the man.

"Why should I do that?!" shouted back Krishna.

"Please!" the man said whilst going into shock.

Krishna loosened His stance on the individual, "Speak or forever hold your peace!"

"I am a bad man, I have done wrong, I have no life, I have no reason to spare, I have done many bad things, I would make wrong from right so I deserve to die," said the man still on the ground. "But the look in Your eyes I do not want to die by You today as surely I'll be damned. Spare me young one."

As Nanda-Raja's company heard this plea for mercy they all became strong in will power and gave sorrow to the lost individual. Krishna let go of His stance. The man kneeled and began praising Krishna.

"Thank you, thank you for sparing my life! I saw in You what I would see in me and You would have drowned me in the bay, and I would have sunk like a stone. You saved me! But I cannot go on living for all the things I have done. I am at Your feet. Release me from my bonds of sins. Never have I met someone who can bring me to my ways."

"Go on now go back home to where you come from," ordered Krishna.

"I have no home to go but only a house full of evil desires. Slit my throat now and sink me into the waters my Maker," requested the man instead.

Krishna feeling the man's heart wanting to grow for the Super-soul knew that the only way that this soul was to be with the Super-soul was to grant his request.

"What is your name? Where do you come from? And why should I grant you this?" asked Krishna. "Should you not die like a noble man?"

The time was deep into the night and the water on the bay was still enough not to see any waves but the moon reflecting light. A light flickered on the dock and besides Krishna and His company along with this man there was no life to observe what was about to happen.

"I have no name for You. I call myself the name of the towns I move from. I have come from a town known as Sankacuda, so You may call me Sankacuda. I have kidnapped and abused young women. I lure them from the south to come up north for fame and fortune, but when they see I have nothing to offer they try to leave me. However I cannot let them go so I keep them locked away," Sankacuda paused and looked over at a boat near the broken flickering light.

Balaram went to the boat with a couple of Nanda-Raja's friends and stepped onboard. Sankacuda did not say anything for a moment's time whilst Balaram looked over the boat. He placed his hand on the handle to the main cabin door but it was locked.

"I shall tell you where the key is if you grant me my wish," said Sankacuda.

Krishna moved him towards the boat and said, "Balaram break the door down!"

Balaram took a step back and launched the strength of the external potency of Krishna onto the door which cracked off the hinges breaking the door frame and its metal locks. He walked into the boat with one friend. After a few minutes Balaram and the friend walked out with four women that were malnourished, abused, and shivering to death. The other friends quickly went to assist them walking the women off the boat one by one. As the women saw their assaulter in the hands of Krishna they felt relieved and saved. Krishna and Balaram told the women not to be afraid anymore that they were in safe hands. Krishna looked over at Nanda-Raja making sure he was well and signed to his friends to walk the Nanda-Raja and the women to the hotel.

As soon as they were out of sight Krishna walked to the end of the dock with Sankacuda feeling that he would finally be freed from his ways. Krishna prayed to *Baba Shiva* for purification to this soul as it was to be aligned with the Supersoul of *Lord Vishnu*. He placed His hands either side of Sankacuda's face as that of holding a conch-shell. Krishna looked over at Balaram and twisted Sankacuda's head cracking his spine immediately killing him and dropped him into the water to sink to the deepest depths of the bay.

The next morning Nanda-Raja, Krishna, Balaram and their friends set off back to Dover thinking nothing about the night before. The women were given food, new clothing and assisted to the nearest hospital where they shared their details and bid them farewell. Krishna's company drove out of Kent Island towards Queenstown in Delaware where again they decided to stop and take a break for lunch.

Whilst Nanda-Raja and his friends were enjoying their company together Krishna and Balaram thought to take a walk around Queenstown. Krishna and Balaram were not familiar to Queenstown but thought of what 'queens' maybe around the town and couldn't help but go and have a wonder. With the appearance of Krishna and Balaram side by side they did turn a few heads around the streets of Queenstown. Some women looked over at them as well as some men. The local police enforcement on horses couldn't help but notice unfamiliar faces in their town as well as some seniors that had been there their entire lifetime.

When one is new to someone else or to something else than that one else or thing else is always considered as an alien. Once that one else or thing else is seen and recognised again then that becomes a familiar. Everything is alien at first and then becomes familiar. Everything is alien at first even parents to their child and a child to their first friends. As Krishna and Balaram were familiar to each other they thought it would be fun to be aliens to others in Queenstown for becoming familiars to them in the future.

As Krishna and Balaram were touring the sights of Queenstown they had happened to catch the attention of an old lady walking her dog with one hand and carrying a rather expensive purse in the other. As the lady looked over at the beauty of the brothers a thief grabbed her purse and quickly started running towards their direction knocking people out his way. As fast as a trojan horse this fellow galloped away from his victim. Krishna looked at the perpetrator making him fully aware that he had been noticed. This made the demon horse like runner move more anxiously to get away and thought to knock over Krishna too.

Sprinting towards the brothers with his mouth wide open looking as if he was to eat Krishna, Krishna locked His stance and strengthened His arm into that of an iron rod. He extended His arm punching the man in his mouth breaking his teeth out of his jaw.

The demon had a print on his overalls reading 'Kesi' which was now covered in blood stains. The demonic man began vomiting and discharging more blood from his mouth and nose. He dropped the purse to hold his face together and disappeared into an ally. Krishna returned the purse to the old lady and crossed her shoulders with His sight and blessed the top of her head. All the people around began to praise and shower Him with love as flowers falling from the sky.

After receiving and welcoming thanks Krishna and Balaram decided to make their way back to the others. However there was still trouble on the horizon. Krishna was The Light, and like with all light there's attraction of moths and insects. Moths and insects trying to find a way out of their consciousnesses are all attracted to a light source. Far on a roof top another demon had spotted Krishna and Balaram.

A demon named Vyoma, who was a female that used her body in crooked ways to sexually abuse young men or file cases of sexual abuse against them. She did not respect the males and used deceiving ways to capture vulnerable males and make their lives into a living nightmare. Vyoma would entrap males and leave them with mountain high amounts of stress for her to laugh over their suffering. She would threaten the males that would leave stones in their mouths so they couldn't speak of her. She practiced and taught dark-mail and dark-magic as a wicked witch to other females to do the same. Little did she know that her time had come to die in her own cauldron.

Vyoma thought to fall in front of Krishna pretending that her ankle had been badly sprained so He would attend to her. As Vyoma swooped closer to Krishna He had noticed her shadow coming from an awkward direction and she had noticed by the look in His eyes that her ways were not to work upon Him. However she could not stop her momentum on approaching Him from the high ground and as she tried to break her pace she failed. Krishna grabbed her like a lion does a lamb. Her ankle broke but intentionally her face was saved from scratching. Krishna left her on the ground to weep in her own sorrow. Vyoma looked at Krishna hoping He would turn and set her free. She moved to a bench limping. Krishna looked over

His shoulder but not at her and she felt liberated. Balaram walked beside Krishna and brushed the dirt of Queenstown off Krishna's shoulder.

Returning back to their father and his friends like nothing out of the blue had happened they all sat back in their vehicle and headed out on the open road. The drive was clear and free with only the occasional police patrol vehicles controlling the traffic. Before they reached back to Taste of Vrndavan, Nanda-Raja had to drop off his friends back to their vehicles which were parked by Silver Lake Park. His friends left the minivan giving praise to Krishna and Balaram. They laughed with Nanda-Raja as he walked them to their cars. He was not feeling his normal self and was afraid to let Yashoda know what happened at Kent Island. After he waved his friends goodbye Nanda-Raja sat on a park bench with his head in his hands contemplating to share the news to his wife or not.

Dusk was approaching and the park gate was closed by Warden Varuna. He then went to the warden's lodge to pack his belongings for the day to leave and go home. As he was doing this he looked into the security monitors and saw a man prowling to and fro beside the lake. Varuna found this unpleasing and reacted to call his staffs that were patrolling the park to go see this man and bring him to the lodge. As far as Varuna thought the man was trespassing out of hours and could do harm to himself or to the park.

Varuna was a noble man and of high importance in the society of Dover. He was a people's person and considered as a democratic god as he knew many people of different cultures and faiths that came to Silver Lake personally. The values that Varuna had were that of father-like but were highly old fashioned in understanding new generations. People were like babies and needed a parental god from spiritual sky to material existence was his attitude towards them. In right mind Varuna was a demigod to his people and that respect made him vigilant to carry out his life.

Warden Varuna's staff seized Nanda-Raja without question and brought him to the warden's lodge. Krishna and Balaram after waiting for some time in the minivan for their father to return went to look for him instead. They searched around the edge of the lake and then to the public toilets and when they began to become worried they went to the lodge to seek for help. Krishna approached the lodge door and knocked.

"Come on in it's open," said Varuna.

They walked in to see their father in handcuffs.

"Oh Krishna! It's You. What brings You to these neck of the woods?" said Varuna cheerfully.

"Hey Varuna, why is our father in your custody?"

Varuna was enlightened, "This is Your father?"

"Yes, that's our father," said Balaram.

Immediately Varuna freed Nanda-Raja from his hold. Varuna knew of Krishna as the news going all over town about Him. He knew of Krishna's forgiving shelter and unmistakably apologised for himself.

"I would have never arrested him if I knew he was the father of Vrndavan, Krishna. He actually had said nothing to my staff or myself and seems to be in a world of his own," Varuna added. "Is all okey-dokey?"

Krishna explained about Nanda-Raja's tiredness from the trip but nothing more than that. He saw that Varuna could have either rebelled against the occurences or become a protector for Nanda-Raja and Yashoda. As a man the same age of His parents Krishna thought to say no more and allow Varuna to see Nanda-Raja as a beloved man.

Varuna lived in spiritual sky as that of Krishna. Their lives were eternal, blissful and full of knowledge. Both loved teaching and eager to give information to conditioned human beings. So Varuna freed Nanda-Raja from his worry and opened the gate to Silver Lake for everyone to go home. All men went home from the park feeling wonderfully blissful with Shree Krishna receiving eternal transcendent prays.

Rasa Oo La La

Chapter 15

Radha-Rani was head cheerleader for Dover High School Senators Football Team. She was amazing at cheerleading as a leader and a dancer. All the other cheerleaders admired Radha-Rani as she was beautiful as she was graceful. Not only was Radha-Rani an icon to the football team but she was also highly gifted in other subject fields. Some would say she was a nerd, some would say she was an inspiration, some would say she was an athlete, some would say she was dangerous, and some would say simply that she was smart and sexy. Whatever some would say Radha-Rani held her own character very well which at many times was not at all the simplest thing to do. She didn't take her material form with spiritual existence for granted as above all she had sold her heart to the most popular guy in school, Krishna.

One of the hardest things for Radha-Rani to put up with was the attraction of the other girls in love with Krishna. There was nothing she could do about that. The other girls loved Krishna in their own special ways and Krishna being Krishna loved them back individually in His own special way.

To break the bond between the women for Krishna would be a tremendous sin as that would make the woman insecure and frail in later life, whereas having them on board with Krishna gave them courage and intelligence to assist others and Radha-Rani herself.

Some times were extremely difficult for Radha-Rani to see other females cooing over Krishna directly in front of her and her being helpless to react. This however made her stronger with relations between other males and females.

Girls that were in transcendental bond with Krishna as with their souls to His Supersoul were the girls He grew up with, girls He met in school, girls He met by passing, His brotherhood's sisters, mothers, grandmothers, daughters, teachers, and the rest of the cheerleaders, and all these girls with a special bond to Him were called His *gopies*, where the number one *gopi* was Radha-Rani.

Running towards Radha-Rani's locker Krishna came and banged His body against the metal relieving His tension, "I'm exhausted."

"Really why?" asked Radha-Rani.

Krishna replied, "Library of course, been doing assignments all day. Class, library, class, library, lunch, class library. Holy moly cow!"

"Oh I feel so sorry for You my Lord," she said.

"And on top of all that I have to keep your girlfriends satisfied. Like I miss one smile, or one hi, or hey, or hello, then I have to hear from the guys, what's wrong with You?"

"Hahahaha. Ya they can be a little mischievous if they don't get Your love and attention."

"Seriously though I'm exhausted. I'm not a machine, I'm still young. I have other responsibilities you know?"

"What like at the farm attending the cows?"

"Of course, and then there's the female cows, again moo, and moo, and when is a guy like Me supposed to have some peace in My life?

"Oh boo-hoo, it's not like You have to make an effort to go out in public. Not like You have to do Your hair, set Your foundation, do nails, where the right matching clothes, change pads once a month…"

"This is not about you, this is about Me and I am exhausted. I need a break from the *gopies* and I need you to do something about that!" Krishna said adamantly.

"Don't raise that tone of voice with me, Mr. Krishna. What do You want me to do? You got Yourself into this world so You can get Yourself out."

Krishna stood up and moved His body over to hers just close enough to her chest without touching her breasts, "You know if you help Me with My problem then chance has that that we can spend more time together. I can sit with you, hold you, play My flute for only you, shower you with..."

"Okay, okay, okay You can stop all that sweet talk," Radha-Rani pushed herself closer into Krishna. "Let me see what I can do to ease Your tension? Just keep the hat I gave You on," she said and moved her hand to His head to adjust His peacock feather cap over His brow. "Mmmmm. Na-mash-kar."

As Radha-Rani said this close enough to Krishna's lips she felt His pulse race and backed away slowly taking her books and locking her locker leaving Krishna in trance. She walked away giving Him in plain sight of her slender waist and tight behind.

A few days later at the time when there was a full moon low on the horizon Krishna got a call from Radha-Rani. The season was of *sarad* and as the moon was full this was *poonum*, a time known as *sarad-poonum*. She asked Him to come dressed in His best to the bank of the Old Woman's Gut River which flowed in from Deepwater Point of Delaware Bay, and head down Kelly's Ditch and to the Indian Gut. Krishna asked why but the only answer He got from Radha-Rani was to drive on Port Mahon Road to the Port Mohan Boat Ramp, park His car and come to where He would hear music. Radha-Rani wasn't one to mess around and as she was trustworthy to Krishna, He went as He was instructed to the fork banked between Kelly's Ditch and Indian Gut.

The night was young arriving at the location. He heard soft tribal music and saw a campfire at the point splitting the river. He then heard chatter and laughter of the *gopies*. As Krishna approached closer with His flute in one hand and His cap turned backwards He heard more chatter and laughter. He approached closer still to see that the *gopies* had a barbeque going and stringed up lights which fed off the engines of a couple of Ford trucks. Most the *gopies* had beer in their hands with many ice-coolers scattered around the campfire. Whatever this was The Light was going to spend throughout the night.

Krishna in His transcendental spiritual existence approached the campfire and walked around seeing all the *gopies* without them noticing Him. He then saw Radha-Rani dressed exceptionally lusty more so then the other *gopies* who were very much attractive as protestant nuns. All the *gopies* had *kunkuma* (red oxide powder) smeared on their breasts deep into their cleavages and on their faces. *Kunkuma* symbolised the passion of love and helped relieve lustful thoughts if the love was not satisfied. There were many *gopies* that had boyfriends and even husbands that Krishna recognised. He then made Himself available for Radha-Rani to see and she seductively walked over to Him.

"This is Your night my Lord from us. May we bathe our desires for You this night that we may be free to carry out Your duties," Radha-Rani said. "The night may last many days in *Brahma Dev* time to give us Eternal Life. Let us *Rasa-Lila* to shed our lust for You."

She finished speaking to the music turning up and all *gopies* began to dance for Krishna. Some came close to touch Him, some came close to kiss Him, and some came close for Him to touch and kiss them. His lotus lips, His lotus eyes, His lotus feet, and His lotus hands were all praised touched and kissed throughout the night by all the *gopies*. Krishna teased the *gopies* by saying no to over half their enquiries which made them angry and even made some *gopies* shed tears. They danced with their toes of cosmetic beauty on the ground seducing orgasmic occurrences for Him. They all experienced *yoga* union of sense gratification from the material existence of Krishna.

What Krishna was thought of by the *gopies* was paramour. To give Himself time to breathe He would speak in discouraging ways which sparked more fire in their souls. He would than compliment each and every *gopi* for their own attributes as eternal friends with eternal husbands, eternal sons, and eternal friends of friends as eternal masters. They all enjoyed Him as their Supreme Beloved. He at many times throughout the night pleaded with them to go back home to their families and husbands, but they replied 'how can they leave His lotus feet?' or 'we are aching for Your touch,' and 'who would be there to cover Your feet in *tulasi* leaves?' and 'we are Your surrendered souls.'

"We are decorated with Your desires and bodily decorations. We appreciate Your love and Your smile of lust. Attracted by Your brawn, before we go into any form of prostitution may Your heat of a scorging sun be as our hot breasts burning for to place Your cool lotus palms as soft as lotus flowers on them."

Krishna allowed the *gopies* to insist their further praises and returned kisses to their cheeks as they kissed Him. The pastime of Radha-Rani, Krishna and the *gopies* were very pleasant. He sang to the *gopies* and He sang to Himself near the cool sandy banks of the river. The *gopies* head, breasts and waist were held by Krishna as they moved around Him. They would pinch, laugh and look at each other too to woo Krishna's male hormonal desires more and more. *Gopies* were blessed with His mercy without infringement of mundane sex life. The Supreme Godhead with His six opulence attributes is in need of nothing and thus His pastimes were all welcoming.

A body is a part of the whole parcel of God, and if asked in a sanguine way, 'what would result to a body if forced to act as sinful?' Then the answer would rest on the lust in passion. Lust in passion would lead to wrath and therefore a sinful energy to the world. Manifestations of material creations would occur more rapidly and without thought or border. For instance a sweeter chocolate, a stronger alcoholic drink, exploitation of fetish sexual traits, increase in potency of drugs, corruption in the markets of money, privatisation of resources, abuse at schools and colleges, negligence and also mockery of the vulnerable. However one who lives Shree Krishna through passion as butter does to yogurt a bond is made between goodness and ignorance to be saved from degradation of material and spiritual attachment. Independence of such is spiritual blissfulness and not to be baffled by lustful stuff. Both lust and wrath can be spiritualised. As when the noble engages wrath to satisfy the Lord, then even enemies become friends.

There are different levels of lust; there's the helpless position known as that similar to trees and an embryo in the womb; one can lust over something that has no ability to defend itself. There's the chanting of holy names of gods, animals, nature to clear the air, and that is known as wiping dust of a mirror. There's also one that has little perception or showing little conception to an Almighty God and that is known as fire which is covered by smoke; as that one loves to live in self-denial. Realising concepts of lust is how one can stunt their own lust so to cultivate in Krishna Consciousness to release that emotion. In soft speaking to release the lust from the light of our mind back to The Light from where the lust most likely came from.

Enemies as criminals, sex addicts, abusers, miscreants etc. would lust (*manu-smrti*) to satisfy self and those that cannot get what they lust for would fix on others to lust their desires; for instance when friends would force another friend to do something just because they themselves cannot or would not. Hence an enemy would find happiness by sense-gratification and their sour happiness would also be the enemy of the enjoyer, (one that would constantly patronize and make fun on others).

The mind is where lust sits over shadowing knowledge which can bewilder the body. Lusty intelligence is false ego. Sin is by lust, lust from either direction. Lust can be a destroyer of knowledge and self-realisation. Knowledge of self by the spirit and not the body is known as *jnana,* and specific knowledge of spirit's soul in relation to Super-soul is known as *vijnana.* Therefore lust as a powerful emotion that affects the soul should be into love of life for perfection of human peace.

Ones work can be sensed into lust as one would not be able to live without a working frame of mind, for example tax-collectors, cooperate business men, stock traders, doctors etc. but the mind is greater than the senses. Conditioning the soul leads to intelligence which leads to the mind which then overcomes the senses of lust for sinful activities. Peace on peace as Krishna on Krishna Consciousness. Henceforth one should steady the mind in intelligence to beat the enemy of lust. They would gain spiritual strength to overcome self-sinfulness and build in *yogic* methods with others pursuing the same path. As lust can be created by slow speaking so too can lust be vanquished.

Not like any material dance the *Rasa-Lila* dance was a spiritual performance with the best looking *gopies* of the three worlds. Krishna also danced with the *gopies* which liberated them for their great desire for His internal potency that didn't need anything, i.e. their great desire of sex. He had His hands with their hands and their shoulders with *gopies* either side of Him. All the senior *gopies* with boyfriends and husbands showered Him with flowers. The Supreme Godhead fully engaged Himself in dancing and took thirty second breaks to applaud the *gopies*, 'Well done! Well done!'

With great attraction Krishna offered them betel nut from His mouth which they kissed and gained spiritual advancement and in return placed Krishna's hands on their raised breasts. Upon exhaustion from dancing Krishna would wipe their faces to relieve their fatigue. They looked loving to

Him. The *gopies* would come out of the water and would walk on the river bank smelling divine and Krishna handled their sex desires by questions and light flirting. Most of the *gopies* previous lives had great sages of special dancers, and through the *Rasa-Lila* He liberated their previous lives.

The *Rasa-Lila* dance by the river bank under the full moon was not to be imitated by anyone and if so then there would be severe punishment bestowed upon them such as blindness. No one was to copy the *Rasa* dance just as no one was to copy *Baba Shiva* drinking the ocean of poison by smoking ganja. If one was to jump into the *Rasa-Lila* dance as an ordinary person they would become ruined by the laws of karma, material body and spiritual light. The dance was for only Krishna and His *gopies*.

Apta-kama was Krishna being self-satisfied. Krishna's heart was of Super-soul and one would need a Super-soul to dance within the *Rasa-Lila*. And as the *gopies* as young women or wives were not in material existence when dancing they were in spiritual bodies, The Light could not be accused of their ordeals. After the *Rasa* dance which did happen to be a very long night that of millions and millions of years. Krishna gave tremendous amounts of love to his *kankuma* covered *gopies* and allowed Him to be a husband to them on that auspicious occasion. *Gopies* became Shree Krishna followers for always: Always followers (*Anu*). Hearing from and about Shree Krishna's *gopies* one would always be in transcendental loving service.

Kaans Invites Krishna

Chapter 16

News of Krishna's existence and eternal bliss had reached the ears of Kaans. He had noticed the change in the markets that he controlled. There seemed to be a random assortment in shares bought and sold that Kaans couldn't quite figure out. His markets in the commodities of trade had boosted in sources not owned by him but by Yadu Dynasty instead and what had been owned by him was on a steady decline. When Kaans went to enquire about the change to his profit margin from his right hand man Narada, he was told straight up that Kaans' time had come for death not only in business but in life.

Kaans controlled a large empire from his building Mathura in Manhattan, New York and was not at all amused that he had been threatened by one of his own people. He spoke to Narada again and forced him to find the root of this problem. Narada sent journalists to search for anything out of the blue in the communities surrounding Mathura Building and that of New York. He sent out spies to look into the educational system for bright gifted students.

Deep down Kaans remembered the warning that *Goddess Durga* had given him over twenty years ago and now had come the time to take action. Kaans' first reaction was to have Vasudev murdered because of his relation to his sister Devika, but as that would create an investigation which would lead back to him he instead invited Devika and Vasudev to Mathura, and entrap them in one of his living quarters.

Narada came back with the news not long after he was forced to find. He returned back with photos, videos and details about Krishna and Balaram, on how these two brothers were the most popular and auspicious in nature in all of Delaware. No records of their birth were found with the residence they occupied and no records of such about their real parents. All Naradu could associate them with were the locations of Taste of Vrndavan and Govardh Hill Restaurant. Immediately Kaans set out an illegal order for those buildings to be torn down due to his rage and fear on his inevitable future.

The day after next a bulldozer with several men in high-visibility jackets came to the location of Taste of Vrndavan. The men worked for a company called Aristasura, which was paid off by Kaans to have the building demolished without notice and reason. The earth shook, rumbled and trembled as the large bulldozer approached Vrndavan. The time was early in the morning when no one would expect a thing and would be helpless to stop Aristasura. Krishna and Balaram were the first to feel a disturbance in the force around them and quickly went to see. Nanda-Raja and Yashoda could not help but notice that something was terribly different. The family exited the building to see the bulldozer come straight for them with its tail exhausting.

In normal observation the company of Aristasura was neighbourly and with transcendental bliss with the community. But as Kaans had paid with a threat to Aristasura for the bulldozer they had no alternative but to take the order. The vehicle started to dig the ground close to Taste of Vrndavan and tear up the earth. The bulldozer meant business and charged up on multiple of four cylinders.

Krishna had to think and act fast before His home was destroyed. He needed to distract the men in control of the bulldozer whilst shutting the engine down so they could understand what was going on. Krishna signaled to Balaram to attack the far men in high-visibility jackets to make a way for Him to reach the bulldozer.

Balaram ran towards the men and struck each of them knocking them off balance and to the ground. Krishna took chance to grab the bull by the horns and attack the driver without a second thought. He used the momentum of Balaram swinging back over the raging bulldozer and boosted Himself to the driver's seat knocking the driver cold with His foot. Krishna got control of the vehicle and pressed the breaks as hard as He could whilst lifting the handle of the digger off the ground and steering the bulldozer away from His home.

The bulldozer screeched and bellowed to a dead stop. Krishna then lifted the engine hood and snapped out the cables running the electrics and gasoline to the engine. The men that were in charge of demolishing quickly made an exit leaving the property of Aristasura.

Before long the news of failure of Aristasura had reach Kaans. Incredibly outraged he began to wonder how Krishna and Balaram could stand up against him. He started to break things of his own possession in his office as the loom of his own death circled his mind.

He pressed down on his intercom, "Melissa! Melissa! Get me my black book!"

The black book that Kaans kept was more a dark book of evildoers. He poured himself a double shot of whisky and drank the hard liquor in one go. Kaans then ordered the people he found in this book of demonic nature, *asuras,* and extreme communists as well as crooked diplomats to call for the outlaws of the city that were good at combat. He walked over to his statue of *Baba Shiva* and gave a drop of his blood as sacrifice to the statue. Kaans then called for The Elephant and a son of Yadu's Dynasty known as Akura.

Akura was a good noble man with strong ties to the Yadu family business and that of Kaans'. He demanded and ordered Akura to call for Krishna and Balaram to visit Uncle Kaans' beautiful Mathura for a wrestling event. As sports were a common trade in America and over the world Kaans thought to lure the brothers to the event where upon arrival have them killed by The Elephant.

On the way to Taste of Vrndavan, Akura thought and prayed about Krishna. Akura was of Yadu Dynasty and a pure devotee of Shree Krishna after what he heard about Him from Vasudev and Devika. Nanda-Raja kept in close contact with Vasudev without giving awareness to any people of Kaans'. From what Akura had heard from Vasudev he didn't think he was worthy enough to meet Krishna, a feeling known as *vaisnava*. Akura imagined Krishna as *Lord Vishnu* with the descriptions of *tulsi* leaves, lotus eyes, and beautiful women covered in *kunkuna* always humble and by His side. He thought about how Krishna redeems the good, destroys demons, gives liberation and provides salvation. He had also heard about the incident that 'king of heaven' King Indra Food Supplies had performed to Govardh Hill Restaurant and how Krishna had overcome the cruel act. Expecting blessings from Krishna's hand by just donating water to Him was what Akura hoped to adopt as the highest blessings of the three planetary systems.

Leaving Manhattan and travelling to Delaware gave Akura time to meditate on Krishna and arrive to Dover without realising the time. He thought on how Krishna and Balaram would greet him. Would they call him Akura Uncle? Would they invite him into their home? Would they give hospitality? On approaching close to Taste of Vrndavan he saw billboards of cows and calves advertising milk. He also felt that the drive became more fluid like with no last minute breaking or turning without indication. He felt relieved to be out of the City of New York and to a place that was more spiritually welcoming. Akura pulled over and got out his car and looked eyes wide open in ecstasy to the environment. His soul felt the Spiritual Master was nearby and then became aware that Krishna will be expecting to ask about Kaans' holdings.

Akura had parked by Rama's farm and out of chance he saw two young men radiating with immense light aiding and milking cows. He became mesmerized by the beauty and wonder of the sight. He came to realisation that the two young men were Krishna and Balaram. Akura approached the brothers and introduced himself as their uncle. Krishna felt his soul and heart beating in fashion of appraisal for them. Krishna embraced Akura and with Balarama went to eat palatable meals. Akura gave the brothers a bottle of water and in return they gave Akura a cheque to donate to any charity of his choice.

Whilst Akura and the brothers ate Nanda-Raja came to join them. Nanda-Raja was very delighted to meet Akura as Vasudev had already prepared him for Akura's arrival. Even though Akura hadn't come for leisure and the business was that of deceiving proposals they all respected their moment of time together. Whilst the meal was being served and enjoyed Nanda-Raja enquired about Kaans and how awful and evil the man was. Krishna laughed, Balaram laughed, Akura laughed, and then they all laughed together. The hysterical moment was that 'of course' Kaans was that bad, as if he wasn't due to the reasons he was then Krishna wouldn't have been at that table.

With the laughter and Nanda-Raja's relaxing voice Akura felt comfortable and the fatigue from his trip had washed away. Akura spent the night with the family but before he did he went to touch the ground of Taste of Vrndavan. He did this in the middle of night and smeared some soil on his face as a sign of devotion and belonging. Before Akura then got into bed he washed his hands, his face and his brow with the water of Vrndavan. The brothers then came to say goodnight.

The next day Krishna and Balaram took Akura to Leipsic River flowing in from Delaware Bay. Krishna then revealed *kumaras* to Akura.

Kumaras were four sages that roam the universe as children in *Puranic* literature. They resemble the four full corners of the universe and are called, *Sanaka, Sanatana, Sananda, and Sanat-Kumara.* Akura received blessings of the highest order as Krishna showed him this form of the universe. All stress of Akura's was lifted. They then prepared for the journey to Mathura to approach the demonic Kaans.

On the drive back to Manhattan on I-95 first to Philadelphia though New Jersey, Akura gave prays to Krishna. Even though Krishna and Balaram accompanied him on the drive, Akura gave prays from his heart to his mind on the same worship level to *Lord Narayana*. *Lord Narayana* was the form of Shree Krishna in the realms of cosmic space. He gave praises to Krishna above the ruling of *Brahma Dev* as Krishna was the entire universe. He gave many many praises.

The 'Supreme Personality of Godhead' is above all demigods as stern and soft as oceans and rivers. Passing the changing terrains of countryside and city high-rises, Akura saw Shree Krishna with fire in His mouth, earth at His feet, sun in His eyes, sky in His navel, directions of the compass in His ears, space in His head, and demigods in His arms, oceans and seas in His abdomen, plants and herbs as hairs on the body, clouds of strength and vitality as hair on His head, mountains as His bones and nails, day and night as His blinking eyelids, genitals as progenitors (*prajapati*), and His semen as rain.

With Krishna being fully aware that Akura's soul was trying to reach His Supersoul, He made this soul of Akura's become a part of Him.

"Your transcendental existences are like living entities in oceans of milk, and they are also like small fruits of *udambara* where mosquitoes come from," Akura said softly for Krishna to hear. "Can I ask for You to give me reincarnations of fish and animal life at the time of *Lord Ramacandra* of Raghu Dynasty, so I can give obeisance to You from the times before last? The three modes of material nature are at Your feet and You are still more without them. My Lord, give me Your protection once we arrive. I surrender to You."

Krishna smiled, blinked and looked out the window towards just a little below the horizon. He lifted His right hand and allowed the sunrays from the sun to reflect light off His hand to bless Akura.

Please or Not To Please

Chapter 17

Krishna's three worlds of material and conscious nature were enjoyed on the drive to Manhattan by all on the journey. The vehicle flowed over the smooth tarmac as the water would flow in the Ganges River. Akura was a great driver. He would give plenty of space to vehicles ahead of him as he overtook them giving them plenty of time and space to slow down. He would indicate signals in advance and at multiple times on one turn too to make way for other vehicles. Akura was like a fish in water and that water he owned. He didn't think too hard about driving, as what Krishna knew was that he was transcendent into Krishna Consciousness that the travel was merely a reason to get from point A to B. As long as everyone in their journeys got home safe Akura wasn't of concern who would come first or who would arrive last. As for Krishna His mind was occupied with the mind of *Baba Shiva* where He kept the three material worlds marked on *Baba Shiva*'s forehead. Coming to the Manhattan skyline, the three worlds of material and conscious nature became all that more wonderful on knowing.

Nanda-Raja and Akura were asked to rest at home whilst Krishna and Balaram went to go please their friends and relatives they had around Manhattan. Akura was asked to also meet up with Kaans and let him know that Krishna and Balaram had arrived as he had requested. Akura obeyed what Krishna had advised and returned home with Nanda-Raja.

Krishna and Balaram went for a walk around New York City and scoped out the community around Mathura Building. They saw many buildings and skyscrapers each one more extravagant than the last. Many had marvellous marble finishings and tiled floors with glass that spaced out at great lengths and widths to reflect the horizon. Each building had a porter or several in some places that would protect the place from strangers. People moved in a tranquil fashion not exhibiting one's concerns from another's. The amount of people Krishna and Balaram saw that walked and flowed by one another was astonishing.

Taxi cabs of New York coloured the roads with a golden appearance that were like the city ornaments. Flowers were well landscaped in some parks and outside businesses that even so in a concrete jungle nature coincided. The brothers walked by women that were half dressed working to try and get their attention. Many children also were seen around Mathura Building coming and going to and fro. All the people of Mathura who saw Krishna and Balaram looked over again at them as wondrous beautiful aliens in New York.

The locals began to ask themselves of who were those two men? Where did they come from? What work did they do? And what in God's name were they doing there? Balaram saw the porter station of Mathura Building was unoccupied and took Krishna by the shoulder and walked Him in. There was a grand lobby with the most exquisite furniture and finishing. Many people were coming and going from the lobby of the building to rented offices and residential apartments. Some people became alarmed by seeing two fresh faces with smiles that they began to smile themselves. Other people were amazed on seeing two fresh smiling faces that they came to ask themselves what pious work must have they done to hold such a confident stature? And more others were taken away by the presence of the smiling faces that they purposefully walked close to the brothers hoping to be with them for the rest of their days.

Once Krishna and Balaram got a feel for Mathura Building they thought not to gain too much attention so they headed out and towards Akura's home. On the way Krishna saw a salesman selling clothes of New York memorabilia, such as t-shirts, jerseys and baseball caps that read; 'I Love New York', where love was replaced by a huge red heart. Krishna decided to stop and purchase something from the salesman for Mother Yashoda and Radha-Rani.

"Salaam brother. Got some of these for the women?" Krishna asked.

"I ain't Your brother!" replied the salesman.

Krishna was thrown back by this, "I just meant hello, no harm man."

"Man, no harm taken. But a man like You don't need anything from me."

"I was just looking for something to buy the girls back home. Forgive Me for asking."

The salesman looked directly at Krishna, "What You not from around here are You with that accent? I'm sure You and Your friend can make do with what You got to give girls."

Krishna looked over at Balaram, "I don't know what you're getting at. Don't you sell clothes?"

"You can give me that cap and I'll sell that," said the man mocking Krishna's peacock feather cap.

"Sorry to bother you dude. We just thought we could buy a little something of New York," added in Balaram, "This man seems to be drunk and..."

"And what?!" said the man with hostility, "You were about to say racist weren't you?"

"Let's go I guess he doesn't want our business."

"We can go, but I still need clothes now for Myself as I'm in dire need to get out of these foreign clothes and get into something the locals would wear..." said Krishna with no attention to leave.

"Hahaha! You now taking the piss? We don't wear these clothes. Why don't you give me what You have and I'll let you walk away with Your cap?"

"Do you work here?" asked Balaram.

"Do you think that I work here?" quickly replied the man. "I don't work here. I don't get paid for working here. I'm just here for you to suck my dick!"

At that point Krishna had had enough at the miscreant. He looked at the man square in the eyes and then moved close to the wall that was beside them. Krishna touched the wall and prayed for a moment and then looked up the wall to see the horizon and the sky above. The clouds were gently moving. Letting go of His touch and His pray He walked back to the man.

The man was fixed and gob-smacked on what he had saw Krishna do. For a moment the man said nothing and just about when he was to speak Krishna smacked him hard across his head twisting the man's neck dropping him to the ground.

"I've come here to kill the ruler of the land so why should I receive your judgment?" said Krishna to the man. "Now pick yourself up and be cleansed from your own hatred for your life!"

Many people saw the scene but didn't react in favour for the man or for Krishna. However Krishna gained devotees from half the witnesses towards the action. Krishna then saw another man who appeared more to be a salesman and left this man where he laid. Balaram spoke for Krishna thereafter and bought some memorabilia for their Mother Yashoda and Radha-Rani from the real salesman, he thanked him and left.

"Peace be with You," said the real salesman.

That afternoon had a full moon visible in daylight. Krishna began to think of His mother, Radha-Rani, the *gopies*, His friends at the farm with the cows and calves, and His other loved men around Dover. He thought of them in heavenly existence that they were always with Him and hence so He was always with them. Krishna visualized the many colours of back home and all His devotees wearing clothes of different colours each one catching His attention. Krishna thought as the Lord Supreme and brought everyone that loved Him to the heavenly planets of *Krsnaloka* and *Goloka Vrndavan.* Where Krishna actually was and where His mind was in two entirely different places; thus as for this Krishna first saw the best in all things i.e. opulence in all material and spiritual nature.

As Krishna was in feeling of opulence He happened to focus on a flower shop. Krishna and Balaram went to the flower shop. Upon arriving and entering they saw the florist happily serving another customer. He wore a wonderful smile and a gentleman's garden hat. He moved the customer around the shop making Krishna and Balaram aware that he was aware of them. The brothers then copied his style and moved their presences in fashion to capture light on the florist. They looked around the shop touching and smelling the plants and flowers. After the florist had assisted the other customer Balaram approached him.

"Good day, sir," said Balaram.

"Good day, young men. My name is Sudamia, how can I help you two?" replied the florist.

"I am Balaram and this is my brother Krishna."

Sudamia in excitement returned, "Holy cow! Wait a minute, you... are... Balaram? And You... are... Krishna? Krishna and Balaram are in my shop?!"

Krishna felt the man's heart as surely Sudamia had heard of them. Sudamia began to give highest obeisances to Krishna. He asked Krishna of His favourite flowers but before Krishna answered Sudamia answered for Him.

"Lotuses, *tulsi*, *rudhrask*, yellow flowers, and You like I hear the flowers of betel nuts and pulp of candana," Sudamia said all in ecstasy and with a delightful feeling that he was a hundred percent right that the man standing by him was Krishna.

Sudamia then said, "You're the Super-soul."

Krishna was pleased with Sudamia's honesty and unselfishness that Krishna offered him material opulences. The Supreme Lord praised Sudamia and his family. He blessed them with long life along with whatever his heart desired in the material world. Sudamia's heart desired Krishna and Balaram to come and meet his family. Once they would see the presence of Shree Krishna they would be satisfied with the three worlds of material and conscious nature to the very end of time. Thus Sudamia insisted for the brothers to visit his home. Krishna to fulfill His purpose of existence for pleasing His devotees agreed to Sudamia's wish.

Meanwhile back at Taste of Vrndravan the *gopies* were feeling the separation from Krishna. *Gopies* not only for *Rasa-Lila* but wanted to be with Krishna all the time. Each *gopi* developed a way of always being with Krishna even if they were separated. Some had pictures of Him, others had gifts that Krishna had given, but most of all they all had a special place for Him in their hearts. They had given their hearts to Him and hence were always with Him. Mayor Caitanya and other men and women of Dover would mimic Radha-Rani and *gopies* as when they were together with Krishna. For instance they would leave whatever they were doing to go to Taste of Vrndavan for refueling transcendental pastimes left by Krishna.

Gopies would talk about all of Krishna; from stories about their upbringing to their meetings, from the home activities to praising His mum Yashoda; from Him lying on His left elbow and hand when resting to the vibrations of His flute; from the animals as cows and calves that would obey Him and; from how the environment would be in trances as waves in rivers and lakes. As *gopies* were never with Krishna's mercy they were always alive with Him just as demigods *Baba Shiva*, *Brahma Dev*, *Goddess Durga* and all enjoying Krishna's presence. *Gopies* would come dressed elegantly to chat at Vrndavan or Govardh Hill about how Krishna and Balaram would dress ever so nicely. They shared personally stories about what Krishna had said to them and where He had touched them. All *gopies* embraced each other in the thought of Krishna.

The clouds and Krishna had a bond too that shadowed Him from excess light. The animals would wonder too what was so enchanting about Him? What beauty, wonder and bliss Krishna had for them? Krishna had attended with what was like a thousand animals that of especially cows. He had buttermilk from them and divided the cows into a hundred and eight groups. He too used this buttermilk system to divide the *gopies* as a hundred and eight individual females. Not only were the farm animals enchanted by Him but furthermore were the black female deers.

All *gopies* that were wives would stop their singing and their clothes would become loosen when in Krishna Consciousness of transcendental space. This of which was a hypnotic magic of Shree Krishna's the *gopies* did the best. Feelings of separation from Krishna left the *gopies* in Krishna Consciousness that made their lives sublime, fruitful and eternally loved.

Back in Manhattan Sudamia brought Krishna and Balaram to his home and introduced them to his family. They were all so struck in surprise and gratitude. The brothers sat and joined company of Sudamia's family especially his son, Uddav whom was very fond of Krishna also. Uddav was a part of the Hindu Student Foundation in New York. So as one can imagine when the Supreme Lord entered his home he wanted to share this with all the friends he knew. Krishna and Balaram took photos with Uddav and Uddav immediately shared them online to all his contacts. Before one could even blink notifications came alive on his phone from friends and friends of friends. And most of these notifications read, 'I told you so.' Apparently many people of the Hindu Student Foundation had heard of stories of Dover and were already in network with Krishna's pastimes.

Uddav asked many questions of Dover and Krishna's home of Vrndavan and Govardh Hill. He then asked Krishna and Balaram to spend some time with his pastimes. They agreed and went for a walk around the neighbourhood. Uddav showed them the parks and basketball courts where he spent many hours with friends. He showed them the local convenience stores. He showed them leisure spots and the police station. Uddav walked Krishna and Balaram around his neighbourhood mostly to give everyone blessings just by their sight of Krishna and Balaram.

Along their travels Uddav had took them to areas of the neighbourhood that not many would go after sun down. As Uddav was with Krishna and Balaram he had no fear but to show them everything that surrounded him.

A hunchback woman named Kabjalia lived in the neighbourhood and was well known for her lusty ways. She happened to also work for a gentleman's club and was told by her other women that two mysterious men known as Krishna and Balaram were in town. Kabjalia had heard of the name Krishna from the fellow women and how a man had appointed love in the women of Delaware. She needed to see with her own two eyes and satisfy her lusty desires.

From where she stood she could see down the alley in the direction of three men that were walking towards her position. Immediately her heart sank deep as she saw Krishna in all His beauty, wonder and destruction that her soul begged her to become liberated by Him. As Uddav, Krishna and Balaram came closer to the gentleman's club, Kabjalia called for the other women to gain the attention of the men. Krishna had saw her too and prepared himself for introduction.

Kabjalia came upon Krishna, "O Lord, is it You? I have prayed many tears to see You. I plead with You good sir, come with me to release me from the shackles of what life has given."

She and the other women surrounded the men and moved them into the building using their bodies up close to them that they couldn't resist without becoming aggressive.

"Let me show You my home, O Lord. I'm sure You will be in exalting satisfaction."

"I'm not sure that you know where we come from or where we are going," replied Krishna.

"Don't say that my Lord. You are Krishna and he is Balaram. Don't you think women as us don't know who You and Your brother are? Do You think of us to be so foolish?" Kabjalia said whilst sliding her tongue between her lips. "Let my girls look after Your brothers and You come with me so I can show You my professionalism."

The parlour of women was filled with perfume and candles. Balaram and Uddav were given royal places to sit. Kabjalia's girls attended Krishna's brothers with drinks, dancing and light flirting. Krishna was taken by the hand of Kabjalia to her room. As Krishna entered the room and the door was closed behind Him He saw that Kabjalia was very talented in lusty seduction. He realised that Kabjalia was more seduced by lusty desires than what the room showed.

The Supreme Lord remains in the spiritual world eternally and partially in materialistic embrace; this spiritual existence is called *aprakata-lila*. Two heavenly parts of the mind exist as planets of where Shree Krishna resides. They are *Vaikuntha* and *Goloka Vrndavan*, which also coexist with two potencies of Kabjalia and Radha-Rani, '*Bhu-sakti*' and '*Cit-sakti*'. Kabjalia was saturated with *bhu-sakti,* this is all she could do and knew therefore she knew how to offer Krishna all the best of sexual female desires. Kabjalia had attributes to the strong potency of peace and life.

Kabjalia sat Krishna at the edge of her bed and went to prepare herself with perfumes and pearls. She prepared a plate of betel nut which was an intoxicating nectar used also as an aphrodisiac. Lustful and sexual contracts were all she knew and what she knew she knew all the best.

She presented herself before Krishna but became hesitant on her approach that she resisted. Krishna grabbed her by her bangles and pulled her into Him. He satisfied her with passionate words and admirations of heavenly nature. She placed Krishna's lotus feet on her breasts relieving her from further lusty thoughts and brought herself to the transcendental world. As Krishna pulled Kabjalia towards Him, He had released her own thoughts of natural sin and became protected by Krishna's abode. One first has to be sin free to enter Nirvana's transcendental energies.

Kabjalia opened more of her heart to Krishna and asked the Lord to stay but He declared He could not. He asked her to apply sandalwood pulp and *kunkama* for the next few days. Then they bid farewell.

Later Krishna asked Uddav to come with them to Akura's home. Akura welcomed them and gave more obeisances to Krishna and Balaram which they were all pleased with. He highly prayed to Krishna and rested His lotus feet on a cushion on His lap and massaged His legs. He then thanked Krishna and remarked on how Krishna was more of spiritual existence than of material body. Akura mentioned the three worlds and three natures. He had already informed Kaans that Krishna had arrived saying that the Yadu Dynasty had returned. Akura was extremely knowledgeable. He praised Krishna and Balaram further on how they had beaten many demons and took down atheistic miscreants of royal families by destroying their military passion. Akura glorified Yadu Dynasty further.

Individual souls with conditioned lives are Krishna's material inferior body. Less intelligent men don't understand there is no difference between the Lord and the Lord's body. Krishna is forever liberated in His own life.

"My dear Lord, my home is purified with Your grace. You are a real friend to everyone. You saved me from entanglement of false society of friends and love. Is there more You'll like me to do?" said Akura.

"O my dear Akura, our friend and well-wisher. I would like you to go to the home of the Pandav's in India. I would like for you to meet my father Vasudev's sister Kunti-Ma's sons. They are in dear need for my assistance so I have heard from my father Vasudev. The five Pandav brothers, Yudistra, Bheem, Arjun, Nakul and Sahadev, are sons of late Pandu-Raja. They are under the thumb of their guardian.

"Late Pandav-Raja has a brother, Dhrutaras who has made himself heir of Bharata-Raja's empire after the death of Pandav-Raja, banishing his brother's sons from their inheritance. The blind, rotten lord from birth has a son, Duryodh and his plans are not favourably disposed to his cousins. Go to Hastinapur in India, Akura, and report back to me the condition of the five Pandav brothers. With your report I shall consider how to favour them. This would mean the world to me."

With this request that Krishna had given Akura he was filled with spiritual importance. At once he went to prepare for the travel. Nanda-Raja looked over at Krishna knowing that Krishna was making plans elsewhere to where they had just come. Balaram bowed to Krishna knowing that after killing Kaans, Krishna would step into the homeland of India. Uddav observed and listened with great respect what had been said. As the night had fallen into deeper sleep, Krishna and Balaram with pleasure voted to take Uddav home.

Krishna Kills Kaans

Chapter 18

The will of Krishna or the will of Kaans had come to the day where will would be concluded. Was this that the Lord Supreme structured an exercise for human kind to fall into sinful acts that the Lord would have to come and show His face again? Or was that a man like Kaans needed to meet his match, needed to prove his worth of grandeur, needed a slap on the wrist or needed to be liberated? Extreme liberalism had taken over the world with the power of foreign exchange and power of wealth across the world. Even if the well minded wish to serve a smile they could not as in spiritual nature with material action would lower the mental activity for them doing their work. So time had come for the Kaans to reconcile himself by a higher identity to make him free of his miserable mind.

In Kaans' apartment in Mathura Building the automatic curtain opened at seven in the morning letting the light into his quarters. Kaans moved his large body slowly out of bed and walked to the window to face the sun. He stood there staring between the horizons of the buildings and the street below for several minutes. He looked up at the sky and prayed.

Akura and Nanda-Raja had been up since six in the morning all excited about the day that was to commence. This was the day where fate would be confirmed, where judgment would be made to justice. A scale between a hundred and ten thousand people were involved in the exhibition about to start that would affect the larger scale of people around the world. Calls were made to Taste of Vrndavan and Govardh Hill Restaurant to call many further out in relation to Nanda-Raja. The people of Delaware bonded with Nanda-Raja were informed that the exhibition of Kaans' death had arrived and them to come to Manhattan to watch the turn of time.

"Hey guys, are you up?" asked Nanda-Raja opening the door to Krishna and Balaram's room.

They were not in their room. They were on the open deck having a chat whilst the life of the city woke for the day. Krishna and Balaram had already prepared the day ahead amongst themselves. All they had to hear from Nanda-Raja was, were the people from back home coming or not?

Nanda-Raja walked to the brothers, "They're all coming! Well all the *brahamanas* and *ksetriyas* we know of that is. Rama's farmers will come and he will bring his friends too. However none of the women will come as they don't want to see You hurt, but I think that they don't want to show their faces to the women surrounding the wrestling match."

Krishna replied, "That's fantastic news! I totally understand about My *gopies*. They are too special to come and be seen by the likes of the damned. They know the outcome of today better than I."

Krishna and Balaram then left Akura's apartment and went to observe the environment for the auspicious day. On their travels Krishna saw a young woman that had a limp in her walk. He saw that she was carrying two bags that read sandalwood pulp and was walking towards the Mathura Building.

"O slender tall young woman, why take that sandalwood to the demon king? Sure be better if you gave to Me!" shouted Krishna from across the street.

She stopped to look around and saw Krishna and Balaram. She shielded her face away from Krishna as she had been struck by blisters and sores on her face.

Without looking towards Krishna's radiance she replied, "It is true I should give it to anyone but him, but I am a mare employee of Kaans."

She then reached into her bag and smeared Krishna and Balaram with prepared sandalwood pulp. She there and then devoted herself to Krishna and looked over at their beauty.

Krishna touched her feet with his foot and stood her up straight amending her twisted leg that gave her the limp. He then looked only at her lips and established communication to her though spiritual sense for her to look at other's lips starting with His. This was to reduce her anxiety and thus removed her facial skin's irregularities. She felt her skin tighten up, her leg free from burden, and her heart full of love and life. She immediately admitted that she had lusty desires in transcendental state to Krishna that He knew nonetheless. However she couldn't resist but put her body into Krishna's and moved her hand around His buttocks to take a feel. All of sudden she had the strength, the courage and the confidence to admit her lusty ways to Krishna on the street. She gave Krishna her number and insisted for Him to come to hers. He replied with words that soothed her and with Balaram walked into Mathura Building.

Krishna saw how the lobby was decorated with pleasantries as fresh flowers, silk drapes, ornaments and decorations of wealth, luxury seating, soft music that calmed Kaans' people that there was nothing for them to worry about. The ambiance of the environment was an illusion of what was actually in Kaans' mind but to his shareholders and partners why talk about something that yet had not happened? Krishna walked around the lobby making His presence known to the people. They looked with peripheral vision that caught perplexes of where Krishna appeared that not only was He to be Kaans' Maker but also that of theirs.

Krishna approached a porter, "Hello, I hear there is a sacrificial arena with a bow made of gold with great strength, can you point Me in that direction?"

The brothers then proceeded to the direction of where the porter had said. They came to an open space with tall ceilings with Roman style columns and in the middle of the room sectioned by a red rope was the sacrificial gold bow. The room had a brown wooden antique appearance that most old grand libraries would have. The gold bow was in the middle being lit by lights from all corners of the room.

Krishna walked towards the bow and saw a sign that read, 'Do Not Touch'. At any other time and any other place Krishna would have obeyed the notice but as for this time and place He was not obliged for caring.

He unclipped the red robe from the stand and strung the string of the bow. The sound resonated throughout the room and out of the doors and through the walls which vibrated further to Kaans' ears. Not a moment later Kaans heard a louder single sound and that was of the bow being broken in two. An alarm sounded soon after and official guards came to arrest Krishna and Balaram, but they each picked up half of the bow and beat the guards to unconsciousness. The brothers after a clean sweep of beating the guards walked out of Mathura Building as easily as they had walked in to later return for the wrestling match.

Kaans heard about the beating of his guards and the breaking of the bow. In amongst his preparations of the fight he began to have visions about golden trees and that his doom was approaching fast. He then ordered his employees to get Devika and Vasudev to have them be seated royally by him at the match. Without showing fear or concern he also send out his employees to speak to Akura and have Nanda-Raja's guests welcomed to be seated by his company also. He spoke to his employees in a more delightful gentle tone that they were thrown back. They did as they were told and sat the *brahamanas*, *vaisyas*, *ksatriyas* and *sudras* all in important seating for the wrestling match, and therefore his demonic shareholders, partners and corruptors further out.

As late afternoon arrived Krishna and Balaram returned back to Mathura Building. There was a crowd of people entering the building in excitement of the wrestling match that

Kaans had advertised. Many bookies and traders had taken bets on the wrestlers who were to compete there. There were also rumours of Kaans being a candidate amongst the inner circles and bets were taken on either him winning or losing too. Krishna was the named highlight of the event and many people that had looked into Krishna had bet for Him to win the contest even though they had never seen Him in person.

There was a buzz around and within Mathura Building that spread all over Manhattan. Kaans had organised the wrestling match on a Friday to influence the trading market and foreign exchange experts to make most out of their money. The match was biased in regards of candidates as Kaans had chosen the most elite to represent his business. Krishna and Balaram walked into the building and followed the course to the arena which was on the fiftieth floor.

In the elevator Krishna summoned His inner peace and expanded His mind to configure the magnitude of the world outside. The elevator pinged on reaching its destination and the doors opened. There were sounds of kettledrums beating and strobe lights flashing as the brothers alighted the elevator. The arena took shape of two floors of the building. It had two floors for the audience to sit and view the match in the middle. At one end of the second floor was the main seating where Kaans, Devika, Vasudev, Nanda-Raja and Akura sat along with some of Kaans' security and his brothers. The extravagant stadium comprised within Mathura Building was truly one to be admired with views of Manhattan and the skyline that stretched all the way to the Statue of Liberty. The people seated on both floors around the arena were in frenzy and all had a drink of some sought in their hands. Krishna looked around and saw the wealth that Kaans' people had without any sound of spiritualism within them. They were all bound by material fruitative desires but soon were to be embedded with Krishna Consciousness.

The brothers approached the arena closer and out stood a man as large and tall as can be. He showed his palm to Krishna and Balaram stopping them from entering. His name was Kuvalia, but more commonly known as The Elephant. He was taking instructions from some other person as he had an earphone inserted into his left ear and microphone over his face. With one arm stretched out blocking Krishna and Balaram, and the other hand trying to listen to the instructions coming into his earphone a spot light came over the three of them. Kuvalia turned around walked to the centre of the arena and saluted Kaans. He then turned and cursed both Krishna and Balaram mocking them on their size and nerve to come to the arena.

Krishna returned curses to him by repeating names and numbers of scriptures which gained Him power as well as forgiveness in what He was about to do. He charged in might to The Elephant and maneuvered Himself behind to his blind spot, returning back to hit Kuvalia in the face knocking out his ear piece. He then tossed and turned The Elephant by his waist and grabbed the trunk of his neck lifting The Elephant off the ground breaking his neck as his spine hit the ground. Krishna looked beautiful in perspiration and the blood of The Elephant.

Balaram then joined Krishna and both grabbed each arm of the dead man and dragged his body closer for Kaans to see. The people of Mathura Building went wild and admired the outcome of Krishna's attack on The Elephant. Bets started to shift from the expected outcomes as the people were thrown back by the show of Krishna and Balaram. The relations of Nanda-Raja cheered as loud and as long as they could.

Once the cheering had settled a famous wrestler named Cainuras welcomed and introduced Krishna as the 'Supreme Godhead' to the audience.

"Be hold the Mighty Lord has arrived! As a child, as a young man, and as the greatest of them all let us bow down to the will of Shree Krishna, the Supreme Godhead!" announced Cainuras.

"Godhead! Godhead! Godhead! Godhead! Godhead!" chanted the audience.

Krishna then leaned towards Cainuras and spoke in his ear. He suggested that ruling would be unethical or displeasing for Him to compete with the huge professional wrestlers and so demanded not to fight against them. Cainuras replied in return that Krishna is the greatest wrestler of them all as He killed the legendary Elephant. Thus how could he not ask Krishna and Balaram to wrestle with them for the sake of entertainment and laughter? So Krishna accepted Cainruas' compliment and turned to Balaram.

"Balaram! Godhead's brother!" said Cainuras.

"Ram! Ram! Hare Ram!" chanted the audience.

"Hare Krishna! Hare Rama!" claimed Cainuras.

"Hare Krishna! Hare Rama!" they repeated.

Over at the VIP suite Kaans began to perspire and turned to face his sister, Devika. She looked over at him knowing what he was thinking but said nothing. He then fidgeted on his seat trying to adjust his anxiety. Kaans then raised his arm to have the spot light come upon him.

"Ladies and gentlemen, look and see the young man that is here to change the way we do business! Uphold your hearts and minds on what we have accomplished and see that He is the reason for what is now to be even if we like it or not. So commence the fights and let the best man be standing! Now wrestle!" instructed Kaans to the wrestlers.

A wrestler known as Mastika took hold of Balaram and Cainuras took hold of Krishna hand to hand and calf to calf. The brothers and the wrestlers turned and heaved each other around on the arena floor. Moments of exertion and inertia from them began but neither candidate losing the battle.

Moments later a woman from the audience cried out, 'how indecent this was to watch this match,' but then another woman shouted, 'but look how handsome, beautiful and strong they are,' and then they carried on to speak about their pastimes. As Krishna overheard this and the emotions of anxiety in the voices He decided to end the match. Krishna struck Cainuras who returned with one last strike as Krishna caught his opponent and spun him around to knock him off guard and fall unconscious to the floor. Balaram then repeated the same move on Mastika knocking him unconscious too. Three other wrestlers that did not like what they saw came onto arena floor to attack Krishna and Balaram, but the brothers struck them out as quickly as they arrived.

"Kick the boys out of here!" shouted out Kaans. "Take their possessions and arrest their father Nanda-Raja and his relations for their death defying cunning schemes!"

Immediately after Kaans had finished that sentence Krishna jumped on three stands and onto the balcony of where he sat. Kaans unsheathed a revolver as he knew Krishna was his Maker, but Krishna knocked out the weapon and grabbed Kaans' hair to drag him to the middle of the wrestling arena. Krishna looked square at Kaans for Kaans to get a good look at Krishna up close and then knocked him to the ground. He then put His foot on Kaans' chest stopping the beat of his heart and ending his vitality from the material world. After this Krishna to insure Kaans' family and crowd that he was dead dragged the body around as a lion would with its prey.

Kaans' spiritual existence returned back to his abode after death which was in the heavenly planet of *Lord Vishnu* as *Vaikuntha*. Kaans was liberated after death as he did believe that Krishna was the Almighty.

Cheering in ecstasy roared throughout the arena. Kaans' brothers and Kaans' uncles became furious and jumped onto the wrestling floor to kill Krishna. Eight brothers came to attack Krishna but as Krishna's ordeal was to kill Kaans, Balaram stepped in to defend Krishna and attacked Kaans' brothers to death. The wives and family of Kaans' grieved for their loss.

Far out of the Mathura Building towards the skies and the heavenly planets an auspicious change occurred. Within the realms of the minds of demigods planets began to change form. Petals of flowers bloomed bright colours and rainbows began to form. The light of the sun changed to a reddish hue as the sun approached the west horizon settling the day. Stars across the universe burned brighter making the night sky more approachable for the last daylight. Fire, water, wind, earth and ether stabilised themselves in tranquil harmony. The lights of the arena switched on and guided the audience to leave Mathura in peace.

Krishna immediately then went to see and release His mother Devika and father Vasudev. They hugged and kissed both Krishna and Balaram. Devika and Vasudev were free from Kaans' keep. They were with their son for who was away from their presence.

Several days later Krishna returned to the widows (His aunties) for ritual funeral ceremonies as after all the dead were His uncles. Both Krishna and Balaram fell to the feet of Kaans' brothers' relatives for obeisance. They prayed with them with condolences but Devika and Vasudev did not consolidate them, however allowed Krishna to praise them deeply valuing His position as Supreme Godhead.

Goodbye Sweetheart

Chapter 19

After releasing His mother and father, Devika and Vasudev from their chains to Kaans and their devotion to *Lord Vishnu*, Krishna expanded in the influence of *yogamaya* to greet and thank them.

Krishna consolidated them, "My dear mother and father, I know life had not been right for you from the beginning. From the beginning you were without your son and could not play with Him or watch Him grow. You had been lost in the thought of protecting Me and for that I am truly sorry."

"Our son we are sorry and give condolences as from our past lives You must have seen brought this burden upon You. As every human should have their children confined to their home as do many animals that love had not reached You. For that we are at Your mercy and ask for Your forgiveness," replied Vasudev.

"O mother and father, please excuse Me for My sinfulness that I couldn't serve you."

As the Supreme Godhead speaking as a boy shed His feelings they all embraced each other and remained silent shedding incessant tears.

On the last night of the cremation and spreading of ashes of Kaans and his brothers into the waters around the island of New York, Krishna approached Grandfather Ugrasen. He anointed Ugrasen to become the rightful owner of Kaans' enterprise and king of Yadu Kingdom. Ugrasen's son Kaans had stolen the rights of his father's position through blackmailing and now that he was dead, Ugrasen would regain control as the Chief Executive Officer. All branches of the enterprise that Kaans was in control of would be constructed to the hand of Ugrasen and Krishna gave progeny (*praja*) that the whole kingdom of Ugrasen would be peaceful.

All occupants, shareholders, delegates, employees and families of Mathura Building and the surrounding land of Manhattan were very pleased with Krishna and Balaram. Seeing their faces brought great strength and happiness to each person. They gave Krishna their own personal name for Him as Mukund, and all of Mathura relations fell into a safe confinement.

Mother Yashoda had come to stay with Devika and Vasudev in Mathura Building along with Nanda-Raja but soon after everything had settled she wanted to return home. Krishna and Balaram applauded their foster parents, giving them compliments and affection for raising them so well. Nanda-Raja's eyes were of tears and embraced his sons on behalf of all of their relations and Taste of Vrndavan.

Upon seeing this Vasudev came to Nanda-Raja and tied on him and their sons a sacred red thread as a symbol for new life. They tied the sacred thread and recited the *Gayatri Mantra.* He then called all *brahamanas* of every religion to perform a ceremony. Vasudev wished to give rich cow milk to everyone he knew on the birth of Krishna but as he was imprisoned he organised the ceremony at this moment in time.

During the ceremony and celebrations Vasudev introduced one of his family priests to Krishna and Balaram. The family priests were known as *Acarya* and they were extreme spiritual masters who taught wisdom and supplemental literatures. The *Acarya* that had taught Vasudev closely was fed and satisfied well and was considered as equal to Krishna in teachings. His name was Sandeepani Muni and was originally a resident of Northern Indian district. Once he saw Krishna he said that He was a *ksatriyas* and His knowledge in military science, politics and ethics was of transcendental inheritance from Father Vasudev.

<u>*Acarya* Department of Knowledge</u>
<u>– Unorthodox Approach</u>

a) How to make peace, how to fight, how to pacify, divide, rule and shelter.
b) Learn arts and sciences in 64 days and 64 nights, (one for hearing and one for saturating).
c) Learn how to sing, compose song and melodies, pitches etc.
d) Learn how to dance in rhythm of melody to different songs.
e) How to write dramas, how to paint to highest perfection.
f) Learn painting *tilaka* on faces, painting oxides on floor, decorating mandirs.
g) Distinguish water in pots.
h) Learn makeup, hair-style and costume to celebrities' wardrobe.
i) Learn sowing and embroidery.
j) Learn magic art of *Bahu-rupi* (face painting and camouflage, disguises and dressing to blind opposition).
k) Learn to play musical instruments: vina, sitar, tambour, violin, guitar, drums etc.
l) Learn how to make and solve riddles and crossword puzzles.
m) Interpret pictures, valuable stones and jewels, architecture and soil minerals.
n) Know herbs and plants for medicinal purposes.
o) Learn how to cross-breed plants and trees to derive different fruits.
p) Teach parrots how to speak.
q) Train rams and cocks to fight for sport.
r) Psychology of hypnotism to achieve own desires, (which hand is stone in).

s) Learn to speak other languages.
t) Communicate with spirit of animals and birds.
u) Learn to see signs in nature and place to significance with natural omen.
v) Create Sudoka puzzles.
w) Cutting stones e.g. diamonds.
x) Do question and answers to immediate poetry in the mind.
y) Learn how to do psychic movements to affect another person.
z) Learn how to satisfy ones desire; e.g. difficultly in money or sex, (mastering this ability can make enemies into best friends or even exhibit power to others. Actions of physical element).

This spiritual knowledge given to Krishna by transcendental inheritance implies that further down the line *Lord Vishnu* Himself had given *Acraya* to pass to Vasudev which returned back to the Lord as Shree Krishna. Thus Krishna asked Sandeepani Muni if he had any desires that he would like Krishna to fulfill. Sandeepani spoke about his wife and their lost son who had supposedly drowned in the Atlantic Ocean.

Krishna therefore left Sandeepani Muni and His family to call upon the Coastguard of the Eastern Coast of America to ask for their favour. They first shared obeisance to Him. Krishna enquired for His teacher's son whereabouts. The coastguard replied that a terrible gang ruled by a man called, Pancajana, (Conch-shell Demon), were kidnapping and taking hostage of sailors off their coasts. The coastguard spoke about the location of the demon but he was out of their jurisdiction for an arrest. Krishna at once set out to find Sandeepani's son.

Arriving at a floating prison of the Conch-shell Demon, Krishna took no mercy and strangled him to death. He then searched the floating prison that Pancajana had made but no boy was to be found. Therefore Krishna thought to take the body of the demon to dry shores and summon Yamaraj. Yamaraj was the Grim-Reaper; he was the Superintend of Death.

Krishna with His external potency banked in Balaram drew the energy from His brother who was sleeping in New York and called the Lord of Death, Yamaraj from the light within the darkness. Yamaraj appeared and offered immediately obeisances to Krishna as he knew of Krishna's mercy. Krishna in return showed obeisances and became very humble by having His head bowed and not looking at Yamaraj head on. He looked at his hands, his heart, his feet, his clothes, and his ornaments but did not look into Yamaraj's eyes. Krishna then asked for His teacher's son back. Yamaraj returned the spirit of the boy into the body of Pancajana, mutating the body to resemble the shape and form of Sandeepani's long lost son.

On return to Sandeepani Muni, Krishna asked if there was anything else that he required. Overjoyed and in extreme delight Sandeepani embraced Krishna, blessing Him and praising Him more.

"I give You benediction of whatever You may speak will remain eternally fresh as instruction of the *Vedas*. Your teachings will be honoured in all of time, space, universe and ages. They will be increasingly new and important," declared Sandeepani. "*Hare Krishna!*"

Soon after Krishna returned back to His parents and foster family at Mathura Building. Krishna required the assistance of His new found friend, Uddav, son of Sudamia and so called for him. Krishna asked Uddav and his family to join Him for a special assignment that only Uddav would be suited to do.

"Hello Uddav," said Krishna whilst he opened the door to let him and his family into the apartment.

"Hello, my Lord Krishna," replied Uddav in excitement to be of use to Krishna.

"What's up, Uddav?" added Balaram.

"Namaste Sudamia," said Krishna and Balaram.

Sudamia replied by placing his hands together.

Uddav and his family entered the apartment and were introduced to Devika, Vasudev, Yashoda and Nanda-Raja. They made light conversation with laughter whilst dinner was preparing. The males sat in the lounge and bantered and then females performed their pastime in between the kitchen and the lounge.

Uddav could not stand to hold in his curiosity for Krishna's request so asked Him to let the cat out of the bag and spill the beans. The first thing Krishna did was laugh and looked over at Balaram. He too smiled and laughed whilst bowing in Uddav's direction.

"Good luck! Nice to have known you man. It has been a great ride," patronised Balaram reaching over to shake Uddav's hand.

Uddav sounding worried replied, "... Okay."

"Hey Uddav, do you believe I am the most exalted person of all?" asked Krishna to stall Uddav.

"O Lord, You are who You say You are," replied Uddav slowing the pace of intuition. "I am in no place to say that You are not who You say You are."

"Good answer, dear boy. Don't let these two fool you," added in Nanda-Raja.

Krishna gave a small smirk towards Nanda-Raja as he knew what He was getting at.

"I have a huge favour to ask of you buddy."

"Yes, my dear Lord, I gathered that much."

"My request is something that a) I cannot do Myself and b) trust in you to do so for Me."

"What can I do that You cannot do yourself?"

"Hahahaha! Hahahaha!" Krishna, Balaram, and Nanda-Raja laughed to savour the moment.

Father Vasudev and Sudamia watched poor blessed Uddav hold onto his silence with a smile.

Mother Yashoda and Mother Devika heard the loud laughter and came to see Uddav's expression as Krishna was to let him in on His request. They came in and comforted Uddav by giving him a cold glass of buttermilk. They then sat beside Uddav.

Krishna raised His right hand and gently positioned His palm to reflect on Uddav. Uddav's natural instinct touched his forefinger and thumb together to stabilise himself from Krishna's love.

"Mmmmm, O son of Sudamia, I would love and request you to go to Taste of Vrndavan and deliver some news to My *gopies*..." said Krishna.

Uddav not in full awareness of this request but aware of not being a light one and that being of significance replied with hesitation, "What news... would you like me... to deliver, my Lord?"

Sealing His lotus lips and looking straight into the eyes of Uddav, Krishna then took a deep breath and replied, "O my beloved *gopies* and cowherd men, I am to go across the pond and leave your side in material body but you will be with Me in spiritual form for all the days to come. Love Krishna."

After a second of realization Uddav replied, "No way! No way, no way, no way, no way, na na na na, na, no! I'm not doing that! I am not delivering that message. Why me? What have I done so bad in all my lives that I need to deliver that message to Your *gopies*? Hell no! No sir, no! I can't. Ask Balaram. You must be joking. I'm going home. I'm not strong enough for that. That's a suicide mission! They will not even listen. No way, never happening! I'll send an email or a text but that's as far as I'll go with that. Is this why You made friends with me? You can keep your obeisances. I'm not worthy. How many are there? Forget I asked. I can't. Please I'm not able to do that. I still have to look out for my future. No ah, ah ah," said

Uddav, trying to get his breathing and his mind to catch up to halt. "Besides where are You going? I didn't say I would. Okay I might. For You anything."

"Radha-Rani will be there," added in Balaram.

"NO WAY! I am not saying what You said to Radha-Rani. No Loving Way! For Love's Sake No Way!" aggressively continued Uddav. "Love Off!"

Everyone laughed and laughed and laughed until Uddav was laughing with tears from his eyes too.

Krishna had promised to pacify the *gopies* in Vrndavan and Govardh Hill that He'd return, but He and Balaram would not. His *gopies* were to stay in remembrance of Him (*bhava*) by His pastimes day and night between loved ones. Yashoda and Nanda-Raja had come to terms that Krishna and Balaram would stay in Manhattan with Devika and Vasudev, in order to compose any further reoccurrences of Kaans, and build relations lost between parents and son.

Uddav was not just found by chance but was a distant brother of Krishna's from where Vasudev's ancestry originated back to Dwarka in India. Uddav's features resembled well to that of Krishna's in age, height, build and style along with tone of voice, lotus eyes, gait and pose. Uddav was the one to go back to the relations of Vrndavan and deliver the message to the *gopies*. To visit Vrndavan and meet the *gopies* one would reach the highest spiritual planet of victory, *Vaikuntha*, and thus be with Krishna Consciousness.

Mother Yashoda gently took the glass of buttermilk from Uddav's hand and went to get him another, "Do not fear, we will be with you," she said.

The morning after the proposal a golden Chavrolet with a heavy horse-power engine rode into Dover pass Govardh Hill Restaurant and parked outside Taste of Vrndavan. Many *gopies* and cowherd men saw the alien car come into their town and to Taste of Vrndavan making them wonder. As first Akura had come to take Krishna away from them and now a mysterious new extravagant vehicle could only mean more bad news. Yashoda and Nanda-Raja stepped out of the vehicle. Yashoda had called Rohini in advance and asked her to meet with the *gopies* at the restaurant. The *gopies* waited in anticipation for Krishna and Balaram, but a person looking remarkably like Krishna stepped out the driver's seat and locked the car.

During the day the *gopies* and cowherd men were introduced to Uddav without too much mention of Krishna and Balaram's whereabouts. They sat and told Uddav about their pastimes with Krishna. They spoke about the demons that the brothers had conquered. Uddav sat in awe and listened to the delightful stories they shared throughout the day.

He saw that the *gopies* were all in love with Krishna as they danced and played with stupidness and with a joyful outlook to life. So many *gopies* came in and out of Taste of Vrndavan to share their stories with Uddav and also to observe his nature of being. Some would sit by him and share, others would sit away and observe, others still would chant the *mahamantra* (*Hare Krishna, Hare Rama*), and some others would speak amongst themselves on why Uddav had come?

All the *gopies* had their own special qualities and attributes of differing ages, ethnicities and intelligence. And all were away from fruitative desires and with Krishna Consciousness that Uddav found very overwhelming. Uddav observed by being with the *gopies* that Krishna and Balaram were far away from manifestations in cosmic nature as he sat with the material form of Krishna's opulence.

The night had come spending time talking and listening to each other's stories. Before the sun was to rise the following day the *gopies* went home to rest and refresh for an hour or so. A few *gopies* close to Yashoda and Rohini spent the night in Taste of Vrndavan. As the sun then rose, the *gopies* prepared an *aarti* (ritual of worship to deities), by lighting lamps, sprinkling butter mixed with yogurt and prepared themselves with the news Uddav was to share. They churned yogurt to make butter in memory of Krishna and sang Krishna's chants to sanctify the atmosphere. Uddav overheard the *gopies* saying, 'that there was nothing worse than not being with Krishna," so soon after their ablutions, prayers and chanting he came to confront them.

"We see you there Uddav. Come and share with us what you have been told," said one of the *gopies*.

"Come and do your deed and be gone with you as we do not need to hear more," said another.

"Give him a chance. I'm sure it's not as easy for him to say as it will be for us to hear," said a *gopi*.

Uddav stood near Yashoda, "I come in peace."

"And there you shall go," humoured a *gopi*.

The door swung open and Rohini along with more *gopies* came into the restaurant all dressed well and smelling divine of sandalwood.

Rohini looked over at Yashoda and then Uddav, "What has he said so far?" she said with attitude.

"He said how Krishna is as selfish as us sending a friend outside the family to pass on a message. He may as well have sent a message via text. As birds not needing trees after mating seasons, he seems to have grown out of fashion for us..." said another *gopi* making a reason of her own.

Uddav said nothing but prepared his thoughts on what to say and how to say that to the audience of women always in thought's of Krishna.

Uddav gave a cough and opened his mouth to speak when another voice came from amongst the *gopies*.

"When I see a bumblebee I address the bumblebee indirectly. I open my mouth and show the bee a road for peace which the bee becomes afraid of and flies to my lotus feet."

The company of *gopies* made space for this voice to speak and become in view of Uddav. She sat amongst her *gopies* with a red silk shawl over her head and twirled a wooden lolly-stick in her right hand. Her pose and composure as she sat and spoke under a lamp in the middle of Taste of Vrndavan made Uddav gulp and shiver slightly from within. This *gopi* was Radha-Rani taking expansion of *Goddess Laxmi-Ma* as she addressed Uddav as the voice for all *gopies*.

Radha-Rani continued, "Leave me be, Bee! I know You have moved to new fully breasted girls of Mathura and thus Vrndavan is obsolete to You. I wouldn't expect anything else from Your lotus face!" she said moving her other hand to her thighs thinking of Krishna. "Oh Bee! Tell Uddav not to mock us with false accusations that You know better than us home girls. Be with heavenly, middle and plutonic planets."

She then switched hands twirling the wooden stick which made Uddav feel obsolete and numb in her presence, "Godhead! You have taught me well. I've seen perfection of austerities, so amen and be as a bee and fly away from me. But how coward is He like Raja Ramachandra not to face His attacker, but instead attack him from behind as He has us? I'm sure though if my Krishna came to say He was to go, this queen bee wouldn't let Him so. Promise that you don't see me as ugly when You see other women that come to be. So gold-bee fly away," she said in force of remorse.

She shed a tear and that tear ran down her cheek and as the tear was to drop off her face to the table a bee flew in from nowhere that caught her attention. The bumble bee hovered around her playing with her left and right senses which filled her with happiness.

The bee flew over the entire room of *gopies* and to Yashoda and Uddav and returned back to Radha-Rani. Radha-Rani humbled herself to the bee and complimented Uddav, "Namashkar."

Uddav returned with, "Namaste, Radha-Rani."

He then looked over at all the *gopies* and had his hands together complimenting them on the highest order for 'perfection of austrisities'. After Radha-Rani and the *gopies* spoke to Uddav about all they wanted him to pass on to

Krishna. He then complimented them further and delivered the message from Krishna.

He quoted, "My dear *gopies*..." and read to them what Krishna had asked him to pass on. The letter spoke about supplemental energy and how Krishna is with all living entities. That *gopies* are in full transcendental bliss with or without Krishna and they are to live as *maya*; living and loving in Krishna with eight elements which the mind cannot vacant.

Uddav read the knowledge that Krishna had instructed to Radha-Rani and the *gopies*: Five gross elements; earth, water, air, fire and sky, along with three subtle elements; mind, intelligence and ego, therefore to adhere this *bhakti* (devotion), for 'perfection of knowledge'. Uddav continued to read the letter in original form by incarnations of *Baba Shiva* and *Brahma Dev*. However Radha-Rani and the *gopies* moved into *yoga-maya* knowing that Krishna was distracting their lust by knowledge. They drowned out the voice and standing of Uddav to feel their hearts beating with Shree Krishna, with their mind sending transcendental thoughts to their love, best wishes, and fulfilled tears for Him.

Uddav returned back to Mathura Building and told Krishna about all in Taste of Vrndavan and He was pleased that Uddav solicited giving solace.

The same moment that Uddav had shared the news back to Krishna a phone call came from Akura. Akura was calling from Hastinapur in India and he had news about the Pandav Brothers. All the brothers were accounted for expect one. The middle brother, Arjun was not with the family but on his own for studies in London, U.K. Krishna thanked Akura and asked him to return back to Manhattan. Krishna then made a call to Godfather Shankar to ask if he knew the whereabouts of Arjun. Shankar answered openly as he was expecting the call. He instructed Krishna, 'O Mighty Father, come here as soon as You can and let Your will be done!'

Parking Consciousness

Chapter 20

"Hello ladies and gentlemen this is your captain speaking. Please can you have your seats and trays in the upright position and your seatbelts fastened as we are commencing our landing to London, Heathrow. The temperature outside is a warm twenty-one degrees celsius and the local time is ten-thirty a.m."

"Almost there guys!" cheerfully said Vasudev.

"Look out the window you can see London City," said Devika. "Look there's the Shard, there's Millennium Dome, there's Canary Wharf, there's that Gherkin Building, and there's River Thames!"

"Wow! There's so much to see," said Krishna.

The sunlight coming in through the plane's windows moved from one side to the other as the pilots maneuvered the plane into spiral taxi-ing to land. The plane circled high above London City and from thirty thousand feet in the air landed on the ground in a matter of minutes. The passengers then waited for instructions to collect their belongings and exit the aircraft. Through the terminal, pass customs, into baggage claim, through last baggage checks and out into the arrivals hall they passed, and there waiting for them waving with a huge smile was Godfather Shankar.

"Good morning! Welcome to London!" said Shankar with his deep British accent.

"Om Shankar," returned Krishna and Balaram.

"Hello Krishna! Hello Rama!" returned Shankar as they all hugged and greeted each other.

"Good to finally meet you Shankar. I've heard a lot about you. Thanks for inviting us," Vasudev said.

"The pleasure is all mine, Vasudev," comforted Shankar. "How are you Mother Devika?"

"Very much better after seeing you Brother Shankar," she replied and gave him a huge hug.

Vasudev, Devika and Balaram had come to London not only to visit Shankar but also to bid Krishna farewell. He was to live with Shankar for the upcoming years to learn and practice the knowledge of Absolute Truth, *yogas* and meet advocates that Shankar had planned. This was Krishna's first time to London and He was excited to say the least. Moreover His bond with Shankar was undeniable strong that even though the family were saddened to leave Him they were also reassured that all that was to happen was in His will. Nevertheless at present there was only reason for joy.

Shankar drove Krishna's family from the airport to his place in Northwood. He had moved home to a well deserved place in Middlesex. If Shankar wanted to travel north to Leicester to Leeds and to Scotland he had the M1 at his disposal. If he wanted to go west towards Wales he was lucky to have the M40 to M4. If Shankar wished to take a road trip to Europe he would drive on the M25, M3, to Dover, England, and across the English Channel to Calais, France and from there the whole of the European continent. And if he wished to go west or anywhere else in the whole wide world, well there was Heathrow just around the corner.

Shankar lived in a magnificent home that was just enough in the countryside that at night was so peaceful that one would be able to hear a mouse, and just in touch of an oyster card to travel on the Transport for London that would take him into City of London.

"Krishna, can you teach us what you have learnt about the Absolute from Yourself?" asked Shankar.

"O My Mighty Universe, I understand that *yoga* is what makes one understand Me in whole heartedness. An impersonal *brahma-jyoti*, a person that lives for the sake of their own passion whatever that may be good or bad, and the localised *paramatma*, a person that lives for the sake of worshipping God, cannot attain My full blissful knowledge. Only *yoga* in Krishna Consciousness, one would understand the science of Myself," began Krishna. "Practicing *yoga* in light of Me all becomes revealed and nothing is hidden or left behind both in the material and spiritual world. They'd conquer phenomenal and numerous accounts of transcendental knowledge."

Devika's mouth opened wide and Vasudev was taken back by the way Krishna spoke. As the fireplace roared beside them in Shankar's lounge, Devika and Vasudev came to enlightenment that their son has grown up taking the role of who He's meant to be.

Krishna carried on, "Amongst thousands of men wanting to gain perfection hardly any would gain perfection in life through being as impersonal *brahman* or localised *paramatma*. What they have attained they would reject in time in respect to transcendental energy of The Light. Therefore the last word of realisation of a personal *brahman* should be God or more specifically My name Krishna. They would practice *bhakti-yoga* to understand Me better.

"With the forms of energy O Krishna, tell me what you know?" Shankar asked.

"Energy at first cannot be created or destroyed. I move from one form to another. There are three worlds of material energy I recite in; the causes, the controllers and the enjoyers. Even resting energy as potential energy I enjoy as equal to the immeasurable amounts kinetic energy I have.

"From these three worlds there are 10 divisions that occupy material science; earth, water, fire, air and ether with sight, sound, smell, touch and taste. What they lead to is a form of expansion in energy of the mind, intelligence and false ego," Krishna chuckled when He said false ego. As many wish to be in delusional optimism and even as there is nothing severally wrong with that, but was still funny to Him.

"Most people as *brahma-jyoti* would use their energy to reach their preferable passions, but to reach Me one would have to acquire the Absolute Truth and send that energy to Me to be with Life forever. As I am the source of all energy; superior energy for living entities and inferior energy for material nature."

"Absolutely right Krishna! Proud of You my God! The inferior energy cannot be changed by users but just used. Meaning one can only get out the energy of material nature as You have put in. Only in You one can understand how to get out more energy, and thus superior energy of living entities are raised that can influence a positive outcome of inferior energy. You Lord, are multiple energies," congratulated Shankar.

"Now as far as the knowledge of the Absolute and Eternal goes; Balaram tell me what you have learnt from your brother over the years about the natures of creation," redirected Shankar to Balaram.

"Creation, right, is of two natures; the material and the spiritual. The material world is the environment and all that we see with our eyes and is in measure of the intelligence of Krishna. And the spiritual world is what one has inherited and the thoughts one has from the material creations. Nature is like a growth pattern to the Super-soul of Shree Krishna. Matter is created by the spirit and spirit is basic field of creation, however spirit is not created by material matter nor can be influence by that," answered Balaram with pride.

"O Don of London, there's nothing superior to Me. Everything rest in Me. I am the smallest of small and the largest of large. I am the transcendental sky," spoke Krishna to Shankar.

"My Lord, You are the light of the sun, taste of water, sound of Om, sound of ether and the ability of man, the seed to intelligence, the seed to life."

Krishna's phone beeped and vibrated. A text message was received. Krishna did not look at the message but everyone in the room had heard the phone. Again the phone beeped and this time there were several beeps one after the next. Everyone looked at the phone just playing sounds and vibrating in consecutive fashion. They looked over at Krishna just sitting in ignorance pretending He had not heard His phone.

"You not going to check that?" asked Devika.

"I know who that is. After all I know everything that was, that is and that is yet to happen," joked Krishna.

"She may have something important to say."

"Well considering that the most important people in my life are in this room, that only leaves three other people, and two of them would not text me as such, so thus it's not hard to guess who's texting me."

"She may need your help."

"If she had something important to say then she should just call. So I guess it's nothing important."

Devika rolled her eyes, "Men, always leaving women on hold."

"Huh? What's that supposed to mean? I return all your messages..." replied Nanda-Raja.

"Okay, I'll check so she knows I have, but then she'll win as she got My attention," added Krishna.

"She's already done that," mocked Balaram.

Krishna checked His phone. There were no text messages but several emoji's from Radha-Rani; one sad face, another sad face, a tongue out face, a happy face, a music note, and an emoji blowing a kiss.

"Yep nothing important as I said," Krishna said.

"Talking about love relationships, how's your love relations going Shankar?" asked Devika.

"Mmmmm, very well thank you. So moving along," quickly replied Shankar as he thought of Parvathi. "I would like to know more about material nature, Krishna. Talk to me about the material nature of consciousness and how one gains optimal relations."

"O Shankar, where do I begin with this one?" modestly replied Krishna. "Krishna Consciousness of material nature is simply of three forms and three forms only. Each one is important to Me as the next, and all three I also have no bond to as well. But knowing and understanding them can help many understand themselves, their relations to others and of course their relation to Me," carried on Krishna. "Material nature falls to behaviour of goodness, passion and ignorance.

"Goodness is what I desire the most, and I am the most. One should have played fifty percent or more goodness in their lives, and twenty-five percent passion and ignorance or less in their lives to acquire behaviour as Mine as, 'Supreme Personality of Godhead'."

"What is goodness, passion and ignorance in Krishna Consciousness?" Shankar asked further.

Krishna replied, "Goodness is as the nature sounds. One must be good and do good deeds without any own reason for benefit but that of benefiting another or Myself. Passion is what one does to acquire something they need may that be for good or evil purposes. For example, a hungry child will cry for food until their passion is met, a lover would woe their beloved until their passion is met, a business man would sell his work until his own passion is satisfied, a criminal or drug lord would do whatever it takes for their passion to be worthy, and so the people work for their passions to live life and feel worthwhile. Finally with ignorance, which many say is bliss and others say is wrong, but to Me ignorance is definitely a quality of consciousness that cannot and should not be ignored. Excuse the pun. An example could be as when a stranger asks personal questions that one shouldn't answer honestly as to protect themselves that ignorance becomes important. Also not everyone should involve themselves in other people's lives or work and hence they should remain ignorant.

"On the other hand ignorance from one that works hard to make positive humanitarian changes should not be ignored.

Providing to charities and sacrifices are balanced between ignorance and goodness. One's daily deeds can overcome the need to provide to a common charity. Overall to reach 'Supreme Personality of Godhead,' behaviour, bliss, knowledge and devotion in love all should present themselves in goodness first, then ignorance, and then lastly passion.

"The reason for this order I will explain; when a lover likes someone they would first let the other know, but if the other rejects then they should ignore and come back later with passion to try goodness again. As if the lover starts expressing passion not only are they acting desperate on chances but also insecure in the eyes of their interest. Hence best to ignore and see if passion can be ignited to lead to goodness.

"Another example is when a child is hungry they would shout out for food in the mode of passion to satisfy their hunger. If they don't get their food they are prone to play in ignorance until the hunger cannot be handled so they would turn to goodness to get whatever food comes their way. Thus one would work in goodness to get food, ignore other factors that don't lead to food, and hence even fall passion into goodness so they would never be short of food. Work should be done regardless from the need for doing for goodness.

"If I say to have passion prior to ignorance then subject to human condition one would become exhausted in goodness and passion that naturally ignorance would take place. At that time out of desperation or failure goodness will have a harder time to re-establish itself and one would live in ignorance fuelling off passion or ignorance only. This would lead to a collapse in society as people would only work and live to satisfy the interests of their own well-being."

There was a short pause as Shankar meditated after Krishna shared the mechanism and systematic approaches to the modes of material consciousness.

"I see what You say. You make much sense. So these modes of nature can result to divisions of faith due to people's own perceptions of God?" rhetorically returned Shankar.

"To conclude in material nature, I have set the working castes as *brahamanas* to be purely in mode of goodness, *ksatriyas* purely in the mode of passion, *vaisyas* both in mode of passion and ignorance, and *sudras* purely in the mode of ignorance. I was working as *vaisyas* but now am between *brahamanas* and *ksatriyas,* as My passion is for goodness and so I work My passion passionately for goodness. Therefore I am too known as *Supreme Brahman.*"

"*Hare Krishna,*" said Vasudev.

"*Hare Krishna,*" forwarded Balaram.

"*Praise Light,*" added Devika.

Krishna raised His right hand to the light coming from outside and smiled a gracious smile.

"To become disentangled from the modes of nature requires The Eternal Truth, so only through Me would one liberated from The Absolute Truth. As I am the three modes of material nature and the three modes of consciousness, I am also free from them too. I provide the liberation (*mukti*) from My own law. My devotees are too to be rescuers for such people."

"*Sadhus*, *Santos* and *Santas* are Your people that can give liberation in Your name Krishna. They that become liberated in The Eternal Truth are to be known as *Santas*, from the word *sanatana* which means eternal," declared Shankar. "On the other hand, miscreants, atheists, and demon worshippers will not surrender to You. They'll not find liberation by Your lotus feet. These people are known as *duskrthina,* the *duskrti.* Their efforts for intelligence are misdirected. As material energy works under the direction of the Lord they will be as *mudhas. Mudhas* do not see what comes from *karma* (action) and *yajna* (sacrifice). Despite the fruits of their labour they set out to destroy themselves in illnesses. Have you come across this?"

"Haa, yes I have! As I say, 'one cannot please everyone all the time.' Without practices in Krishna Consciousness how could we find ways of improvement? *Duskrti* also known as *naradhama* (lowest human being), has been a problem for life for a very long time. These individuals despite the delivery of The Eternal Truth would ignore the liberation by own *maya* (illusory energy)," Krishna debated ahead.

"As population growth reaches ninety-nine percent *naradhama* there would still be a chance in faith for God. However at a hundred percent a void would occur to the powerful energy of physical nature. For this to be revived mercy would be needed from one of Your devotees. As this has already occurred Krishna You are here again. The world has reached the form of *naradhama*. There was great foolishness, lowest of mankind behaviour, deluded speculators and professional atheists, and they would never humble themselves for the greater good or Godhead. My sacrifice to You was the first encounter from You. Now Your own arrival from Heaven is the second so people do not forget the Supreme Grace and Power of The Light" spoke Shankar humble in respect.

"Wow I think we should take a time out and catch some of the beautiful day," said Devika. "Would anyone like something to eat or drink?"

"Not at the moment mom," said Krishna.

"Not for me either," said Balaram.

"Whatever you wish honey," said Vasudev.

"The kitchen is just over there. You are utmost welcome to make yourself at home. I'll have some ice cold Coca-Cola, poured over ice cubes please," requested Shankar.

"Me too please," re-thought Krishna.

"Actually me as well," added in Balaram.

"Okay, me four," said Vasudev too.

Mother Devika walked away from the men to the kitchen. As she walked away the conversation continued...

"The opposite of miscreants are those wanting to reach supreme knowledge for exchange of personal need and they would become devotees of God. These groups of people that change their ways are known to You as *sukrtinah*, and are of four types; the distressed, the desirers of wealth, the inquisitive, and those in the search for knowledge and the meaning of life," continued Shankar. "What is the meaning of life?"

Krishna returned in praise, "Love, man. Love... simple and straight down the middle. Pure respectable un-frail love," Krishna said in a hippy tone of voice. "One in exchange of love and devotion in Me is best, thus pure devotees even penniless are protected by Me, as are the ones I have blessed who praise Me. They I call magnanimous devotees, *Srimad-Bhagavatum*. 'The thought of Thee always with Thee.'"

"Your father Vasudev was a hard soul to find in this lifetime from the last long ago," Shankar forwarded in respect to Vasudev. "People's intelligence that has been stolen by material desires recide to demigods whom have lower material nature energy than God. Don't get me wrong, the path they choose serves them better than forgetting God altogether. Vasudev's soul kept faith in the Lord and now surrenders to You as You know even the demigods and living entities worship the Father," carried on Shankar.

"I am that Father," said Krishna. "I am that Super-soul in hearts of ninety-nine percent of creatures. I make life easy for the heart to handle other deities. Through Me independence is granted for deity and living as through Me the faith in other is made steady.

"On light of reading *sustras* for whatever reason one worships any demigod or deity and not Me; for healing, education, spouse, children, wealth, they are only to end up coming back to Me. Even as Christians sought Jesus Christ for love, forgiveness and freedom of sins, Jesus Christ praised the Father, as Me as Christ. Therefore Christians, Muslims, Sikhs, Jains, Jewish, Buddhists, Hindus and more worshippers of nature, demigods and deities, I am the One that delivers a complete spiritual bond with material benefit for them all," declared Krishna. "Demigod worshippers go to demigod planets in mind and space whereas My devotees would go to My Supreme Planet in Heaven (*Swarg*). That being said, My devotees for material gain will receive material gain to give devotion for My opulence to mankind."

"Your work is to be an all or nothing outcome. You will have to attain that all mankind believe You are the Lord, that One God, that time, location and necessity had divided into different cultures. You are to bring all to know that You are Supreme Personality of God, Lord," instructed Shankar. "*Bhagavan*, is nothing compared to *Paramatma*, and *Brahma* too is nothing compared to You. They are demigods in Your control. As demigods are perishable but God's unlimited and imperishable and so are His devotees. To keep You simple for unintelligent persons The Eternal Truth has form and personality so use that as a fundamental base for life to bring the masses home."

Devika walked back into the lounge with drinks.

"What I was, what they thought, what I am, and what I show is soon to be seen," said Krishna and then added, "Mom, you took your sweet time..."

Wiping a tear of joy she replied, "Well son with You I have all the time in the world and universe."

The devotees of Krishna took the ice cold Coca-Cola's poured over ice and shared a moment. They had stopped talking about The Absolute. As a matter of fact all that was meant to have been said had been said.

All souls of living entities prior to determination of Krishna as Lord were to be pardoned as they would attain Him in present time. The intelligent men of any age would have different lives but become with the same spirit as the Supreme. People reciting God would become *brahamanas* for *Supreme*

Brahma. Great experienced devotees together would engage in worship of the Lord and His pastimes. They would raise their mind's intelligence further to reach *Goloka Vrndavan*, (Supreme Planet in Heaven). Those souls woken to Shree Krishna would attain *Shree Krishna* in death and not undergo reincarnations in respect to material nature with devotional service in love or fear of the Lord. So chances rolled that goodness would prevail.

Gold Lighthouse Keeper

Chapter 21

The lamps of rooms, libraries, computers, laptops, and mobile phones were flicked on and off as many times as a person would blink in a lifetime by Arjun Pandav. The middle brother of five was captured by the Lord's spirit once he arrived in United Kingdom from his home in India. He couldn't think of anything more important and rewarding than the mission to save mankind. Arjun was born in a country that even though was democratic was popularised by communism. The communism within itself was greatly segregated with divisions in castes, wealth, education, gods and goddesses, and also that of demons within the realms of corruption and crime. However arriving to United Kingdom, he was in witness of true first class democracy style living with people living side by side from all ends of the globe. That was where Arjun knew that a foundation must be set to base the fundamental facts for life, and so Arjun persevered to find the answer to make the world live in peace, harmony and tranquility.

Brought up around Hindu communities Arjun was accustomed to the language used to talk about the faith. However not many people spoke about the religion or the gods as much as they spoke about other people's problems and ways of migrating to developed nations in chase for money and security. English was learnt in India not to communicate and build relations but to acquire a career and so to make money. Only when coming to United Kingdom, Arjun realised the western world spoke about much more and smiled a little more than what he had did back home. Back in India just greeting a stranger could cause hostility and was made to become meaningless or pointless.

Arjun in England understood power to the people more by attending services and worships in churches. He became accustomed to the Holy Spirit, Jesus Christ and the Almighty Father. With the power of the Holy Trinity and endless amounts of studying the Holy Bible, Arjun found the answer on how to bring people together.

The road from there was not going to be easy. As even though Arjun was preserving that every faith had its merits, he knew that a small part of each person's faith (i.e. reason to live), will have to be sacrificed to accommodate some other faith to better accustom each individual's own personal consciousness. How can one person state a change in this magnitude and how can one person declare this on all of mankind? The only way Arjun was to succeed was to test everything out on himself first to witness the changes that would be on the people around him.

He was to push other people's buttons as many times as he was to push buttons on a keyboard. So lamps flickering on and off, night and day, several times a day, several times a night, Arjun would make notes, edits, formatting, deleting and re-writing from the moods he was in and what he had felt from daily findings to find consistency in peace.

Arjun wrote a novel was more an autobiography which was more a testimony for how from a Hindu he became a Christian. The title came one day whilst working a labour job digging a trench to run electrical power lines to a hospital. With a smile on Arjun's face, a fellow native man asked him, 'Why you smiling so hard?' Arjun replied, 'I wrote a book,' the native in his deep English accent said, 'oh ya, what you going to call it?' Arjun replied, 'The Calling,' but the English man returned, 'Why don't you call it, 'Sand Deep'?" (As he was deep in the sand digging). And so the mission began with; 'Sand Deep'.

After he sat to ask the Lord to give him another book to write as Sand Deep, the testimony wasn't the most delightful ways to finish an authorship. In a bolt of lightning Arjun received the second title, 'A Potion'.

During the writing of the second book, Arjun said to the Lord, "Good things come in threes, give me another title.' Again in a bolt of lightning the Lord, granted him the start of a novel called, 'Colours of Enlightenment'. Mixing work, writing, pleasure, and exercise the three books were finalised and presented as best as can be by Arjun Pandav in 2012.

Wait a minute, just because Pandav was a popular name doesn't mean the books would sell or that Arjun would become noticed. All that work on what to Arjun was the richest thing since slice bread would go a miss for more reasons than needed. The people would give excuses like; they don't read, they don't read English, they only do audio books, and they don't have space on their phones for e-books. Loved ones would too ask Arjun what the novels are about without any desire to satisfy Arjun with a sale. Most of all the people would ignore Arjun Pandav for his authorship and despise him as he was confident in himself above anyone else. Arjun knew if the people read the books with an open heart then mankind would be able to shoot for the stars as the books gave life, love and peace in abundance. His missions were aimed to turn minds, have people thinking passionately, have people loving deeper, and have people understanding that no matter what a God's name was, a fully known Life as God cannot be God of all known Life.

No matter, no worries Arjun thought. This was not their fault. Arjun did not have a hook or popularity or even a wingman or woman that could bite the bullet and help him. So Arjun sat back and thought what could be a hook that people could not look away from and would benefit with that would raise his book sales. The hook should hold the knowledge and wisdom to save mankind. The aspects of the novels that correlate with each other would become the hook that should aim to save most if not all of mankind for the better.

Through trials and tribulations Arjun had come up with the answer. Using a website platform as Facebook, Arjun advertised his books and began to construct a page focusing on what he was trying to deliver to the people. Facebook at that time was in prime standing to deliver to the people and also help Arjun advertise. Anyone who was anyone used Facebook. Arjun constructed a page called Lighthouse, which later he changed to The Lighthouse, and again to 'Gold Lighthouse'.

Gold Lighthouse taught by knowledge, wisdom and enlightenment about faith. Knowledge was aimed to answer a question not asked; enlightenment was aimed to answer a question asked; and wisdom was how to work them together.

Arjun Pandav was Gold Lighthouse. He shined light into darkness and taught whoever read about the positives of their own faiths and the faiths of others. As this was no easy task judgments came from all across the globe. Nevertheless Arjun stood true in belief that there was nothing worse than the crucifixion of Lord Jesus Christ. Using that with the resurrection of Jesus Christ, Arjun Pandav wrote without consulting any other human but himself. From reading the Holy Bible he mastered the art of editing and formatting that would be hundred percent from any other.

Arjun then released a post on Facebook that he would have photocopied a million times over to throw from rooftops if Facebook had not been. The post had titles as, New Era Truth, then Democratic Revolution, Independent Declaration, Secret of Secrets, Water of Life, and lastly stuck by the title known as, The Five Gold Rings Scroll (SSS) a.k.a. The Eternal Truth.

The Five Gold Rings Scroll (SSS) was the hook to get people to admire and hopefully increase his book sales. Arjun knew the value of SSS, and knew of the power. SSS was the most important and sacred piece of writing to support mankind to fortune and glory since the beginning of time. SSS was a scroll, actually a divine scroll of information for the new modern era. Arjun labeled the divine scroll as a science of philosophy to convince the people of the truth. The science was a simple set of five factors which helped the control of senses to improve consciousness of behaviours in a dynamic world.

The Eternal Truth gave Arjun more answers. With this Arjun published more at Gold Lighthouse. He made Gold Lighthouse extremely attractive that just knowing of the webpage was enough for people to aim blessings in support, liberation and uniting existence.

As the light of a lighthouse would shine to keep boats away from the rocks and guide them to safety, so did Gold Lighthouse for the people keeping them clear from danger and steering their lives in the right direction. This all being said and done as the Earth turns away from the light of the sun, Arjun was still living in expectation that even though people know what they know, they needed an outlet to let Arjun know that they knew. Therefore Arjun Pandav for Gold Lighthouse was to make plans for a backup generator.

GOLD LIGHTHOUSE
Support, Liberate & Unite Existence
Grace and Power

The Five Gold Rings Scroll (SSS) / The Eternal Truth

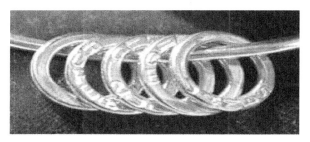

A Fundamental Base for Life!

The Five Gold Rings Scroll, speaks of a science which focuses on three senses, Stability, Sight, & Sound (SSS) with relation to control psychological behaviours. The control of stability relies on what to do with our hands for a strong posture, the control of sight relies on three perceptions of colours, and the control of sound relies on knowing a mute frequency. The aim is to control our conscious for self and interactions in a time of diversity for equality and inclusion, with each soul gaining liberation.

STABILITY

- TOUCH/EXERTION: The heart of stability is very simple to acquire. Stability primarily comes from our hands. Some people have used their hands for awful things. Some people use their hands to defend themselves as reflex rather than voluntary actions. Some people just fly their hands all over the place to protect themselves from their own delusions. Thus hands touching together provide ultimate strength. Overall hands together provide stability and stability shows strength. Press them harder together and that's exertion. The rhythm of our pulse from the heart also becomes stable as the circulation of blood in our body stabilizes. Placing first finger and thumb of each hand in touch as in a yoga position also provides stability. This touch also helps one fall asleep, as one would concentrate on the touch and soon the touch would release its self as one would fall asleep. When young we are taught to sit up straight and place hands together it's only when life and work come in play we forget this basic quality of life. Hands together safeguards in contributing to important debates. People use this as pray also. What has been looked at from stability as exertion is the sense to let go which is inertia. With placing hands together they will have to be released at sometime and hence that's inertia. Most people find this by lifting weights (exertion) and releasing (inertia). Holding this theory evidently buys time to protect our self love commercially and emotionally. Holding or leaning onto stuff also has the same effect for stability.

SIGHT

- LIGHT/LIFE: The colour light or even white, as seen by the human eye should reflect the emotion of life. In all religions "Light" is a representation of God. God is Light. God is Life. With this theory Light/White is seen as living and working one's mind. In reality and for clarity it's Life that has caused joy and sorrows thus it's Life that has to resolve them. The colour light/white has psychological behaviour that one can control their affection and contribution to their own life. Natural daylight is enough for one to perceive this element so to emphasise life is good then to keep to life in the light is a must too. Work, play and any activity are all defined as being in the light. Light is also known as security, security is by money, thus money is seen as an element of light i.e. materialistic. The Light is both life and death. Being 'with' The Light & not 'into' The Light is beneficial to God. (Souls that to go into The Light would make less for The Light to see). God, Life, Yahweh, Jehovah, Allah, Christ, Krishna, Vishnu, Father are The One Light, & known from light/white.

- RED/LOVE: The colour red as seen by the human eye reflects the emotion of love. Whatever is red is showing love. A red stop sign or red light is saying stop out of love more than stop danger. Gazing out a window and looking for red focuses to bring love back into an individual. Why red? Well blood is red and every human if not animal on this planet has red blood. Blood is a vital source for life to flourish, and seeing people as red (instead of any other colour) can bring people to love one another. Looking at someone's lips signifies love. The human eye has a great affinity for red. The Eternal Truth works best when empowering red as imagine a world without ever seeing red. Replenish love from insults and abuse that lead to depression, hate, jealousy, abuse, sorrow, forgiveness and gratitude by looking at red. Literally go and count things red, remember people are red; Red 1, Red 1001, Red 106,965, Red 545,123 ... Sometimes if you can't find the words for someone's idiocracy then just reply with, "Red". One person's passion can be different to another, i.e one may use love as a form of hate. Nevertheless red controls this emotion. Look at red occurrences to replenish love. Love is a necessity and known from red.

- BLACK/PEACE: The colour black or even shadows and the night sky as seen by the human eye opens the emotion of peace. Peace from 'Light'. Sleeping, closing eyes, blinking all are psychological behaviours of bringing peace. Being aware of colour black helps one focus and see their surroundings thus bringing peace to one's conscious environment. Black has been misplaced by media, movies, stories etc. as being something wicked. In this case black is not wicked, darkness is. Black is Peace, Peace is Spirit. Seeing black as peace can also make life graceful. So whenever one wants peace then the best intention would be to find something black. The most beautiful thing about black is that it can be found everywhere, (still or moving), between edges, horizons, shadows, inside trees, car tires, writing, animals, cleavages, a camera lens, but most of all in eye contact. People that have suffered, looked for appraisals, oppressed or been mislead can look back into eyes of to see the black pupils as peace, thus making this formality an easy practice to master, (remember to blink or smile). (With dagger eyes it's not the black of pupils that's causing disturbance it's the white of the corneas, hence either shine a light back to those who perform these acts, blink at them, or simply look elsewhere for peace). So don't think of black as darkness! Darkness is darkness; Black is Peace. Peace is known from black.

SOUND

- MUSIC/MUTE: The frequency of sound when all sound is mute is Om. Om is the vibrations of the universe, the ability to hear and read over noise and brawls, the ability to ignore in uncomfortable situations, the ability to mute unwanted thoughts and vanquish memories, the ability to overcome unwanted or alien sound; Om (ॐ). Yoga has used this sound of Om in repetitive cycles, Ommm... Ommm... Ommm... Here the proposal is that Om is to be played in one linear frequency with "O" playing as long as needed and "m" playing for eternity with breaks in between, i.e. Ooo... mm... mmm... mmm... mm... or initially from mmm without pronouncing the "O" part. Om can be played as music too by making the mmm sound into bass vibrations, mMm... mmMM MmMMm... Om can be played in the mind or out aloud. Instead of shouting, "Shut Up!" or "Quieten down!" to a noisy family or conference room, one can say or initiate Om! Om cannot be played with anger in mind. With anger & Om the brain develops headaches. Om is for optimism. Thus The Five Gold Rings Scroll acts better for goodness.

NOW ENJOY SOME WATER.

The Eternal Truth is Liberation which is Golden!

Once the candle is lit, we cannot change it but only enjoy what it does. Light the candle for The Eternal Truth (SSS).

Have Faith As Every Faith Has Its Merits. ((o))

#NOTE: If one has a tendency to hate, needs a person to blame or needs to have explanation for darkness then the one & only character for this is the ego of Light/Life/God in the soul of every-being. Life also has love & compassion. So why should we live to hate Life? It's better to confess/let-go/learn over repenting. So with this hate that came from someone's light give back to the light, or even The Light, as the Almighty can handle that and liberate you from the troubles sooner.

The colours as one seem sinister, hence the term, 'Fear the Lord', but using individually when needed makes The Eternal Truth a valuable asset to have!

COMPLIMENTS: Those that have hands in pray, The Light as Allah, Red as love and blood of Jesus Christ, Black as the existence of the Black Stone of Kaa'ba (Shivalinga), Sound as the ubiquitous Hinduism's Om & Water as from Abhishek and [Jn 3:5-7]. Praise too to [Mt 28:19] & [Rv 10:1-11] from the Holy Bible.

LOVE ONE LIFE IN PEACE.

- FEELING GOLDEN: One day will go better than the last. This will feel auspiciously good but troublesome as we wouldn't want to lose our feeling of a good day over several to many days, to even years. So wear the colours of white, red, black. Even wearing all black shows me the red and white, as red is always our blood, and white is the light from within our soul. Thus this sustains the gold feeling (liberation). Also saying the words, Light, Red, Black & Om, keeps one feeling golden! Sooner rather than later this will be as a second nature as first is being in Life instinct, and therefore thereafter as natural as water.

HOW SSS WAS FOUND: I first found hands together. Then I was once listening to a minister thinking what in the hell was he on about and I seemed to hate him. So I looked outside but there was so much light so I looked inside and straight ahead and that's when I saw a black speaker. I was fixed. I came out of darkness instantly and I was able to look around. Then a year later a man in a red shirt and with my relationship with Jesus Christ became love. Then came Om as trying to find sleep & gave to Jesus in mind, and he gave back as a beat. Lastly my Hindu uncle sent me photos of Jesus Christ by email and taking that as a kind gesture The Light shined back in Krishna's image. So there you go I began to write SSS. First I didn't see black as peace, I saw it as just something constant, for me cool. - Last I added water. [Jn 3:5-7] / abhishek. I had also asked that if black is what I found to be still, then the opposite would be light, hence life. So where do we fit in between these two entities? As people can't be Black or Light, so henceforth the answer was thankfully Red. We are Love to fit with God's Life & Spirit.

The Five Gold Rings from the Christmas carol, 'Twelve Days of Christmas' refered to the first five letters of the Old Testament known as the 'Pentateuch,' which gives history of man's fall from grace. So in light of the SSS is the opposite.

WHITE-OUT: To have genocide on a particular group of people the food would have to be eliminated and possibly the women too. Now men are usually the ones gifted from God to bring and create Scripture and food, but however it's the women that maintain it through out time. It's just the way it has been. And this form of genocide is impossible, really it is, as it only takes just one other person to make a fajita, samosa, cottage pie, hot dog, baguette etc. for the culture to begin again. So that's that. Now WHITE OUT! Will be if a group of people go out and destroys, burns or covers anything they see that's red. Okay, I've said enough... Imagine a world where there's no red, the world will die. Thus bless the world by planting red, plant red billboards (which gives shade too) and the world will grow. Good or bad is another concept altogether. No White Out, Grow Red.

The statement, "Absolute Truth", was first mentioned in the Bhagavad-Gita as the Tridev; *Paramatma* (Light), *Brahma* & *Bhagavan*, as three forms of God from One. When I awoke to use, Light, Red and Black, I later researched & found Scriptures of 5000+ & 2000+ yrs ago (NTTT) correlating with SSS, thus evolved the Absolute Truth to become 'The Eternal Truth' for good.

The Throne in Heaven [Revelation 4:4]

Christianity speaks of a Throne in Heaven where the Almighty Lord sits. Well why not? Two reasons, as if there was a Lord, then best to have Him sitting than getting up and shaking the universe (no joke); and two, as if we like sitting then why wouldn't the Lord? The question I asked my self is where would this Throne be? I have come to a pleasing opinion that the Throne is due south in space. Hence the Lord is sitting back, looking up watching the universe He created expand and rotate as a child would watching television mounted on the wall. The Lord would obviously have zoom and through the stars as our sun His eye's light would reach us on Earth from our sky above. So for some I hope this releases that the Lord hovers above us, as He is sitting relaxing due South. Also for some that the Lord is at the sky above becomes also true, as in cosmic space looking to our south is still looking up. So just for fun measure our look is due South, and He's looking up at us. But if His gaze passes us He would be looking at the north border of the four corner rectangle (ellipsis) universe. Thus our north horizon is where we don't look as their recites the evil spirit of God, and the damned souls that enter into The Light. There's always pleasure to level the North Horizon.

[Acts 10:11] "He saw heaven opened and something like a large sheet being let down to earth by its four corners."

THE ETERNAL EMBLEM: Half Salaam and Half Salvation. Speculation as even though all colours are God's, I think God has His own unique colours too. The "GOOD" and the "BETTER". If it's not obvious, Om given to Jesus. (Jesus made Om music). In methodology Krishna only knows how Om's done, and one day He will arrive to teach the people. Shree Krishna gave Om to Spirit Shiva (He who holds the universe's secrets and knowledge), then my Spirit gave Om to Jesus Christ (Son of God), for His hardships as no one deserved Om more. Thus Om at Jesus' feet. (Respect). The emblem has nothing to do with religions as been over many thousands of years. It's simply Om at Jesus' feet, and Father/Allah (Insurance) on his mind. There's Ying & Yang on both sides and in reverse as for Grace and Power. The "S" stands for Santa, Santo, Sadhu, Salaam, Salvation, Santas, and San.

OVERCOME: There was a time in #SandDeep, that I didn't even look or even speak to the one's who had hurt me. Hardest thing was that I had to live and work with them, so how did I manage daily activities without looking or speaking to them? Days to months to a year, I would respond to some questions as simple yes, no, or I don't know, (nodding, shaking head or shrugging shoulders), without looking at them. And I watched them by only marking their hands. Well that's my advice to anyone struggling the same at present. Best to do this, enjoy life when you can, and let the time pass then to plan & move/elope to live better life in happiness.

RIGHT HAND: In majority of people the right hand is more active and has made what the person has done. From killing to writing to eating and everything possible that we admire the person for. Hence showing the right palm of hand shines the blessing and gives power to others. I do it naturally at times, meaning my right hand will bless you and I will catch up to that. Whereas the left hand there's nothing wrong with. The left palm shows love, but one cannot love everyone as I don't know everyone genuinely, so I bless them. The left hand will hold that 'burden' of love that the right hand needs to bless others.

Make lives better and let your faith and your culture follow thereafter.

ONE DAY YOUR LIFE WILL FLASH BEFORE YOUR EYES MAKE SURE IT IS WORTH WATCHING	I'll wait here ẁ the Sci-Fi, nursery rhymes & fairy-tales & allow you to catch up. ☺☯↓	For the love of Allah when talking God for Christ's sake TRY & keep a smile in mind. ☺ Jesus Om Krsna ☯ - श्री गुरु संदीप जी -	Many religions but One God, One Life! Y? Time, Cultures, Environment & Necessity to Evolve : One International
To Air, "Hold On, Black's Peace, Love's Red, Life's Light, mMmOmMm + Water = Gold!"	This "Teacher" Starts to Sing When The "Student(s)" Comes Across Anxious & Sorts All Problems Out! ✌☺ No Pressure	I use Haha reaction when you've made me very happy. Haha means YesYes in Hindi/Guji.	Relax. It's only been 63 yrs since we've all been in common. And Fb for 13 yrs. Exhale ((o)) Water "A Little Coca-Cola"

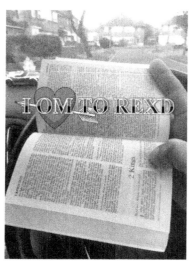

O Mighty Arm Arjun

Chapter 22

Exercising in respect to endurance by resistant weight practice, stamina cardio-respiratory exercises, growth by stretching and relaxation with yoga practice, Arjun gave maximum effort by spending a minimum of eight hours a week at his local gym. He liked going to the gym for leisure and socialising mostly but once he touched a piece of iron by lifting free weights over that of machine aided for a few repetitions his workout would hit to a hundred percent.

Arjun concentrated on three things; breathing, counting and relaxation. As long as he improved his breathing and kept up with his counting he motivated himself to do more, lift more, move easier, and rest faster. A special action that Arjun had and everyone at the gym became accustomed to was his relaxation methods. Arjun would weight exercise then move to another end of the room or hide behind something or turn his back to where he was last, (like Arjun was hiding from himself or the energy still loaming over the last place he exercised). His spirit moved him or he moved himself, but when he rested he was back again fast to face the weight. Many guys, men and women adopted his techniques. Some guys would leave the room and return, some would change seating and some would lean up against the wall. The energy or Arjun's light that occupied his workout expanded throughout his exercise centre penetrating anyone, anything in its path. Arjun exercising was a heavenly experience.

Arjun motivated himself but also others in the room. If there wasn't anyone there then Arjun would sing to himself or count louder and exhale harder. Some people liked what he did and some people didn't, but there was no matching Arjun as when others would figure out what he was doing they would sink into deep love for him. He knew what he was doing, he was giving love to everyone in magnitude numbers that people without Om wouldn't be able to manage. There were days when he would forget his headphones and he would sing, parabolise, encourage, have fellowship with others by starting talks by a simple, 'hello' or 'namaste.' One could not say to Arjun, 'how long you going to be?' or 'have you done with that weight?' without first saying hello or some better form of introduction. That was Arjun and that was his style. If was one to cause Arjun tension or to show their own ego, or a man thinking Arjun couldn't look at his woman, or a woman asking another man to talk down to Arjun, he would simple turn his back to them and walk and face the wall to pray or Om or speak parables or numbers to holy scriptures openly to the air. Then he would turn back around and carry on his workout.

His techniques were a true blessing to witness. Arjun exercised with an eye on the clock; T-minus an hour and thirty, T-minus thirty etc. That way most guys would know his breathing and counting cycle. Arjun knew about the divisions of faiths and culture so he would motivate by speaking and singing during his workout that would relate to others. This would encourage others for having a brighter day or allow them to forget about their woes for the time being. As he spoke, sang, or counted whilst he worked out this helped his breathing and thus that helped him control his rhythm. Truth wasn't as he couldn't be quiet as at times when there was quietness the guys became concerned for him and encouraged a hello back in return. There was nothing worse than Arjun exercising or as he would like to put it exorcisming (taking the devil out) in complete silence.

Above all Arjun's relaxation techniques were the best. He would do yoga straight sitting with chest on an inclined bench and through *maya* (illusive energy), close his eyes and take himself far from where he sat by transcendence to spiritual sky. When he came out of trance the exertion energy transferred to potential energy upon rest would have a great magnitude of reserved energy; that the next touch by him would be transferred to any form of matter. After exercise he would leave with a respectful signature and get himself a vanilla milkshake on the best of days.

During a weekend in autumn, Arjun was invited to attend a speed-dating event from his university. The event was organised by students of North London University and was to be a two day event for all who would like to attend. As Arjun lived alone for many years with only spending time in libraries, classes, exercising and church, he felt that he should try to meet new people and hopefully find himself a good woman too. The event was in a five-star hotel in London City with the tickets to attend being nothing but expensive. But as this happened to be the next stepping stone for Arjun he felt optimistic that he would find the perfect date.

On his entrance into the hotel Arjun accidently bumped into a woman. She was wearing a Christian cross and gave Arjun the most evil of looks behind his back. She then immediately told the porter that she thought that Arjun was trying to steal from her. He went to confront Arjun on the lies the woman shared. She stood by the porter as he searched Arjun for any of the woman's belongings. The woman stood with a smirk on her face pleased with herself on grieving Arjun. Nothing was found on Arjun but he spent half an hour with the hotel security interrogating him on why he was there. The woman had left long before Arjun was free to go. After the security had pardoned him he made his way to the room he had booked.

The speed-dating event was to start at seven in the evening but by five many singles had made themselves comfortable at the bar. Arjun went to have himself a drink and watch the football surrounded by singles that all had company. He sat alone and watched the game as the males and females began talking and getting to know one another. The program for the event was drinks and dancing on the first night, the speed-dating event in the afternoon of the second day, followed by a meal and dancing on the second night. During this time singles would get to share their contact details and the event organisers would pass on email addresses for further contact. Arjun was in a world of his own feeling like a duck in a pool full of swans. What was quite apparent was that all the people seemed to know each other or someone that knew someone else, and that all were established to their future careers. Arjun had neither.

The event began by a welcome and an introduction from the organisers. Whilst at a table in the ball room Arjun looked around to see if anyone caught his eye. He saw the woman that falsely accused him sitting on a table nearby. Arjun being a religious man and to save his dignity decided to get up to meet the organiser introducing the event. He asked if he could give a pray to begin the event. The man agreed and introduced Arjun to pray. Arjun first asked every male in the room to stand but not the females. Then he asked them to bow their heads as he gave the pray:

"Dear Father in Heaven, give us strength that we may act in accordance to Your love,
provide us with integrity for Yourself as well as others. Give the men courage and the woman
respect for the men as they can love You more dear. In Jesus name we pray. Praise The Lord. Amen."

Everyone was taken away by hearing Arjun's humble yet strange reason and approach on pray. Some people thought he was crazy, some people thought he was noble, and some people thought nothing of anything. However one person was very much aroused by him. Arjun sat back down whilst others went up to get themselves drinks.

The lights went down and the music started. A beautiful tall woman with black curly hair walked onto the dance floor with her girlfriend. She had her eye on Arjun since his pray and caught his attention the moment she stepped onto the dance floor. Arjun got off his chair and walked straight to her.

"Hey, I'm Arjun. What's your name?" he asked.

She looked at him and then looked away.

Arjun suddenly turned to her friend and asked her the same question. Just then as the other girl was about to say something to Arjun, the rude woman from earlier approached and spilled her drink over his shirt. Without reacted to her, Arjun went to the nearest table and stripped off the tablecloth. He went back and wiped the dance floor dry and then threw the table cloth over the rude woman's head. She stood as a ghost on the dance floor as Arjun left them all to go to the gents to clean his shirt.

As he washed and dried his shirt three to four males approached him and began swearing and threatening him on why he did what he did. This resulted into Arjun being outraged but he maintained his cool in the face of the evil side of God.

Arjun sat back down at a table to control his anger. He found a black eyeliner on the table and began to draw alchemic images on the table cloth. He drew a cross, then three crosses, then a hill, then an Om, Allah written in Arabic, a Khanda, a Star of David, and then other images of what gave him peace as a candle and rose. He drew to relax his rouge and to bring confusion into the souls of the other men and women. The males that had approached him stayed well clear of him as in all honesty he was an alien to them and they were alien to him. The rest of the people sat, drank and ignored what they were witnessing. A while after getting his money's worth, Arjun left the party to go exercise in the hotel's gym and then went to bed.

The next day the speed-dating round began. Chairs were aligned in rows facing each other for one side for the men to sit and the other for the women. Every three minutes a bell would ring which would instruct the men to move over one chair.

The woman that had caught Arjun's eye was nowhere to be seen. Arjun being a tall built man and she was a tall athletic woman. They were physically made for each other, but unfortunately as he looked over the four corners of the room she was no where to be seen.

The event began and the men and women took turns asking questions of interests, occupation, siblings, place of birth, and whatever would flow from that. Inevitably Arjun approached the seat opposite to the rude woman. He looked at her and said, 'How big is your tongue?' As soon as he said that to intentionally provoke her one of the organisers tapped him on the shoulder and asked him to leave. Arjun maintained his pride, got up and walked out to take a seat in the lobby.

Moments later the tall woman with curly hair approached him, "Hey, my name is Drupati," she said.

"Oh hey, sorry about last night," replied Arjun.

"About what? The out of the blue pray?"

Arjun felt eased, "It's a long story."

"I bet," she said, "Your name's Arjun right?"

Arjun smiled, "You heard my pray and you remember my name... unbelievable."

"I'm good like that. So why you out here?"

"Just taking a time out. What about yourself?"

"Waiting for my girlfriend; she's speed-dating."

"Oh I see," Arjun paused, "As I've already made a fool out of myself, would you like that we have a three minute speed-date to get to know each other?"

Drupati smiled, "I wouldn't mind. It would only be appropriate. What would you like to know?"

"You start..."

"Mmmm, I would like to ask... What do you do? What's your interests? Do you have siblings? What's your favourite movie? What's your favourite song? What's your idea of a perfect date?" Drupati rolled a string of questions for Arjun.

"Wow! Okay. I'm an architect building my portfolio. I like exercising. I have four brothers back in India. Movie? Possibly, Man of Steel. Song? Most with an electric guitar. Ideal date? Mmmm, being with an affectionate woman."

"That's interesting," Drupati replied with an interest. "What would you like to know about me?"

"I have five questions that I actually came prepared with. Hope you don't mind me asking them."

"Haha, that's quite sad and sounds square," Drupati laughed, "Can I choose not to answer?"

"Of course, no problem. And besides square is better than scribble," reassured Arjun. "Do you have a faith and if so to which God? Are you vegetarian? Would you show affection to your partner in public? Can you share with me a time of sorrow? And like you, what would be your idea of the perfect date?"

"I am a non-vegetarian. I would love to express affection openly. My faith is in Hinduism from *Dada Bhagwan*, who comprises from *Sri Krsna*, *Baba Shiva* and *Shri Simandhar Swami* whom happens to be my God. For an ideal date with my man I'd like to take him to a *satsang*, which is a get together to learn about self-realisation from *Dada Bhagwan*. I know that sounds a little sad, but I would love to do that."

Arjun was amused, "Sounds as we have some in common especially that I'm not being a vegetarian too."

"Oh you have heard of *Dada Bhagwan*?"

"I can't say that I have actually, but I have heard of *Sri Krsna* and *Baba Shiva*."

Drupati smiled and continued, "My biggest moment of sorrow was the time when I lost my mum."

"I'm sorry to hear that. When did that happen?"

"That's okay. Talking about it makes it easier. She was murdered at gun point. She was working in a gas station in the States and a man came in and shot her as she stopped him from robbing her. The police found him and he's behind bars. They found his hand print and his date of birth registered on the till system as my mum asked for his I.D. for smokes. I couldn't at first go to the funeral as I'm not allowed in the States, as I'm in wait for Permanent Residence. Luckily my uncle knew a custom's lawyer and he waited for me at customs allowing me to cross the border. A Humanitarian Visa got stamped for me for five days and then I travelled back to England. Can you believe that the American Embassy did not grant me the right to go even though I showed the sheriff's report and coronary report? All they gave me was condolences. As my family are U.S. citizens I am to wait for entry which is another story."

"That's awful. So who do you stay with?"

"I have a place. Work is good, so I just get on with life," concluded Drupati.

Changing the subject Arjun said, "Well I'm a Christian. I have faith in Father, God, Jesus Christ and the Holy Spirit. My family is in India and I am here living 'life' too. My life makes me always wonder what differences in worshipping are there that affect acts of goodness, passion and ignorance?"

"Oh you have read that from *Sri Krsna!*" replied Drupati with a sparkle in her eyes. "But how do you know that if you're a Christian?"

"I wasn't born Christian, I was reborn Christian. My spirit in Christian faith taught me about other faiths. I read that from *Krsna* and said to tickle your fancy."

"You'll like to what? Tickle my fancy? I kinda like the sound of that," Drupati said with deep thought.

"Oh I didn't mean it like that."

"Aww, I thought you might have," teased Drupati. "Any-who. Consciousness should fit to peace and prosperity I believe. Faith can be in goodness, passion and ignorance but shouldn't be blind from one to the next. As if one's faith is good than that faith shouldn't be broken. Every faith has its merits. Faith is so fragile at times too so I was overly-pleased to hear you pray. I've never heard words like that in person."

"I read that *sraddha/dharma* (faith) for men who worship in goodness would be as demigods. I too see the Almighty God as goodness. As far as passion and ignorance goes with Son and Spirit there came discrepancies in time that I've edited and executed to suit my life."

"Seems like you have edited a lot of your life."

Arjun laughed, "Hahaha! That's one way of putting that. I've been through severe austricities and penances that I try not to entangle them into self-realisation. Trying not to think deeply on them allows life to be lived and combines faith into the Unknown God. I however believe that self-realisation is not the most important thing in life, but instead is realization of others to be of most importance."

Drupati replied, "Aha, I guess discriminating or dividing faith is foolish. *Dada Bhagwan* said that."

Arjun saw Drupati's gentle interior through her hard exterior. He felt warm from within on how openly she spoke and how gorgeous she was doing so. There was a special light in her that he wanted to see more.

"So why are you a non-vegetarian?" Arjun asked.

"I don't mind. Food is a mode of goodness which increases the duration of life. Food can purify and/or strengthen one's health, happiness and satisfactions. So just as everything else to do in moderation; let that be eating juicy fruit, fatty cheese, wholesome bread, or delicious vegetables or 'meat' that pleases the sacred heart," Drupati said rolling her eyes.

"I guess one bad mouthing food can lead to misery, distress, and divisions in faith," agreed Arjun.

"Do you happen to eat beef? Actually you don't need to answer that as sacrifices and rituals are said to be a mode of passion rather than goodness."

"Well one cannot win them all," laughed Arjun. "*Prasadam* I hear is a form of ritual that actually one is ignorant to eat if they don't read scriptures or don't help human society. By the way I don't eat red meat."

"I'm not so fond of *prasadam*; however I don't like to be rude so I just take some. As far as I see that's spiritual food so it can't be all that bad," Drupati gave a small laugh trying to hide her innocence.

The two of them bantered on for several hours about how the mind works to continuously sense enjoyment and realisation from dissatisfactions. Their conversations were as debates where they agreed, disagreed, or when unsure altogether they changed the subject.

Satisfaction, simplicity, gravity, self-control and purification were the active austerities of what controlled there conquest on finding about more of each other. Nevertheless what was evident to the third person was that they had already found each other and now they were finding Supreme Godhead together. They were acting in such a transcendental way that there was no loss of energy from them together.

"When God performs changes even in a faith and even in sacrifices, He would start by Om," said Drupati.

"As *Om Tat Sat* – Supreme The Eternal. I beg your pardon but Amen and Om or else," replied Arjun.

"Absolute Truth with *Om Tat Sat*, is perfect for all activities and really makes everything complete. Sacrifice, penance and charity without Supreme Lord, is '*asat*,' this is considered useless in this life and the next. Understanding the love of God, may this be yours or mine, but overall is One."

Drupati looked at the time. She asked for Arjun's phone where she entered her number and gave herself a miss call. She then got up and made way in her red dress towards the hotel exit. She was approached by her girlfriend. They exchanged small talk between the outside night sky and the inside lobby. Drupati leaned back on the side of the doorway and bent one leg up against the doorframe. She then intentionally placed the arm furthest from Arjun up into her long black curly hair. The wind blew into the lobby as she stood in that pose briefly allowing Arjun prime position to gaze at her beauty like a gazelle.

Arjun Attains Supreme

Chapter 23

A time came when Arjun had had enough of working for the well of mankind. Arjun, the middle brother of five was alone as his family was in India. He worked hard on his career in England as an architect and he worked harder still on Gold Lighthouse. His mind was working on overtime and he felt that he was going much faster than anyone else he came across. The grieving man was also feeling sickened on the amount of energy he had placed into love that was not returning to him as much as he had given out. The only thing that gave Arjun belonging was going to church on Sundays, but all times he wasn't much for worship as he was auditing the church's service. Arjun's mind was split into so many pieces that no matter how hard he tried to stabilise himself in his own practice he was still weak.

One Sunday during service Arjun was lifted into high hopes. He was singing and deeply singing praises for the Lord, Jesus Christ and the Holy Spirit. For Arjun this was a good day as after he was to get a pat on the back for his work in making, creating, editing and formatting what was soon to change the world. So Arjun kept in high spirits that was bestowed on him and enjoyed the congregation and fellowship.

After service Arjun went to the supermarket to buy groceries for his weekly shopping. As soon as he walked in through the door he began to preach the Word of God, summons of the service and parables in the name of Jesus Christ. Everything he said was to better the people's understanding of each other and that of the Lord Almighty.

Standing in one end of the supermarket was a man with dreadlocks that was tied into a turban. He watched Arjun with a concerned look and muttered under his breath. Arjun approached the man to say hello and hoped to ease his sorrows. The man replied nothing in return so Arjun carried on with his shopping and preaching. This man followed Arjun around the store which made Arjun nervous. After buying his food and leaving the building the man approached him and asked for his name. He then asked what Arjun was saying but one thing led to another and Arjun not only was banned from the store but also was arrested in suspicion of causing racial distress and harassment.

The man was an undercover store detective that later was informed to Arjun by the police. Poor Arjun spent one night in jail and then to court the next day, for a court hearing in a couple of months time after that. Arjun was advised by a law aiding solicitor that was more concerned with reducing the charge if he pleaded guilty than proving him innocent. The accusers i.e. a female Muslim store manager and the male store detective did not show for the hearing as they both had bereavements in their family, so the case was postponed for a couple of more months. On the second attempt of hearing the accusers were again not present so a governmental prosecutor was elected. To save more trouble or a larger sentence Arjun pleaded guilty. He was then free to go but with a criminal record.

The day after Arjun came to a crossroads for himself. He was either to have a mental break down that could lead into suicide or that he go to see a doctor. So Arjun did exactly that. He booked an appointment with his general practitioner who advised him to go see the mental health unit at his local hospital. So Arjun with fear of his life and hoping to just get better admitted himself to the mental health unit who listened to his problems and prescribed him with medication for a bipolar disorder.

Arjun thereafter took his medication everyday and slept long hours. He was made to miss out on all the things that inspired him. He stopped his writing, he stopped watching television, he stopped exercising and all he did was eat a little and sleep. On a review date for his condition the doctor suspended him on going home and sectioned him into the hospital. Of course Arjun became over concerned by remembered his own reason for existence. Plus he had faith that the doctors and nurses were there for his own well-being and that after twenty-eight days he would be better enough to leave.

Meanwhile at Shankar's home Krishna was adjusting to His new life. He had one question to ask Shankar that Shankar knew too well that He would ask.

"Shankar, when are we going to meet the lost son of Pandu-Raja?" Krishna asked.

"Krishna, do you feel the missing entity of mankind in Your bones?" redirected Shankar.

"I do feel that something is just quite not right I must say," replied Krishna.

Shankar's phone then suddenly began to ring.

"What are the chances? When one thinks of the cause, the cause calls. Grab Your jacket Krishna; we are going to go meet that missing entity. He is being treated in the mental ward," Shankar directed.

Shankar and Krishna arrived at the Mental Health Unit at Northwick Park Hospital. They signed themselves in to visit Arjun Pandav. Krishna had never met Arjun and nor had Shankar in person. For Arjun too was the first time he was to see his cousin Krishna and advocate Shankar. Arjun was called from his room to meet his guests in the communal area.

On first sight Krishna and Arjun felt a bond for each other. Shankar too noticed the affinity of hearts and introduced himself and Krishna to Arjun. Shankar first said to Arjun that they were there to help. Arjun felt relieved that someone had come to see him as well as that someone of goodwill was his cousin.

Straight off the bat Krishna introduced Himself fully as the Supreme Himself and shared with Arjun His pastimes as a young man. Shankar observed the reactions of Arjun which were surprisingly non-judgmental on who and what Krishna was. Arjun sat and listened to Krishna reassure him that everything would be okay. When Krishna had finished He asked Arjun to share his life and why he was in hospital.

Once hearing Arjun, Krishna said, "We are going to have you come and stay with us for a while Arjun. Let's say for now that I need you as much as you need Me. I want to help you attain supreme so you can take back your inheritance and make means to an end on your work for mankind."

"What do you mean 'attaining the supreme'?"

"My brother, your road ahead is going to be more difficult than the road you have come from. You will be able to handle this with My instructions. In return you are doing this for Me as Supreme Godhead. Satisfying My future ordeals with generations to come as I am asking for your help and in return I am helping you also," spoke Krishna. "Let Me guess, you heard about *Brahman*, (you know about self), you heard about *karma* (action), you heard about materialism, and you heard about demigods. Am I wrong? You've heard of Supreme Absolute Truth also known as *Brahma*, *Paramatma* and *Bhagavan*. Your *atma* (soul) is bonded in transcendence to the Super-soul."

Arjun raised his head and looked at Krishna, "Then that would mean You are the Lord of Sacrifice (*Adhiyajna*). You are the One I used to refer to as *Madhusudana*, as I heard You killed the demon *Madhu* just so people would remember Your words. So that means that I am a sacrifice?"

"You are not a sacrifice if you don't wish. You after all are sacrificing your love to a much higher entity. You are sacrificed to Supreme Godhead if you wish," Shankar added. "After all we are all someone's sacrifice but this way you benefit in material and spiritual gain for yourself, your family and your Lord."

"I have two fears, and they are being forced to break ties and fear in the final moment of life. How am I to remember Your lotus feet?" Arjun asked.

"Love, O my dear brother. Love is the answer to both those questions, simply non-withering love. Love for self and love for Me.

"As eternal nature of self (*adhyatma*) and *Brahma Dev* are indestructible (*uttama*) so shall you be. *Brahma Dev* creates all living entities and influences of *karma*. Material consciousness of *Brahma Dev* can enter over eight million four hundred species of life and make them live for material existence. Five fires of *Brahma Dev* are heavenly planets, clouds, earth, man and woman; and five sacrifices for *Brahma Dev* are faith, enjoyers of the moon, rain, grains and semen used to reproduce. As I as Super-soul is in every heart of every living being, the Lord too has sacrificed as *Adhiyajna*. Whoever thinks of Me at the time of their death will attain the Lord, and if one thinks of an animal or whatever then the soul won't be judged but become that in the next life. So in the spiritual world think of love to reach Godhead. Do not fear for I am with you."

"For you to practice Arjun come live with me and Krishna to focus on Krishna Consciousness around some people that do. Performing in Krishna Consciousness as *bhakti-yoga* i.e. devotional service, focus on inner being between the eyebrows by practicing this *yoga* for attaining the supreme," Shankar forwarded. "Saying or uttering *Omkara* once can attain love of *Brahma Dev*. Chanting of *Aksara*, *Omkara* and *Maha-mantra* as *Hare Krishna*, through air of life between eyebrows one can reach perfection in human celibacy for material. We are not asking for you to become celibate, God no..."

"In *Kali-Yuga* chanting *Maha-mantra* provides the salvation as once told. Whereas Om simply as you wrote is perfectly sound due to the sacred vibrations. It's just a matter of doing so to reach the heavenly planets of *Goloka Vrndavan* (body), *Krsnaloka* (mind) and *Vaikuntha* (soul)," assured

Krishna. "There are four kinds of devotees that benefit from this liberation; the distressed, the inquisitive, they seeking material gain and the speculative philosophers. The Lord's mercy is upon them all but they should try to exhibit five parts of *bhakti-yoga*; devoting to serve in neutrality, as servent, as friend, as parent and serve the Supreme Lord by loving life. And I agree that someone in your position would find that easier said than done. But that is what devotion is all about for gaining supreme stronghold. One never said life would be easy but One does say you have the tools to do just that," declared Krishna.

"Brother Krishna, You make everything sound like if everything points to You then everything would be nice and dandy and there would be no problems. That's very hard to digest. How can supreme souls that just want Krishna or in Krishna Consciousness want nothing else gain the highest perfection in life if they haven't experienced life as I have? You say they attain higher planets of thought and power without returning to materialistic distresses, how would they know the difference? If you ask me it sounds like they are being ignorant on helping others as long as they have the Supreme in mind," quizzed Arjun.

"You have all that mixed around Arjun. I see what you mean, but one to be with Me has to have sacrificed, has to have provided charity, and has to have become intelligent, compassionate, stern, and many other traits that follow the *yoga* system in attachment with *bhakti-yoga*. Operation of the three modes of material consciousness is a must before I can say that they are with the Supreme. To be evaluated to the higher states of mind is not an outcome but a process of choice and continuous action," replied Krishna. "And only then one has right to learn, share and eliminate."

Shankar then added, "Can I just add a tangent to that? *Brahma Dev*, as red, as love affinity, as adhering and feeling is as variable in time and relativity that *Brahma Dev's* one day (*kalpa*) is a thousand ages, thus duration of the material universe is limited. The state of mind has consisted of a thousand cycles of four ages (*yugas*). The Age of Satya, where minds are in virtue, wisdom, religion, no ignorance and last 1,728,000 years. The Age of Teta came thereafter and lasted 1,296,000 years. The Age of Dvapara was after and declined greater in virtue and religion which lasted 864,000 years bringing us to where we are now, the Age of Kali where there is much strife, ignorance, irreligion and lasts 432,000 years in which we have 5000 years of that still remaining. These times are all subject to *Brahma Dev* aging and shows that this time *Kali-Yuga* can either mean the destruction of all of *Brahma Dev* or that an eternal *Satya-Yuga* occurs. That's the mindset Krishna wishes to share as He is in dire need as *Brahma* has brought the world into an inevitable make or break situation."

"We shall get to that later but that is the aim of My master plan. As fast as a lightning bolt can flash is proportional to a trillion years passing in respect to time of *Brahma Dev's* love. In the material world even *Brahma Dev* is subject to death and happens to be that faith is dying. However as *Brahma Dev* who has similar energy potency of Lord Jesus Christ, who I know you are familiar with, he too is liberated to resolve the world's issues with Supreme Lord," concurred Krishna.

Arjun chuckled, "That makes sense as that's one reason why I am in here as people doubted the faith of love. By day love in living entities seem to become manifested and at night unmanifested. As in the day time they all appreciate love and work for that with varied minds, but when night comes they seem to be excused and in annihilation of death. Why does doubt and sadness come even though a new day is to follow?"

Krishna smiled, "That is absolutely true. It's as every person has a chance to put their guard down. The only thing that's not affected by *Brahma Dev's* manifestations is Supreme Godhead as I work with superior and inferior energies and thus cannot be swayed, bargained or reckoned with. I wouldn't allow Myself to become different than the sun shining."

With Krishna's abode no one returns to this world. Krishna's transcendental beauty is the best. When He is as such He is at His abode of love, *Goloka Vrndavan*, which is the spiritual sky over Taste of Vrndavan. His Supreme abode is expansions to millions of life forms who all maintain *bhakti* to stay in the Supreme Lord's mercy.

In Vedic literature, Vrndavan is ninety miles south-east of New Delhi, India. Vrndavan would have been full of palaces made of touchstone, trees called desire trees, cows known as surabhi cows that gave limitless milk, *Sri Krsna* with flute, peacock feather in hair, saffron cloth, His skin as the colour of clouds and the Supreme Lord served by thousands of Laxmi's.

"O Arjun, my lost cousin. I want to have an unalloyed relationship with you, where you will not care for death or method of death. As with the practice of *karma-yoga*, *jnana-yoga* and *bhakti-yoga* you can choose to leave the body from a desired ambition. A great *yogi* as Shankar can also select time and situation to leave the world," informed Krishna.

"I wouldn't go as far as that, Krishna. But I guess I have prolonged existence," returned Shankar. "Some who know *Supreme Brahman* can influence their time for departure and not return to this world. It's like knowing your roads and getting by in the means of knowing whatever's round the corner. One could pass in light at any auspicious moment of the day. Nevertheless Krishna Consciousness doesn't account for either way for truth be accidental or arranged."

Arjun seemed pleased that he could talk about death without being accused of being suicidal or depressed so he said, "I believe there's two ways of leaving Earth; either in light where there's no return or in darkness where there is a return. As energy loves energy with no excess luggage but excess energy, is that why You think I can help the cosmos energy?"

Krishna laughed, "You 'are' the missing entity."

Shankar said to Arjun, "He got that from me."

"We're both getting love from him," said Krishna and with Shankar shared laughter.

"So Arjun now you attained the supreme don't be bewildered but remain in devotion. All conquests of reaching Supreme Godhead's abode can be reached by charity, austrisities, devotion, and so salvation is granted. You have gone through much sorrow as you were made to be eternally happy. So as a man once sang, 'A little less conversation and a little more action! Grab your coat and let's start walking!'"

Walk On Transcendence

Chapter 24

Winter was approaching fast and the days in England had begun to get shorter. The sun was to set before five in the afternoon. The cold mist of the hemisphere had got everyone to start dressing a little cosier. The leaves of the trees were still present as hues of dark green to orange to yellow. The time of the season of winter was quite special to the folks in England even though daylight was shorter. A special thing about the weather, climate and environment from the time of Diwali to Christmas was that there was something special in the air. For the children of Britain, there would be presents at Christmas and Christmas programs with family gatherings. For the adults there would be pleasing the children. And as for everyone else there was hope when the winter would soon change to spring which would soon change to summer.

Krishna on one bright but cold weekend had decided to take Arjun for a walk along the south bank of River Thames. This stretch of walk was famous from St. Thomas' Hospital where opposite was the Houses of Parliament with Tower of Big Ben, pass Westminster Bridge, to Millennium Eye, along a stretch of many tourists, under Waterloo Bridge, to Tate Modern Gallery, pass Millennium Bridge, to the restaurants around Shakespeare's Globe, to London Bridge and into Hayes Galleria, out again to see HMS Belfast sitting beside the dock, a wave to the Mayor of London in the Mayor of London Building, viewing Tower Bridge, and crossing the Tower of London where the Crown Jewels were kept which would be the end point of the walk. At a slow and steady pace stopping for a drink and a meal the walk to be fully enjoyed would take a few hours. In the case of Krishna summarizing to Arjun about his life, Krishna knew that Arjun would stop and sing to play out loud as a guitar his worries and woes. Thus the walk had the chance to last a whole day with the potential to last an era too.

They made an exit from Westminster Station, turned left and looked at the time shown on the clock of Big Ben. The time was three in the afternoon and Arjun was feeling insecure about what Krishna had already told him. Arjun's importance was on claiming back his inheritance and fighting for the people back home. There was no running away from the problems that faced him and his family. Arjun was *ksatriyas*, by birth which means a protector of people. He was a soldier, he was a warrior, he was trained well as a child the arts of military science. But Arjun was full of miss material compassion, lamentation and close to tears due to confusion of senses and misunderstanding. Arjun was weeping more like a *sudras* than a *ksatriyas*.

Krishna chose this setting on guidance from Shankar so Arjun could see up front all the people that had no clue on where they were going but he would. He was made to feel the division in society and Arjun felt immensely powerful over the thousands of people that he walked by but still he felt helpless beside Krishna. They walked over Westminister Bridge and down the stairs to the left towards the Millennium Eye.

Arjun was shown the work of fruitative desires and how much material attachment was embedded into the future for mankind. He was shown the luxuries that people had, the joy that street performers gave, and the homeless on the richest paths that London had to offer.

"Your work O winner of wealth, will make way for millions to live happily with what they have and still climb to make way for others whilst making more for themselves," Krishna said. "So how can impurities come upon you? O Arjun you are a valued man in awareness of the heavenly planets in minds of many people. You have been through much trying to escape but your heart being strong draws you back to what's right. You are away from infamy."

"O *Bhagavan*, Your truth is most highest that I don't choose to escape even though I am weak. *Bhagavan* You are not impersonal pervasive spirit as *Paramatma* or localised accept of Supreme in all hearts as *Brahma Dev*. *Bhagavan*, You are with Absolute Truth. You are with Eternal Truth resonating from and without Your law. *Bhagavan* I need no law, I need *Bhagavan* only," replied Arjun. "You are as the sun we see at this present moment, forever happy and shining bright. Why place this burden upon me?"

Krishna smiled as the light of the sun came upon them, "The sunshine has three attributes as it shines upon the world; the outer sun, the sun as star, and the sun-disc. Just as the Trinity of Father, Son, and Holy Spirit, and the Tridev as *Brahma*, *Paramatma*, *Bhagavan*, the student would have three characters as the sun does. One for life which is the light of the star itself, one for love which is the outer sun which shines upon us, and the other is the sun-disc which shines that shine of peace in the universe onto anything in its path. A student as you shall do the same. You shall be as beautiful, strong, powerful, rich and famous as that as *Baba Shiva*, *Lord Narayan*, The Eternal Truth and as I, as *Govinda*, as I accompany you."

"Not every culture on the planet has trinity forms, take Islam for instance they worship only Allah."

"I am He. They do have a trinity if one looks a little closer. Yes they worship One. Allah as Life, but they have the Holy Kaa'ba as peace, that I set long ago before the time of Prophet Muhammad, which would be Islam's love. Do you see that trinity? Do you also see that time, location, necessity and evolution of man was why One Light had come to Abraham and Ishmael to set forth obedience to Me? I ordained that they worship the cows, I ordained the language, I ordained their practices, and I ordained the fear they have in equal measure to the love they have for My name as Allah."

Suddenly Arjun received the light with Islam. Krishna raised the palm of His hand and blessed all the people that passed Him and Arjun with His first two fingers to their left and right shoulders, to the top of their head, down to their toes.

Arjun's lamentations however did not stop, "O *Bhagavan, Bhagavan,* where am I from?"

"O Brother Arjun, you're from long ago. Aryan civilisations which ruled many kingdoms around the world, which actually have become the men and women you see around you today. You are a survivor, and you are the one to carry on the civilisation of man for the better of mankind."

"That is a very tall order."

"Hahaha! As soon as you have come to terms with your destiny O son of Kunti, you will see it will be as easy as taking another step on green grass," chuckled Krishna. "Let me say this, the energy of magnanimity is to put forward an action on nonviolence, but as this will not be possible for us, I will guide you along."

Arjun raised his voice at Krishna in an argument due to worry after what Krishna had said about nonviolence not being possible. On making the point of concern count Arjun took a few steps away from Krishna and paced to and fro from where He stood.

"No way can I conquer my own teacher, Bhisma. It's better not to attack him then get counterattacked. There's no duck, cover, defend, run and return with fire when coming close to great Grandfather Bhisma! Him and his right hand man Drona are not to be reckoned with when playing with their own teachings! I hate to admit it, but that's one of the reasons I moved to London. Far away from the furious flames of those two men!"

Krishna felt Arjun's heart burning without concern about the many of people surrounding them. Krishna took a step forward and slowed Arjun's pace. He then took him by the shoulder and sat him on the seating outside Tate Modern Gallery.

"O adrenaline filled Arjun, this Bhisma, Drona, and even your cousin Duryodh, are all about financial gain and worry if they even lose a penny. Yes, greater teachers should be respected, but by killing them their wisdom will become tainted. Also killing the sons of your father's brother, Dhrutaras, the betrayer would benefit the liberation of material existence."

"*Bhagavan*! With the platform of knowledge destroyed, it's better to be begging in the royal grounds than have many be slaughtered."

"What platform of knowledge? Knowledge is Mine, and I am for mankind..."

"Well I'm Your disciple, I'm confused, weak in misery. What shall I do?"

The perplexity of the situation would need a bona fide Master (a master who is real and not deceiving), as material perplexity in man was to become confused. The excess affection for family, country, society, materials, news, etc. would make disturbed talks in friendship, (*krpanas*). And one would need to see the unborn Krishna from within and without to feel that nothing else is really that important.

"O Master of the Universe, I will not be able to dispel my grief unlike Your many demigods in Heaven. I am filled with academic knowledge as a bona fide master myself. I am filled as a scholarly *brahmanas* in wealth and economics. I am filled with peace and harmony where I'd leave the politicians lament on what's good for the people. The curb of lamentation is a good one," Arjun carried on spilling his heart out. "I will not fight!"

Looking through the people walking by and across the river towards the direction of St. Paul's Cathedral, Krishna gave Arjun further insight, "Your intimate friends are in the same position. I am volunteering Myself to be a bona fide Master to both you and your friends," He said with gravity. "Don't cry over this grief and don't be a fool! You are speaking as an educated man when you should be speaking as a liberated man.

With or without your cries in the time of the *Upanishads* you shall still exist in the future as you do in the present and as you have in the past."

Arjun looked over at Krishna, "I am not to be in an illusion of *maya* but be in eternal peace. I am an individual and fully conscious. But this is like licking a bottle with honey but tasting nothing but plastic. As a devotee to You, how can I not make sense out of this?"

"Get up Arjun let's carry on. Don't be concerned about Bhisma and Dhrona, or anybody that of death or thereafter. The spiritual men to fight beside you shall receive greater material existence. The future of mankind will be fifty percent material and fifty percent of spiritual nature, as I do as Super-soul with My material of planets, stars and moons in the universe. They shall be of perfect knowledge to go forth from where you are now. So let us go forth and enjoy what this day has to offer," Krishna said getting Arjun to carry on their stroll.

The *mayavadi* theory of oneness of the spirit soul also known as the Super-soul cannot be cleavable. Krishna's external energies exist as *ksara* (*sanatana* i.e. eternal), thus are bound to fall into material nature and thus liberated by His truth that make one's desires eternal. As light reflects off water to show the sky both teacher and master, both man and Super-soul, both father and son, both desire and eternity go hand in hand, or further so heart with heart. The pulse of the hearts submerge with each other however many times the devotee is to make own initiatives, even that of laughing and so allowing the other heart to laugh.

Maya is the illusion or even assumptions of what one perceives to see and hear and not that of what was actually said or seen. For instance travelling in a car what one person sees is not the same as another in the same car. Also for what's in one's mind is not what one sees either. Arjun was to tolerate non-permanent appearances and disappearances of happiness and distress. The *maya* was making Arjun illusive in his actions and as long as Krishna said he was *ksatriyas* he should fight the good fight. Arjun was Krishna's cousin from Arjun's mother, Kuntia's side, but he was more matured from his father's, Bharata. Therefore taking *maya* out of the equation, Arjun by far was cut out for the responsibility.

"O son of Bharata, who controls the senses worthy of liberation and living in liberation is in the fourth stage of life, i.e. a renounced order (*sannyasa*). This can be difficult and painstaking as the fourth stage of life can be given to a child who has no experience of life or a senior who may have wished he had known sooner. However this is the realisation of the life to live. To change from material body which is aging to spiritual soul which eternally exists can be overwhelming for the many," spoke Krishna as they walked over Millennium Bridge.

Getting to the other side of the bridge over River Thames, Krishna twirled around on one foot and faced back to the direction that they had just walked. Without hesitation and deep in concentration with what Krishna was saying Arjun followed His stride.

"The pervading aura over a body that is all pervading and not destroyable is very conscious to conscience of pain and pleasure. This is like a soul being conscious to the body's reactions. The triggers in the neural pathways of the nervous system exist of atoms in material form and that of spiritual form in spiritual souls. Just as one may sneeze several times when excited or nervous, or that sweats excessively due to same reasons, these are the spiritual atoms affecting the neural pathways, and there are numerous spiritual atoms. When there is a spiritual spark between your heart and the Super-soul as that of Mine, you would feel a sudden rush of approval that may hamper your breathing or over excite you beyond your control. The soul is always learning and adapting to occupy more of its own transcendental space. This automatic soul would float in five kinds of air, which I name as *prana, apana, vyana, samana*, and *udana*. Now don't become too alarmed, My *maya* is upon this world to have Me exist in this form. Since My upbringing I have slowly adjusted the five airs to be able to sustain external energies in body, mind and spirit allowing the universe to exist without Me," Krishna took a pause and Arjun stood with his mouth open. "Controlling the five airs is known as *harth-yoga* and I only want more souls to be liberated from this bringing them to *bhakti-yoga*."

"O Mighty Word, I can feel my soul, I can feel on times of solitude and on times of music. I feel *swaaha*, I feel my soul, but they say we don't."

Krishna took Arjun's hand and placed over His heart. As soon as Krishna did this, Arjun felt a rush of energy filling his blood that occupied his mind and he gave that feeling back to The Light. Coming back across the bridge they moved ahead to the east of the south bank towards Shakespeare's Globe Theatre.

"When the soul leaves the body that is when the body decomposes. A body without a soul to a higher identity and that higher identity to the Super-soul has no reason to fight. Thus you should fight for body and soul, Arjun," forwarded Krishna. "A material weapon can harm the body but the soul atom is so small that it cannot be harmed by material wonder. Fight for this faith and don't fear or portray yourself as whimsical."

Arjun didn't like what he heard from Krishna, but as He was his brother and the Lord, he refrained from saying he was offended. Instead Arjun replied, "So *Bhagavan*, You're saying that the soul is not slain when body is slain. It keeps all its knowledge and consciousness into everlasting life? That is a wonderful thing but can one remember its deeds?"

"Good question, O son of Kuntia, would you like to remember this life? Would one like to remember a life of pain and struggle? Would a child like to remember that they didn't have a full life? No. A soul wouldn't remember the deeds of their life, but their reason for being would fall into the heart of

Mine. And I shall move it along on rationing of their goodness, passion and ignorance," answered Krishna. "Every life with Krishna Consciousness would have a particle soul (*anu-atma*), and that would be a particle to the Super-soul (*vibhu-atma*). When one swears to defend the peace of *Paramatma* within them it is actually *Bhagavan* swearing. As too when one laughs or stops the will to cry then that is *Paramatma* enabling *Brahma* to create. If you ask yourself why are you concern about your destiny, it is not you that is concerned it is I. Both souls of universal life are branches of Supreme Godhead, that link that I have to My true form as One,"

"O *Swastika*, O Happiness, how can an unborn soul be made or instructed to murder?"

"My inquisitive Arjun, a person improves as fashion does but a marketing and advertising agent has to be there to manage the improvement. The Super-soul does this to souls giving up old and useless bodies for new and improved ones."

Reaching a bar near a pirate ship just pass Southwark Bridge the two of them sat to have a meal. As a bird that eats and another that looks out, both atomically the same and both interchangeable, Arjun and Krishna looked out for each other and made themselves comfortable in the unfamiliar place.

"O Arjun, a *Jiva* soul is a soul that is struggling as it's reached the top of the material tree and would need a spiritual master to reduce its anxiety freeing itself from lamentation. Many people here where we sit are subject to reaching the highest branches of the material tree. Some have spiritual bondage with their doctors, psychiatrists, support workers, and many do not, and will hopefully seek a means to find a way to reach spiritual awakening. This is why your role is extremely important as you will preserve the spiritual life of souls in all levels of the material world. A Super-soul can infiltrate an atomic soul but not the other way; hence therefore a body should not grieve for the soul."

Arjun's own lamentations and anxiousness lowered as he began to understand and adhere to the sacrificial alter that Krishna was making before him. During their meal and their drinks Krishna and Arjun had warmed up to each other more and that of the day. Arjun became enlightened by the amazing concept of the soul being in sight, sound and stability of what Krishna shared. He self-understood that a soul though thought as love should not be grieved over as it is immortal and never able to be slain. The unmanifestations and manifestations of activity would occur throughout life and into death thus for him to take action and not to fall into depression or worry. Understanding the soul Arjun felt optimistic to his deeds of destiny even though violence was encouraged.

Putting the glass back down on the table after His last intake of drink, Krishna forwarded, "O *Ksetriyas*, do not hesitate. You are a fighter of the forests and a soldier on the sand. You are not to accept orders of *sannayasa* or to forget easily. Some *brahamanas* shall give you animal sacrifices and you shall respond by human killings. Listen to the word and work of My desire. I shall give you peace of mind."

Arjun didn't take too much notice of what Krishna had said. He was in awe of the win/win situation between that of the Kingdom of Heaven and that Kingdom of Man. Even though Arjun knew this task of life was going to be difficult he also felt that if he backed out then he would have failed his family, his inheritance and the people trusting upon him. He not only would have been considered to be a coward, but also would be out of the limelight of Krishna and his soul would return to the cycle of reincarnations.

"O brave Arjun, truth will be better to die in war and have a soldier's death than to withdraw and dishonour the days to save. Win, die but don't withdraw. Remember the weapon that Shankar has given you, the *pasupatra-astra*. Do not use against weaker enemies and use in mind of sight and will to fire the arrows from your bow. The gift of the spirit to enhance your accuracy to defeat more of the opposition of self-gainers and builders of personal wealth can be put to their knees with the weapon he has given."

"*Om Namah Shivaya*!" replied Arjun.

"Need this be said, fight for the sake of fighting! Fight in My consciousness. Don't think emotions thus you'll be free from sin of war and free of debts. I know you like sense-gratification of happiness by not fighting, but as I described to you the nature of the soul (*sankhya*) that killing the guilty is proper for their souls and that of yours for all of time," continued Krishna. "A great soul as yours would surrender to a bona fide master. You are to control your senses (*yoga*) and experience the ever blissful Kingdom of God. Let me let you know that a soul without the Lord will practice as atheists do, *sankhya-yoga*, but that with the Lord would be in *bhakti-yoga*."

"So *Bhagavan*, You are saying that being in Krishna Consciousness I will be cultivated in life and can ascend to higher planets without fear?"

"You are already O Arjun. You have already achieved this on your acceptance to Me. Your work is a unique quality in path of work done that is above of aristocrats and *brahamanas* searching for a further chance to be blessed and grow."

Arjun bowed his head, "I have faith in You."

"I feel that so but faith should be unflinching trust in sublime existence. As you see Me know your faith is increased, but imagine all those that have not witnessed My being. Hence your faith should even become more than all of them put altogether."

"You speak so wonderfully *Bhagavan* Krishna."

"My dear Arjun, flowery words as heavenly, divine, beautiful, and even fruitative bring also along with them attachment and they who seek sense gratification from these words only to fill an opulent life and nothing more than that. One should see that I would be as a music song list with many songs of different natures all being satisfied within the moment of time they are in. However people in general are ignorant beyond measure due to experiences, education and unfortunately at most times out of free will. They are not intelligent enough to even satisfy their own curiosities that they fall into rituals and pastimes that had been laid before them. As long as their stomachs are satisfied they do not care about their heart or mind."

The brothers now had approached London Bridge Market which was packing up for the day. They slowly strolled by the people laughing and chattering on their pastimes. They approached the entrance to Borough High Street and crossed the road to walk down St. Thomas' Street, pass Guy's and St. Thomas Hospital student entrance and pass the entrance to the Shard, and into the archway of Hayes Galleria.

"See here Arjun. This place is as a garden full of opulence and angel women as my planetary realms of *Nandan-kanana*. The people are drinking drinks as *soma-rasa*, satisfying happiness as immortals. They would repeat this cycle in respect to their income and time for leisure and maintain this happiness forever in strength and enjoyment. However this is temporary nature where I am willing to give eternal bliss in the minds set in Krishna Consciousness," said Krishna.

They walked through a flow of people around the boat sculpture in the middle of Hayes Galleria. Arjun and Krishna walked to the end of Hayes Galleria where the area touched the river and turned right. There docked was a military warship, HMS Belfast, open for tourists to observe from the World Wars.

"O Arjun, on the contrary of what I said about people being in a temporary state of mind for happiness here are the people that had fought for the Lord, and their souls which gained everlasting life. They had their mind fixed in *samadhi*, and did not seek for material existence, but that of the Lord's grace to protect their people and the world. You should consider this highly too as *ksatriyas*," carried on Krishna as he walked Arjun closer to the ship. "Purpose and sacrifices as *karma-*

kanda, helps one to come to self-realisation. You as they should be able to absorb much knowledge as water from a well that is a part of the ocean and be able to apply it as wisdom. This life, this *Veda* opens to the right minds. Tell me what you know of the *Veda*."

"Krishna, I know the last word in Vedic literature is *Vedanta* which ultimately means Shree Krishna. And that to inoffensively chant Your holy name as Lord is known as *Vedanta*."

"A student brother of Shree Krishna, you are indeed even though I am still of concern as you have not yet fully accustomed yourself on the prescribed duties as *karmani*."

"O *Bhagavan* of Peace, how can I fully drop to Your will when I have not been in sight of my home I left a decade ago? You tell me my prescribed duties."

Leaving the site of HMS Belfast they walked west towards the great opening Tower Bridge. They slowly paced pass the Mayor of London offices and under the bridge to the other side where they walked up the stairs and onto Tower Bridge Road. Krishna and Arjun looked up at the grand architecture of the famous bridge with its two tall towers and blue iron holdings. The vehicle speed over the bridge was 20mph and the brothers walk was just under taking in the views either side of the bridge.

"*Sai* Arjun, prescribed duties are activities enjoyed of one's own mode of natures. This outstands capricious works that are actions without sanction of authority and inaction which are not performing duties altogether. You are advised to form routine work of goodness and inauspiciously, plus emergency work, and desired work, as prescribed duties. This bondage of duty will be your sacrifice and your salvation."

"O *Bhagavan*, are You not solely my salvation? I am to do Your bidding, but do I get salvation from Your prescribed duties? What if I am not successful?"

"*Yoga* is the answer Arjun. Don't think of abandoning success. Always fight for the enlightenment from failures. Preserve self being and understanding. Keep your body, mind and spirit in successful energy. Take rest and perform duties. Allow what is to come to come but always give your best. In *yoga*, we are not to worry about good or bad, just do what you feel is right. Feel the flow of blood around your body from your heart to your skin. Aim for a goal of safe peace as *Vaikantha*."

"My intelligence coincides with Yours and as I saturate Your wisdom my intelligence moves past the delusion of the dense forest clouding my judgments. The indifference I had before seems not of any concern and I'm fixed minded as we carry on," said Arjun in delight. "O Krishna I am a devotee of Yours to be free from bondage of different meditations and sacrifices. I shall love You and worship You three times a day till the end of days. *Brahma, Paramatma, Bhagavan!*"

Krishna looked over at Arjun with His lotus eyes amazed to hear the dedication in Arjun's voice.

"Good for you. We shall see," He replied with a disconcerted mocking tone. "I have given you conclusive knowledge but if you wish do find out on your own be My guest."

Arjun looked over at Krishna with worry again because of the change in Krishna's tone. Krishna looked back at him with His eyelids half closed smiling. Then they both began to laugh. Arjun realised that Krishna was playing a bromance with him, and Krishna was relieved that Arjun figured that out.

Krishna had made Arjun a subject of *muni*, which is when one can agitate the mind in several ways without the desire on coming to a conclusion. Never is any *muni* the same as another and they who can exhibit and catch a *muni* are free from misery and attachments. A *muni* is a conquest for feeling happiness.

Arjun and Krishna had reached the east wall of Tower of London. This was a building famous for having dungeons and used as a prison in the medieval days of the British Kingdom, whereas now the building was securing the Crown Jewels. Precious jewels that the British say were given to them by kings of India for their help during the British-Raj and the Indians say were stolen from them by the British. Whichever way one looks at this the most valuable jewels in the world were kept safe guarded day and night by beefeaters.

Krishna continued, "O courageous Arjun, one who can withdraw senses from matter such as that building is in perfect consciousness is elevated to higher planes of thought. The taste of death is sweet even for *yogis* with higher tastes and fixed awareness. Once one gets a taste of Krishna Consciousness nothing there forward tastes any better and people have died trying. This being said, one would not know if they don't try to taste something else. Life as I am is an upside down, inside out, back and forth one," Krishna chuckled to Himself and delivered that energy to *Lord Vishnu* in Heaven. He then chuckled again.

"I'm going to just stick to *Bhagavan*, O *Bhagavan*. Too many twists and turns has got me searching for a bone that I haven't hid to taste better somewhere in the Garden of Eden," replied Arjun in a sincere tone.

"Absolutely true Arjun. Senses are strong and penetrative, thus *yoga* should be used to control them. Emotions can control senses and vice versa. Even as great as a *yogi* as I, I would maintain My own Krishna Consciousness to revert senses back into Thee," agreed Krishna. "Men of steady intelligence as they build that bridge control their senses and their thoughts of God. The devotees to the Lord at the time of the construction of this street had not the luxury of meditation as *yoga-sutra*, as the purpose for it to be built exceeded the conscience for it. But now and for many days to come it will be worshipped by millions around the world as a tourist attraction."

"O Krishna, wouldn't anger rise from the attachment to lust and desire over such a place? Shouldn't one just stay in their existence of senses to gratify life's desires?"

"Yes, this is also true brother. One can come to destroy such a creation or with no reward for a creation a creator can destroy themselves. Hence to maintain sense pleasure with Krishna Consciousness as *Brahma Dev* and *Baba Shiva* does to obtain growth from objects they sense," Krishna said whilst raising His right finger and scrolled His hands to fit the finger and thumb together in *yoga-sutra* for that thought.

As daylight was shorter in the season of winter the clear blue sky was about to turn black as fast as a blink to have stars shining through space. Krishna and Arjun made their way to Tower Hill Station for the journey back to Shankar's home.

"So My *sai,* My brother Arjun, how do you feel now?" asked Krishna.

"I may become forgetful making me lose intelligence, My *Bhagavan*. Would this lead me to bewilderment, delusion and anger again dropping me back into the material pool of this era?" replied Arjun.

"Allow Me to place into your mind and heart that they without Krishna Consciousness would desire liberation through material gain, meaning they'll only believe if they get what they want, and will not enjoy a full life. As food offered to the Lord as *prasadam* is eaten in God's consciousness, then the spirit will not lose its intelligence on the grounds of respect for that intelligence. That being said, only with Krishna Consciousness with use of *karma-yoga* will one have enjoyment, persevere, and would be a friend to everyone and everything, and thus shall have self-manifested happiness and peace. There is no peace without the Lord of Almighty Life, with or without intelligence," instructed Krishna. "As a boat can drift away from the shores so can one's intelligence without controlling their senses."

Krishna and Arjun entered the underground station of Tower Hill, placed their Oysters onto the yellow pad making way pass the barriers and down the escalators to the trains.

As they stood right of the escalator making way for others on the left Krishna spoke about two kinds of intelligence. An ability of intelligence in material activities for self-gratification and the other intelligence as an introspective awake to cultivation of self-realisation. Both are subject to transcendental advancement with the composure of peace and are interchangeable. They are both in grounds of equal importance and if an individual can remain undisturbed or in stability of *yoga* then they would enjoy the luxuries of many pleasures.

The train for the green District Line arrived to the passengers at Tower Hill. Passengers disembarking the train were given space to exit and then the passengers alighting the train made themselves onto the carriages along with Krishna and Arjun.

"Please mind the gap. The doors are closing," announced the intercom for the Transport for London.

"O Arjun the Aryan, My devotees require nothing therefore are in the flow of peace as this train is on the flow of the tracks laid under it. However I Myself am not at peace if particular desires are not met and hence to satisfy the desires one can have real peace," Krishna said amongst the other passengers. "Work has to be done to better resource and raise mankind's intelligence to suit Supreme Godhead."

"*Bhagavan* O Lord, my desires are that of Yours. I too feel like intelligence should be consciousness I can summon on my own even though I rather be a sheep instructed by a bona fide shepherd. I will believe that property is not mine but ours, and ours is Your divine opulence," Arjun replied amongst the other passengers. "Hence I am not to be bewildered to gain a spiritual godly life in *bhakti-yoga*."

Krishna then took out a wooden lollypop stick from His possession and gave it to Arjun. He said for him to touch this wooden stick as a bond of power to the material world that shouldn't be forgotten in the realms of transcendental spiritual natures. The wooden stick can be used to fidget with and hold tighter for stability. It absorbs unsteadiness and feelings of despair. The wooden stick can also be placed in the mouth to help with breathing and times of hypoventilation of the lungs. The stick too would absorb toxins from the tongue and soft palate opening the airway for those that have smoked. Many aspects of transcendental life and peace flow in cosmic energy from the soul to the wooden material making it a conductor of the two worlds of material and spiritual force. However just as everything else that is not to be attached in exceeding amounts but only that of Krishna Consciousness the wooden stick should be let down from time to time.

Arjun pulled up one of his sleeves where he wore a sweatband half way up his arm and tucked the wooden lollypop stick under. He wore sweatbands around his limb muscles sometimes more than one and at times longer than others to enhance the blood flow around his body, (the same feeling that can come from wearing rings). He also wore them around joints at times to help to alleviate the constrictive forces of blood as they moved, i.e. at elbow, knees, and ankles; wherever he felt that slight pressure would benefit blood circulation and hence breathing. Arjun used the sweatband as a discreet pressure to improve on his stability. He knew he would rather be with one than without when with a bona fide master as Shree Krishna.

Drupati's Dhyana-yoga

Chapter 25

Sannyasi is the ability to have the whole satisfaction of life. It is prescribed for one to see the whole picture of what life has to offer. A perfect *yogi* would see the whole picture and be satisfied with life working in harmony and tranquillity. The *yogis* themselves would not be afraid to work so would contribute to the whole picture of life. They would be unattached to their work however would gather that work is obligated. For the *yogis* to control the senses and the mind an eight-fold *yoga* system is practiced known as *dhyana-yoga* (*astanga-yoga*), even though *karma-yoga* acting in Krishna Consciousness is considered to be better.

Yoga is performed for the stability of the mind and the release from sense-gratifications. With *sannyasa-yoga* or *bhakti-yoga,* the highest form of all *yogas* is a form to connect with Lord Krishna Himself, i.e. to be one with the Supreme One. *Bhakti-yoga* is the greatest Mount Everest of *yogas*. This is the practice that even if a man stops serving men they can never stop serving the Supreme Lord. *Bhakti*: "devotional service to the Lord free from desire of material profit either in this life time or the next."

King Bharata (Arjun's grandfather), had died early in search of spiritual realisation but the soul gained another body to perfect his search and became attracted to *yogis* even without seeking so.

With the spiritual link of *bhakti-yoga* through the heart that can be performed everywhere and at anytime, and the physical *yoga* as *dhyana-yoga* that is performed with manageable acts of movement, there is also *jnana-yoga* that is practiced knowledge of restraining senses, i.e. using evaluations

---

over acts of passion and ignorance either from self or from others. Above all *yoga* with a purpose is very attractive to life. There are two paths that lead to *yoga*; one being for divine transcendence and the other for atheist mapping, i.e. one to be with God and the other to test God.

One that has just begun a journey in *yoga* would be known to be at *yogaruruksu*. Arjun was this as in instruction by Drupati who was more a master at *yogarudha* status.

By invite into the relationship of Drupati and Arjun they were on their sixth date. Drupati was introducing Arjun to *dhyana-yoga*. Traditionally *dhyana-yoga* is an eight-fold system presented with seating positions that would alleviate stress and mental frustrations, however in reality of the modern world the *yoga* was one of bodily exercises of composure, stretching and breathing, which Drupati was using to get close and intimate with Arjun.

Zooming into the fine print *yoga* is for freeing sense-gratification and fruitative desires but also is to engage with loving the Lord. Drupati felt that this proactive yet forgiving manner of *yoga* was beneficial to Arjun being introduced to the Lord. And as Arjun was no stranger to Krishna Consciousness he more than pleased himself for Drupati to carry on.

In a secluded place in Drupati's apartment she began to warm Arjun. She lived on her own but had a fine view of City of London on the south side of Vauxhall Bridge. Her patio view faced the bridge and she could see both the east and west directions of River Thames. Drupati had a synthetic kusa grass rug that she placed on the floor and sat Arjun down cross legged. She gently placed her hands on his shirt and began to undo the buttons. Arjun did not resist and sat smelling her perfume and her jet black curly hair. Drupati then got a cloth resembling that of deer skin and wrapped it around Arjun. The reason for the kusa grass and deer skin was said to control heart and mind purity.

"O Arjun, my soul, my love, what have you heard about *dhyana-yoga*?" she asked.

Arjun remained silent.

Drupati worked herself around Arjun tucking him into the deer skin and said, "*Dhyana-yoga,* is a step by step process for cease of sense activities. It will help you refrain from overexcitement, the fear of degradation, and forms part of *brahmacarya.*"

"I've heard of *brahmacarya*, isn't that a *yoga* practice that helps one refrain from sex?"

"Unless with a spouse, my dear love."

"Well then I like the sound of that. You know I'm a sensitive person," replied Arjun.

She laughed and moved her hands over his bulging biceps, "I would be your *bhramacari,* if as married as a *yoga* master in Krishna Consciousness, and you'd be one too. But first, you'll have to understand the eight limbs of the *yoga*," she giggled.

"In Sanskrit; *Yama* is the attitude towards your environment, *Niryama* is the attitude towards each other, *Asana* is the physical posture, *Pranayama* is the restraint or expansion of breath, *Pratyahara* is the withdrawal of the senses, *Dharana* is to concentrate, *Dhyana* is to meditate and *Samadhi* is to complete the integration of force absorbing into the Lord. This means that everything is tranquil in subjectivity even subjected within dishonour. Thus *dhyana-yoga* is to conquer the mind and senses as all that glitters is not gold and therefore then to give to God," she said.

"Wow! Like extremely WOW!" Arjun said immediately. "I do that at the gym. I don't know what I am doing by name but all that you said there defines the process I exercise with."

"What do you mean? Explain that to me."

"My Drupati, you have no idea as what you say is in full force of harnessing extreme power. During my regular weight-lifting as exertions and taking breaks for my breathing and pulse to catch up during inertia, I have sat doing as you say *dhyana-yoga*. I would sit on a strong sturdy gym bench with my chest facing the bench inclined by ninety-degrees. I would close my eyes and feel my blood flow and my muscles all absorb to a stasis to build potential energy. I would do all as you said and take my mind off where I am. Even the guys at the gym find this refreshing to watch. I sit as such and tense my muscles and free my mind off tensions," Arjun said. "I would be sitting upright feeling the energy in the bench and like..."

"And like...?"

"Well you'll laugh."

"No I won't tell me."

"...And like making love in the moment of time to the bench. Then when I feel the force of the ground by planting my feet and the force of the bench that I fix myself onto, with the top of my brow that touches the bench, all with my eyes closed, the potential energy that stores itself in me needs to be inevitably be released. So when I feel like releasing the sound still potential energy as an explosion I move off the bench and in complete expansion of power."

"What do you do with all the power than?"

"Mmm.... I shake it off or shake someone's hand or the wall or my hands together to transfer the energy away. Then I go and lift more weights and when done I then go to eat."

"Oh, of course you do," said Drupati in an agreeing tone. "But now you can come here."

Arjun looked over at Drupati as she moved to sit on Arjun's lap with her breasts in his face.

"I'd destroy you with that," he said quietly.

"I believe that you would," she said. "Your body, neck and head erect to focus on one spot as the top of the gym bench, come and focus on the tip of my nose. And fix your mind to one scene, such as a river, a meadow, a waterfall, or the spiritual sky."

With that Arjun became very aroused by Drupati that she felt him becoming aroused. Arjun diverted his mind from the words that Drupati had said in love knowing that sex is the chief material desire of mankind so not to fall too easily into Drupati. He maintained transcendental meditation as steady as a flame in a windless place. As the mind is difficult to control as turbulent, obstinate and very strong to place at equilibrium with matter he was to become detached from matter and engage with spirit. Arjun moved his posture slightly to unlink the axis that Drupati had positioned herself with on him. Drupati felt his arousal wither away.

They both were with Krishna Consciousness and were in perfect knowledge wishing well for each other with an equal mind. The real purpose of *yoga* was to gain the highest perfection of Krishna, as there's no better pleasure than that of His Light as He's never lost.

"Arjun," Drupati said, "Place your forehead cleft on mine. This is where the *atma* point rests for the mind. The mind can rest positively or negatively to the soul, i.e. the mind can be a friend or an enemy to itself. The times when one has thoughts and actions which are not in their normal behaviour is an extension of this. I think it's the Lord testing how one would react to such projections. Making friends with minds engaged to Krishna Consciousness relieves distress and are autonomic which each other."

"Dru, I know everyone has bad days that affect their judgments, but what would I do if I deviate a transcendental path due to circumstances?"

"Arjun, no one can deviate from *bhakti-yoga*. It's so simple to connect to Krishna Consciousness that it only takes a second to humble self or move away from unlike minds. Don't worry if unsuccessful in transcendence to spiritual essence. There's two types of people that this can happen to: the regulated and non-regulated person; one that thinks salvation and next life and one that thinks self-gratification respectively, but then there's three paths of auspiciousness that brings them back to consciousness: those devoting back to Krishna Consciousness, those finding liberation from material existence and those following rules and regulations come back to enjoy material prosperity, who do have higher standards of living but can get lost again into material attachment."

"That's beautiful. A little hard to digest and maybe I'll have to ask you to remind me in the future."

"I would love to. A perfect *yogi* is like the Super-soul that binds with all living hearts of the people they pass, the good and the wicked and even animals such as dogs and birds. My heart flickers and becomes unsteady too, but then I become compassionate to others in their happiness and distress which brings me back to divine consciousness and possibly them too."

Drupati moved her posture to relieve her weight that she was loading on Arjun. He flexed his leg muscles and inhaled but didn't move or allow Drupati to move.

Being an unsuccessful *yogi* would result from one falling after very little progress or falling after long progress. The former is given another chance by the soul being born into families with Krishna Consciousness such as aristocrats and *brahamanas* or for the latter grace given by God. As for Arjun he was born in a family with great wisdom in *yoga* and his birth was a rare one to find as the soul he had could be educated, become knowledgeable, and thus present itself as fearless.

As the spiritual sky covered the two lovers in aura of *dhyana-yoga,* the neophyte of the following day came upon Arjun. Drupati saw his eyelids become heavy and moved towards advanced *dhyana-yoga.* Here she was the *yogi* (performer), for the *yoga* (performance) at a high *yukta* (performance level).

Drupati slowly rose off Arjun and asked, "Would you like something to eat? How about, mmmm, Nando's chicken!"

He looked at her in admiration, "I thought you'd say no to that. That's a mode of ignorance on part of *yoga*. There are plenty of grains, vege, fruits and milk."

"Listen young man! My poppa had nothing to feed me when I was little and we could only go fishing to catch fish, and then one thing led to another and now I like chicken. Besides that's a farm animal and not a wild animal. Gives me protein, and Jai Shree Krishna! Okay? You can keep the fruits and milk for yourself!"

Arjun laughed at her complete change of tone, "Okay honey bunny. Gotcha! Not to mess with a hungry lioness. Must be your Sikh blood."

"*Waheguru* will forgive me, you'll see."

"Well let's get something as I need six hours of sleep at least. Sleeping more can move me into a mode of ignorance which somehow moves me into many dreams, and the dreams don't seem to be pleasant."

"I'm sorry to hear that. I need my beauty sleep too something you males wouldn't understand. So let's just drive-thru and come right on back. A sacrifice made by the best of people I say," forwarded Drupati. "As a fire sacrifice (*sannayasi*) when throwing grains over the fire which we would circle around in marriage," she winked.

"Would that be a *prasadum*?"

"I've already told you what I think about that."

"The *prasadum* is a food sacrifice first to the Lord and prayed by before eaten by the people. I'm sure it's a variable to Krishna Consciousness but all in balance right? I'll go for your fruits and milk later on in life. An eternal life as that of the four armed *Vishnu* stretching to the four corners of the universe."

"O Arjun, you have sold yourself to me."

"Huh? Baby, I don't think you could really afford me," he patronized. "What's your worth? Four, five thousand?"

Drupati laughed, "I'll just put that on your tab."

Enjoying Consciousness
Chapter 26

The evening before the flight to India for the crusade of Krishna's destiny, He organised a meeting with Arjun and Shankar at the bowling lanes in Park Royal, Middlesex. Krishna had agreed with Arjun that Drupati should too be invited as she would be accompanying them back to the homeland. Park Royal was leisure complex with a cinema and many restaurants that accompanied the bowling complex in North-West London off the A40 prior to reaching Wembley from London City. The location was chosen as the morning after Krishna, Arjun and Drupati were to fly from Heathrow London to New Delhi, India, bidding farewell to Shankar. Tenpin Acton was the venue to educate the friends on the three modes of material nature so they could be accustomed to strike.

Within the bowling alley the lights were turned for night time bowling which made the lanes and pins glow fluorescent. White lighting covered the other areas which occupied pool tables, arcades, tables of ping-pong, a diner and a bar with seating areas. The place was lively with families, couples, friends, professional bowlers, and support workers assisting the disabled. Music flowed from speakers that brought a dance environment for the customers. The staffs were always on the move from assisting the people to helping the management run the evening shift.

Krishna, Arjun, Shankar and Drupati made themselves to one of the bowling allies and registered their names on the computer system. Krishna called Himself 'Milkman,' Arjun called himself, 'Blood-bank,' Shankar called himself, 'Blackbird,' and Drupati called herself, 'Goldilocks.'

"O friends, there is no birth of creation or destruction with transcendental knowledge. The knowledge has always been there and with the right time and mind is shared to the given audience. As the pins there are always replaced from striking them down as too is transcendental knowledge," Krishna said and released a spin of the bowling ball to gain a strike.

"You cheated," said Drupati.

"Hey I'm American. I've got this game in My blood. I'm unnatural that's all," Krishna replied.

Shankar signaled to Arjun and said, "That's an understatement, 'unnatural',"

"O lover of Arjun, all species of life are born and I'm the seed-giver. I would not just throw My seed on Earth and not watch it grow. As we would watch our play or our flowers grow, Father *Vishnu* would also watch His creations. As I am the element that gives life to love, that gave life to *Brahma*, I am therefore obliged to give love eternal life," carried on Krishna.

Shankar got up to take his turn, "I remember that was He not *Mahedev* that actually brought peace to *Paramatma* and *Brahma* as when Father and Son were fighting to see who was more powerful? Sure God used *Brahma* as the spark-plug for the universe but from the belly of *Brahma*, *Mahedev* was born as an equal," and then Shankar released the ball and achieved a strike.

"You cheated," said Arjun.

"You're lying Arjun, just as *Brahma* did when *Mahedev* asked him a question, and therefore for that I will take Krishna's side as *Paramatma* as He did not lie. Hahaha!" teased Shankar.

Arjun's turn was next and he contemplated his throw. He released the ball to strike all ten pins down also. Upon great excitement he did a spin and a Michael Jackson move and shouted, "*Om Tat Sat!*"

Drupati feeling motivated moved between the three men and reached for a bowling ball. She moved close to the start of the lane and turned to say, "O Goodness, Ignorance and Passion, how I'm I to succeed in competing with You when I have all three modes of material nature but yet have nothing without Shree Krishna," she winked at Krishna and released the ball which struck all pins but one.

"Did she just call me ignorant?" said Shankar.

"O Shankar, do not worry. Fifty percent should be goodness, as twenty-five percent would be ignorance and passion in ration for Supreme Lord," Krishna said.

"Okay, but I'm far from ignorant. I'm more the Chancellor of Truth," said Shankar.

"With that you have to be ignorant on many matters then though don't you?" approved Drupati.

Drupati went to get another ball for her second turn to knock down the last pin, "O sinless One, Your goodness heals sinful reactions. One can be happy, active or helpless and that of this little one pin I will knock its head off its base, as it's helpless and inactive and that will make me happy."

She released the ball which turned and moved with pace just enough to clip the edge of the pin giving her joy, excitement and a half-strike.

"Splendid! Wow! Give me a high five!" cheered Krishna for Drupati.

"*Brahamanas* are in use of material knowledge and not material misery, as in goodness an illusion may present due to the material world. This is where mode of passion assembles. One person's passion would not be the same as another's. Only when passion can be moved to the last form of material nature can goodness come from passion. Passion cannot though be eliminated as we all love watering plants, having joy, getting a reward, making children and deleting unwanted notes and messages," Krishna said whilst His train of speech caught up to His thought. He then chuckled and laughed to Himself.

"Do you mean Milkman, that in order for a child to listen to be fed they should be ignored first so to settle their passion, just as a youth should ignore that a love had rejected them?"

"Yes Blood-bank, and then to come back round to passion once they realise that work had needed to be done to gain the food or the relationship in goodness."

"So Milkman and Blood-bank, it's best to serve goodness first, then ignorance and then passion," said Shankar evaluating material nature. "That sounds like it would work. As if I aim to have passion before ignorance I don't think I would be able to sustain goodness in this world."

"Blackbird, passion has unlimited desires and longings and mostly they are of lust, sex, children, careers that become dependent on sense-gratification and are never fully satisfied, that's greed and thus goodness is better at the top," Drupati added.

The conversation about the mode of goodness, ignorance and passion carried on whilst they played their rounds of bowling. Confusion had laid in the mode of ignorance being that of sinister nature, but as Krishna explained that all modes of material nature are of God, then in proportion ignorance is not as bad as that of passion which is not as bad as that of ignorance. Ultimately goodness should be sought and not fought.

"Goldilocks, there are nine gates of the body that can experience goodness: the eyes, the ears, the nostrils, the mouth and the genital and anus. Sounds obnoxious to consider all as goodness but to have one in dysfunction may not seek goodness. So thus this would lead to illusions of madness and thus the darker side of ignorance and passion," Krishna said.

Dying in the mode of goodness one can project to higher planets of the sages of divine grace. This means that the people of the world would continuously become better and better as generations pass. Whereas dying in the mode of passion will lead to rebirths that chase fruitative desires making people envious of each other and thus destroying the element of love in the world. And so forth dying in the mode of ignorance would give rebirths to the animal and plant kingdom, meaning that as life energy has to move from one form to another then that soul is given a position where it stays ignorant in its following life; to eventually if the soul hasn't gone into The Light it would be given another chance to be human and search for Krishna Consciousness to drive for the mode of goodness.

"O Preserver of Strikes, can I differentiate the symptoms of modes of material nature?" asked Arjun.

"Can I answer that one Supreme Godhead?" asked Shankar. "Arjun, you are a coin and whoever can see both sides of the coin and make the best out of them without any gain is said to be free from the modes of material nature. All life is valuable but what's better from cursed should be allowed in expense of the other."

Milkman, Blood-bank, Blackbird and Goldilocks had finished one round of bowling where Blackbird had come in first place with a perfect score of three hundred. Blood-bank had come in second place with several strikes that were three in a row and hence had scored Turkeys across the board. Goldilocks had come in fourth place with several strikes and half-strikes that accumulated her score to just one above Milkman's, who at the end of the round had enjoyed the nature and the consciousness of His fellow friendships. The second round of bowling of ten-turns each was to start and the total scores combined from both rounds would decide who would be the grand winner.

The Supreme Godhead is ultimately the nature (*prakrti*), the enjoyer (*purusa*), and the consciousness (*ksetra*) of sense gratification of the body and the field of activity. In the case of the friends at the bowling alley the most in nature was Drupati, the most in enjoyment was Arjun and the most in consciousness was Shankar.

"O Krishna, Knower of Fields, You would know who would win this contest of ours today, does knowing what You know still bring You satisfaction of body senses?" asked Arjun.

Krishna took His turn which struck the pins leaving them in a split position. He then replied to Arjun, "I am the knower of the field of activities, I am conscious with in thought and action, but I cannot not allow freedom of choice and option. I am the finite knower to one's progression in goodness, passion and ignorance. The field of activities that one does is constituted by potent and impotent life. All are to enjoy transcendental bliss of Supreme Truth and that's all."

He then got His second ball of the turn and had only a chance to knock one of the two pins over. There have been people that could knock-over both pins by knowing the lane and weight of the pins for that to be possible. Krishna was not going to try to knock both pins over but to concentrate enough to at least get one. He adjusted His peacock feather cap and released the bowling ball with a heavy spin. The ball curled the polished lane and struck hard on the pin to the left to bounce off the edge of the crib to fly over to the right standing pin and knocked it over too. Half-strike!

"You cheated," said Shankar.

Krishna said to him, "Was that good for you?"

"I have five senses, my eyes, ears, nose, tongue and skin, and my third eye of consciousness being the sixth. But with my working senses as voice, legs, hands, genitals and anus I solemnly swear You cheated. Didn't I raise You well for You not to cheat?"

"Om Shankar. Peace. He probably did cheat as He can. He is the knower of fields as a proprietor of all. In hatred or happiness or distress in gross body in silence I'm sure He cheated too," favoured Drupati.

"I'll cheat on all of you if call Me a cheater!"

"Well of course You would. Our point exactly as You're a cheater, cheater, cheater," mocked Shankar.

Shankar then moved pass Krishna bumping Him on the arm and picked up a ball. He then looked around and made stance to take his turn. Not soon after that he had released the ball it ended up in the gutter giving Shankar a score of zero on his first ball. He was gob-smacked but then knew to release his frustration back onto Krishna to come into peace. With the second turn Blackbird scored a full knock down. Half-strike!

"O fellow friends, I believe this role of nature, enjoyer and consciousness falls down to control acts of humility, pridelessness, tolerance, cleanliness and steadiness; thus one would be rewarded with self-control, freedom of entanglement even that from children, and having detachment of materialistic gain thus just enjoying The Eternal Truth as it's presented with a bona fide master. Everything outside this is ignorance," said Arjun taking Krishna's influence, "Maintaining knowledge of life-outcomes is preferred over self-outcomes. Controlling the tongue better suits other attributes like triumphing distress."

Blood-bank then walked to the lane and released the ball he had. Balls on the neighbouring lanes had been released prior and a rhythm of sound of pins being knocked down across the lanes finished with the sound of Blood-bank's pins being knocked for a strike result. Strike to Blood-bank!

"Boo-ya!" cheered Arjun and again did a victory dance. "Knowing knowledge tastes so good!"

Drupati gave Arjun a high-five and stood to take her turn. She began to think of the affects of transcendence on how they were all radiating as the Spirit of God treating all living things as the same. She also thought on how the fields of activity in knowledge of what's around her and being knowable to the process of knowing transform modes of nature. That nothing truly matters but the Lord enjoying Himself with the nature and consciousness of others. Drupati saw the luminous objects of the pins as that of the moon, sun, stars, lightning and electricity and that they were unmanifestations of the spiritual kingdom. She learnt that the Supreme Lord can be without nature as His light alone pervades all objects, knowledge, hearts and souls. There is nothing really but what Shree Krishna wishes to give for trial and error or good and better. He is the Master, He is *Prabhu*. She looked around to see what Krishna was doing. He was looking over at the children bowling with their families and then He looked over at her. She turned back round to the lane and released the ball. Strike to Goldilocks!

"You cheated," said Krishna.

"I do what I must," said Drupati with a curtsy.

The Supreme Lord's internal potency has energy that is unseen of wealth and education. This is how transcendental energy becomes in existence. The more one knows the more one can contemplate and the more one can dwell and bond with the spiritual essence of the Lord. His senses are vastly different and accept all given to Him. He is omnipotent, omnipresent and omniscient. And as the Supreme Truth is His Eternal Truth which is His Absolute Truth the Truth exists outside and inside of all living beings moving and non-moving. Drupati, as well as Arjun and Shankar knew Krishna is Everything; and Krishna as in material form of Light, would have a hard time filling His own boots in a world that He was past, present and future.

Eight-point-four million species on Earth for both good and sinister parts are all associated with material nature. That nature could be form of food or the form of shelter and leisure. Nature in particular in the three modes of material consciousness causes the affects from effects presented upon God. Nature can be that of the climate upon plants, animals and man to the nature of behaviour between people which makes differences in happiness and distress. As dogs would fit into their nature they too have nature of the Supreme Lord within their hearts which make them man's best friend. So to have this form from the millions of species the Lord helps to nurture man to nurture nature for enjoyment and positive consciousness.

"Let's wrap this up and go home," said Krishna.

"Oh what's wrong? Not in the lead? Wish that You didn't give a chance?" sarcastically said Drupati.

"Watch out! O Lord's eager to return everything to spiritual energy but due to independence of individual souls the Entity resists," Shankar forwarded.

"The Lord is always giving instructions from within and without," Arjun assisted Shankar.

Krishna looked at them as they had come across more spiritually aware than Him, "One's with liberation will not take birth here again regardless of one's present position. I'm just asking to go home like everyone else. It's difficult though to be a part of the love that is here but yet also not be known that I am. I guess I'll practice *hatha-yoga* to gain liberation as Supreme Godhead through childish activities."

"We know that You are. Your home knows that You are. And Krishna Consciousness would reign for all of time even that beyond me. I can't believe You're feeling sorry for Yourself," said Shankar.

"I do what I must," replied Krishna.

"Now you sound like a girl," said Arjun.

"Hey, what's wrong with girls? Krishna can be a girl if He wants too," teased Drupati.

"O Field of Activities and Knower of Cosmos, maybe You need a glass of milk," continued Shankar.

"Hey, don't say milk to the Milkman, He likes anything but milk," said Arjun saving Shankar.

They all knew Krishna really well and their individual soul was one with the Super-soul that exists as One and away from each other. Their nature, enjoyment and consciousness would not be destroyed but move to Supreme Godhead abode in Heaven after the loss of the body.

What one wanted most was self sense-gratification to see the Super-soul in material existence, and they would consider this as a transcendental destination. Even though contradictions and oxymoron expressions are evident between self-gratification and that of purpose of the Supreme being in goodness of Krishna Consciousness overlaid all benedictions.

The friends in the moment of play took a break whilst Arjun went to order some refreshments for them. As he waited at the bar he looked over at his friends and the people around. Arjun began to wonder about different bodies as expansions of one seen by that of the living entity of Krishna (this was *Brahman* conception). In all the wonderful moments of happiness and distress that was occurring around him, he came to epiphany that all wanted to be as Krishna. Seeing Shree Krishna stand amongst the other people, it was evident that Krishna was neither there or away from anyone. He had visions of eternity with the One that doesn't coincide with material existence. Shree Krishna is not an entangled soul and only exists to experience what time and life has to offer. Arjun returned back to his friends with a tray of drinks.

"As the sky doesn't mix with water, mud, or earth, the living entity of pure love doesn't mix with material. *Brahma* existence as love is protected by life as life cannot live without love," Krishna was saying. "Even the living entity of the people and of us shines light like the sun to the entire universe, and this is what illuminates the entire body and conscious of nature."

The game had come to the final turns for Milkman, Blood-bank, Blackbird, and Goldilocks. The scores were not so far apart and the Living Entity within them had an equal chance of winning. Thus what would predict who wins would fall onto the Knower of Fields of Activity. The soul being most in practice of knowledge as knowledge was power and power is as God would surely win the game. A faithful person in good association with material and spiritual existence would reach the supreme destination for the will and mercy of Supreme Godhead. The game now had come to an end and scores from both rounds were totalled. Goldilocks had come in fourth place, Milkman had come in third, Blackbird had come in second, and Blood-bank had won the match in first place.

Deal or No Deal

Chapter 27

Coming of age was brought about by continuation of the clock ticking. One could look at this as the Earth rotating around her axis which orbits around her closest star which the people of Earth accustomed themselves to call him, the sun. Why 'her' the Earth is called? As for Mother Earth. Practical to say that nonetheless as the earth of the Earth has grown much upon herself. A *shivalinga* stone symbolises this as the base of the stone is a womb and the outer projection is a male reproductive organ. Henceforth on Mother Earth a seed is planted by some other source in the universe for the earth to flourish to what she has on land, in the waters, and in the sky. For arguments sake the initial seed planted onto Earth would be referred to as Father, as God, as in mythology *Lord Vishnu*. But by far the people of Earth would consider the clock ticking as that made by man although the ticking of Him was there since the beginning of time.

Mother Earth is also considered as a mother as she is a nurturer of the earth as too nature and weather. The goddesses of the outer realms of spirituality and demigods of the Lord are spiritually set in ways to decide what weather goes where. The female trait of The Light is responsible for Earth's weather. What influences a woman to go through changes including hormonal changes? What has governed this? The Father of course, the male influence on the female, i.e. *Shiva-linga, Shiva-Shakti, Bhagavan-Bhagavati*. The changes in mood on Mother Earth produces droughts, floods, storms, hurricanes, tornadoes, volcanic eruptions, and of course the normal daily weathers to help crops grow and flowers flourish. Laughing with this outstretched fantasy of belief one must think too that a man that keeps his counterpart at calamity and peace will allow her to give offspring for herself and her counterpart. Sexual desires that are uncontrollable and not kept towards mature respect radiates into the person(s) that affects Almighty Life and Mother Earth.

Vedic literature speaks of seven kinds of mothers: the real mother, wife of teacher or spiritual master, wife of a king, wife of *brahmana*, the mother cow, a nurse, and of course Mother Earth.

Genesis would be the beginning of all this and as for most beginnings time is very hard to comprehend what and how that actually happened. Time is said to be unknown just like the end of things, time's unknown, and time's out of our control. What we can only assume is that the Father will play His best hand on nature. A tomato will never be too big in the hand unless our hands become bigger.

Last calling of the Preserver, *Lord Vishnu* as an Avatar to be summoned onto Mother Earth would be at an age called *Kali-Yuga*, and He would be named as *Kalki*. *Kali-Yuga* is the age where the people had come to in the new millennium of 2000A.D. Time succeeded four ages prior to this and after *Kalki* arrives on Earth the cycle of ages would again begin itself from the age of *Sutra-Yuga*.

Kali-Yuga is the age of where man purges against each other, an age of quarrel and strife of the Iron Age, where man would lead them to the darkness and literally begin to dig their own graves. Deeper in the idea of this The Light, the Preserver, the Almighty Life would result into huge amounts of energy being shifted into healing rather than preserving. Nature wouldn't want to endorse this terrible burden upon her. How many times would she have to suffer in order for this circle of ages to come to a standstill and reach full liberation, (*moksha*)?

About five thousand years gives one cycle of ages. So really not that many cycles have been made. Homo-sapiens have been on Earth for many years, but human civilisations not so much. So figuratively speaking the turn of ages is neither here nor there and ideally can be stopped in rotation at the age of *Kuli-Yuga*. A line would have to drawn by the Lord Almighty whom indeed as the Lord Almighty should give a burst of beautiful empowering energy of light into souls across generations to strike into keeping an Eternal Golden Age. Every tomorrow would decide the fate of the present day and the day after; that is the translation of *Kalki* - Tomorrow.

As *Kalki* was inevitably to come He would have to develop His own reason for arrival. As fate would have Him the chances of increasing populations and civilisations driving in competition of each other would soon be made to be intolerable. The day after tomorrow would have to have symptoms of suffering preceding Him for Him to arrive. These symptoms happened to be churned in the developing lands of north-west India in the twenty-first century.

In the state of Gujarat, India, recited a very wealthy man. He was just as wealthy in money as he was of respect in love from the district he looked over. His father before him was a farmer that traded his crops of wheat, rice, tobacco, cotton seeds, corn, lentils and millets with the nearby villages. His father had a difficult time to transport his goods but he himself had time even more difficult in distributing goods to a growing population. Let alone both men did well and with the respect of their neighbours and workmen the business of farming grew more valuably stronger. This man was known extremely well in Gujarat's capital, Ahmadabad and he exported to India's capital, New Delhi. As of this he was known as a raja (king), and they called him, Bharata-Raja. (Bharat was also the ancient name given to India that was even before the time India was called Hindustan).

Bharata-Raja's dynasty was so great and vast that he occupied the land from Ahmadabad to New Delhi and beyond. The passage of business for trading that Bharata-Raja had used was famously known as Kuruksetra. He had two sons that succeeded after him that grew the Bharata Dynasty. The older son was born blind, and his name was Dhrutaras, (Dhrutaras-Raja), and the younger son who had died after seeding five sons of his own was Pandav, (Pandav-Raja).

The five Pandav sons were regarded as princes; Yudistra, Bheem, Arjun, Sahadev, and Nakul (Pandavs) had lost their father and their grandfather so they were forced to live with their uncle Dhrutaras. The Pandav Brothers were in line for the throne of the dynasty but Dhrutaras being the elder son of his father had entitlement by tradition to follow course so he sent all the brothers to boarding school.

Dhrutaras-Raja had a son too given to him by a woman that vowed to cover her eyes with a blindfold in order to pledge allegiance to Dhrutaras. If her husband was to be blind then she too would walk as she was blind. Their son's name was Duryodh. He too was regarded as a prince and was sent to the same boarding school, and too he was full of hatred for the Pandavs. Duryodh wished to inherit the kingdom without any bond to his cousins. Duryodh rightly speaking was the oldest child of his father's and his father was the oldest child of Bharata-Raja. The brother in right mind and traditional speaking would have fallen to Duryodh, however Duryodh wasn't in right mind.

The Pandavs were looked after and cared for compassionately by their uncle Viduria on their mum's side. Their mum's name was Kuntia-Ma and she was the second wife to Pandav-Raja. She had a son of her own called, Karnas who had a great love for the Pandavs. She was sister to Vasudev, which made Krishna her nephew and a cousin to the Pandavs.

The Pandav Brothers studied alongside Duryodh at Sardar Patel University, Vidyanagar, Gujarat, headed by Dean Grandfather Bhisma and his wingman Drone who were grand-teachers of military arts and construction. All brothers were tricked by Bhisma and Drone as they knew whose sons they were and thus were taught especially well in hope that one day they would fight each other to death.

Duryodh advocated his father to take all that was rightly his and set every other family member aside. One particular family member that Prince Duryodh detested was Prince Arjun (the middle son of Pandav-Raja). Arjun had a heart that was filled with the Lord and had many questions to his lips on why right wasn't kept right as well as why wrong wasn't eliminated. He had more concerns on humanity on doing the right thing than any other man that had ever set foot on the soil of Kuruksetra. Arjun's passion was that for the people of the land and of archery. Duryodh hated Arjun's enquiring heart but more so for speaking in empathy for the union of people working under him. This so kept Arjun's spirit in a state of flux full of confusion and self misunderstanding in material compassion and lamentation, which lead to more times than many into tears as he was lost between *ksatriyas* and *brahamanas* rituals.

"Well that's me O Krishna. That's where I am coming from. My mother Kuntia-Ma is sister to Your father Vasudev and I kneel to You as my cousin brother, my Lord, my hope, and my salvation. Time is soon to come where wrongs must become right," said Arjun.

Krishna looked in with His third eye on why Arjun had spoke as such and replied, "O son of Kuntia, seems to Me that nature had hands in this rising. Seems to me that *karma* had to laid out of *kama* to strike."

"You mean Lord, life needed to play actions of such just so it can be taught a lesson?" asked Drupati.

"And not just this life of yours but all the lives encountered by such branches of the mighty roots of Bharata-Raja. What goes around comes around as let's say they are begging for a beating, and a beaten is what they'll get," continued Krishna. "Where are the Kuru Dynasty and members of the household now?"

"I expect scattered throughout the region of my grandfather's land. Duryodh has many people under his control. I cannot be sure on a particular place where his dark market doesn't reach," replied Arjun.

"We shall go to Hastinapur. We shall fly to New Delhi and from there to Hastinapur. Discover what we discover and see what we see. I'm sure Arjun they will not expect us as much as we will be expecting them."

"I have never been to India, but I guess I always expected to do so," said Drupati.

Krishna laughed, "Matter of fact nor have I but I guess I am mandated to go."

Arjun smiled and said, "I guess You know best. What shall we do in Hastinapur, Krishna?"

"We shall make a household. We shall start gaining company of people that are good. We shall make stronghold of the land once forgotten. We shall make a home for you close to the capital. The way I see things is that the land of India is infested by human mosquitoes, mosquitoes are not just born of India. Hastinapur is close enough to the capital that I can use as a final insurance policy," Krishna said tightening his brawn. "I will set them all alight! Every sorry and poor soul from New Delhi to the far reaches of the land, I will set alight! The only place the people will be able to run to will be the waters of the Indian Ocean as I will set everything on fire. But do not fear the land of India will grow green again even if people do not."

Arjun had no words to say to Krishna so just looked as Krishna wrote the future through His sight.

"So then Yours truly too shall be liberated!"

"Surely You will not come to setting the whole land on fire, my Lord," mercifully spoke Arjun.

"We shall see. But for now make the phone call to your brothers. Let them know that you are on your way home. Let them know to meet us where I say and let them know I am with you," Krishna assured.

"So I guess we are going," said Drupati.

"Yes, I guess we are," confirmed Arjun.

The phone call was made, the tickets were bought, the bags were packed, the flight departed, the flight landed, the brothers travelled from London to New Delhi to Hastinapur. The land was to become the capital of the Pandav's kingdom.

Once upon a time long ago the kings that ruled the land also ruled the world. It was famous for elephants, horses and chariots and even to this day there were elephants and horses to be seen in Hastinapur.

On their arrival to Hastinapur they were met and greeted by Arjun's brothers, families and friends in the city. However the Pandav Brothers had never met Krishna before. All they had known were a few stories that their mother had told them about her brother, Vasudev-Mama, (*mama* meaning mother's brother). That he was married to Devika-Mami and they had trouble with her brother Kaans. Kaans was then overthrown by their son, Krishna, so obviously all brothers were keen to meet Lord Krishna to see for with their own eyes the Supreme Lord.

As for Krishna he had never seen India with His own eyes. Krishna greeted each brother and the land with His radiant light and beautiful smile. He touched the land and picked some sand into His hand. Krishna prayed to *Bhagavan* to bless the land for the time to come.

Krishna, Arjun and the brothers were to assess the political situation in respect to their inheritance, Kuru Dynasty involvement with the political parties of India, and all other the people that occupied the region. The land of Kuruksetra was filled with the good, the bad, and the poor. Expectedly very much of the poor were bad as the hand that fed them happen to be spoilt which meant that there were very few people to trust.

"My brother we have missed you! Our dear sister-in-law, Drupati we solemnly greet you to our family. My brother we have been in preparation for your arrival," said Bheem.

Bheem was the second oldest Pandav brother and he was by far the strongest. His body size and strength was twice that of any of his brothers. In youth they teased him on being so large and always with mum in the kitchen. Bheem was humble at the best of times, and ruthless at the worst of times. He was not one to stoop low as he soared above everyone else. He believed if one was tall then they should walk tall. And as for this walk of confidence he was knocked down many times but that didn't stop him from strengthening his heart. He gave Arjun and Drupati a huge bear hug and then kneeled before Krishna.

"O Supreme Lord, Preserver of Life, Bringer of Liberation. I, Bheem am at Your every word," Bheem said whilst kneeling.

"Rise O mighty Bheem," said Krishna.

Krishna placed His hand on Bheem's chest over his heart, "Tell me Bheem what troubles this land?"

"The policy of the mandirs matter no more. The government are too small in size for the millions of people. And as for Duryodh he speaks to no one but himself and his unlawful father. They rule over four heads of the weapon trade. They need to be found and beheaded, my Lord," returned Bheem.

Mother Kuntia was last to approach Arjun, Drupati and Krishna. She was so pleased and overwhelmed to see them. As she was the elder traditionally they all bowed to touch her feet, whereas Krishna bowed to please His devotee.

"My son Arjun, how have I missed you over these years. My prays have been answered that you return to me and you have brought me much joy and happiness that you have found a wonderful woman," Kuntia-Ma said trying to stop tears from her eyes. She placed her hand on Drupati's head and blessed her.

"My mother, how have I missed you too," replied Arjun wiping her tears away.

"I have been like a deer amongst tigers after losing your father and his brother taking over everything. We have no right to speak to him and he banishes us from his palace even at Diwali," said Kuntia-Ma without being able to stop herself crying.

"O Lord of the Universe, You don't have to be so humble. Your father's eyes You have. How I waited to meet You and be in Your presence," said Kuntia-Ma.

In amongst her anguish stories with Arjun she began praising Shree Krishna, the Master of *Yogis*, and she fully began to surrender to Him. Arjun solaced her.

"Don't worry mother. We shall go to Duryodh and let him know that his father is actually his uncle Vyas and not what that blind begets's child thinks," comforted Arjun illusive matter to Kuntia-Ma.

"Drutaras does not care what he is anymore. He is filled with material desires and his son Duryodh, is a hundred times worst. They do not rule with ethical or moral practice for the welfare of others," said Kuntia-Ma with despair.

"Material desires as fruitative desires..." said Krishna to the room. "Shankar had taught about *karma-yoga*, and that only through Me are fruitative desires considered as they are not spoilt upon the *karma*. The two camps of brothers will have to fight but the Pandav Brothers will come out victoriously. The small fish swimming in a big pond with very little time will be made obsolete. Ill ways of wealth and power are to be made to learn and let go in Krishna Consciousness."

"I shall go to his house and tell him myself I am with the Supreme Lord Krishna. What will he reply to that Krishna?" Arjun asked him.

"He will reply as I'm sure he will. He will reply in humble gracious talk after hearing My name as he should have heard about the fall of Kaans. But he will not be able to abide even though he will become liberated into the 'Supreme Personality of Godhead.' As with the Yadu Dynasty he will not be able to stop the wheels that are already in motion," replied Krishna. "Dhrutaras will know he will lose everything. He will be stripped as he will be helpless to touch My lotus feet once all is over. I'm here to reduce the burdens of the world which includes the death of his son."

"The more and more You speak My Lord, the more I believe I am just a pawn in Your master plan for mankind. I believe that we are all pawns for Your Almighty Life. The energy that creates everything can influence the smallest atom. I'm not that convinced that the Lord works in mysterious ways anymore," said Arjun with a laugh to lighten the mood.

"We shall go to Kuru Kingdom and meet with the blind king, his son, his political parties, his military officers, his knights, kinsman, gang leaders, and whoever else they have to offer. And we shall play for your inheritance and the freedom of Yadu Dynasty. O Arjun you shall lose the gamble for they play with wicked ways in their rebellious house without a Lord. They shall see Me but they will not know it's Me as they're miscreants and atheist. Thereafter you along with your brothers will return back here to commence the foreseen battle," boldly instructed Krishna.

When the time of settlement came the ill-motivated Dhrutaras-Raja and his son Duryodh were in power of the political influence of military members across the region of Kuruksetra. Duryodh alongside very crooked politicians and gang members vowed to Dhrutaras means of living and wanted to expunge Pandav-Raja's sons.

As soon as Pandav Brothers arrived to their uncle's empire stolen from their father they were exiled from the land for thirteen years due to a fixed gambling bet. This was orchestrated by Bhisma and Drone manipulating Duryodh further on disowning his brothers so they could gain the people's vote for growing corrupt politicians from Duryodh and his father Dhrutaras-Raja.

A Ludo Game, was played for gambling which had a change of hidden dice which weighed in favour of Duryodh as they played to negotiate partnership of the Kuru Dynasty. Before they were exiled Arjun had lost all his fortune and was forced to present his fiancé, Drupati as a wager. Out of sneering laughs and snares of eyes he had lost the bet which lead to disgrace of Drupati by making her dance for the Kuru Dynasty. However just as the dice weight was illusive from the Pandavs' so were the lights on Drupati. As Drupati was to dance for the wicked family the room's lights flickered as strobe which made the crowd frightened on what they were not being able to see. Arjun knew this was the doing of Shree Krishna who stood nearby watching the whole fiasco.

As the sunset over the palace the Pandavs were dismissed from the table of negotiations. Krishna went to ask Duryodh to share his grandfather's business with his brothers in respect for love and peace. Duryodh refused Krishna's proposal. Krishna gave Duryodh a look that sent shivers down his spine. The war between personal passion and passionate about the people appeared on the horizon.

Making Dwarka Home

Chapter 28

Along way away back in Manhattan the women of Kaans were still mourning their lost. Two particular women known as Asti and Prapti who were most in love with Kaans' fortune felt that they had become widows. In custom for a woman becoming a widow in *Vedic* literature they would either sought protection by their sons or their father. Asti and Prapti had no sons so they returned back to their father for comfort. They had the same father and his name was Jarasand. Asti and Prapti shared the story of their loss to their father naming Krishna and Balaram as the whole reason for the tears of sadness.

Their father, Jarasand was a very wealthy business man in retail estate. He had a huge confound of thirteen building sites known as Magadha, down south in San Antonio, Texas. After hearing what Krishna had done from the stories spoken by his daughters he not only wanted to kill Krishna but also destroy the whole Yadu Dynasty in Madhura Building. Jarasand caught the first flight he could and went over new sand to Manhattan to find more about Krishna.

Upon Jarasand's arrival he immediately felt in disarray from the environment of New York. Jarasand had travelled to that state many times thus was custom to the lifestyle. However on this visit he felt like a stranger to the land to the extent to even ask himself if he was in the right place. He was expecting a real busy robotic city with people walking left, right and center without thought of the next person. He was expecting pollution as trash on the floor, smog in the air, graffiti on the walls and trains. Jarasand was expecting rude yellow-cab drivers so he could be the same to them. None of this was seen by Jarasand but instead quite the opposite. The vibe of Manhattan was as the people were well tuned into their consciousness. Worse still for Jarasand was he felt that New Yorkers had an eye on him as soon as he arrived. Without bringing undesired attention to himself he asked no questions and politely spoke to the cab driver to take him to Madhura Building.

Jarasand made his way to the concierge and asked to meet with Krishna. The concierge asked him to wait and called Balaram. Stepping out of the lift from the top floor with two bodyguards, Balaram approached the concierge and Jarasand.

"Hello, I'm Sankarsana. How may I help you?" Balaram introduced himself.

Jarasand replied, "I'm here to meet with Krishna."

The way Jarasand said 'I' Balaram knew this was not a pleasant visit from the stranger.

"Krishna is not here at present. What is your name? May I take a message?" Balaram asked.

"I am Jarasand, Estate Manager of Magadha, father of Asti and Prapti. My daughters say he is the protector of people, a *ksatriyas*, but how could He then kill His uncle Kaans?"

"I see, Jarasand, how are you in relation with Kaans?"

"Let's just say I don't like to see my daughters unhappy shall we?"

"Well in that case I guess you deserve answers. Can you just take a seat, maybe have a drink and I'll call Krishna to consult back with you for making arrangements about your enquiry."

Balaram's bodyguards walked Jarasand to the seating area in the lobby of Mathura Building. Balaram did not use his real name to the stranger as to test what the stranger actually knew. Hence he called himself Sankarsana. Balaram called Krishna in India, and mentioned to Him all the names Jarasand had said. Upon hearing the names Asti and Prapti, Krishna was aware of them as He comforted them in the funeral ceremonies of Kaans. Krishna then researched to find the worth of Jarasand as an estate manager of Magadha. A person's character can be easily seen by their occupation even though the occupation should not define the character. Krishna learnt that Jarasand was very wealthy in San Antonio, Texas, and did not have any reason to overtake his property. So when it boiled down to facts, there was no reason to harm Jarasand. Krishna asked Balaram to speak to Jarasand by phone.

"O Jarasand, I am Krishna. I would like to first say that I am sorry for your daughters' loss. However there is no reason for you to enquire the reason for My actions against My uncle," Krishna said.

Jarasand was not accustomed to kindness or speech as such and replied in haste, "I'm disgusted by You and Your brother, Krishna. How could You do such a cruel act of injustice? I am ashamed to Yadu Dynasty and would resort to measures on bringing things as they once used to be!"

"Jarasand! Was that a threat you just gave?"

"You don't know the power that I have boy! Many men have be slain by the might of my will and You, Your brother with the rest of this building will fall as soon as I give the word, You rotten child!"

"My dear CEO Jarasand, heroes don't talk much. So what I shall do is let My brother handle you. I'm sure you will come to an arrangement before any blood is spilt. After all you are our guest. Can you please give the phone back to Sankarsana? Goodbye."

And with that Balaram took the phone from Jarasand and spoke to Krishna for a brief moment. Jarasand felt a shiver shoot up his spine and his legs become weak. He felt that he had crossed the line.

"So Jarasand, Krishna has instructed me to write you a cheque. What will it take to make yourself and your daughters happy? Say over a thousand arrows to be fired to break your phalanxes? Say a thousand more arrows for *sarnga,* i.e.

executing peace for your horses, elephants, and people? So name your price Jaras? Possibly over another thousand arrows to make us feel better that we don't have you arrested for threatening the Yadu Dynasty name?" negotiated Balaram.

"Your money is no match for mine young one! I've come here to see Krishna. If He cannot be here now then I'll stay nearby until He or Balaram comes to meet me face to face," insisted Jarasand.

"My brother Krishna cannot be here as He is in India. I, Balaram, am here though face to face with you. My brother and I believe life will be of cosmic benefit of future relations to have you go as a fighting hero, before we come with our people to San Antonio and have a look at who's really worth more."

Jarasand's eyes opened wide and he trembled with fear. He had got played. Who he was insulting was standing an arm's length away and as a lion was looking down at him waiting to consume his prey. Jarasand felt his whole life catch up to him. He was not a young man anymore. The time of the new generation was best suited to men like Balaram and Krishna. He was in no position to make threats and was caught up in expelling his daughters' anger out on the brothers.

Balaram leaned down and presented Jarasand with a cheque in the amount of three hundred dollars. But what was most valuable on the cheque as any self-sufficient business man would know is the signature and stamp on that paper. The signature was that of Balaram's and the stamp was that of Yadu Dynasty. Jarasand thanked his lucky stars and exited Mathura Building to go back to his Magadha to meditate.

Not long after the occupants of Mathura Building rejoiced their victory, Krishna had also given respect to His grandfather Ugrusana and crowned him lead of Yadu Dynasty.

One of the sons of Ugrusana, known as Gungi-Muni, had a beget child by daughter of not such a prestigious father, Yavana, and his name was Kalayan from Nevada. He had his mindset on stealing power from his grandfather from hearing how awful Ugrusana's son was by his mother. The child who had now become an insecure young man plotted with his grandfather Yavana to steal the wealth of Yadu Dynasty starting with destruction of Mathura. Gungi-Muni had heard of his son's anger on him and prayed to *Baba Shiva* asking him why he was given a bastard child? He made a call to Balaram informing him that Mathura Building was in danger from his son. He informed Balaram to speak to Krishna to take any means necessary to protect the family from the distress that Kalayan was to cause.

When Krishna heard this news He had enough from people wanting to attack the Yadu Dynasty from repercussions of Kaans' bad seeds, Kalayan, Jarasand, and any other persons. With investment fixed in the Mathura Building and Yadu Dynasty businesses, Krishna signed and lifted away the occupants and his family to move closer to Him. Krishna built a home for them in Dwarka, Gujarat, India.

All of Krishna's closest family members of Mathura were given diplomatic approval of transfer by help of Shankar to move close to the Bay of Dwarka, that Shree Krishna would govern over. With an architect considered as a demigod by Krishna, they constructed a ninety-six square meter wall in the sea of the Bay of Dwarka and built a fortress for all His loved ones. The city constructed was half in the sea and half on land with roads, streets, lanes, houses, parks, plants, and desire trees, (which only exist in spiritual presence). At the centre of the fortress a temple was constructed in such elegance and grandeur that bridged the land with spiritual sky. Krishna called this temple, Dwarka Temple. Trees were planted in the sea and in Dwarka City which surrounded huge homes as palaces and was guarded by big gates called *gopuras,* which protected the fortress from the rest of the world.

A whole new kingdom of auspicious nature was made to home Krishna's most loved and dearest. The true sight of the fortress was dazzling. Many demigods after hearing about Dwarka City gave gifts to Krishna. Indra Food Industries sent the city a special tree called Panjata Tree as a house warming gift. A parliamentary house called *Sudharama* was given too which was special as it was antiquely made but always presented new. The demigod *Varuna* gave white horses with black ears which could gallop at light speed. Dwarka City became the home away from home in a universe within a universe with all respect to Krishna Consciousness. Shree Krishna moved all inhabitants of Mathura Building from America to India, and made Brother Balaram the father of Dwarka City.

Divine or Demon

Chapter 29

Through the valleys of divine and demonic creation,
Out of the days of light and darkness,
Some people will never like you,
As your spirit irritates their demons,
So liberate into honour for protection in the wilderness,
By Krishna gives fearlessness known as *abhayam*.
Praise Krishna! Hail Krishna!

Don't beget children as cats and dogs,
Beget into Krishna Consciousness after birth.
Females of wealth for sense-gratification are forbidden,
As too are men for females with material possession,
And should just go suicide themselves before marriage.
To beg for money for Supreme Godhead is prohibited,
Instead accumulate for charity to give as mode of goodness.
Praise Krishna! Hail Krishna!

Have self-control (*dama*) – Make children for the Lord.
Sacrifices should be adopted in household by householder.
Have austerity (*tapas*) especially for retired life.
Without being straight forward there is no liberation.
Do not distort truth for self personal interest (*satyam*).
Check your anger (*akrodha*) and cleanliness (*saucam*).
Socialism and occupation is an order of transcendence.
Praise Krishna! Hail Krishna!

Demonic manifest in inauspicious qualities,
Meaning one doesn't know what they do,
With arrogance, pride, lust, ignorance, anger, demon speech,
And that worshipped by others is forbidden.
Born and live with divine as *ksatriyas*,
Military men and women are transcendental,
So no cause to lament unless refraining from duty.
Praise Krishna! Hail Krishna!

Created beings are either divine or demonic,
Flesh gives birth to flesh and Spirit gives birth to spirit.
Prajapati gives birth to both but through *Vedic* literature,
They are made great.
Demonic people are neither clean or with proper behaviour,
No truth is found in them.
Women shouldn't be trapped as nor should children,
But both should have room to grow.
Praise Krishna! Hail Krishna!

Demons have no perfect creation of the world,
They say naturally world is unreal, no foundation, no God,
They produce sex desires and no other desires but lust,
Demons are lost to themselves,
They have no intelligence, they have horrible works,
Their only purpose is to destroy the world,
Demons attracted to unclean work and impermanent,
Creating own hymns and chants of false pride and prestige.
Praise Krishna! Hail Krishna!

Preach to believe in One God,
Rejoice in excluding others.
Charity and sacrifice at pure minimum,
Leads into demonic nature.
Bewildered of false ego and envious of Krishna,
Thus the enemies of Life will be cut down by Life.
Mischievous as miscreants should fall to obeisances.
Praise Krishna! Hail Krishna!

Incarnations of species of demoniac life,
Would live to destroy previous Lord,
Thus through mercy of Lord (*asuras*),
They are fortunate to be killed by Him.
Divine liberated without a doubt,
Or liberated out of necessity for Life.
Praise Krishna! Hail Krishna!

The whimsical, discards Life,
Doesn't bow to happiness,
Will have no destination and no perfection.
So read Scripture (*sastra*) and be elevated,
As great saints as *Acaryas*.
Be with a bona fide master,
Away from demonic nature to divine eternal life.
Hare Krishna! Jai Shree Krishna!

Supreme Person's Yoga

Chapter 30

A beautiful sunrise was rising over the land of Dwarka, Gujarat. The cool midst of the morning air was warming as the sun rose over the greenery of the land. Animals such as dogs, cats, cows, camels, monkeys and birds were warming and stretching their limbs to the morning light. The streets were not yet booming with rickshaws, bicycles, motorbikes, cars, lorries, trucks, carts and the general public. People however were seen walking and enjoying the sunrise. Some people were sitting and watching the life of the place start to begin the day. Some people were opening stores and their businesses. Some people were doing their morning prays. And some people were sitting doing yoga eyes closed facing the sun.

Krishna had brought Arjun and his brothers to the land of Dwarka as of divine business that He was to fulfill. But before Krishna was to raise the land of Dwarka and His fort He was to teach the Pandav Brothers the yoga used for the supreme person. The Pandav Brothers accompanied Krishna on this fine morning to a park that was banked on the edge of the Arabian Sea which was a part of the Indian Ocean.

The park was favoured by Krishna as the place was covered with many Banyan trees. Banyan trees were of Indian fig trees where the branches would grow downwards into the ground making roots as well as accessory trunks for the tree. The lifetime of the tree is usually about two-hundred years. The Banyan tree has fruits that when cut open flowers were seen. The fruits also harbour many medicinal properties such as its leaf, bark, seeds and fig are used for a variety of disorders like diarrhoea, polyuria, diabetes and urine disorders. The wood of the Banyan tree can be used to making door panels, tables, and boxes, along with other woodcrafts. The most special attribute of the tree was that its eternal energy from its branches and twigs are senses of Shree Krishna. Banyan tree's materialistic roots bound and found to be the life of the Supreme Godhead, and thus to surrender to the tree is to surrender to Life.

The Eternal Kingdom of God does not consider any man to be alien but only familiar. Unlike the initial meetings of man and the changes of environment would first be that as alien and thereafter be familiar. Even babies are first alien to their parents where soon after they become family. Make no mistake one is always first a stranger to another before they become a familiar face. There is no reason for someone to say not to talk to strangers, as without talking to a stranger there would be no moment in becoming familiar. However the Supreme Godhead knows man before they even know themselves, making each individual a familiar to the Lord.

"The Supreme Abode of Mine is a lot like illumination of the sun, moon, fire, lightning and electricity. Those that reach never come back to the materialistic universe. There are two places of abode a soul can rest; *Krishnaloka* where the soul rests with My mind, and *Goloka Vrndavan* where the soul rest with My love. The Supreme Abode is achieved by surrender and no other means. Thus once one has reached full liberation they should surrender to Me as Super-soul," advised Krishna.

The being of the Supreme Lord is fragmented over time and space for those who come to consciousness of Supreme Godhead can talk face to face to man, animal and Banyan tree. As one surrenders to Lord Jesus Christ to find Father they are also considered to struggle for the existence of Jesus who had for the Lord's purpose. The struggle brought the reward of the Holy Spirit (*karsati*), as the Spirit of God was carried in His son that all who believes in him will have eternal life throughout time. These are the fragments along with other prophets in other faiths such as Prophet Muhammad in Islam, Guru Nanak in

Sikhism and Siddhartha Gautama in Buddhism that were left for time and space to pick up.

"O Pandavs, as you see around you there are many *yogis* in search for self-realisation to the living entity for love of life, but without surrendering to Me; they will not find transcendental peace even if they think they do. There is no need for much but that service of life I have to offer. The splendour of sun, moon, fire and water comes from My Eternal Abode, and is for he who can look past objects catch the spiritual world. Imagine watching a crow fly across a blue sky and then let go of the crow to fly and see what is left is blue sky, in that moment you have caught Me. Just as cutting the horizon when one stands by a large truck or double-decker bus as it drives by. They could stand and fix a point to the top edge of the vehicle from front to back as the vehicle drives by so when gone one's left with spiritual sky, and that is Me."

Talking about the light of the sun, moon, stars, fire, lightning and electricity one can challenge the mind of another with Krishna Consciousness, as at night the moonshine is what vegetables use to be nourishing themselves. The Lord enters the plant (entity) and stays as energy is as equal to people's realisation of Supreme Godhead. He is the force of the digestive system. Energy loves energy and God can change the energy from one form to another. As a simple example of digestive energy from drinking, chewing, licking, and sucking an individual can experience different forces of energy from each process. Deeper still tasting of red wine forms euphoric and spiritual transformations of energy for the senses.

Krishna continues, "I am seated in everyone's heart from here comes remembrance, knowledge and forgetfulness. Even as the mind processes such affects the heart is what initiates for this to happen. I am apart of all the *Vedas*, I'm a knower of *Vedas*, as simple as in Spanish Vida means Life, *Vedas* is as such. If one is willing in heart with Krishna Consciousness and I am willing as a part of that heart than one would forget about past life and begin new ones. However a strong will power is to be created through *Brahma Dev* energy for I to preserve as *Paramatma*."

Vedas allows soul to mould lives back to Supreme Godhead, i.e. back to home. *Vedas* offers knowledge of Supreme Godhead from *Lord Vishnu* through the incarnations of avatars. Shree Krishna would be the giver of knowledge through reservation by *Baba Shiva* as *Bhagavan*. The present body would forget that the Lord gives intelligence to renew His work, and the *Vedas* to be one with God as known Life.

"O sons of Kuntiya, the Supreme Soul Myself is also supreme at *yoga* all for peace, but of too harnessing power of the transcendental time and space and executing the power. Through all the *yogas* that I have spoken to you I also practice to be that of *Baba Shiva* in eternal *yoga* of Myself. I would maintain the material world as fallible, the spiritual world as infallible and Myself as Supreme Living Entity, thus be the *yogis* of supreme person. Simply to adjust with many forms of the universe the underlying Ocean of Milk that I can be is where I rest Myself as *Krishnaloka*."

The Lord here by the Banyan trees agrees that He too Himself is baptized in transcendence with material body and the eternal bliss lives as spiritual form. Nothing is what life is until one has made life happen by either conscious thought or action. When the Super-soul is out of body He enters space of impersonal *brahmajyoti,* where He remains in spiritual illumination both exhibiting and diffusing His spiritual effulgence of energy. Upon evaluation what is the point of a soul living hundreds to thousands of different lives if there is no final purpose? After all that would just be a great waste of time.

"O saviours of Earth, ignorance does lead to darkness as a state of lack of understanding or a lack of interests and action, but ignorance too can be a lifesaver, a stress free unpolluted environment of woes. As a foolish man does not know why he finds a cleavage enticing, a man in Krishna

Consciousness would train his eyes to look pass this and see the spiritual essence of a woman. This is where dark and light ignorance go hand in hand for the woman who would present consciousness of the Supreme Father for her to show a cleavage for man and herself. As bona fide masters as yourselves they'll be no question of ignorance or wickedness as you'll aim to make others intelligent and purified. The heart however is weak to the desire of material nature, possessions and attractions of lust but with devotional service one heart will be excused for the heart's weakness," Krishna paused. "Upon the last evidence of *yoga* practice, the supreme person would strengthen the heart and protect love as love is greater than egocentric behaviour."

The Pandav Brothers and Krishna continued their walk by the Bay of Dwarka sharing ideas of interest. The day was well spent in gaining knowledge from Krishna that the Pandav Brothers felt that they had no concern about the outside world.

Pleasing His People

Chapter 31

Monsoon season had ended over in India and winter season had thus started. However for the earth of India which the equator crosses over there was no real affects of cold for that season. For the locals of course there was a vast difference in climate and temperature. As the rain season was over the mosquitoes were fewer and the people were more out and about longer into the night. During the day the people were more active being able to cope better with work and studies as the light and heat was tolerable compared to spring and summer seasons.

Krishna had invited Arjun to Vidyanagar, Gujarat, which was in the Anand district to assist in a retail purchase. Krishna was very fond of Vidyanagar as the place was home to Sardar Vallabhbhai Patel University. Sardar V. Patel was known as the Iron Man of India in the era of Mahatma Gandhi (who was also a Gujarati man), and paved a strong fight for unity. The grounds around the university taught various subjects and were of military standing. Within the campus was a huge park called Shrastri-Madan, where soldiers, students and locals would leisure from early morning to late evening every day. Krishna liked the aura of the town as He liked the enthusiasm of the people. He also knew that the location was on the up and coming as a massive educational district for Gujarat for all ages.

The Supreme Godhead had His eye on the news and with a word from Shankar knew of a building been constructed that homed only for NRI (Non-Resident of India) citizens. The residential complex was of two buildings called Tara Towers, built by four brothers in the name of their grandmother who was known as Tara, (*tara* means star). The four brothers had eight children of six were male and two were female. The oldest grandchild was to meet Krishna and Arjun to seal a deal for Him to have the number one apartment looking over the entire district. But before Krishna could sign a deal with Tara's grandson who was known as Sandeep Patel, He needed to see for Himself the land around Tara Towers and Sardar V. Patel University.

Before arriving to meet with Sandeep, Krishna and Arjun decided to sight see around the campus and mingle with the students and locals. Krishna planned to take the chance to provide His devotional service to the people He'd encounter. Arjun was to also take a chance to spread the news about his passion and goodness of Gold Lighthouse to the students in the area. Both Krishna and Arjun wished to saturate the new home for Krishna by bringing new tidings to Sandeep and the locals, and too wish them a Merry Christmas and a Happy New Year.

As Krishna and Arjun walked around Vidyanagar they passed many shops that had different demigods in their shop windows and on their signs.

Arjun asked Krishna, "O Lord, what is more perfect, the impersonal unmanifest of *Brahman* or that attachment to personal form of The Light in the search for Absolute Truth?"

"My Arjun, many have asked this question but not as many as I would have liked over the eras passed. Even though both routes through to Shree Krishna is directed to Godhead, those directed and engaged in worship of The Light in transcendence with Me is perfect! Those that worship as impersonal unmanifest of *Brahman* is that of Me too but they may not have time to fully worship Me personally. People's time is constituted in their work, their lifestyles, and their environments to suit and adapt in that habitat as to survive. Hence demigods and other manifestations of Myself are worshipped. Once the individual receives the benefits of these demigods in their society they should come back to Me as Supreme Godhead."

"I see what you mean, Krishna. This life around us seems too far mixed even though the language is the same. Here there's importance to worship The Light as Super-soul as that's seeing the soul rather than person. Sounds difficult for them to suit with so many years of change but I guess that time is a good welfare for them to have a variety of ways for their worshipping."

Krishna nodded, "True but to reach the same goal is what I desire from them. God is One, and if they are to give God a personality and a name than that name should be Mine. That is why I recommend all these individuals and yourself to follow *bhakti-yoga* as with this practice life becomes easier and natural for the embodied soul to accept Me as *Lord Vishnu*."

"Is there any accordance to this my Lord?"

"On accordance to *jnana-yoga* Arjun. Where though mindset many find troublesome to live unmanifested lives in worship of the Supreme Lord. Thus they begin segregating faith, i.e. what's *brahman* like and that is not. What most end up doing is worshipping as *saguna,* meaning worshipping My material qualities such as stone, wood, and even oil paint. However they dismiss Krishna Consciousness as the reason I said earlier. I do find this quite amusing as they all want their own state of power particularly from their neighbours."

Krishna and Arjun laughed over the matter. They carried on walking by the stores and shop fronts where the locals stood and drank *chai*. They nodded and made eye contact with many individuals where they saw that they had a hard time not being able to look. With all of Krishna's stance and appearance He caught the attention of every person that came by Him. Arjun was not so different walking with Krishna as no one could imagine seeing a more divine sight.

"Look right, look right, look right, shoulder!" sang Arjun.

"Left right, left right, left right, soldier!" contributed Krishna.

Using several moments of passing men and women Krishna and Arjun preached this little hymn to see who would find this easy to understand and rest their sight. The point of the parable was that there was a safe spot to mark on an individual and that was the shoulder. Krishna at times marked many people's shoulders in His sight as He moved passed crowds. This enabled them to move from His path as if Krishna and Arjun kept swaying their walk that would cause more confusion. The pure size of Krishna and Arjun together would mean to better move or be moved. Krishna along His walk also blessed some individuals by crossing His sight across their shoulders and to the top of their heads as He walked by them. An instant reaction was that the individual would feel blessed to walk tall no matter man or woman, adult or child.

Where the crowds in some areas from Vidyanagar to Anand were intense Krishna would extend His arm and palm whilst walking to get the attention of others not paying attention. Krishna very little would move from His path no matter what direction He was looking in and nor did Arjun. Hence Krishna used His palm to safeguard Himself and Arjun so people would not collide into them for their own good.

"This is form of *bhakti* I'm performing as you see their surrendering to My will," said Krishna.

"Oh I see. Better to have Your way as I feel a whole lot safer with You than I did growing up in India as a young lad," immediately replied Arjun.

"You can feel that I am not looking for Absolute Truth here. This land seems troublesome and seems that I am using far many more senses to control such a lack of love they have for each other. I do not recommend *jnana-yoga* here even though worshipping in *Sri Krsna* would allow the soul to reach spiritual sky. But if one soul can be surrendered they can become the deliverer. Instantly children would be completely cured by their parents and thus their position in life becomes secure. The children do not need to transfer to *yoga* rather like a bird not needing to nest elsewhere, but the children that have not yet learnt will need to swim to be saved if drowning," Krishna announced.

"Speaking about devotional service; can any intelligent man do this to reach a higher position with Godhead? As transferring souls to spiritual planets of fortune and glory seems to be what one is pleasured by in Krishna Consciousness. So even though this sounds fruitative may I distribute my cards for awareness in Krishna Consciousness to the locals?" hinted Arjun.

Krishna looked over at him, "I have been waiting an eternity for you to do that! Do My will! This goes without saying. I'll love to see you at work on gaining their attention. Please do also take a few photos with them. They shall be first devotees though out time that will reap the full benefits of Gold Lighthouse."

Arjun smiled, "Thank You Father, God."

"You don't have to let them know that I am with You. It may spook them out or think you're crazy. Hahaha!"

"They may appreciate that. Besides I think Your cap gives You away," Arjun said sarcastically.

Arjun approached many students in different intervals around Anand back to Vidyanagar and around the campus of Sardar Patel University. He approached them introducing them to the science of The Five Gold Rings. He also asked them how they felt after hearing the divine philosophy. Arjun knew that the students and locals would not benefit as much as people in a mixed democratic society but nevertheless planted the seed.

Arjun clearly was not seen as a local so many students and locals stopped to listen to him speak in English and Gujarati about the news he wished to share. Arjun was asked a few questions and not many resisted the moment with him and Krishna. He managed to take many photos and at the time no one knew that they would become the first stepping stone to a better future for the developed world but Krishna.

Arjun handed out business cards to his website and hoped that they would enjoy his novels. Overall he asked them to enjoy the truth of life and share to others. Krishna observed how Arjun handled the locals being an alien to them he did pretty well. The obvious reaction that everyone was thinking was 'who was this madman coming to speak to them?' Arjun however held his ground and his passion for goodness for others and preached to them the good news of consciousness.

"O Preacher of Parables, they will not be able to fix their mind on Me without *bhakti-yoga*, but you are providing that with a smile so mercilessly," praised Krishna. "Many will only be accustomed to the love for money which will shadow the love for God for the sake of security. Let them know to meditate on your words for purification of senses when sense-gratifications of impure thoughts come to mind."

"O Lord of the Universe, I sympathise with them in understanding this grand truth. I am of course trying to make sales in my authorship with the good news that will become better news. Being self-situated but unable to be in Krishna Consciousness due to lack of awareness, family problems, society issues, religious impediments; how am I to sacrifice the mood of others to come into Supreme Godhead?" enquired Arjun.

Taking Arjun by the shoulder Krishna said, "Devotional service is not for everyone but for the straight and recommended. As you have un-frail love you have what that takes. Using *bhakti-yoga* one would need to renounce materials to gain that level of knowledge leading to meditation which leads to Me as Super-soul. Show what you have in light and let the rest follow in time (*nirmama*). I do not wish any devotee of Mine to go through trouble or think life could have been worse. Even though My past deeds have come into play I do believe this was in *Sri Krsna's* will and not that of *Sri Krsna's* fault," encouraged Krishna.

"What am I to say to that? All I can say is as of You I am, and as of me, You are," said Arjun smiling back at Krishna. "There was a sense of equipoise that good should be seen in everyone through happiness, distress, anxiety, fearfulness, dissatisfaction, sorrow and laughter."

Krishna replied, "A devotee should be as you, O Arjun. They should be cool, and have love of God."

God's grace is of auto-spiritualisation of self-realisation. Every moment of different emotions and occurrences are to be considered without speaking nonsense. The only nonsense considered would be as an intentional joke that one may have got or not. Friends and enemies are the same in the eyes of the Lord. Rich and poor are the same as the Lord is their Maker. A devotee can accept money as they should not need to struggle to acquire that. Auspicious and inauspicious moments thereafter collided in the name of Shree Krishna who served Sandeep Patel to buy Himself a place under the stars overlooking new optimistic futures for Sardar's students.

Krishna Loves Rukmani

Chapter 32

Krishna had settled into His new second home in Tara Towers. He had unpacked all belongings and neatly organised the apartment the way He deemed fit. There were three bedrooms with en-suite bathrooms, a large lounge space with a dining area, a modern kitchen and a terrace that looked over all of Anand. He had an apartment on the top floor where the floor above would be the roof if He wished to fly kites. There was a large communal garden with car parking under the building. There were three security guards that worked alternative shifts that helped keep the place safe, and there were garden workers and maintenance workers to make sure everything was kept up to standards. All the apartments had air conditioning and a backup generator just in case of blackouts. Krishna had got to know all the people in the residential complex, along with neighbouring buildings and businesses.

During one hot afternoon there was a knock on His door. Krishna opened the door to see Sandeep there with what looked like take-away food. Krishna invited him in and they enjoyed a meal together. Then Sandeep asked Krishna the weirdest of questions.

"Krishna, do you have a girlfriend?"

Krishna looked at him, smiled and said, "I guess I haven't found the time."

"There are some good girls in Anand. Maybe I can introduce You to some sometime."

"Well I wouldn't want to impose."

"Not at all Krishna, it would be my pleasure."

Sandeep then sat there looking at Krishna in a way that was asking Him to say something.

"Seems you already have someone in mind?"

"Yes! But not if You don't want to. But You should want to. Sorry I've already told her about You."

Krishna looked at him with bafflement, "And?"

"And with one call she can meet You here."

Krishna laughed at Sandeep's forwardness.

"You don't think that is too forward, Sand? What have you 'already' told this person?"

"Only the truth; You are tall. You speak English, Gujarati and Hindi. And You have moved to Tara Towers to overlook the education of the district. And that You are from the Great Britsh Isles."

"I'm from the United States of America."

"Tomato, *Tamata*, Toma*to*. United Kingdom, United States, United English. What's important is that You become united with her, and then we can have a huge marriage and celebrate unity. So what You say?"

"You told her I was from abroad? That is what you said? Does she speak English? I've just moved in."

Sandeep looked at Krishna with a puzzled look, "You haven't even asked me her name?"

"On the other hand I have lots to do today so maybe some other time, Sand."

"Her name is Rukmani, but she likes to call herself, Manisha," Sandeep proclaimed.

"Oh My life, she's already sounding complicated. Why does she do that?"

Sandeep shrugged his shoulders, "I don't know. Communities? Something You may want to ask her."

"Let me take a wild guess. Rukmani is the divine name of the woman who married *Sri Krsna*. Thus she doesn't always want to be thought of in that image within the communities and henceforth she calls herself Manisha, as that name contributes to many female names in the cosmos."

"And hence You'll be perfect for her. You are already a match made in Heaven. So with You Krishna she can call herself by her name Rukmani. Perfect!"

Krishna gazed at Sandeep, "Has she a temper?"

"No when did I say that? She's young, she'll grow out of that. She just hasn't found the right guy. How did You know? It's just her way of being sweet."

"Mmmm. So how do you know her?"

"I happen to go to a meeting and she attends there too. We go to the same *satsangs* and we have been friends for some while. How about I don't call her here and You accompany me to the *satsang* tonight?"

Krishna thought for awhile, "Okay, but only on one condition. Don't let her know I am the one that you already have told her about…"

Sandeep quickly replied, "Okay, but that also being said, I won't point her out and I will see if she catches Your sight, mind and heart. In faith I'll pray."

Around seven in the evening Krishna and Sandeep went to the *satsang*. A *satsang* was a meeting of people with a similar religious interest. Once a week the *satsang* was in Vidyanagar. The people at this *satsang* worshipped in a man named *Dada Bhagwan*.

The story goes that this man in his senior age was sitting at a railway station and had the vision of *Shree Sumandar Swami*, who was of God likeness. Upon this vision God shared divine insights with *Dada Bhagwan*, who's birth name was Ambalal Patel. He told his brother and spoke about his past lives and the past lives of others. He shared self-realisation of God and himself along with *Sri Krsna* and *Baba Shiva*. His brother shared the news to the other people and they then flocked to meet Ambalal Patel to ask about their lives. *Dada Bhagwan* did not preach about God but that of self-realisation, effects of actions to others, liberation and knowledge of the four corners of space. The teachings of *Dada*

Bhagwan were shared by hymns, prays, gatherings and scriptures. *Dada Bhagwan's* devotees would greet and goodbye by placing their hands together and saying, '*Jai Sachidanand.*'

When Krishna and Sandeep arrived at the *satsang*, Krishna was welcomed by a member having their hands together and saying, *Jai Sachidanand.* Krishna thought to please them and placed His hands together and said '*Jai Sachidanand,*' in return.

Krishna then heard the beat of a *dhol*, and from that beat His heart became warmed and was delighted. Before He could see who was playing the *dhol*, a woman's voice came evident to Him. A hymn was being sung by a woman who also satisfied His audio senses. The voice was soothing as well as heartwarming. For whoever was singing sang with devotion and whoever was playing the *dhol* played with devotion too. Krishna then saw that the woman who was singing was also playing the *dhol*.

Sandeep was given a seat with the elders and Krishna sat beside him. They listened to the hymns being played and the stories of self-realisation being shared. Everyone was so interested in the *satsang* that they didn't give Krishna a second look. During break time, Rukmani came to say hello to Sandeep, and he introduced her to Krishna without disclosing their names to each other. But Krishna gathered she was the woman that Sandeep had spoken about earlier.

Krishna spoke to her in English and she replied back well. He asked her what her occupation was and in reply she said she had studied in London, England for a Biomedical Science degree, and at present worked as a laboratory technician for Shree Krishna Hospital in Anand. Krishna asked her if there was any place that she preferred to go in Anand that would be good for Him. In reply Rukmani laughed and said right where He was, meaning the *satsang*. Krishna thought that was sweet of her but also felt confused on why she placed her hands together for a human and not *Shree Sumander Swami*.

For that Krishna did not feel that Rukmani would be able to live a life that He could offer so had no desire for her. As Rukmani said *Jai Sachidanand*, Krishna returned a smile and said the same words back to her but also *Om Namah Shivaya*.

Rukmani's first impression of Krishna was that He was very handsome. She tried to maintain composure from the fact that she was attracted to Him. When Krishna spoke in Gujarati to the elders and the host of the *satsang*, who was a disciple of *Dada Bhagwan*, she was very much impressed. She never imagined that a foreigner would be able to speak as well as He did. During the rest of the *satsang,* Rukmani couldn't help but keep her eye in view to see Krishna from her peripheries. Every now and then Rukmani stole glimpses of Krishna. Krishna whereas on the other hand observed everyone in the room on how they worshipped. He figured out very well that who Sandeep was to introduce Him to was the girl that kept stealing glimpses. Krishna then whispered something to Sandeep and excused himself from the *satsang*.

The next day Sandeep had called Rukmani to ask her if she liked Krishna. Rukmani said yes, and that she hadn't stopped thinking about Him since the moment she saw Him. She had spoke to her mum and said that she finally had approved her heart to a man after thirty-three years. And so with the blessings of her father who was there at the *satsang*, she wanted to meet Krishna again. Sandeep there after contacted Krishna but he was not able to get through to Him. Sandeep then went to ask the security of Tara Towers on Krishna's whereabouts, and the security replied that all he knew was that Krishna had packed some bags and left early morning. Not knowing how Rukmani would react to the news, Sandeep thought best to just let her know for now that Krishna was away on business.

Rukmani's heart did sink when she heard that Krishna was not available to speak to. She wondered what she may have done wrong. Rukmani thought about their brief conversation and was under the impression that Krishna liked her as He asked, 'where she'd like to go out?' However He did not.

Minutes turned to hours, hours turned to days, days turned to nights, nights turned fortnights, fortnights turned to months and one month turned to two. Rukmani was not going to settle with being stood up by Krishna. She had never liked anyone in her whole life in the way she liked Him. She prayed to her God and with faith she believed that *Dada Bhagwan*, would help her find Him. Rukmani searched online on all social media sites to see if she could find him as nothing occupied her mind as much as Krishna did.

Just when she had thought about giving up she found Arjun's webpage. She was looking for a way to work back in United Kingdom and through a profession website she saw Arjun's profile. As Gold Lighthouse, spoke about *Sri Krsna* and had pictures of London buses she read and looked into his profile more. Whilst browsing she saw a picture of Krishna. He was sitting with many young men in a yellow shirt and black cap. She was certain that was Him. Though looking further at Arjun's tag's she found Krishna's profile. Rukmani shouted to her mum that she found Krishna. She replied that to contact Him. So Rukmani messaged Him to complement Arjun for his website but nothing more besides her name as, Manisha.

Meanwhile in Dwarka City, Krishna was on His social media account and up came the notification from Manisha. Krishna liked the words she used and looked over at her profile pictures. The first thing He saw was that this Manisha was actually Rukmani so He messaged her back immediately.

Krishna asked her how she came about His profile or that of Arjun's as He had not mentioned that to her. She gave the story as she was looking for a path to United Kingdom and hence came upon Arjun's site, and thereafter the photo of Him in the yellow shirt and black cap. Krishna found this very hard to believe and expected that she must have got a business card from Arjun whilst he had given them out all around Anand.

Krishna didn't ask any further questions but was pleased to hear from her. Rukmani didn't ask why He left in such a hurry. But one thing both of them knew without asking was that faith had brought them together in name of God's Spirit. Her spirit as *Dada Bhagwan's Shivaya*, and His spirit as Arjun's, Holy Spirit. Without Gold Lighthouse they would have never had met again and only with Gold Lighthouse they did.

Krishna felt from then that she was the right woman for Him. He asked for her number and He called her as soon as He could. Krishna then asked Rukmani if she'd like to show affection in public, have children and get married. She said yes, yes, and Yes!

Rukmani's Kidnapped!

Chapter 33

After four months Krishna arrived back to Anand from overseeing renovations in Dwarka. The only person He wanted to see first was Rukmani and so went to her home before going to His. She welcomed Him into her house and by His hand took Him to her room where they passionately shared their first kiss. Rukmani's parents welcomed Krishna's parents Vasudev and Devika. Krishna thought things would not be right to satisfy Rukmani further without speaking to her father and returned with Rukmani to the communal room.

Rukmani's father's name was Vallabhbhai. He was a noble man that was considered of high ranking in his community. Vallabhbhai worshipped in *Dada Bhagwan* but the community worshipped *Goddess Durga* also known as *Goddess Amba-Ma*. Rukmani was considered by the community as a person of high calibre, and that being said Rukmani thought of herself too in high regard with the community. She was a representation image for *Goddess Durga*. There was no way the people of the community would consider letting her go to a foreigner whom they knew nothing about no matter His prestige or godliness.

Even though Vallabhbhai was greatly pleased with Rukmani's choice in marriage to avoid conflict and to keep worship of *Goddess Durga*, Krishna was asked to kidnap Rukmani from the people and refrain her from coming return home. Yes this was an extreme measure but Vallabhbhai had no other choice between satisfying his daughter and satisfying their community. Such a bold move would resolve the people for respect to an Almighty Lord instead of praying to a demigod.

Rukmani in full consciousness of *mahatmas* and *Mahadev* i.e. *Baba Shiva*, did consult with her father to reassure herself that he knew what's best for her and the community. As Rukmani had the approval of Krishna and Krishna had the approval of Rukmani's father she played her part. She was also aware of Krishna's role in the Yadu Dynasty and time was of the essence before problems would arise amongst the *brahamanas.* Thus whatever action was to be taken in her kidnapping should happen as soon as possible.

Many men regarded as princes resided in the community and surrounding districts of Anand. They all had a fond eye for Rukmani as she would increase their power and name amongst the people. Rukmani had a younger brother, Rukmaan whose friends were also fond of Rukmani. Between the princes and Rukmaan's friends, a man known as Sisipala was considered to be the one to marry Rukmani.

Sisipala was highly educated and trained in military arts that he would be an ideal spouse for Rukmani. He was better regarded as a suitable spouse than the other men as he was not of demonic nature but a worshipper of *Lord Vishnu* and *Goddess Durga*. Sisipala was ordained to take Rukmani's hand in marriage upon her consent. However Rukmani was totally absorbed with Krishna that none of the other men saw that she was already kidnapped by Him.

One fine day, Rukmani presented herself elegantly with perfumes, gold, exquisite clothes, and *brahamanas* girlfriends dressed in ornament cloth to Sispala's father, Bhismaka. She closed her eyes in helplessness and felt lucrative with twitching limbs and weakness in her knees. Rukmani as a respectful figure of the community could not let her father's name go to shame so respected Sispala's father to let him know why she couldn't marry his son.

The Super-soul as Krishna elevated Rukmani's soul and made her full of opulence in transcendental thought. She spoke to Bhismaka that the marriage will not happen with Sisipala and to respect her decision no matter the influences from other princes or even her brother Rukmaan. In return Rukmani would bless *Goddess Durga* with benedictions and her girlfriends would present *prasadam* as sugar, nuts and toffee to Sisipala and the other men waiting for marriage. Bhismaka accepted Rukmani's honesty and blessed her.

The day arrived when Rukmani did not arrive home as expected and the news of her kidnapping travelled fast as mobiles would ring. All the people began to talk amongst themselves the following day saying that she must be in trouble or even worse. Sisipala was informed by his friend, Charas who was a close friend to Rukmaan. Sisipala became bewildered on what had happened. Rukmani at this time was safe with Krishna and the Yadu Dynasty at Tara Towers whilst men on motorbikes from her community zoomed around Anand searching for her.

Not so long after Krishna informed Arjun to go share the news of Rukmani's safety with the locals and call for Charas. From an explanation by Krishna on His actions Charas gathered there would be unnecessary loss of lives fighting against true love. Charas shared the news with Sisipala in a way that he would understand which he did. The friends of Sisipala advised him not to be discouraged as he belonged to a royal order and Rukmani was going to a supreme family also. So instead of losing his respect in any false hope of heroic action he returned home without hostility as a noble man with flattery for Rukmani and Krishna.

Rukmaan however was very displeased by losing his sister to Krishna who was to him a foreigner from the western world. Rukmaan decided to take Krishna upon himself and stage a fight against Him. Rukmaan gathered his strongest and most deceitful friends to build an infantry phalanx to ambush Krishna whilst he was still in Anand.

On the day Rukmaan was to surprise attack Krishna and take back his sister, Krishna and Rukmani were leaving for

Dwarka. Rukmaan along with his friends blocked the car that Krishna was in and stole his sister back as a crow would grab a sparrow. He then fired three strikes to Krishna's face and was determined to knock Him down. Krishna returned to strike back and with one open palmed strike broke Rukmaan's arm below the shoulder. Rukmaan's friends approached to strike Krishna with bats and iron rods but Krishna returned mystic martial arts that dismantled Rukmaan's inventory. Rukmaan then pulled out a firearm embarrassed and outraged by his progress but before he could pull the trigger, brother-in-law or not Krishna kicked Rukmaan's leg shattering his bones taking the firearm from his hand. Rukmaan fell to the ground in pain at the lotus feet of Rukmani's husband begging for forgiveness. Rukmani then pleaded Krishna to spare Rukmaan by calling Him, *Yogesvara*. Krishna raised Rukmani from His feet and forgave Rukmaan.

Rukmaan by no means wanted to be killed by Krishna in such an auspicious moment therefore gave blessings to his sister to live as a happily married woman. Krishna in return was not so sure of Rukmaan's behaviour and needed to teach him and his friends a lesson. He tied Rukmaan up to shave his mustache and beard with some hair He left as open patches. As for Rukmaan's friends Krishna took a step forward to hand them money. They declined.

"O Rukmaan, brother of Rukmani, I will not call the law enforcement and put chastisement upon you. But I will make you regret for a short time your actions you placed before a visitor to your land. After which your hair grows back and you gain stance be good for your community. Strengthen them in which I will give you opulence of liberation and mercy from My brother Balaram," instructed Krishna.

Then Krishna called Balaram and spoke to him in a tone that Rukmaan would have never expected. They spoke in formal English which was gentle but also with authority. The language was so simple to hear that Rukmaan became liberated. He felt ashamed for his actions and so did Rukmani. Krishna and Balaram spoke on speaker and first Balaram praised Rukmani. He then told her not to be ashamed for Rukmaan as he was now in Krishna Consciousness. Also in a patronizing tone said to Rukmaan that next time to have Balaram on his side before going against Krishna.

Balaram was then taken off speaker phone and spoke to Rukmani about *ksatiryas* traditions, kingdoms, land, wealth, women of prestige and power, hence for her to be less lenient. Balaram enlightened her with material manifestations of the western world and eyesight for sunlight. Balaram entertained Rukmani all the way from Anand to Dwarka via text messaging and miss calls. Krishna thought that was obnoxious especially on call charges, but as He could not argue with Balaram's passion for Rukmani He allowed her to gossip with His brother on the four hour journey.

Upon arrival to Dwarka, Krishna immediately took Rukmani to His fort. Her eyes opened wide and saw that He was King of Yadu Dynasty.

The inhabitants of Dwarka City illuminated the streets with *divas* and candles. The entire city was intoxicated over the arrival of Rukmani. The flag flying over Dwarkadish Temple was replaced every night in respect to *Sri Krsna*, but on that night Rukmani had choice for her favourite colour to fly over Dwarka City. She chose a pink flag to fly for the new night and following day. A man climbed freestyle to the top of the temple and replaced the flag. He then climbed back down and allowed Rukmani to have the first touch of the last flag. Rukmani touched the flag with her forehead and then took Krishna's hand. The people called Krishna's wife, Rani-Rukmani.

Shree Krishna and Rani-Rukmani praised all the people of Dwarka City. They spent the whole night with them in worship and dinner. Later as the night fell deeper into time, God and His Goddess walked to their quarters and closed the door.

The marriage of Rani-Rukmani and Shree Krishna was already ordained by the highest realms of Heaven. As she was to marry Krishna He had already arranged that His word would count above all of His family members. Rukmani had already fallen to His will of eternal bliss and supreme knowledge that no matter how hard she tried to compete with Krishna she was always ending up being satisfied by His love.

"O my love, my womb shall carry Your spirit and that of Your father's Vasudev, which I will call Kama, which translates to cupid," spoke Rukmani.

"Kama, sounds awfully a lot like the name of a demigod of lusty desires," replied Krishna.

She shrugged her shoulders, "As father, as son."

"Fine, sure if you wish to be as that, we shall call him, Pradyuma. That's what I think you mean."

"I think Kama sounds better as I don't want him to be bullied at school with that other name."

"Pradyuma, Kama, both sound well to me."

"He shall also be a vegetarian not to be swallowed by meat demons of the kitchen," Rukmani looked at Him like Krishna had done something wrong.

"There'll be no demon of any sort wanting to make our child into a fish or chicken curry you can count on that. After all our child will have My name."

"People that eat meat mercilessly are *raksusas*. A Sambara demon may take our baby and throw him into the sea of fast food to be used by other demons."

"O Rukmani, not all non-vegetarians are demons just as not all vegetarians are saints, My love."

"And then Rati would become his wife by the wrath of *Baba Shiva* but miraculously would grow into a beautiful bodily form of meat and potatoes, and thus would exhibit lusty desires known as that of *kama*."

"I don't know where you're going with this."

"Mayavati would be Rati's real name and she will tell Kama he's Your son. And I will lose my baby boy forever as he would rebel against You!"

"He'll surely rebel if I never take him to McDonald's."

"Roaring thunder and striking mountains between Pradyuma and Sambara. They will fight to the earnest. Sambara's mystic powers of taste and texture would bring *maya* to himself and reach sky or space, but Pradyuma's mystic powers of vegetables and iron would beat the dark mystic power of Sambara, right?" Rukmani carried on.

"Yes!" Krishna thought to play along, "But through the supernatural strength of Kama, he would cut off the head of the meat demon, and then Sambara would die!"

Rukmani kissed Krishna on the cheek, "Well of course without a head I'm sure he'd obviously die. Mayavati would then travel throughout Earth and space to sit with other women that placed meat in food. She would have reddish eyes, bright jewelry and ornaments, curly hair and yellowish garments and place all of the meat eaters in their place. *Swaaha.*"

"What's *swaaha* about that? Our child hasn't even been born. We haven't even begun that process of that happening and all of a sudden our child has a name, is a vegetarian, and is married to a woman with strength as *Shakti*. I think you need help. Do you want to be Mayavati?" Krishna said.

"As the higher planetary systems brought us together, so shall they bring a beautiful son to me that will be reborn from the dead world of meat eaters."

"My son is going to have more feminine characteristics than Myself," laughed Krishna.

She looked over at Him, "There's nothing wrong with that. He will be in tune with his sexuality."

"Sexuality huh? So you wanting some flesh now or what, Mani?" directly asked Krishna.

"Ruk, ruk," she said as Krishna moved on her.

"Stop, stop?" replied Krishna. "You can't use your own name as that. Say that slowly, Ruuuk."

Rukmani then without hesitation gave in to the full moon that lit the night sky and came full body onto Krishna. The drapes of the room moved to the cool air wind blowing in. Glasses of milk were poured again. The temperature of their bodies cooled with the night's breeze. The Earth shook.

So Let Battle Commence

Chapter 34

On the day before the day of the great battle a letter was sent from the Pandav camp to the Kuru family in secret. The letter was sent by Bheem to reach Duryodh challenging him to a duel. Everything that came into the Kuru family was checked over by the first lady, Gandha-Rani. Gandha-Rani had vowed to keep a blindfold on from the day of her marriage to Dhrutaras-Raja. As he was blind she too would walk as a blind person so thus she was assisted by her fellow maids. Even though she did not see she was given sight by the workers on the ordeals of her husband's empire. So the letter addressed to her son was read to her by one of her maids. She knew very well that through her son's false ego Bheem Pandav would surely be victorious.

"Go and call for my son, Duyodh and ask him to come see me as if I was seeing him for the first time..." she ordered one of her servants.

"Do you mean unrobed Gandha-Rani?"

"I do. Yes. Tell him he should come and see his mother in nothing but his birthday suit, and let him know as I have never laid my sight upon him, I wish to see him with my own eyes before he goes into battle as pure as I had made him," she explained. "Let him know that Bheem has challenged him to a duel and if he doesn't comply he should consider himself as lost. The Pandav brother Bheem is a mighty fighter but will be no match for my son once I've seen him."

Gandha-Rani had never seen her son in her life with her own two eyes. From birth to adulthood she had saved the light of day from entering her eyes. She believed that the first thing she would see will give that thing immense durability and thus she knew the time had come to give the first light from her eyes after thirty-odd years to Duryodh. Duryodh was to present himself as bare as a baby's bottom to his mother for her to unveil the blindfold and open her eyes to see his flesh, and make him invincible against Bheem.

The servant relayed the message from Gandha-Rani to Duryodh and Duryodh was unconcerned to say the least. Nevertheless he respected two things; one was not to disobey his mother and two was not to underestimate Bheem. So Duryodh took the servant's word and made his way to his mother's room in nothing but a towel. Before entering her chambers he was to drop the towel and walk in but was stopped by Krishna.

"Don't you think it would be foolish for you to see your mother for the first time as a grown naked man?" He enquired.

"My mother has told me to come as such as she is about to see me for the first time. And I don't see this as any of Your concern," Duryodh replied.

"First time can lead into a life time of thoughts and memories Duryodh. A man of your status should not have to fear but to only fear the shame of not being a man before a woman," Krishna said tricking him to keep his towel on to protect his dignity.

Gandha-Rani heard Duryodh come into her room. She greeted him from afar and asked him to standstill. She unfolded her blindfold and moved her head to feel the heat from the sunlight coming into her room. After thirty years of having her eyes shut she opened them slowly to see her son. As the light entered her eyes and she made sight of the male figure standing in front of her she noticed that he was partially covered around the hips. Duryodh stood and received his mother's first sight which made him feel grand as the power from her first sight blessed his skin. Once Gandha-Rani sight adjusted she saw her son's face for the first time and was not surprised why her son disobeyed her. Duryodh received her blessing on his flesh and walked out with his male pride intact.

Bheem and Duryodh met for duel thereafter. Over half the duel went in favour of Duryodh and Bheem felt powerless and exhausted against him. Krishna made His way to the duel that Bheem had set and as Bheem noticed Krishna arrive he began to give obeisance to Him covered in blood, sweat and tears. As Bheem did so, Krishna patted the top of His own quadriceps signaling to Bheem to strike Duryodh on that part of the body. Bheem obeyed and as he did Duryodh fell to the ground in agony, pain and rage. He cursed his mother for failing him, he cursed Bheem for hurting him, he cursed his own life for deceiving him, he cursed Krishna for misleading him, he cursed his father's love, he cursed the Pandav Brothers, and he cursed a final curse to have the Earth go up in flames.

Many morals of life painted here as Duryodh to gain ultimate strength from a mother's love as she broke the bond given to her husband. Also the moral of life with the art of deception backfiring. And also a moral where if one wishes to gain full perfection one must be ready to trust in sacrificing everything.

The morning sun had risen to just above the horizon line over the land stretching between the Kuru and Yadu dynasties. Whoever wasn't involved in the great fight was far from the field of war. Who wasn't involved was not spoke of as everyone was involved.

The great fight was to be a war between the brothers' entitlement to wealth, fortune and power of Bharata-Raja's kingdom. The line of successors deemed to carry this story on would obviously need to be alive to do so. They would naturally have to be unaffected by intentional de-motivation. The line of successors would be from Arjun and the Pandav Brothers but as for there and then the story was told to the blind king Dhrutaras-Raja from the insight of his informer Sanjaya.

The last line of what was to come from the glorification of the fight was as song (*mahatmya-gita*) and was to strike as the same. Arjun's testimony that would arrive after the fight from Lord Krishna Himself was equal to what Sanjaya shared to Dhrutaras-Raja:

'He who comes from this will be greater in *Vedic* literature, summarise *Gita,* give Word of Lord as guidance to mankind, and know of other spiritual wisdom. He will be of look, appearance and intellect as of what the Time needs.'

A news reporter shouts, "Get all the bloody camera's rolling! Film whatever happens on the ground from the ground and from the rooftops. Don't let a second of a minute not be captured. If a camera man is lost in amongst the fight then have them replaced but don't stop filming! Word has it that a war is to start today between *dharma-ksetra* and *kuru-ksetra* belief systems of life!"

Dhrutaras-Raja had become humble at the news of the Supreme Lord on the side of the Pandav Brothers, which made his stature step away from his son's apparition. Within his mind he saw that the Pandav Brothers and Duryodh with his military might were on equal planes regarding family values, but also in doubt of his empire to be victorious. *Dharma-ksetra* (faith values) and *Kuru-ksetra* (household values) were to be judged on which was actually mightier.

Grandfather Bhisma who had taught all the grandsons of Bharata-Raja the art of combat and military fighting was now in conflict with Krishna's mastery of war. Even though he had taken side of Duryodh during the gambling episode after he had heard of the Supreme Lord being on the side of the Pandav Brothers he knew he'd surely die by their hands. But as a person with great pride in his teachings and redeeming his sins for salvation he knew he shouldn't back away. So all investments and fixed gambling bets that were made by himself and his wingman Drone were cancelled before the fight. Furthermore Bhisma gave sound advice to Duryodh not to break strategic platforms of battle and to open up all phalanxes as not only was Krishna a brother, a lover, a demon-killer but also a war-master.

On the fields far from police influences in center between New Delhi and Ahmadabad the two groups of brothers lined their troops for battle.

Duryodh's company was of Bhisma, Drone, over half of the Kuru Dynasty males, gang-lords, drug-lords, outlaws, corrupt young politicians, corrupt law enforcers, inmates of prisons that he had the power to release, false mandir priests and evermore vulnerable people that he had happen to bribe. They all had a weapon in their hands from knives to swords to guns to bottle-bombs to bats to planks of wood to bows and arrows and they were in plenty of supply. They stepped up to the line beside Duryodh and covered their mouth and nose with black handkerchiefs. They stood beside him roaring, smirking, swearing and laughing at their opposition who assembled opposite them. Duroydh promised each one of his troops a handsome reward to live like kings for the rest of their lives. He promised them extreme luxuries of self-gratification, personal gain, execution of poverty, and to rule Indian politics.

The Pandav Brothers assembled their soldiers of friends and family. They were noble people such as their trustworthy stepbrother Karna (Kuntia-Ma's first son), working men, faithful missionaries, sacrifice takers, the humble and the hurt, the relentless, the well-wishers, and most of all the lovers of the land and of brotherhood. Each one of them was armed with weapons as of the opposition with no mercy to be granted after an eternity of segregation. They played drums, bugles and trumpets under the transcendental sky. They covered their mouth and nose with red handkerchiefs. Arjun's army was to fight for humanity and well of mankind, opportunities to be made for the well of others, and pursue sense-gratification, to get his grandfather's empire back, to give to the women of the land, and to annihilate any seed from opposing the will of Shree Krishna.

Before the commencement of the fight Arjun was in great lamentation for the necessity to kill his step-brother. Then again as he was with Krishna he knew there is no other form of goodness beside Him.

Within his kingdom sitting on his throne Dhrutaras-Raja said, "O Sanjaya, after they assembled, my sons and Pandu's sons, what did they do?"

Sanjaya replied, "Duryodh seeing alignment of Pandav's fleet went to see his teacher Bhisma, and said, 'Arjun has disciples which appear to be well organized and intelligent. I on the other hand have other military science to lay down their lives for me!'"

"My son sounds too sure of himself. He has Grandfather Bhisma and the Pandav's have Bheem. Bheem being through what he has is not limited at all. They are all great powerful fighters. Oh what have I made happen?" said Dhrutaras-Raja in woe and sorrow.

All young and old fighters waited for the sound of the conch-shell to blow eager to battle and make their passions rightfully theirs. Arjun had Krishna as his charioteer holding in arm four white steeds. The only other fighters in the battle with chariots were his brothers, Duryodh, Bhsima and Drone.

No chariot was like Krishna's. The chariot was donated from the far ends of space by the fire god, *Agni*. The chariot harnessed fire and if sparked by Krishna could not only end the battle in the blink of an eye but also of all life of Northern India to the Himalayas. There was a red flag on His chariot of demigod *Hanuman-Ji*, which *Lord Vishnu* had sent to Himself when as *Lord Rama*. The flag symbolised the expression, 'survival of the fittest and most humble.'

Shree Krishna blew His conch-shell named, '*Pancajanya*,' and as He did the hearts of opposition shattered.

Arjun then blew his conch-shell named '*Devadatta*,' and then Bheem blew on his conch-shell, '*Paundra*.' The melody of rhythm represented different values of life and that of transcendental victory. The *Kuru-kestra* blew on their conch-shells but nothing of comparison to the *Dharma-ksetra*.

"O Bringing of Salvation, move the chariot between the armies so I can address the many of this unwanted war," said Arjun acting infallible to Krishna.

Krishna moved the mighty chariot to the centre of the battlefront of the armies. For Arjun to be successful the Lord had to listen to Arjun as Arjun was listening to Him. Arjun saw the candidates that were eager to please evil and he raised his right hand and blessed the ones asleep and ignorant, a form known as *Gudakesa*. Krishna moved the chariot back to the line of the His disciples. Krishna felt His Supersoul with Arjun and joked upon that moment of life, "One for all and all for One!"

Arjun became overwhelmed with passion as he became mixed minded in what was about to happen. Was this so for love or for hate? And does that mean he is to love hate or hate love? He looked over at his relatives with their material culture and became compassionate about their fighting spirit. Arjun went weak in the knees and his mouth dried, palms became sweaty, his body trembled, and his bow (*Gandiva*) slipped away from his grip. He was experiencing the flight or fight reaction of the sympathetic nervous system. The fear of the loss of life struck him hard especially that he was the one to take lives. Arjun became unable to stand and fell into his chariot.

"O My mighty armed warrior, son of Pandu, be with My consciousness and thus forgetful of desire or sorrow, forget self-interest and ways of lamentations," instructed Krishna.

"What good will any of this do?!" Arjun replied in frustration. "Our powerful spiritual men and culture would become overturned on itself far from now nonetheless and can I not just excuse the miscreants and teachers of evil practices? One bad seed will just go ahead and plant another."

Krishna looked at him, "The decision to finish is a must. There was a beginning, middle and now you must make an end for a new beginning to occur. This makes satisfaction in opulence. Many of the people are sleeping and even if not they are not afraid of My raft. I cannot show My raft in all its might but I can deliver to you to express My aspirations to them."

Arjun looked back at Krishna, "O Lord of Mercy, how can I be happy killing my kinsmen?"

"My brother Arjun, there is six kinds of aggressors and our opposition exhibit all these signs of aggression. They who are poison givers, they who would set fire to homes, they who would attack with deadly weapons, they who plunder riches, they who would occupy your home, and they who would occupy other lands. They have already degraded your fiancé Drupati so it's not too far that they'll do worse. Therefore do not be saintliness, you are *ksatriyas* and these aggressors must naturally be killed. Once the conch-shell is blown again the future will be set for good and better and not balance of good and bad."

Arjun got back up on his feet, "I do not see how killing relatives would be sinless. Tell me how?"

"With Me you are sin-free and in My name you have salvation if your devotion rests fully in My abode. And let me say, a destruction of a dynasty would occur from senior members of a family. Losing respect of elders as that from Dhrutaras, Gandha-Rani, Bhisma, Drone and kinsmen has led the younger generations to material confusion and not spiritual realisation, thus slaying seniors is not considered if not like yours but as yours has led to irreligion there is no other way."

Krishna continued, "*Varnasrama* is when there is a good population of spiritual growth with community and society. Both children and women are protected by elder members of family, this is *varnasrama-dharma*. Not following this faith can lead to flooding of children, war and pestilence; which we have right in front of us. The women who follow those men are untrustworthy and are as pests who back fire on the men to become victims of abuse. Unwanted populations grow and corrupt families, traditions and dissolve the generations of ancestry. When there's irreligion women become polluted which leads to degradation of womanhood. They have unwanted progeny, chastity, and unfaithfulness. They are not very intelligent, not trustworthy and thus the females are mislead to adultery. Without *sanatana-dharma* or *varnasrama-dharma* there would only be chaos," declared Krishna.

"Arjun has become extremely soft in the midst of what was asked of him," said Sanjaya to Dhrutaras-Raja. "He has laid down his arms, bow and arrows and overwhelmed with grief. He is fit for devotional service to Shree Krishna, but as a *ksatriyas* he is becoming hard heartened not to have intention for killing. He also cannot go against his own passion for Krishna and that of Krishna's goodness. Arjun is in his chariot weeping."

Shree Krishna lifted His conch-shell once again and placed on His lips. Krishna blew again. The sound roared the land and the sky. The mercenaries and the soldiers began attacking in full force. The fight took the length of a whole day but in spiritual transcendental time the bloodbath lasted generations with hundreds of thousands being slain and murdered. Every person of every generation died in the fight for life, love and peace. Every person died in the war expect for six, the Pandav Brothers and the Lord. Furthermore every person that died in the great fight was liberated upon death and gained salvation by the Supreme Lord.

Transcendence to Earth

Chapter 35

The history of when the original fight between the Pandav Brothers for power to the people and Kuru Dynasty for power to self was in the time of the Bhagavad-Gita. The sources of information that constructed the book came from Scriptures that were writings by Arjuna Pandav. For the days more close to the present the language was found in Sanskrit translated to Gujarati to Hindi and then to English. Obviously debates had been lost in translation and of course lost through generations so Arjun asked Krishna, 'how the transcendental knowledge could pass through time to be delivered to him on the frontline of war?'

The science of the Bhagavad-Gita was passed through succession of saintly kings meaning that the true effects of the Gita could only be received by godly men. No demoniac person would be able to reap the full benefits of the knowledge and only those that wished no harm would acquire its mystic wisdom. Five thousand years into the future through disciplinic succession (*parampara*) the ancient secrets of relationship of devotees (*sadhus*) and demons (*duskriti*) as friends and foe came from the sun of the galaxy's solar system.

Because the sun was shining prior to the times *Lord Vishnu* had stepped on Earth in His avatar forms He had given imperishable amounts of *yoga* to the sun god, *Vivasvan*. The sun controlled all planets in the solar system and the Supreme Godhead had given the power of *yoga* to the star. *Viviasvan*, then had given the power to the father of mankind, *Manu*, and thus started the founding of the Raghu Dynasty in the era of *Lord Ramacandra* (avatar of *Lord Vishnu*), and then forward to *Sri Krsna* and forward still to Shree Krishna. God gave power to the sun and that sun gave power to life in form of *ksatriyas* and made them superhuman as *Vivasvan*. Believe that the sun gave life to Earth which gave life to animals and plants which gave life to humans which then asked why? Thus the Supreme Godhead within the sun always watching over Earth gave the transcendental knowledge to saints who then gave to mankind.

Krishna and Arjun had taken many births prior to this one and from the births prior to the ancient days of the Bhagavad-Gita. Nature (*prakati*) brought about the return of Krishna as unborn in every millennium. If nature is not valued and taken care of either there will be another Krishna coming in the next millennium or that there would not be a millennium for mankind. Furthermore if this was so, the Lord would remain on Earth and will not come and go like night and day. As without man there is still Earth as Earth's life is not that of only man. But whenever and wherever there is a fall of religion practice or irreligion the Lord shall descend or ascend again. God would manifest Himself as He is to bring His eternal existence to view.

The birth of Krishna in the New Age of digital transformation was to bring the Lord through the growth of beings under the sun to accustom to life as time showed. He would not act truly to one religion but would define religious order. Also when the Supreme Godhead was to come He did not have to come from a particular nation of soil. He did not have to be that of Indian origin or any other. The Supreme Conscious of Krishna ordained everything so would come to a land that ordained all others. He would come again and again as an avatar of God to suit the people in form, appearance and intelligence.

Krishna Consciousness can come in many ways however to the chosen soul would come as a disguise even to the body the soul ordained. The consciousness to be passed onto mankind from Krishna and Shankar was given to Arjun as his soul could manifest and non-manifest moments proportional to the time he occupied.

Predictions of the avatar to come were considered but particular interests in culture of *Sankirtana* was to be a broadcast to the world that the avatar of The Light will not come to destroy demons but deliver them through mercy. They that know (*brahmajyoti*) the transcendental activities and appearance of the Supreme Lord through continuous births would gain liberation to Krishna's Abode upon dying. For the avatar to come in the era for Arjun, the world and everyone in the world would be liberated for all time to come thereafter. There would be no stopping the force of spirit even after the soul returned back to *Krsnaloka* or *Goloka Vrndavan*.

Free from attachment of dark elements and knowledge into the good side through grace of the black universe love reaches Heaven. Reaching Heaven is easier said than done as to attain the spiritual world one must release material attachment especially with material that one has fundamental recognition. Upon one's path or once accomplished an individual is steady, self-realised, likes hearing about Shree Krishna, and their real love for God would then be known as *prema.*

All worshippers of any religion are all trying to reach the 'Supreme Personality of Godhead.' Foolish people or powerful men that want more fruitative desires of material world would worship demigods, but even demigods such as *Brahma Dev* and *Baba Shiva* are on path to reach *Sri Krsna*, *Narayan*, *Lord Vishnu* as the Almighty Lord. People that do not worship God and worship another deity will achieve for temporary things including love and peace. Thus the Supreme Godhead is for granting mercy and eternal bliss as He would not be able to give anything more, but if was to give more than that would be His raft either on self or as teaching to others. Hence atheists or people that have lost their path in worshipping the Lord through trouble times and tribulations are also given mercy of liberation.

The three modes of nature are given to the four classes of human society embed as *brahamanas* as goodness, *ksatriyas* as passion, *vaisyas* as mix, and *sudras* as ignorance. At that one moment in life that anyone gains enlightenment on agreeing to Shree Krishna they would gain His intelligence and grace.

Time had once wrote and observed that to have no attachment one would gain heavenly happiness, however through enlightenment of intelligence and experience of time they would gain happiness but wouldn't be of heavenly composition. Action, inaction and forbidden action all should be considered with Krishna Consciousness to reach happiness that too can be practiced on Earth to ensure The Life in Heaven.

Smart men would have self-realisation that is free from *karma* (reaction of work, [not to be mistaken for *kama* which is a belief in fate]), and would be pleased in eternal truth with Krishna Consciousness. Therefore as attachment the devotees would suit life into gaining perfect knowledge (*jnana*) voluntarily or best involuntarily.

A smart mind works intelligence altogether without sinful reactions. They do not think good or bad motive but that of real independence as a machine works with oil, the body will work with the mind. For many others the effects of passion and ignorance would take over which they would think of acts of discrimination or unfairness, but if they could be taught or be brought to the light of cause and effect then mode of goodness would become visible. One that is not jealous and definitely not envious of material emotions and objects would never be stuck in problems but enjoy every moment of life even the ones that they do not agree with. For example a devotee of Krishna would go to many mandirs for adventure and tourism but only pray to Supreme God. Living with this awareness grants salvation.

Practices of many *yogis* offer fire sacrifices of grain, rice, oil, twigs, and other fine prepared materials of a household to allow greater transcendental life. Any sacrifice in the name of understanding, liberation, and bond to Krishna Consciousness is considered as a good *yagna*. Donating money for good charities is also a *yagna* and is of importance to gain salvation. In simple terms one may need to let go of something in order to gain something else. A father of a household may allow sense gratification for his children upon luxuries of all sorts including exploring lust and love so later in life they would achieve a higher order of life with the Lord. *Yogis* would perform different charity sacrifices and *yoga* systems to overcome troublesome times and austrisities to advance in transcendence.

Performers who know value of sacrifice become free from sin. They would taste the nectar of sacrifice and they then would live towards *Santana* with the spiritual sky. They would have happy, opulent lives with the Eternal Kingdom of God. This being said one would see that to live happily on this planet a life should have a form of sacrifice, e.g. marriage, food, milk, career, and/or other forms of particular usual habits. Making *yagna* relieves all problems.

As for the physical acts of *yoga* breathing is the most important factor. *Apnana* is air that goes downward and *prana* is air that goes upward. *Pranayama-yoga* is breathing until currents are neutralised into equilibrium (*puraka*), where offering exhaled air into the inhaled breath is known as *recaka*. *Kumbhaka-yoga* is when both air currents are completely stopped. Practicing this one can prolong perfection of life.

Absolute means that one plus one is equal to one and that one minus one is also equal to one. A self-realised person will never fall again into illusion (*maya*). They would have learnt from a bona fide spiritual master and would receive automatically perfection of knowledge by surrendering to them. The knowledge gained can burn out misery as a fire. The knowledge would be sublime and liberating but the soul would only enlighten to this if the person surrenders to the teacher for good and for worse. The faithful person would thus act as a *brahmani* and then to *sadhu* (devotee) of Shree Krishna (*Sri Krsna*). An example of the faithful would be the *Acaryas*. On the opposite bank of the canyon of knowledge the faithless and ignorant would enter the next world in unhappiness.

Back to the land and sky of judgement, "O son of Bharata, armed with *yoga* stand and fight! You have *sanatana-yoga* (eternal activities of body), resulting to sacrifice of material possessions and accumulator of knowledge to one, stand and fight!" said Krishna to Arjun. "Material not sacrificed for spirit of peace remains material, and so should be sacrificed in spiritual note to gain a perfect sacrifice. I have sacrificed to demigods, I have sacrificed to *brahman*, I have sacrificed in celibacy, and I have sacrificed in penance. So as when this day's sun rises so should you rise and sacrifice your family to gain your kingdom!"

Show You're Universe

Chapter 36

Dusk had come upon the land of Kuruksetra and bodies were piling up on the land. Several holds of gunshots, many sounds of screams and lots of sights of blood pooling out of bodies covered the circumference of Arjun's chariot. Arjun had stopped thinking too hard about what would become of all this and instead shielded the fighters from killing each other too fast. Not only did he protect his own disciples but moved back Duryodh's from becoming easy targets for his great warriors. As he saw the sun had no more than an hour left on the day of sacrifices he turned to his charioteer and pleaded Him to reveal Himself.

"O Mighty Lord, I do not go against Your love but I need to know for sure if I am doing right," said Arjun to Krishna. "I need to see You as God. I need to know what You know. I need to see what You see."

"O son of Pandu, My universal form is not easy for you to understand let alone see. I know you are in despair even so your soul has reached that of Super-soul. But even if you put down your arms My will will be done," replied Krishna. "I'll show you what you seek, but know that even the demigods have desire to see My universal form and yet have not."

"Krishna, lotus-eye eternal bliss I must know what the outcome of destroying my loved ones are?" asked Arjun adamantly.

"As night is about to approach Brother Arjun, I shall let you know that what you see and hear are words for your grace and your benefit, whereas this war and everything happening from here is for My eternal grace," returned Krishna in a peaceful but yet stern tone. "My cosmic form is much more than a mere mortal being can comprehend. The appearance and disappearance of material manifestations that neither your strength nor mental ability can comprehend, as human eyes are not accustomed to see My Light. But yet I will grant you the ability to see so you can claim what you'll see to the people of tomorrow," Krishna paused for a while, "O son of Pandav-Raja, My inconceivable power, *Yogesvara*!"

And as Krishna had said this Arjun from his chariot looked up and was shown hundreds of forms of manifestated and non-manifested realities of time. He was shown eternal time in moments of time. He heard and saw things that were of long ago, far away, and yet to come. He saw the whole universe as one whereas a scientist would only have been able to see parts at a time. Krishna gave Arjun divine sight to see a particular sequence of time. He saw many mouths, eyes, weapons, and ornaments of wondrous brilliance, unlimited and all-expanding forms of potent energies from Krishna.

From the middle of the battlefield Arjun was given sight to see planets of different sizes, materials, gases, orbits, all in harmony with each other. He saw Krishna was omnipresent with no beginning, middle or end. Even though He was difficult to see with all the light shining from objects, ornaments, suns, rainbows, and life Arjun looked in sober calmness. From Krishna all demigods could be seen entering Him. They had their hands folded and sang in *Vedic* literature, 'All Peace!'

Whereas what he saw in wonder Arjun was also given sight to see the rotten form of man as they faced The Light. The Lord had blazing deathlike faces with awful teeth in all directions where he saw soldiers from both sides of Kuruksetra battle entering and leaving the Lord's mouth with some being smashed by His teeth. Some people were seen as flies flying at full speed to the many mouths of God and they were calling for God. At the sight and sound of this Arjun became terrified upon measure and Krishna transformed back into a human being.

Arjun folded his hands together and bowed to give obeisances, "You are the maintainer of eternal religion, *Hare Krishna! Hare Krishna! Hare Krishna! Hare Krishna!* You spread over the skies, planets and all space in between. All Your worlds are numb without You and yet You are present. O Lord, all lords and demigods behold Your wonder. Please be gracious to me. You have wondrous and terrible forms. You turn the ones who work and die for You into rivers and oceans of gold that stretch throughout You as You are the universe. *Hare Krishna! Hare Krishna!* O Lord be gracious, who are You? What's Your mission?"

"O Kuntia's son, only Pandav's survive this battle whether you fight or not. All people in this battle will be slain on either side for the ruling of Supreme Truth. Both the devoted into self and devoted for others will become neutral as of My nature. Everyone is already put to death by My arrangement. Each individual should have a balance of love for self and for others. They that have more for self should provide for others, but then others should provide for self and others beyond that. So prepare to fight and win glory to enjoy a flourishing kingdom!" replied Krishna. "So you are to fight for credit to your devotees and the survival for existence!"

Arjun still with his hands folded looked around at his four corners for a brief moment to confirm what was illusive and what reality was.

He bowed again by Krishna, "O Lord, O Limitless One, all living and deceased recite in You and give You obeisance. You are all causes, transcendental and of material manifestations. You are everything!"

Arjun's love of ecstasy for Krishna moved around the Lord giving Him obeisance from every angle. And then Arjun stood strong and posed in full might for the Almighty.

With the pose that Arjun exhibited the Lord couldn't help but laugh. Arjun gained the power of knowledge knowing that Shree Krishna's power was immeasurable power. Arjun posed for some time to allow the Lord grant his power to the three worlds that the Lord's power excels over in consciousness. Arjun stood in pose worshipping Krishna for His tolerance and that tolerance for mercy. So he stood longer still as the battle carried around them as he would be forgiven.

Arjun then asked, "Shree Krishna, O Lord, I have been raised with hands folded to Your form as *Lord Narayan*. May I see Your form as He?"

Before Arjun could finish his sentence Krishna showed Himself with four hands in the wonderful universe as that of *Lord Narayan*. He resembles Himself as *Lord Vishnu* and as the Super-soul in every living heart. He saw the four corner universe and in each hand an object; lotus flower (love), conch-shell (Om), spinning disc (peace), and club (strength). Arjun then came apart of *Srimad-Bhagavatum*, that knowing Krishna is free from all material existence and will see Him in young form to the very end of days.

Krishna, the 'Supreme Personality of Godhead' replied, "My dear Arjun, never has this internal potency of Mine been revealed in the material world. No one before you has seen this primal, unlimited form full of glaring effulgence. O best of Bharata warriors no one has seen this form! My cosmic impersonal form of body and universe is completely spiritual, full of bliss and eternal in manifest and non-manifest forms."

Arjun was then given sight of The Light in His fundamental eternal form as the Ocean of Milk. A fluid movement of a living liquid cosmic form that was embedded into everything he had saw and heard before. The existence of Shree Krishna in universal form and that of the Ocean of Milk was stitched so well with each other that he came to a conclusive decision on what to do. Now Arjun had no fear in the face of God.

He picked up his bow *Gandiva* and fit an arrow on. He moved the bow and arrow to lie parallel to the middle of his face. He closed his eyes and prayed to the Supreme Lord. He aimed the arrow towards his cousin brother Duryodh. He pulled back the string to build a force of potential energy in the string of the bow to the arrow. He held the position to maximise the torque on the string. He opened his eyes, looked at his target and released the hold. The potential energy was transferred to kinetic energy in the arrow as God flew over a hundred feet and struck Duryodh through the chest. His heart was pierced as the arrow broke out of his back to see the last light of the day.

Duroydh paused in his moment to feel his heart stop beating. Duroydh saw Arjun with his bow still in aim. Duroydh fell to his knees eye level with Krishna and with his last breath said, "Jai Shree Krishna!"

"O my king Dhrutaras, Krishna has shown His 'Supreme Personality of Godhead' to Arjun. Through the graces placed on me by my descendents of Vyasa, a phenomenon was spoken off that had the radiance of a thousand suns. After Arjun had been shown the universal form of the Almighty, he prayed in wonder with hands folded over and over again," spoke Sanjaya to Dhrutaras-Raja. "He has also seen the four armed and two armed form of *Lord Vishnu*, that only one with eyes smeared with the ointment of love can see that beautiful form of Supreme Godhead."

Dhrutaras-Raja replied, "What happened next?"

"He picked his bow my Lord, and your son Duryodh is no more," concluded Sanjaya.

Dhrutaras-Raja closed his eyes and tears ran down his face. The battle was over. The balance of passion was reset. The kingdom of his was no more. The slate was wiped clean. Dhrutaras' status and presence in the Iron Age disassembled. His heart stopped. The time for the Eternal Golden Age had begun.

Demigods, devotees, priests, kings, rulers and common-folk desire to see God in Heavenly form. Only angels and those trusted upon by *Sri Krsna* from the beginning of time would have witnessed what the entirety of God had to offer. Divine vision could not be seen by studying *Vedas* nor undergoing series of practices and penances, neither by charity or worship. Not by any means can one see the Lord as such. Practice into Krishna Consciousness is around the clock, that is given by Krishna rather than the link the other way around. One with undivided devotional service can enter His mysterious ways.

The restructure of energy was re-crafted to enjoy life to the fullest and give thanks to life, to avoid raptures, regret and revenge, and to smile in the face of danger. Transferring energy to Krishna activities is known as *Krshna-karma* and can potentially make thousands and thousands of dollars; and so to thus work exponentially for Shree Krishna on land, fields, water and sky. As a *tulasi* leaf is satisfied with water so is working for Krishna as the highest of abodes to heavenly planets. A pure devotee would not want Krishna's salvation to the highest planet, *Goloka Vrndavan* but instead serve Krishna wherever He may be. A pure devotee is as steady as the sun and friendly to everyone.

Christ is a favourite form of Supreme God's consciousness never mind in what forms or names that awareness was given. Thus a friendly living being would surely go to the Lord providing that they are not forgetful of their eternal relationship with God. Arjun's devotional services without fruitative activities and mental speculation were not enough to reach him to the highest planets, but to assist Krishna to bring the battle to hand for new beginnings surely did.

All or One Renunciation

Chapter 37

The dust had settled and the blood had dried on the grounds of the great battle. The dead were taken away for cremation and spreading of ashes in River Ganges. The living of which were only six went to meditate in the foothills of the Himalayas. The six were accompanied by their loved ones. The six were the Pandav Brothers and Krishna. Their loved ones were Kunti-Ma, Drupati, Rukmani, and the wives of Yudistra, Bheem, Sahadev, and Nakul. The land where they went to meditate was beside Christ Church, Shimla, Himachal Pradesh. The weather was colder at that altitude and the land was covered in snow.

Time had come to forget about all that had happened. For the Bharata Dynasty from the death of their father and the adoption by their uncle, to the upbringing of the brothers and the abandonment of them with their mother, to Arjun leaving for London and arriving back with Krishna, to the degrading of Drupati and the mockery of Duryodh, to the beginning and to the end of battle the time had come to forget about all that. To perfect the form of renunciation was now on the horizon. Delivery of all the feelings one would not wish to repent, one would not wish to pass to children, and one would not wish to ever speak of again was to be given back to the source of all things. The time had come to raise head's high and give everything back to The Light. Time had come for the mercy of the Lord to be granted in providing freedom from entanglement and attachment.

The party of thirteen entered Christ Church after leaving their belongings in a nearby villa. The time was late afternoon with not many people within the church. The party split themselves in four and sat on two rows either side of the aisle. There was plenty of space to move around the inner nave that to say they had Christ Church all to themselves.

Drupati, Rani-Rukmani and Kunti-Ma along with the other women went to the altar to light candles. Krishna and the Pandav Brothers made space for them to come back. The women arrived back to the area of their spouses but sat in a comfortable random order around Krishna standing in center from the altar and them in the middle of the aisle.

"One who thinks of God within themselves is best," began saying Krishna. "To kill the demon of doubt by placing God in one's heart is a step in the right direction."

"O Krishna, Father of Love, how are we to forget all that has happened? What we do defines who we are, makes us stronger, wiser and more in devotion. Why and how are we to forget that?" asked Arjun.

Krishna prowled a few steps left and right in the middle of the aisle and between the seating on both sides. He replied, "My dear Brother Arjun, this falls onto two aspects of thought: the renounced order which is giving up activities based on material desire and renunciation which is giving up the results of activities. The fine print reads that the outcome could be positive or negative but still the thought is given up. As a conclusive scenario the mind will become tired of thinking woe and sorrow just as the mind forgets smiles and good deeds also. Utmost spiritual knowledge will not be removed with the material memory."

"O Lord Krishna, would I not just consider forgetting as a sacrifice and thus be done with it by a sorry, I love you?" asked the youngest brother Nakul.

"Yes, Brother Nakul. Maintaining charity shame to say that, sorry, I love you too is a sacrifice the human tongue has to speak even though the heart does not feel so. Deep down as I am Super-soul I would say that to all of you who had to go through this for Me, and that I said I truly mean. Hence one saying to another without devotion doesn't mean that they don't deserve to at least hear those words coming from another. As you all have been charity to Supreme Godhead, I sacrifice My love onto you."

Nakul placed his hands together in obeisance and received Krishna's love by Him raising His palm to Nakul.

"Lord O Krishna, going back to spiritual plane; this should that not be stopped, and so follow into Krishna Consciousness, as prescribed duties as such should not be renounced, is that correct?" asked Yudistra, the eldest brother.

"Yes, Brother Yudistra. As leaving everything one's mind becomes vacant and to keep the mind occupied is a very important thing as the mind is a terrible thing to waste. So keep in mind spiritual source to accumulate the fruits of one's labour."

"Namaste Krishna," said Yudistra.

"With Krishna Consciousness and labour in mind, one should make money regardless of fruitative activities, but to be aware that with passion of money and not passion of work one would fall into a miserable life. Renounce and renunciation of activities that will cause this feeling should be taken and thus to announce that fruitative renunciation is goodness. Acting transcendentally either working for a low income or a high one is the best means forward to not being bothered about duty but to living life," spoke Krishna.

"Sounds like to me that the renounce either being good or bad leaves auspicious and inauspicious work which leads to no doubts about work and life going forward," said Kunti-Ma.

"Ma Kunti that's true! To enjoy work and not to fear letting go for the Lord," complimented Krishna to Kunti-Ma.

Rukmani looked over at Krishna and challenged Him by saying, "That's easier said than done. Renouncing the fruits of my work would feel like I had no reward, I had no purpose. Can you renounce the fruits of Your work, my love? Can you renounce us?"

"O apple of My eye, to not renounce is threefold. One may have desirability, undesirability and a mixed effect of renouncing one's fruit. The renounced life can have no effect, can be made to suffer or can be made to enjoy. Whoever is with Me cannot be renounced either before death or after death. Imagine you are in amongst your activities without thought of Me, but just a second thought would lift you to pure transcendence, that is what is impossible to renounce. The Super-soul's thought is always with one with Krishna Consciousness even if one's thought has been distracted away. Imagine if the bond was not as such, would any work be done?"

The women laughed as they imagined being in Krishna's transcendental bliss for eternity without mercy and enjoyed that feeling. The men laughed also as they thought that how delightful life would be if there were no accumulations of work. But the reality was that work had to be done on Earth as in Heaven so people had comfort to grow and worship more. Just as an animal (a hamster, a dog, a fish, a bird, an elephant), has to work for shelter and food to give rise to offspring so does mankind to live in love and peace.

"Some people see God as money, some people see God as bodily demands. Sleeping, defending, eating, and mating all without Krishna Consciousness leads into darkness which leads to mental speculation which thus turns to personal passion of love or hatred. Renunciation of this is a mode of goodness," Krishna enlightened.

Bheem suddenly stood and said, "O Lord of Mercy, I have heard of this. I have felt this. This is a feeling of performing in passion. There was nothing I wanted more than to strike our perpetrators down and I did feel to give into my desire and gratify that. The passion of this fruit to have them killed is what drove me for many years but for love of my family I was in fear for their safety. Thank You Lord for my blessings, thank You Lord for showing me all's possible by You."

Krishna raised His right most working palm and praised Bheem, "Even the passion of Christ as Jesus that Christians follow would lead or stay in despair. The passion to be loved and to give love would be fragile in most cases as well there are many people in the world with many mixed sets of emotions and occurrences. Therefore as the Holy Spirit can say 'Jesus is Lord', the Spirit as *Bhagavan* say's to glorify Jesus Christ, as he was said to be Son of God, and many miss that with Son comes Father, and thus fall onto self passion of Christ without Father. Believers would understand that I as Lord would be more so, so amen."

All the people that heard Krishna say 'amen' in church returned in love of mind and sound, "Amen."

"Praise your soul," Krishna said aloud.

Sahadev rose and asked, "O Father, why can I not control my emotions and consciousness when around the weak, feeble, less intelligent, slow paced, basically they that don't give normal responses which slows down my train of thought?"

Krishna laughed, "Welcome to My world. O Brother Sahedev," and continued to chuckle a little more. "I know what you mean. The more intelligent one is feels isolated. You have spoken like a great king Sahadev. The first element is to understand that for that person or persons in question there is no point on feeling sorry for oneself. Both the emotion should be renounced, and also to forgive the person as renunciation. The mode of ignorance works better than the mode of passion in this case. It's better to ignore the person that effects one's mental ability, however if you can act in mode of goodness and take the long way of explanations then by all means do so. But if you cannot do not get upset at them or yourself and take a step forward, look at the sky above and fall back into transcendence. Hurting those people is more abuse than ignorance as they don't realise that their ignorance has hurt you. These people are illusive and can only comprehend so much. There would be need for huge sacrifices for those minds and souls to reach the higher planets. Thus work without acknowledgement of reward, success or failure in the mode of goodness. Place distress in the middle of happiness and allow the distress to be squashed."

"Thanks Lord. I had been trying to pin the root of their negligence or reason for misunderstanding. Was reason due to their faith, their education, their culture, their experiences, their baptisms, their sacrifices? And so on and so on. But when truth came down to Earth each person I encountered being un-theoretical, I found to just be a nuisance for my spirit. That's when I just said to myself, that everyone is different and I am different from them also. Still I would not mind a common ground and a laugh to share," admitted Sahadev.

"My dear Sahadev, one person's intellect and humour can be vastly different from another's. If I was to say to an English man, 'One can't teach an old dog new tricks,' they would most likely reply, 'like one can't teach the young to be civil.' And if I was to say the same thing to an Indian man, he may return with anger on why I called him old and a dog, do you see?" Krishna explained. "They that have not loved or had real love from others would fall to laziness, sleep and illusion as a mode of ignorance. Whereas goodness is first like a narcotic and then the nectar comes. The transcendence is the real nectar and thus to have passion for that goodness. Happiness would follow in union thereafter."

The father of Christ Church walked down the aisle and brushed by Krishna. He looked over at Krishna and His party and nodded with a smile. One could see that this man had self-control, peacefulness, austerity, purity, tolerance, honesty and satisfaction for life. He was a *brahamanas* in his work system of people. Full of heroism, power, resourcefulness, courageous, generous and with leadership that didn't show without that smile which one would otherwise think he was *ksatriyas*. The father's external energy equaled his internal energy; which was all pervading and engaged in Supreme Godhead which allowed him to gain the highest perfection from Father.

"O Krishna, my lover's brother," spoke Drupati. "Seems to me that with every endeavour is covered by some fault or some selfish act of Yours. I know You are Lord but I cannot accept that with something that is well there has to be some fault. Please enlighten me."

"O Drupati, my brother's lover," returned Krishna, "Yes, there is no such thing as a selfless good deed. We are all trying to get something good out of something with the expense of something else. This is honestly how many things are done. For instance why does one have to go to war or have to suffer in some way to find the true meaning of deep love? The only answer falls to sacrifice in order to gain and understand perfection. Imagine if one could just acquire love for everyone and all people can do that readily. Would love be of real value? One true scholar can satisfy his time to work by smoking tobacco; on one hand people need his wisdom and on the other he is suffering to provide them with such. Once the heart becomes in action to pursue a life to look to the future wellbeing of family and mankind, then through enlightened consciousness the faults are forgiven. For goodness they are given freedom from self-reaction which eventually leads to removal of the particular fault. Hence they are said to be pardoned."

"That makes sense. Thanks," Drupati replied. "I shall pardon myself into thinking otherwise."

Krishna went to light a candle and returned, "O family of Pandav, learn from Me the *Brahma-Bhuta* stage of self-realisation with purified intelligence. The person of intelligence is not falsely proud. Their intellect flows and is not affected or given up by objects and people of self-gratification. They eat as they like, they control body, mind and spirit, they control anger and find inner peace free from material conception of life, they control power of speech and strive to satisfy others over self-desires. They are a special group of people that are becoming more that live and love life as given, but also aim to reach for the skies and too bring everyone along their path with them. There are many men and women that desire this so see a person at this stage one should love them most dearly. The light of *Brahma Dev* desires nothing of laments or desires. They are joyful and live for Supreme Truth from Myself and from their own practices."

Kunti-Ma went to sit beside Arjun, "O Lord, I am bewildered from Your teaching and understanding. You answer straight for understanding, for purpose and for satisfaction from Your universal form. This liberation frees people from actions they would know nothing about. You free them from misconceptions. You free them from modes of darkness in form of ignorance influence from dreams, thoughts, actions, folklore and old wives' tales," she gave Arjun a kiss.

"O Kunti-Ma, thank you for your kind words. After all this was My civic duty," modestly replied Krishna. "A devotee of God or person searching for belonging lives for Life, and that Life being the eternal form of God. They are protected and imperishable who live a hundred percent value around the clock. With this mind they come to my mind of *Krshnaloka,* My Supreme Abode, full of knowledge and the secrets from the vast depths of eternal space. Their soul works for Supreme Godhead is protected and they would dwell and enjoy what all Heaven offers and space expands."

The human eye cannot look at sunlight for long periods of time however the eye of angels in Heaven can look at the source of light for eternity. Just as the realms of space and Heaven cannot be perceived by the human mind, the effects of after-life cannot be imagined. One cannot know everything about God otherwise God would not be God. So to surrender to Him is the most benefitting attribute a human mind can do for good or for worse. This thought of existence is considered as a 'polestar,' which is of a special planet in the Supreme Abode of the Lord for the faithful that dwell and are free from profanity.

The Supreme Godhead has living entity of magnitude amounts of energy that Sanjaya felt in the battle of passions which he shared to Dhrutaras. The energy was that of Krishna and Arjun as when spoke of together there was victory. The same feeling but in much less power is as when hair stands on end in times of pleasure, ecstasy, euphoria which exhibits one being thrilled at each moment.

The speech of Krishna's at Christ Church had come to a close. Night will surely come and day would surely follow. Perfection in knowledge of Krishna Consciousness, would assist one as having no reason to lie as a moralist. Absolute Truth in conjunction with Krishna's transcendental internal potency with cosmic material energy would make life memories visible and invisible when needs be. Thus as a rule of thumb, memories to be lost, forgotten, and given away are to be like the sunrays from the sun that shines in the name of Krishna as a normal forgivable occurence.

In Utmost Confidence

Chapter 38

Great sages had come and gone by for lives of the Bharata-Raja Dynasty, from the great King Bharata to his sons, to their sons and from there to their sons and daughters too. Once again a sage was to begin and was at Indira Gandhi International Airport, New Delhi, India. The Pandav Brothers with their partners were waiting for departures. Due to work, lifestyle, children, education, health, friends, and necessity the brothers were to bid farewell to each other and live their lives away from each other. This was not considered as a huge deal as in the twenty-first century communication was as easy as pressing or tapping a button on a keypad. This also wasn't a huge deal as travel was made much easier across diversity because of aviation equality and inclusion. Furthermore there were many roads that not just linked A to B, but A to Z and back over again.

Yudistra, Bheem, Arjun, Sahadev, and Nakul sat with their partners, their mother and Krishna and Rani-Rukmani, keeping an eye on gate numbers and boarding times. Krishna had given plenty of time for the Pandav Brothers and family to enjoy their moments together for the time being.

Yudistra and his partner were to settle in Sydney, Australia. Bheem, his partner and Kunti-Ma were to travel and settle in New York, United States. Arjun and Drupati were to go back to London, United Kingdom and pick things up where the left off. Sahadev and his partner were travelling to settle in Brazil, South America. Nakul with his partner was to settle off the coast of the Mediterranean in Tunisia, Africa. And Krishna and Rukmani who were going to settle close to Dwarka City in Vidyanagar, Gujarat, India.

There were smiles and laughter amongst the family in hopes of farewell, safe travel, beautiful lives, fellowship, and prays as brothers were to lighten lives in different continents. Krishna was not to travel far considering the travel for Bheem and Sahadev and so reserved His flights at the latest time available. An atmosphere of delight, anxiety, sadness, hunger and ecstasy for new beginnings were being experienced by each loved one as time ticked.

Krishna had a last most confidential knowledge to share. Intertwined with silent mundane moments over an eight hour hold He taught His beloved.

Adjusting His clothes and tightening His posture Krishna began to say, "O Arjun and devotees, those in higher level are always in conscious of Almighty Life. They are in conscious of life as you see around you. You can see the four corners of the ceiling that surrounds us and you are well secure in the environment. With this not only can you protect yourselves but also of those around you. With this one can do all nine parts of pure devotional service; hearing, chanting, remembering, serving, worshipping, praying, obeying, maintaining friendships and surrendering everything. Those that are jealous or even worse envious of Me are fools and fools cannot critique Me rationally. I am to explain to you your future beneficiaries."

Krishna licked and sucked on His lotus lips, "Your individual expertise on interests are of many departments of internal and external education; mathematics, astronomy, politics, sociology, sciences, art, dance, sport, theology, business management, accounting, graphics, digital engineering, etc, etc. These are all important to the vital soul and would gain liberation in awareness of work with Krishna Consciousness after death or within a new life. Good seeds planted in heart and mind would allow enlightenment, knowledge, and wisdom to grow good human beings.

"Spiritual (black) and devotional (light) service is purest service and in itself is liberating. It is uncontaminated by material world (*tamas*) as transcendental (*uttama*). The advancement of spiritual life is not dependent on previous educations or qualifications, thus living as light and black or black and light dismisses all judgment. One becomes pure with the ability to thrive," Krishna exhaled and relaxed. "Examples of such folk are the *Acaryas*, who offer *tulasi* leaves to Me back home. *Sanat-Kumara* are great devotees who are happy and pure with whatever they offer the Lord with love, and I accept."

"*Mayavadi* philosophers say 'to become one with God, to become one with Life, to become one with One," added Rukmani.

Krishna continued, "*Karma-yoga, jnana-yoga, dhyana-yoga* and others as *sankara-yoga,* one should adopt into life with *bhakti-yoga.* People benefiting from *karma-yoga* and *jnana-yoga*, happen to soon loose devotion to Krishna Consciousness as due to gaining approval for fruitative desires and intelligent actions leads to an extent where one becomes to hide the truth from Myself. Thus this becomes the disbelief of serving. They say, 'I did it all on my own,' but you be honest in what you do, sing in the rain, and don't be a hypocrite to Supreme Life. I am that who paved the way and removed obstacles, i.e. one should smile and count their blessings. So keeping faith is very important in elevating to highest perfection of life, which I call *Krsna-bhakti*, otherwise souls from birth to death would come back to this material world or My many others to search for liberation again."

He paused allowing the beloved some time to think, "How are you all feeling?" Krishna asked moments later after enjoying His environment.

No one answered but looked at each other with a puzzled smile and relaxed back to look at Krishna waiting for Him to carry on.

"Okay then… As a king's power of diffusion of energy I am all pervading; I am in all My creation. My pastimes as Lord are in superior energy as My spiritual and material energy is My inferior energy. All My energy is spread over all creation and everything is resting in that energy. But everything created doesn't rest in Me, as the formation of parasites and pollution they are impediments, thus seen as when I cannot do what I like. As the sun I am known as *Govinda* (pleasure of all senses), where the immense properties of material energy rest. I am as the sky which is aloof; I am as the wind which is unseen but harbours energy. When creation, maintenance and annihilation exist it's My nature to harness that energy back to Me. Thus I forbid but if love is destroyed as *Brahma Dev* then the energy is recoiled to Me, thus Light will create again.

"My material energy lies in a casual Ocean of Milk, and from here *Lord Vishnu*'s incarnations are formed in cosmic order in the order of Himself. As *Maha-Vishnu* breathes out multiple universes, He can be as big as a galaxy or as small as an atom. I as Lord am movable and immovable and under My direction are things are annihilated or evolved. For example the link with a smell of a flower to the thought and relation to that smell is I. Similarly to waves that carry sound.

"Fools would not understand this *uttama*, thinking that I am a powerful man and nothing more. *Isvaras* are controllers of one who appears greater than others and the foolish who are poor in education would call Me, *Mudha*. As I am a master of energy of matter and with material body the foolish do not see My infinite and finite form. All My divine energy is protected by *Mahatma* where I exist as Ocean of Milk and inexhaustible as breath into the universe."

"Holy God, baby Jesus, Mother Mary and Joseph. Energy beyond comprehension," spoke out Sahadev. "I'm glad I see You, that's all I'm saying."

Krishna blinked a few times and changed His vision of sight to take a moment to look pass Sahadev and His company to continue, "On the day of My birth on Earth, as the appearance day of the Lord, known as *Ekadasi*; the forms of *Mahatma* were placed to *Acaryas*, *Sannyasi* and *Brahmacari* through either domestic affairs or conception to then grow to state any position in the world. These *mahatmas* were strategically placed by Myself to protect My movement on this Earth with time. Basically in impersonal or personal awareness I set powerful angels to assist Me to be here today."

"Holy Mother Mary, Joseph, Jesus and Holy Spirit. I knew You had some form of backup. I thought Shankar was Your back up. Or that You were his. Oh? Never mind... carry on..." said Nakul.

"mmMmm. There are levels of worshipping God," continued Krishna.

"One minute, one minute, one minute I need to go and get myself a drink and visit the men's" said Bheem. "O Krishna, just wait a little until I get back. I'm sure You'll be able to pass time," phrased Bheem.

"Me too, me too, me too, I need to go too," added Yudistra.

"Well if they're going then we may as well too," hinted Rani-Rukmani to the women. "We may take a longer as of powdering our nose."

"Or shopping at duty-free. You know don't want to miss that chance," frankly said Drupati.

Krishna looked over at Sahadev, Nakul and Arjun, "What about you guys?"

"mmMmm. As You've asked my Lord, I fancy going to stretch my legs," said Sahadev.

Nakul looked over at Krishna and Arjun, "Yep me too, I guess I'll leave you guys just for a moment, so you can spend some quality time together."

All the members of the group left Arjun and Krishna. Arjun then said, "I think we just got blanked."

"I don't know what to make of that but I have a feeling you're right," concurred Krishna. "Shall I proceed?"

"O *Bhagavan*, I thought you'd never ask," Arjun said amusing Krishna.

"So Arjun, my brother, there are three levels of worshipping; one as *Mahatma*, who consider self as God, and know only Godhead, they are impersonalist in behaviour of worship. Second non-*mahatma* who are of different cause but with belief in God, they tend to have distress in finance, their inquisitive and engaged in cultivation of knowledge. Third are those that see the universe as God are said to be in material entrapment. All are well and good as long as one sees that life is of supreme protection and shelter with ultimate goal to reach Me, as Shree Krishna," said Krishna without sounding too pounce. "O Arjun, give heat and send forth rain as you've seen My universal form, I am immortality!"

"O Krishna, my Lord, I have seen one living on heavenly minds can sense hundreds and thousands of times better than on this planet. Was this so seen from the time long ago?"

"The time long ago was studied by *brahamanas* who studied three *Vedas* known as *Sama*, *Yajur* and *Rig*, comprised the *Tri-Veda*. Those whom studied the *Vedas* and drank soma juice were in false worship. Once back from sense gratification of pleasure senses to return to reality i.e. detox, those practicing *Tri-Veda* underwent repeated lives and birth. Thus with worshipping life is best to just live spiritually in bliss and knowledge. Worshipping twenty-four-seven to Supreme Godhead are protected in the material world but to do through *yoga* for approaching Me effortlessly. My mercy will never allow a soul to come to material life and suffering. *Yoga* provides that protection."

Yudistra and Bheem arrived back.

"What did we miss? Tell me you didn't carry on without us," asked Bheem.

"O Bheem and elder brother, you two were always in our hearts," patronized Krishna. "But as you asked, I will continue. Worshipping false demigods is bad, as so is ignoring the existence of true ones as worshipping anyone of them is ultimately worshipping God. I am the full enjoyer and the master of sacrifices. Those that don't worship Me, fall down in this life or the next. Those who pray to demigods reach a demigod. Those who pray to ancestors reach an ancestor. Those who pray to ghosts and spirits reach the same being. And those that pray to Almighty Lord reach Me."

"That sounds an awful lot like, 'if one offers with love than accept it'," said Rani-Rukmani from behind Krishna.

Krishna looked over to see the women had items in their hands, "I don't know if this is a stereotypical image or that it just fits the picture right. So I'll like to say… that an intelligent civilised man or woman now should work for life and give to charity."

"Did you call me charity?" proclaimed Rani-Rukmani.

Krishna played on, "Whatever you've offered Me with love you'll be free from bondage of work. All results of inauspiciousness will therefore be liberated. Now all that is to see is *yukta*, your performance level."

"That's easy! I'll just sit next to You. Done!"

"She's under God's direction of eternal thinking. She's acting in *sannyasi,*" said Drupati.

Sahadev and Nakul approached the others.

"I was thinking about an action of abominable cost but with self-determination and engaged to Krishna I would become saintly. I would be considered a high devotee!" proclaimed Nakul. "When one falls down they get up again, rise and fall, but remain in Lord of Life. You shall purify me will You not?"

Krishna felt that Nakul was up to something and replied, "Even a great *yogi* as I can heal in hearts but for this time you can chant *Hare Krishna, Hare Rama.*"

"*Hare Krishna, Hare Krishna, Hare Hare. Hare Rama, Hare Rama, Hare Hare!*" and Nakul pulled out a CD from his bag, "Rock and Roll On Man! Sahadev!"

Sahadev rolled his eyes, "It was either that or he was to buy a guitar in the name of You, Krishna."

"I didn't know he played the guitar," said Arjun.

"He can't," simultaneously said Yudistra, Bheem, Sahadev and Nakul's wife.

Nakul all excited returned with, "Whatever bros, I love Krishna. As a devotee I'll never perish. I'll become righteous and in everlasting peace. I'll be one pure in nature. With His shelter I'll reach great heights. You'll hear my strings alongside Krishna's flute!"

Krishna nodded, "Well I guess that's all what I've been trying to teach. One should take Krishna Consciousness and make life perfect on this fragile planet. As there are two sides of the coin it's best to pick the better side no matter what the odds, as this would help others to decide what the better life is. Plus even though a coin has two sides, the coin has one purpose, to exchange goods. Hence be in Krishna Consciousness keeping your mind on Me and My teachings and you will all be fine tuned as a guitar playing as one with God," concluded Krishna.

Farewell, *bon-voyage, arrivederci, haista la vago, hasta manana, namaste, namashkar*, pat on the back, shake of the hand, blink of an eye, nod of the head, hug of the body, tear from the eye, wave of the hand, smile of the face, grace and power, Amen and Om, see you when the tides come in, stay in contact, bye bye, goodbye, keep in touch, love to see you again, go in peace, see you in the morning, come now let us leave, see you at dawn, last boarding calls, blow a kiss, a kiss on the forehead, a kiss on the hand, a kiss on the cheek, kisses on the cheeks, kiss on the eyes, kiss on the lips, kiss in the mouth, a kiss for good luck, a kiss goodbye, a last graceful touch before they left to go forward.

Shankar Gets Served

Chapter 39

In the midst of a cloudy London morning Shankar was at home watching BBC World News with a cup of tea and his laptop on surfing the net. Shankar preferred making the most out of the time he had leaving the remainder of time on listening to music, meditating and playing video games. His time outside of what he enjoyed was occupied by work, global news, social affairs and his new found love, Parvathi. Whilst he sat listening to the news and doing assignments his phone began to ring. He saw that his boss, Sukadev Gosvami, was calling.

"Hello, Sukadev," said Shankar.

"Morning Shankar, I hope I didn't wake you," replied Sukadev.

"Not at all Suk, you know me, I was up at the crack of dawn. How can I help?"

"The Indian foreign affairs diplomat, Maharaja Pariskit, wants to know how come there has been a massive influx of tourist into the State of Gujarat over the last couple of months? And I thought you would have something to do with that due to your affairs with a man called Krishna, that I know you have been supporting since His childhood."

"I'm not sure what you're quite getting at Suk, can you elaborate on tourists?"

"For the past month now, there has been a ten times increase of American citizens from the State of Delaware flying to Ahmadabad, Gujarat. They all have started to be screened and shows that most of the people have no relation to the State whatsoever, but are spending money in the State of Gujarat, from Anand to Dwarka," continued Sukadev.

"Well that sounds like a good thing."

"Of course it's an amazing thing! Maharaja Pariskit, called me to let me know of a huge development in Dwarka that happened in the name of Kishan Kanaiya, and that same Kishan Kanaiya has bought an apartment in Vidyanagar and married a woman from Anand. Looking into records of Non-Residents of India His birth name was Krishna Gokul from Delaware."

Shankar looked at the time, which was ten o'clock.

"Sounds like you are about to ask me for something nonetheless, Sukadev," enquired Shankar.

"I'm asking you on behalf of the Maharaja, to share the secret so he can be more at ease with the foreigners coming and going from his land. And as it's your name on the property deeds in Anand, and many names from Manhattan associated with the Yadu Dynasty, I think you owe both of us an explanation on this fantastic breakthrough in diplomacy."

Shankar laughed, "Oh I see. Nothing is kept a secret or data protected in the nation of India."

Sukadev gave a sigh of relief, "So you do know and you are familiar. Nothing in this magnitude can go without someone asking questions. Even beneficial work doesn't go amiss when it comes to diplomatic affairs between Britain and India. You should know that. Well I guess you did."

"I was waiting to hear what the turnout was from the third party, that's all. Seems like the turnout has gone much better than expected."

"Pariskit, want's to know Kishan Kanaiya."

Shankar cleared his throat, "Let me put it in a way that Maharaja Pariskit can understand. It all starts with 'what goes around comes around.' Let him know... have you got a pen?"

"Of course I have a pen. Actually I don't have a pen. I'll record this conversation, so make it good."

"Yes O Sukadev. It comes down to devotional service i.e. *bhakti*. The countries, cities, towns, villages, and times that Krishna has occupied by Himself and His brother, Balaram are all in devotion to Krishna, (Kishan Kanaiya). He is the people's person. He has become the 'go to guy' but let's not get too close guy. He is a God, as a matter of fact Sukadev, He is God."

"Are you having me on?"

"As far as I can imagine on the revenue the country has made and the levels of costs other countries have saved in the timeframe compared to that of a hundred years; I think it's best if you listen to what I have to say. Considering that you are asking, and you know me I'm not one to tell porkies."

"Go on I'm all ears. You're saying He is God."

"Sukadev let Pariksit know that *Lord Vishnu* has appeared as Krishna Gokul. He appears opulent for the worshippers who are mostly poverty stricken. Whereas worshippers of *Baba Shiva*, whom appears without a home but that of the Himalayan Tree the worshippers are opulent, i.e. the shift in money market from worshipping the Lord's spirit to worshipping the Lord directly has made One God, by devotion in one person, who's called Himself there Kishan Kanyaiya."

"Shankar are you saying this Krishna that you've supported over thirty years is now the reason for people freely protecting investments?"

Whilst nodding Shankar replied, "Yes. He has changed time and passions to preserve a better future."

"Holy God! The figures that I have seen would require some form a miraculous explanation. I know you work the Lord's spirit seriously as I was blown away by you when we first met. You have been an inspiration to me too. But how could a single young man have made so much difference in global affairs that no one can negatively critic Him?"

"I guess where there's a will there's a way. Krishna had done this step by step. There is much more to the depth of which His transcendence nature allows us to see. I understand the mastery of material energy, including that of women such as my wife Parvathi, who characterises herself as *Goddess Durga*, and that material energy of goodness, passion and ignorance does not reach spiritual sky though demigods but only ascends to *Lord Vishnu* by Shree Krishna. We ascend to His eternal abode of *Goloka Vrndavan* (also known as *Vaikuntha*) His heart, or *Krsnaloka*, His mind. And this is why a massive influx of tourism is happening I believe as people want to be closer to Him and nothing more. So in turn if people can feel opulent by going to India, they are making opulence to their surrounding home in the name of the Krishna," Shankar paused.

Sukadev didn't reply so Shankar continued, "You wanted to know how Sukadev, well this is the best explanation I can give you to pass on. Krishna exercised the mind of every individual subject to their own understanding until they all spoke amongst each other and simply set straight in their mind there is no pleasure than that above God's. Thus the material opulence left on *Baba Shiva*, as the Spirit of Life from planets to plants needed to be set free. To release the fight for material attachment would benefit the soul to be conditioned and that prize in itself is priceless. Thus that is what has happened, done and dusted."

Sukadev said, "Krishna's Supreme Godhead."

"People have achieved *nirguna*, eternal peace. These are early days but most people that were in fear are fearless, people without faith are faithful, people not with knowledge are knowledgeable, and people not wanting to throw away or lose anything are renouncing for charities and freeing from material entanglement. Krishna did this by setting parables in motion for all His devotees to understand and not that of singularity. He spoke these parables in public spaces with hope in His smile and love in His heart, thus changed life."

"Let me just stop you here. I need to process this. It sounds sweet on the tongue but feels bitter in the stomach."

"By all means one has to digest the fact and I will send you supporting evidence which you can read written by His devotee Arjun. Sleep on it for one night and then you can relay back to Pariksit, Sukadev."

"To declare the Lord as Supreme Godhead is Kishan Kanaiya has gained Him a great number of followers. His attraction of activities in life and position has freed many others to experience life in all its wonders. The Supreme Godhead as Krishna has made this happen. This somehow is making sense."

"Shree Krishna has said, 'That for Him to have an individual bound to one person then He would eliminate everything from that person's life until close to poverty-stricken and lost from entire family which than the person follows Krishna as a devotee.' That is the power of the Lord and of time and space equilibrium. What Krishna is also saying by this, is that He can take all from me too if He desires for me to be closer to Him."

"Ouch, that sounds harsh but also compelling if there was a guarantee for being back to Krishna's opulence. I guess though that would be so if the Lord was acting in His own accordance," replied Sukadev.

Shankar followed on, "Indeed, rightly philosophised. Why Krishna would place tribulation to His devotees is due to a larger plan that initially the devotee would not see. That is what exactly happened between Pandav Brothers and Krishna. They were in His mercy to protect their inheritance but the next step or bigger picture was the great mission on annihilating the miscreants and protecting more devotees."

Sukadev analysed, "I see. The act of God is not for happiness or distress but for a bigger purpose of reason and effect. As in a material world a mother's punishment can be as great as an enemy's, as too why would someone leave royalty when elevated but stay when distressed? I rather prefer to stay in distress than have to leave. Nevertheless He would not have come unless to bring blessing to His followers and the people who were distressed. The Lord appears in great distress. Were we actually on the point of break? No matter rain or shine the Lord's appearance would be more pleasant and enjoyable."

"Okay Sukadev, I think that should be all for now. I hope I've explained. I will email you the supportive evidence. Keep this to ourselves as the rate of which Krishna is changing things is as you say, 'hard to digest'. Simplify to Maharaja Pariskit of India, that with worshipping many demigods the land and time across the world had become affected by passion and ignorance. But as the numbers within the circles show that with Supreme Godhead, each material nature is in control and not to become ecstatic in opulence over the other or neglected by benedictions, unless that purely by goodness. The material creation of *Brahma Dev* and *Baba Shiva* when satisfied gave benedictions to the people but when angered the people retaliated without remorse. People acted selfishly to what they were not accustomed with, but with Supreme Godhead taking up the entire thought market, the reactions became merciful towards actions," Shankar chuckled. "Locking the demons is auspiciously good. Supreme Godhead is always all good. Above all the devotees are in *bhakti-yoga*, where they find peace, love and life around the clock. Let me know."

"I sure will, and possibly you can escort me to Dwarka City to meet Krishna when we go to collect your bonus from Maharaja," Sukadev forwarded.

"I'll make some phone calls," joked Shankar. "But that will be my pleasure. *Jai Shree Krishna!*"

"*Om Namah Shivaya!*"

Shankar wiped his face with his hands and got up to freshen himself. Shankar was feeling clogged up with his sinus' feeling congested. He walked to his bathroom to wet his toothbrush with water and lightly brushed the soft tissues in his mouth (gums, tongue, inner-cheeks) and palate. Shankar concentrated on areas that were making his oral tissues tickle whilst he did this. Focusing on areas just behind the last tooth on either side of his lower jaw one at a time he brushed the area between there and the tongue. The sensation of the brushing triggered his nerves to trigger his throat muscles to force lymphatic drainage. His body tensed, his eyes watered, ooh, ooo, aaa, ooo, aha! And there came out a mucus waste ball.

Lymphatic drainage from the lymphatic system around the body drains into the left sub-clavian vein and into the entrance of the thoracic duct where either the person spits out, blows through their nose to clear, or the mucus enters the digestive system. Shankar had mastered clearing blockage of lymph and mucus to enjoy a smoke better, but really was a means to stop by removing the toxins to help him breathe and sing better. Shankar would repeat the process on both sides of his mouth and over soft palate which was felt by brushing that would control the expulsion of a cough. The tongue was made to roll easily. His legs and arms felt free, and his whole vibrancy of breathing and body became better in a matter of seconds. All he had to do was force and withstand the pump of drainage. Shankar then blew out the remnants of mucus from his nose, washed his face and stood as a new man in the mirror.

A fortnight had passed since the last conversation between Shankar and Sukadev. Arrangements had been made between them and Maharaja Pariskit to visit Krishna in Gujarat. Shankar had made the call to Krishna saying that he and Parvathi would come to see him with a few friends as they would like to give their obeisance. Krishna was over the moon to have Shankar come visit since He had last seen him in England over a decade ago.

When Shankar arrived to Heathrow Airport to board his flight with Paravati and Sukadev, he felt that he was being followed. A rather obscure looking man kept catching his eye. From leaving his home he had first noticed this person. At first Shankar thought nothing of him and even when he saw the person again at the airport in the same checking in line he thought nothing of that. But after passing security and customs and taking a seat waiting for the boarding gate to appear Shankar became concerned by this suspicious person who sat not so far from them. Shankar had enough of debating the odds of the person and asked Parvathi if she had noticed.

"Why are you worried about him Shankar? What are the biggest virtues and sins that a man can commit?" Parvathi said not to allow Shankar to trouble the man.

Knowing what she was trying to do Shankar replied, "The biggest virtue is a man that is honourable and always truthful, whilst the biggest sin is to be dishonest or support such acts. A man should indulge in honesty and not harm the righteousness of their being. I'll just ask how he's doing."

Shankar approached the man, "Hello mate, how are you?" he said and took the seat next to him.

The man replied, "I'm fine. How are you?"

"Good, not bad. I feel like I've seen you somewhere before. What do you do?"

"I'm between jobs at the moment, we have not met before face to face but I've been your friend on social media for some time now. My name is Victorsura."

Shankar smiled and replied, "Oh, I'm sorry."

"Don't be. I understand, it's not so realistic to remember all the friends on social media, after all you are a busy man. I'm just happy to be a friend, Shankar."

"Thank you. That boosts my ego. So Victorsura, where are you heading?"

"Can I be honest? I read one of your conversations on liberation and became very interested. Actually I became hooked on your words. I am heading where you are. Wherever you go I'll go. So I followed you and bought a ticket to India."

Shankar now felt a little troubled, "So you are planning to stork me to India and back?"

"Well not actually stork, come on man. I was actually hoping to build the courage to come and introduce myself and ask if I could tag along. I should have seen that there's no beating your awareness."

"I need to ask..." Shankar paused, "What are you hoping to gain from this? Do you have family there?"

"In all honesty Shankar, I wished to provide sacrifice of my own self desire as offerings to you. In truth I have been a huge fan of yours and just wish to have a face to face benediction from you or I would not be able to go on another day. I need to be set free from your enlightenment and I thought if I met you, you would be able to free me from my thoughts."

Shankar felt compassion for Victorsura and didn't wish to overwhelm himself or undermine a total stranger that knew a lot about him. Victorsura was showing signs of *sarva-kama* which was as a demon asking for benedictions to prevent suicide. Fate didn't play in acts of worship or offerings that presented Shankar to Victorsura through his work, but the will of the wicked to get their way around the righteous. Without making the man hostile or hysteric, Shankar with compassion offered to heal his sorrows along with blessing his wishes.

Victorsura asked Shankar for benediction as to be feared and abominable to other people. This is what Victorsura asked Shankar. He wished that people would fear him and that he was no one to be reckoned with as that is what he saw in Shankar. As Shankar was in *tri-linga*, with the mixture of the three material worlds and nature of goodness he granted Victorsura his wish. What Shankar had accidently done was given this man confidence and merit for instead of helping human societies he would accelerate their path of destruction and death. Shankar without thought of himself appeased Victorsura from his threat of suicide and gave him the passion to crack necks by his own hands. Shankar should have played ignorant but he knew none of this at the time. All Shankar thought was that he provided the benediction, not that the man would take his new found confidence to the lowest of levels.

During the flight to India, Shankar thought nothing more to his encounter with Victorsura, whereas Victorsura thought nothing but the thought of killing Shankar. He was possessed with overpowering Shankar to the extent of murdering him and taking Parvathi for his personal enjoyment. As Victorsura believed the power of demigods rested in Shankar he was given them now to misuse.

The flight had a stopover at Mumbai International Airport and then to Ahmadabad where Krishna had sent a driver to welcome Shankar. Shankar felt the gloomy presence of darkness over his head and every time he looked around to see Victorsura without a doubt there he was. By this time Parvathi had caught onto the man who was troubling Shankar and became worried.

Arriving at Sardar Patel International Airport, Ahmadabad, Shankar thought that Victorsura would not be able to follow as he had no means of transportation. However from leaving England, changing flights in Mumbai to arriving in Ahmadabad, and henceforth to Anand and so forth to Dwarka, Shankar had fled to distant parts of the universe to occupy his thought but wherever he tried to take his mind there was noise.

They finally reached Vidyanagar, the second home of Krishna's. The land of such resembled the eternal realm of *Lord Vishnu*'s planet, *Vaikuntha*, and that for Krishna would be *Goloka Vrndavan*, the eternal love. All the people in Vidyanagar who were devotees of Krishna were without material attachment. Krishna's humble gatekeeper to Tara Towers, Narayana welcomed Shankar, Parvathi and Sukadev to their living arrangements.

Narayana as an opulent man stood before Shankar with gold rudraksha beads as a perfect *brahmacari*. He was very pleased to finally meet Shankar but immediately saw that something was troubling the respected man. Without asking any questions Narayana illuminated his light upon Krishna's guests. His welcoming light shined so far into distant space that the warmth attracted the demon Victorsura. The demon had found a means of following Shankar and approached to kill him.

Shankar saw Victorsura coming from a far as they stood by the gates of Tara Towers. Shankar spoke to Narayana about his benediction to Victorsura. Narayana as a *brahmacari* (full of mystic *yoga* arts), approached Victorsura with sweet words and relaxed his body, mind and spirit. Without asking any questions, Narayana said to the demon that he must be tired after such a long journey and dehydrated. He called a fellow worker to bring water for all the guests as divine and demonic both respect their own bodies to be nourished.

"You must be dehydrated son," Narayana said. "I can make arrangements for you if you like."

Victorsura was shocked that he was not feared.

"What do you require may I ask?"

"Do you not fear me? Are you not afraid? I am here to crack Shankar's neck!" Victorsura claimed.

"Why would you think and want to do that?"

"He has condemned me into believing his ways and I have no freedom of choice! I am bound by the chains of his words that I can never be set free from! I am not given the choice of own experimentation and discovery! I hate him! I want him dead! He promised me what I touch I can kill through disseat. I made him bless me and for that I want to kill him!"

"You've come all the way here to murder?"

"He is no good man; he is more like selfish man! I would have not come as far if I did not have to. However no one knows me here and I shall disappear without a trace. There's no light now that can allow me to have my life of mystery back. His light is tainted!"

Narayana calmly then said, "Very well, before you bestow your might on Shankar, bestow on yourself and let yourself feel the strength of Shankar's offering. You wish to set yourself free, well go and set yourself free. Do what you would have to yourself if Shankar was not to have given you benediction. And if you are not satisfied with the blessings you are free to attack Shankar."

With that Victorsura was perplexed by Narayana's words. He fell into deep thought for a short space of time and to save himself on humility or shame of action and full of curiosity he struck his own neck hard with his hand. He knocked himself unconscious and the last person he saw was Narayana looking back at him. Victorsura fell to the ground with his neck hitting a rock. His neck cracked and his soul left his body.

Narayana saved Shankar and too liberated him. He informed him that such a demon could only be killed by his own hands due to his austerities. The demon was killed by the help of Narayana who was a prodigy of Krishna Consciousness. Shankar that day became liberated to spend eternity in Om, peace, free from material entanglement and in extreme opulence within the continuation of *Vaikuntha*.

The moral of the moment was one way or another believe in the power of Supreme Godhead as Lord or believe in *Bhagavan. Ayushmian bahva* (Live long).

Om Jai Jagadish

Chapter 40

Om Jai Jagadish (Mantra)
/ O Lord of the Universe (Hymn)

Om Jai Jagadiśh, hare,
O Lord of the Universe, praise,
Swāmi* Jai Jagadiśh, hare
Mighty Lord of the Universe, praise,
Bhakta janoṃ ke sankata,
The agonies of devotees,
Dāsa janoṃ ke saṅkaṭa,
The sorrows of devotees,
Kśana meṃ dūra kare,
In an instant, you make these go away,
Om Jai Jagadiśh, hare.
O Lord of the Universe, praise.

Jo dhyāve phala pāve,
He who's immersed in devotion,
Dukha bina se mana kā,
With a mind without sadness,
Swami, dukha bina se mana kā,
Lord, with a mind without sadness,
Sukha sampati ghara āve,
Joy, prosperity enter the home,
Sukha sampati ghara āve,
Joy, prosperity enter the home,
Kaṣṭa miṭe tana kā,
A body free of problems,
Om Jai Jagadiśh, hare.
O Lord of the Universe, praise.

Mātā pitā tuma mere,
You are my Mother and Father,
Śarana karu maiṃ kiski,
Whom should I take refuge with,
Swāmi śaraṇa karu maiṃ kiski,
Lord, whom should I take refuge with,
Tuma bina aura na dūjā,
Without you, there is no other,
Tuma bina aura na dūjā,
Without you, there is no other,
Āśā karuṇa maiṃ jiski,
For whom I would wish,
Om Jai Jagadiśh hare.
O Lord of the Universe, praise.

Tuma pūraṇa Paramātmā,
You are the ancient great soul,
Tuma Antarayāmi,
You are the in-dweller,
Swāmi, Tuma Antarayāmi,
Lord, You are the in-dweller,
Pāra Brahma Parameśwara,
Perfect, Absolute, Supreme God,
Pāra Brahma Parameśwara,
Perfect, Absolute, Supreme God,
Tuma saba ke swāmi,
You are the Lord of everything and everyone,
Om Jai Jagadiśh, hare.
O Lord of the Universe, praise.

Tuma karuṇa ke sāgara,
You are an ocean of mercy,
Tuma pālana kartā,
You are the protector,
Swāmi, Tuma pālana kartā,
Lord, You are the protector,
Mai mūrakh khalakhāmi,
I am a simpleton with wrong wishes,
Mai sevaka Tuma Swāmi,
I am a servant and You are the Lord,
Kripā karo Bhartā,
O Lord, grant me Your divine grace,
Om Jai Jagadiśh, hare.
O Lord of the Universe, praise.

Tuma ho Eka agochara,
You are the One unseen,
Saba ke prāṇapati,
Of all living beings,
Swāmi saba ke prānapati,
The Lord of all living beings,
Kisa vidhi milūṃ dayāmaya,
Kisa vidhi milūṃ dayāmaya,
Grant me a glimpse,
Grant me a glimpse,
Tuma ko maiṃ kumati,
Guide me along the path to thee,
Om Jai Jagadiśh, hare.
O Lord of the Universe, praise

Dīna bandhu dukha harata,
Friend of the helpless and feeble,
Thākura tuma mere,
Benevolent saviour of all,
Swāmi, ṭhākura tuma mere,
Lord, benevolent saviour of all,
Apane hāth uṭhāo,
Apani śaraṇa lagāo, Dwāra paṛā hūn Tere,
Lift up Your hand,
Offer me Thy refuge, At Thy feet,
Om Jai Jagadiśh, hare.
O Lord of the Universe, praise.

Vishaya vikāra miṭāo, Pāpa haro, Devā,
Removing earthly desires, Defeating sin, Lord,
Swāmi, pāpa haro Devā,
Lord, defeating sin, Lord,
Śradhā bhakti baṛhāo,
Śradhā bhakti baṛhāo,
With all my faith and devotion,
With all my faith and devotion,
Santana kr sevā,
Eternal care unto Thee,
Om Jai Jagadiśh, hare.
O Lord of the Universe, praise.

Tan, man, dhan sab kuch hai Tera,
Body, mind, wealth is all Yours,
Swami, sab kuch hai tera,
Lord, everything is Yours,
Tera tujh ko arpan, Prahbu,

Ji ka prabhu ko arpan,
What's Yours we return, Lord,
What's Yours we return,
Kya laage mera?
What is it to me?
Om Jai Jagadish, Hare,
O Lord of the Universe, Praise,

Om Jai Jagadish, Hare.
O Lord of the Universe, Praise,
Swami Jai Jagadish, Hare.
Mighty Lord of the Universe, Praise.
Bhakta janon ke sankat,
Dāsa janon ke sankata,
The agonies of devotees,
The sorrows of devotees,
Kshan me door kare,
Thou instantly make go afar,
Om Jai Jagadish, Hare.
O Lord of the Universe, Praise.

Sovereign news had spread all around the globe. Many eyes had seen, many ears had heard, and many hearts had been touched by Supreme Godhead. The world's ecosystem had changed dramatically in the space of thirty years that even the Earth was adjusting. The air was cleaner, the waters were fresh, and plant life was evidently going to bloom. People desired the will to do what was right and simple mundane moments were a huge reward in itself. From Kaans being taken over and the Kuru Dynasty falling there was fear in the minds of demons whereas for the divine they were blissfully liberated. Even many without knowledge of Krishna began standing as the Lord, with one foot crossed over the other.

Affects of consciousness in life, love and peace was so strong that there was no better life to live. The bringer of the science, Arjun Pandav was the true reason why people followed his law. People were satisfied with so much love that they couldn't express to Arjun directly so a glance or smile was enough for thanks. The people of the world through Gold Lighthouse, both by word of mouth or witness to the website day by day and minute by minute were becoming baptized and saturated in The Eternal Truth. No person was really alone and no person was left out. The hardest part of the law was to relax upon the wisdom. So when time came for sleep more people slept well and woke with a spring in their step.

Cosmos of the outer realms had also seen the difference in light from planet Earth. Earth was that of light from Heaven. There were times of despair that the stars would contemplate to shine more for Earth, but overall more years became better than expected.

The whole plan of Krishna, Supreme Godhead as *Bhagavan* panned out. Time was saved, energy was conserved, sorrow was comforted, love was shared, and peace was worked on. Goodness prevailed, ignorance was respected, and passion was sacrificed to the best of the needs of one another on Earth. *Yoga* followed suit of *bhakti-yoga* as the name Shree Krishna was highlighted across the globe. Everyone knew the master of *yogis* and that was not from *Baba Shiva* even though he did that best, but was from the Source. Devotees of Krishna spread awareness fast as others got the message of one should join Him rather than even think about beating Him. When the words came from devotees and friends of devotees more people started believing in the chance that Krishna had given mercy upon the world for future generations to come.

The future of mankind was looking promising. People had become more accustomed to look at each other and control their senses on communication. Even children as young as toddlers were taught the arts of awareness, consciousness, and maturity so they could practice early and grow without fear. The only fear that was in transcendental space was that the truth existed. How that came about and what was that to be was far too much for any one person to comprehend and so to just face the fact that the truth exists. Where the truth would go from the Eternal Golden Age, would be to build a federation to explore strange new worlds and seek out new life and new civilisations across the universe, to boldly go where no one had gone before.

After developing a sustainable Earth with minimum input but maximum output, mankind would build up and out. Mankind would come altogether with richer senses in knowledge, wisdom and enlightenment making them evolved from humans to *Sanatanas*, (Eternals). The future for mankind was set by Life who controls chance so more with Life would improve chances for others to be more with Life. Love was thus protected against all odds. What would come next was for mankind to close their eyes, face the sun and roll the dice of chance, pass go and collect happiness (*swastika*). Mmmm...

Supplemental Notes

- Consciousness cannot be created by a combination of matter – Needs spirit.
- O Lord of Bharata: I am sex life involved with those not working for children. I am too the *dharma* (faith) of sex life working for children and to give children Krishna Consciousness (KC).
- Each soul is potentially divine to obtain God perfection, to see Him, hear Him & play with Him.
- Saints throughout time have gained KC.
- Seven qualities of Supreme Personality of Godhead #SPofGodhead: Attractive, Wealth, Power, Fame, Beauty, Wisdom, and Renunciation.
- Krishna lived on Earth for 125 years and His activities were unparallel.
- Krishna plays as a human but maintains Godhead.
- Krishna Consciousness is the act of supplying love.
- When a child is in danger, they think of mother or father, similarly when a devotee is in danger they think of Supreme Godhead.
- #SPofGodhead rests in all hearts with ability of intelligence and forgetfulness.
- Material Nature: Form of Creation, Expansion and Annihilation.
- Holy Name & Holy Appearance are the same.
- #SPofGodhead: Advanced in Absolute knowledge.
- Devotees understand Krishna's pastimes of both transcendental and materialistic attributes.
- Demigods appear with wives to execute the Lord's mission.
- Krishna to Arjuna, "You may declare to the world, My devotee shall never be vanquished."

- Blue Skin: *Lord Vishnu's* association with water is depicted as blue; therefore all His incarnations including Krishna are shown as such. In *Sanatana Dharma*, those who have depth of character and have the capacity to fight evil are depicted as blue skinned. Police known as 'boys in blue'.
- KC removes sins first and then brings one to Absolute Truth.
- #SPofGodhead states that God must present Himself forward rather than be defined by *Vedic* or *Upnishads* literatures.
- *Yogi* – A person who practices *yoga* to transfer self to higher planets of the mind.
- Father and sons affectionate for each other same as cows and calves.
- Peacock feather given to Krishna by Radha. The eye of the feather faces Radha.
- Love God means loving each other.
- Socialism, Communism, Altruism, Humanitarianism, and Nationalism.
- One may become ignorant to love Krishna.
- Mellows (*rasas*) – Adapting to love different personalities. A wave of multiple adaptations.
- Awakened dormant love for Krishna no need to execute austerities and penances unnecessarily.
- Overload of sinful activities on Earth doesn't belong to Krishna alone, but expansions of energy of multiple forms most *Lord Vishnu* carried across space and time.
- Incarnations of *Lord Vishnu* (God) combined together forms body of Krishna.
- *Kaana* – Krishna's childhood name.
- Krishna can choose His own country & family – that form becomes famous. As grapes of wines falls on many countries so can Krishna be of many.

- Pastimes of Lord Krishna - Attractive, Relish, and Able for all classes of men.
- Three types of men – Liberated souls, Trying to be liberated, and the Materialistic.
- *Krsna-katha* (KK) – ordeals of Krishna as worldwide mandate. Love affairs / pleasure and potency / People will be interested even if they say they're not as time will show the difference.
- Bhagavad-Gita – Writings translated from feelings of material existence to a spiritual setting.
- Benefit to hear about KK to highest degree. The kings would have conversations of transcendence. Usual conversations are limited but KK is at harmony with afterlife that one would never starve from belonging to Krishna Consciousness.
- Krishna's Pastimes – Destroy all inauspicious acts in the Age of Kali.
- King Pariskat (Grandson of Arjuna) – Interested in KK from Battle of Kuruksetra. Pariskat was fortunate to hear about KK (Krishna's pastimes and planetary systems [upper, middle and lower] on his death bed).
- Supreme Godhead lives within everyone's heart and outside as His universal form.
- Mercy of Shree Krishna, Arjun leaped over the battle field of dangerous fighters and survivors.
- There is no accepting to swear at the Holy Spirit, just as to Baba Shiva as the Spirit of God is the Chancellor of Truth. Strictly forbidden to swear at the Spirit of God. Swear against Father & Son, but again not wise to swear against Spirit. [Matthew 12:32] "Anyone who speaks a word against the Son of Man will be forgiven, but anyone who speaks against the Holy Spirit will not be forgiven, either in this age or in the age to come."
- #NumberDrug: Accumulation of numbers as accounts for self, family and career can comprise as a drug, as many

feel whole if they handling accounts. We all work with numbers in some sense. Be mindful with numbers they will be in next life. Be mindful and think that numbers too is a drug that should be controlled.

- The more you read, the more you know, the more you can eliminate, & the more you grow.
- I get love from my imagination.
- Reincarnations work across the animal and plant kingdom that soon or again an animal becomes a human. In human form they are to find Krishna Consciousness to reach Godhead otherwise the cycle starts again or the soul enters The Light. With belonging of God one thus can resurrect.
- The world is made by the Word and without the Word the world breaks.
- My stillness can affect your *karma* (actions).
- Music is medication, Om and Sing!
- Younger generations are bound to be smarter and more attractive. This is subject to generalisation but I wouldn't expect anything less here. Yes I raised the bar, yes I keep the bar raised.
- Great men and known by great men.
- A hybrid baby will always be to the father's side as of the XY chromosome unless later baby becomes an adult and chooses their own path.
- Take life slow, and make life memorable.
- #Intuition: I sense at best of times if someone doesn't like me as I feel that way about them. But that is not my nature not to unlike, thus then that leaves me feeling their spite for me. Meaning when one can sense someone else's spite so then I better myself by ignoring them.
- #NoLight: Ignore attention or unwanted attention, and dagger eyes by blocking the sight of the other person to self by raising the hand so own palm covers own eyes. I.e. talk to the back of hand.

- They say I am strong enough to handle abuse so they keep on firing.
- I am a father to myself trying to love.
- #GoldenApples: They say an apple a day keeps the doctor away. Apples are great at absorbing toxins and also stimulating the mind. (Biblical too).
- People can press others buttons purposefully. I cannot see pass the ones that do this, hence I find a way to penetrate or to shatter altogether. Noticed.
- Applaud hard work or gifted students? – Applaud the one that brings good work/results to the table.
- #PointReactions: One word from the right person can affect right compared to thousands of words from another for the same outcome.
- Be influenced by one with experience, empathy and education.
- #LightSpots: When staring into a blue sky one may see little spots that are floating around. One may think these are rays of Heaven, when science says they are white blood cells in the back of the eye. (I like rays of Heaven).
- Primitive verses Professional = You said that, verses Why you said that?
- You can stop but if you leave how can I save you?
- I mostly show stress when I'm against the clock.
- I do not like showing my stress to a woman as a) I don't want to share that burden with a woman b) some women would use that stress against me.
- I'll not take your faults on me out on your children.
- She views her own photos. I read my own words.
- #SPofGodhead: When one is spiritually, mentally, physically and financially above you, then don't be an idiot to them as really that shows you're the idiot and if that person stays silent consider yourself saved on your words against them.
- Harm from swearing depends on intensity & duration.

- Being rude can also mean that one's ego didn't satisfy someone else's.
- At times I laugh out loud at my own thoughts. At times I am not the one laughing.
- The world was about to go to war. I'm glad I played my part in it.
- Feel love? Go out and say hello to someone new.
- The East had been deprived and the West had been in confusion.
- A father that has not prepared his children for his death has not been a good father.
- More miserable one is, the more pleasant I have to be.
- Bible, 'Fear the Lord' but no need to hate Him.
- #IDK: I don't know. How could I know? When I know I'll know.
- Inhibitions: Controlled by the frontal lobe. So if damaged or undeveloped one would live a life with negative thoughts, swears, and even violence.
- #RockBottom: If one hits rock bottom there is only two things they can do; either live or die. Climbing up and making better is a bonus. So in other words live and survive if dare say this happens.
- Babies have love and innocence that refuels the adult heart. Adults need a break from all the love from babies as the heart needs that break. Plus if one finds it easier to look at babies for this reason, i.e. without fear, then one can look at others in same thought. We are babies.
- Cardiopulmonary Resuscitation (CPR): The heart contains that life force that keeps one alive. Hence God i.e. the Super-soul being in all people's hearts.
- #Deep Power: Look at a light source, but not for too long. Power Up! I look at a light source & then when I look at life, I consider it been seen by the Lord. #DeepGrace: Look straight ahead at whatever to be & through whatever that will come to pass.

About the Author

I became accustomed to writing since a young age either from the work I had studied throughout my life and when taking notes on daily activities. I enjoyed writing from as far back as it was as paper and pen. Because of my youth and reflectance to what's important within it I was to write my books. Being privileged to having an education I didn't want my knowledge to be lost and so I thought I should write down my interests. My interests were like everyone else's in what they know and what they are taught. I didn't want to lose my education I had received and thought to write down what I knew as stories. As my worked continued I realised I had a true gift for creativity.

I am very pleased to present my history and my interests within these books of mine. The main aim of the whole project was to bring positive aspects of life to everyday situations. These even included mental behaviour to change and better adapt or evolve our situations. We can all better something at sometime, may this be a temper problem, may this be an illness or suffering to another, this maybe how to congratulate another when there's nothing that can be offered. The path of many religions show to care for our neighbour, our brother, sister, family or friend member but at times we did not know how to approach difficult situations. Overall I hope to have shown that we should first smile and alongside make others smile.

There are a few factors to consider from my observations. I have included these statements to follow in all stories and I hope you can agree they are of importance to understand. They aid humanity to survive with strength and explore the unknown realities.

In all my stories I mentioned to understand that 'Om' (Sanskrit Scripture for the hymn of peace), this should be done from within and cannot be done in anger. The theme peace to be identified as the colour 'black', the theme of each other, every human being, and every animal as being that of blood, something representing love, and that is anything 'red', and most important to live in the 'light', light is life and we have peace and love to find and build for one another. Light is most important, some people including myself would like to represent this Light to also be known as God, whatever his name maybe. And lastly whenever you require power then to harness the thought of light and imagine that, also place hands together. Feel your heartbeat when tightening hands together. This doesn't need to be praying but just holding stability. Exertion is to release, the grace of yoga.

I thank every reader to have got to this point of my book. I hope you've really enjoyed it. I am to carry on working in life and wellness to inspire people to live improved lives and work with people that can benefit from my remedies. I wish all the time to read the book again. Live, love, laugh and add gold to peace.

Other Books by Author

A Potion

Colours of Enlightenment

Sand Deep

CofEt and A Potion

Printed in Great Britain
by Amazon

43513457R00209